Chasing Peace

CHASING PEACE

ALAINE GREYSON

ISBN: ebook 978-1-7332621-1-8
ISBN: paperback 978-1-7332621-0-1

Any references to historical events, real people or real places are used factiously. Names, characters, and places are products of the author's imagination.

Front Cover image by Triumph Covers
Edited by Brian Paone
Book Designed by KH Formatting
Logo by Kevin Harless
First Printing Edition 2019
Published by Creative James Media

www.alainegreysonauthor.com

Dedicated to Patrick, my son and biggest fan
and to my Dad who is my hero

CHAPTER 1

Samantha Barrett wanted to die. At least that's what it seemed. She grew up in Bracken Point, a sleepy little town fifty miles from the Chesapeake Bay. Her twin sister, Elizabeth, thought it idyllic. But its lack of entertainment made some search for enjoyment in other things. In Samantha's case other things weren't always wise.

Alone in her room on a Friday night, she did her best to suppress the ghosts of her past. Like every night for the past six months, she raised a crack pipe to her lips and took a hit. She was breaking the rules, but she didn't care. Even though she ran with a crowd that loved to party—cocaine being the drug of choice—they had rules to ensure safety. Michael—her current boyfriend—was a strict believer of the rules. He wouldn't approve of her smoking alone. But it didn't help when she spiraled at home without him.

As she lowered the pipe, a knock at the door startled her. Who was awake this time of night?

"Samantha, wake up!" Cassie Roberts—her housemate—shouted through the door. "It's gossip-and-whine-fest time. Elizabeth has news to share."

Elizabeth—or *Lizzie*, as only Samantha called her—was the mediator of the three. She called their meetings whenever they had gossip or exciting events in their lives. Samantha used to love their talks, but they lost their luster when they turned into interrogations and lectures about her life.

"Can it wait until morning? I'm exhausted," Samantha said.

"No. Meet you in the living room in five minutes," Cassie said with a hint of amusement in her voice.

Samantha sighed. She put the pipe on the headboard and crammed the bag inside Mr. Rabbit, her tattered stuffed bunny. What news did her twin have?

Annoyed, she trudged to the living room, hoping the announcement would be short. She covered her eyes as she entered, wishing she were somewhere else. The front room had been Elizabeth's first attempt at interior design and Samantha's least favorite place. Elizabeth had painted the walls a bright yellow and had decorated with red velvet furniture and cherry wood end tables. The garish design had been completed with a claw-foot coffee table Elizabeth found at an estate sale. The design gave Samantha a headache, but she wasn't in a place to change it.

Three glasses of champagne sat on the table, obviously for some celebration, but Samantha wasn't interested. Her days of wine and girl talk were done. She graduated to the harder stuff.

She settled on the couch, tucked in the corner of the room. She covered her eyes with her hands, her long blond hair cascading over her face, and hoped they would forget she was there. Cassie and Elizabeth stood in the middle of the room. Elizabeth's large frame towered over their friend. As Samantha watched, they gushed over something. Craning her neck to listen, she put a few words together and deciphered the meaning.

"So, Mr. Perfect proposed. That's why I'm here, in hell, instead of my bed. Couldn't this wait until morning?"

Samantha closed her eyes and sank deeper into the couch. Her sister was engaged, how nice. Another reminder of her sister's perfection and her own failings.

"Where did he take you, anyway? Aren't restaurants in Bracken Point closed after ten o'clock at night?"

"They are. We went to Kingsford, by the bay. It was gorgeous—the moon overhead, boats skimming in the water … the perfect evening," Samantha's mirror image said.

"Glad you had a good time. Now for sleep." Samantha stood and yawned. She pulled up her pajama pants and headed toward the hallway. Sleep wasn't part of her plan, but they didn't need to know the truth.

Without warning, Cassie sprinted in front of her, preventing her departure. Her smaller stature didn't reach Samantha's height, but she compensated with an intimidating stare. "Don't be selfish. This is a big deal for Elizabeth." She placed her hands on her hips, daring her to speak.

"Okay, Okay." Samantha raised her hands in defeat and returned to her perch on the couch.

"Ignore her, Cass. She's being grumpy. Need coffee? It'll perk you up," Elizabeth said.

"No thanks. Get on with it." When Lizzie suggested coffee before Samantha abused drugs it meant bonding time. Now it meant lectures and interrogations. Was Lizzie primed for a confrontation tonight? Samantha wasn't up to one. She moved to the edge and feigned interest. If she played along, she could return to her high sooner and escape Lizzie's wrath.

Cassie refocused her attention to the reason for the gathering, her mousy brown hair hanging in waves down her back. "Let me see it again. I still can't believe he proposed." She gushed, reaching to gaze at the diamond. "Tell me everything. Was it as you imagined?"

Elizabeth's green eyes shone, and her smile widened. "Well, I never expected Jeremy to propose, so I never thought about it. I suppose it was like any other proposal—dinner, wine, dessert. He got on one knee in front of everyone. He looked so embarrassed. I said *yes*—"

"Because you felt sorry for him." Samantha finished her sentence and stretched out, her frame filling the space.

"Not exactly sister dear. You may finish my sentences most of the time, but you're wrong on this one. I'm happy with Jeremy." Elizabeth shot her twin a warning glance. "If you can't be happy for me, go to bed. I'm sorry I disturbed your precious sleep."

Samantha straightened herself, meeting her sister's gaze. "You want me to be happy? Okay, I'm happy for you, but not for Jeremy's sake. You know why he got promoted at Mother's company? He's one of her puppets."

Their mother, Portia Barrett, owned Barrett Cosmetics, the largest employer in Bracken Point. Portia delighted in her contributions to the town and never let anyone forget. Jeremy was another Bracken Point resident who rode her coat tails to the top. His family valued their connection to Portia. This was another way to secure their place in society. And if Lizzie married him, Portia could still control her daughter as she pleased. Lizzie was blind to Portia's manipulation, but Samantha was too familiar with it.

Elizabeth shot her a disparaging look. "Jeremy worked for his promotion. Stop being a jerk."

Samantha rolled her eyes. Her sister wouldn't relent, so she played along. "Show me the stupid ring. The light in this room is giving me a headache."

Elizabeth brightened and displayed her manicured hand. The glare of the diamond blinded Samantha as if she was staring at her reflection in a pool on a sunny day. Her stomach reacted, churning in disgust—or was it jealousy? She stifled her thoughts and concentrated on the object in front of her.

"Gaudy, don't you agree?" Samantha raised her eyebrows at Cassie. "It's bigger than your hand. I would want something far simpler." She grabbed Elizabeth's hand for further inspection, scratching her neck with her other. "I'm sure Mother will approve. Did Jeremy talk to her before he proposed? She will never forgive you if she's the last to know."

"Mother knows. Come tomorrow. There's a luncheon at Mother's around noon. Jeremy's family will be there. I want you to meet his sister Amber. It'll be fun, drinking mimosas and planning the wedding. There's so much to plan—dresses, theme, venue. I would love your input."

Elizabeth's eyes pleaded with Samantha, a tactic that usually worked.

Of course, their mother knew. She probably orchestrated the whole proposal. Portia wasn't one to let things happen by chance. How would she react if Samantha showed up uninvited? Lizzie might want her there, but, without a Portia seal of approval, she wouldn't allow her through the front door.

She looked away. Lizzie should know better. Her presence only spelled trouble. Did Lizzie want the Martins to discover the truth about their dysfunctional family? Samantha shook her head and looked at the ground, shuffling her feet. "Weddings aren't my thing. Cassie has more style sense than I do. She should go. I'm not interested."

Elizabeth grabbed Samantha's chin. raising it so their eyes met. "I don't care about your style sense. You're my twin. I need you there. It's not the same without you."

"Would Mother let me in? I haven't received an invitation to her events in months. Despite what Cassie thinks." She shot Cassie a biting look. "I don't want this to be about me."

"Everything will be fine. I'll make sure. Remember, it's my engagement party. I get to have my way. And I want you there."

Unable to conjure another excuse, Samantha relented. "Okay, I'll go. But if she says one negative thing, I'm gone."

Elizabeth wrapped her arms around her sister and whispered in her ear, "I love you. You needed to hear that." She stepped backward and looked in Samantha's eyes, now lined in dark circles. "I hope you find peace one day. When you find it, chase it, and don't let it go."

Peace? Is that what Lizzie had? Samantha hadn't known peace since her dad had died when she was six. Life had been calm then. Their dad had stayed home, playing games and reading stories while their mother worked to build her company. Samantha and Lizzie had been close and had shared everything, especially their dad's attention. When Robert Barrett had died in a car accident, it destroyed their world. For the first time, they were alone. Portia had spent most of her time at work, neglecting her daughters. Lizzie had learned to cope, but Samantha had not. She had taken his death hard, and Lizzie had tried to fill the gap. Samantha loved her for it, but she never filled the missing hole.

Through it all, Lizzie had never let Samantha's bad attitude ruin their bond. Even when she had been at her ugliest, Lizzie was there. And Samantha had done everything to push her away.

"Thank you for your concern, sister." She yawned, walking toward the hallway to her bedroom. "But I'm fine. Nothing to worry about. Cassie, remind me to paint this room when she moves out. A nice shade of black will do."

Once in the hallway between the living room and bedrooms, Samantha leaned against the wall, hoping to listen to Cassie and Lizzie's conversation. She smiled, knowing Lizzie would put Cassie in her place.

"She used to love staying up late talking. I don't understand what happened. It's like she's a different person now," Elizabeth said.

"She's selfish. She only cares about getting high and partying. I don't understand why you let her get away with it. If you keep saving her, she'll never grow up," Cassie said.

Elizabeth sighed. "She's my twin. I'm responsible for her. I'm the only chance she has. Be patient with her, Cass. The Samantha we know and love is in there somewhere. She'll come around."

A tear streaked Samantha's face. Lizzie had never given up on her. Even when Samantha had given up on herself. Her emotions overflowed. Anger, sadness and loneliness mixed until she couldn't decipher how she felt. One thing would deaden the pain.

She tiptoed to her room hoping to hide her activity.

Elizabeth appeared from nowhere, inside her bedroom doorway.

Samantha jumped. "Shit. Are you trying to give me a heart attack? How did you get here so fast?"

"You don't remember my stealthy ninja moves? You could never hide from me. Twin telepathy and all that. Want coffee? Come to the kitchen and let me pour you a cup."

Defeated, Samantha trudged behind her sister. She couldn't escape the lecture this time. Samantha leaned on the island and watched Elizabeth busy herself brewing coffee. Smells of vanilla filled the air—her favorite.

Elizabeth's long blond hair swayed as she worked, retrieving plates and filling them with fresh-baked cookies. She placed the plates on the island next to a vase of yellow roses.

Samantha stroked the petals, waiting for the inevitable.

Elizabeth filled them both and handed one to Samantha. "I'm glad you were home tonight. I couldn't wait to tell you."

Samantha took the cup of coffee and a plate of cookies, settling herself in the window seat.

Elizabeth slid in next to her. She looked content, but Samantha didn't believe it.

"Why? I mean, why Jeremy? Are you in love with him?" Samantha said.

"Are you in love with Michael?"

Samantha recoiled. "No, but I'm not marrying him. If you're not in love with him, why marry him?"

"There's more to life than love. He's successful, well-connected, and devoted to his family. Plus, his sister needs someone to look after her."

Samantha sipped her coffee and took a bite of cookie. Was Lizzie replacing her? She shuddered at the thought. Losing Lizzie to Jeremy and his sister cut deep, and she didn't know how to respond.

"What's on your mind? If you're worried about me moving out, don't," Elizabeth said.

"You're not moving in with Jeremy? Long-distance marriage? Would he go for that?" Samantha smirked and raised her eyes over her coffee cup.

"That's not what I mean. I am moving out. But Cassie agreed to let you stay here, rent free."

Elizabeth stirred her coffee and gazed out the window to the backyard.

The stars twinkled in the moonlight, throwing a stream of light on the garden of yellow roses.

"How can Cassie afford that? She can't pay the mortgage on her own. She's in school," Samantha said.

"I'm covering all your expenses. Just like always."

"And Jeremy approves?"

"Jeremy doesn't know, and he won't find out. I may marry Jeremy, but he doesn't rule me. I still make my own decisions, and this is important." She paused and looked into Samantha's eyes. "You are important."

Samantha shook her head. Her twin tried, but she didn't understand. When she stepped in, Samantha felt more like a failure. Sweat formed on her brow, and her stomach turned. She had to get out of here. The walls closed in around her, and she couldn't breathe. In a panic, she slammed the coffee cup on the table, ran down the hallway to her room, and closed the door.

Settling herself on the bed, she grabbed her stuffed rabbit and loosened the back stitch. She reached inside and removed the bag from earlier. She propped herself on the pillow and filled the pipe, emptying the bag. This will do … for now. She raised it to her mouth. A white cloud formed around her as something forced open the door.

Samantha jumped when Elizabeth entered the room.

"What are you doing?" Elizabeth loomed over her, eyes cold.

"This is my private space. Get out." Samantha sat and turned toward the back window.

"It's Cassie's house, and I pay your rent. You're unbelievable."

"If it's bothering you so much, go tell Cassie."

"She went to bed. We need to talk." Elizabeth sat on the bed next to Samantha, swatting the white cloud away with her hands.

"You can talk, but I don't have to listen." Samantha folded her arms and turned away.

Elizabeth sighed and changed her tone. "This weekend should be gorgeous. Spring is the perfect time for picnics. We should go to the lake. Picnic next to the water, relax, bring your camera. You used to love the lake."

Samantha snorted. She used to love a lot of things, but they didn't matter anymore. Picnics, hikes at the lake, photography—favorite activities from the past did nothing to erase her pain. Only crack did.

"Cut to the chase, sister. You want to say something, say it. You have my attention." Samantha propped herself against the headboard and stared at her twin.

"Can you put that thing away?"

"This is the last of my stash. I'm not wasting it. Besides, it calms me." Samantha took another hit, drumming her fingers on the pipe.

Elizabeth took a breath and wandered to the closet. She retrieved Samantha's camera and spun it in her hands. "This is collecting dust. You haven't used it in months. Your photographs, they were good. Professional. You could have opened a photography studio. Destination weddings, pictures of kids and families … Made something of your talent."

"I'm smoking crack in Cassie's house, and you're concerned about my photography hobby? Good to know you approve." She took one final hit before placing it on the headboard.

"I'm not fine with it. I suppose I'd rather you do this here, where I can look after you, but, when I move out, who will make sure you don't overdose? Whenever you go to Michael's, it scares me."

"Michael has rules. He makes sure it's safe."

"Rules? How does that help? It's lethal no matter what you do. I'll pay for rehab, if you agree to go."

"You don't understand. Your life is perfect. It's always been perfect. Go away."

Elizabeth grabbed Samantha's hands and looked into her sister's eyes. "You think I don't understand, but I do. When I look at you, I see the same wounded girl hiding in the bathroom the day Dad died. So much hurts inside you, I don't know how to reach you anymore. If you had a healthy release, things could be different. Rehab, or at least counseling, would help. And this …" Elizabeth held up the camera. "Getting into your old hobbies. Maybe taking pictures again would help. Maybe you wouldn't need cocaine. It makes sense. You replaced your passion with the addiction. Photography gave you the same high the cocaine gives you. Replace the bad habit with a good one."

Samantha looked away. It wasn't that easy. Smoking crack gave her a high with no effort of her own. Photography was a different story. It came easily enough, as she had a natural talent. From childhood, it had been her passion, but her mother never understood. Portia considered it a hobby, not a profession. In college, Samantha had an opportunity to present a collection of photographs in the Kingston Art Gallery. Valerie Covington—the gallery owner—offered space to aspiring artists every spring. But Portia convinced Ms. Covington that Samantha wasn't ready for that honor. Portia's influence went far and crushed Samantha's dreams. Without her mother's approval, Samantha had decided it wasn't worth her time. Portia would stand in the way of any success. That knowledge took away her joy. Samantha shook her head. Lizzie didn't know. She thought Samantha hadn't been picked. It was one of many secrets she kept from her twin.

"It's a hobby, nothing more. Ask Mother."

"It's more than a hobby. And Mother isn't always right. You need to share your talent with the world. It's what you're meant to do."

"You mean well, but you don't understand. Mother never disapproved of anything you did. Why would she? You followed in her footsteps, working in her office. I ran from that place. Desk jobs are too constricting."

"That's why you need to follow your passion. Tomorrow tell Mother you are pursuing photography. I'll get you set up. I can rent a studio, do advertising."

"No. I don't need your money or your pity." Samantha gathered a few pieces of clothing from the floor and stuffed them in a bag.

Elizabeth shot her a confused look. "What are you doing?"

"What does it look like? Packing. I'm sleeping at Michael's tonight." Samantha continued to add items to the bag.

Elizabeth latched onto one corner and pulled. "As your older sister, I forbid you to leave this house."

"Forbid, huh? First, I'm twenty-six years old. You can't forbid me. Second, you're only two minutes older.

I don't think that counts." Samantha tugged on the bag, freeing it from her twin's grasp, and headed out the bedroom door.

Elizabeth sped after her and tackled her sister onto the living room floor. "You're in no shape to drive. If I have to sit on you until you sober up, I will. But you're not driving anywhere."

Samantha struggled. "Get off me." She slammed her fists into the ground and kicked her feet, hoping to throw Elizabeth off her.

"Throwing a tantrum won't help. My will is stronger than yours." Elizabeth adjusted herself so she sat squarely on Samantha's back, restricting her ability to move.

"I'm not a child anymore. You can't make me stay against my will. If you're worried, Michael can pick me up."

"On a Friday night? He's probably in no better shape than you."

Lizzie was right, but she couldn't stay here tonight. Not when her thoughts and emotions were out of control. She needed somewhere to relax and be herself, with no pressure. Michael's house made sense. He didn't care about her shattered dreams, only about having a good time. And that's exactly what she needed.

Summoning all her strength, she reached behind, grabbed Elizabeth's arm and bit, sending her reeling on the floor with pain.

"What the hell? You broke the skin. Are you mad?" Elizabeth held her arm, examining the damage.

Samantha shrugged. "I told you to get off me." She leaped to her feet and gathered her belongings. "I'll see you later, sister dear. Don't wait up for me."

She spied a tear in her sister's eye but kept walking. Not even Lizzie could keep her from her next high.

CHAPTER 2

Even addicts have rules. That's what Cole Weston told his clients and friends. And that's what Michael taught Samantha when she attended his parties. Rule number one was most important—don't smoke crack alone. But Samantha had already broken that one.

Then there was rule number two. Since Cole controlled the cocaine scene in Bracken Point, he had little need to enforce it—unless someone tried to target his territory. Samantha entered such a conflict when she arrived at Michael's house.

She pulled beside his small mobile home, reeling from her fight with Lizzie. A crowd had gathered outside, surrounding Michael, Cole, and their close friend Liam Masters. Cole's involvement hadn't surprised her, but Michael avoided these confrontations.

Cole faced Liam, his long brown hair plastered to his face and his eyes glassy from a night smoking crack. He donned a crazed look—one that frightened Samantha whenever she saw him. She wondered what caused Cole's latest outburst.

Distracted, she pulled between two cars, almost hitting him. She exited, wanting to apologize.

Michael waved her off. "Get back in the car Sam. This isn't a good time."

This made little sense. The three had been friends for years. What went wrong?

She froze outside her car door and stared, trying to understand.

"We have rules, Masters. You know that. We don't mix drugs. Take your speedballs and leave." Cole stood an inch from Liam's face, his eyes menacing.

"What's the difference? Cocaine, heroin, speedballs. It does the same thing, right? Everyone wants to have fun," Liam said.

As the two argued, Michael approached Samantha from behind and pulled her to the porch. His green eyes shone in the moon light, complementing his jet-black hair.

"What're you doing here? I didn't know you were coming."

"Long story. What did Liam do?"

"He brought speedballs and you know that's against Cole's rules."

Speedballs were a dangerous mixture of cocaine and heroin. Why did he bring them? Everyone knew Cole's rules. He did his best to help people have a good time, but he also didn't want dead bodies on his hands. What was Liam trying to prove?

Samantha returned to the argument and stared at Liam. Defying Cole took guts. He had a reputation of turning violent when it involved money. If Liam had sold speedballs to Cole's clients, a turf war was imminent.

Liam's blond hair shone in the moonlight. He stood inches from Cole's face, his finger wagging. "People get tired of the same old high. I'm offering them something better. Afraid they'll leave you? One day, you'll be irrelevant." He spit on the ground.

Cole reached behind him and removed his revolver. He cocked it and pointed. "Leave, Masters. And don't think about coming back with that shit."

Liam backed away and got into his car.

Cole lowered his revolver and released a cackling laugh. "That's right chicken shit. Run." He put his revolver in his back pocket and approached the porch.

"Do you believe that fucker?" He slapped Michael on the back and entered the house.

Samantha shook her head. "One day he'll shoot someone with that thing."

Michael laughed. "You think so? I'm not even sure it's loaded. But don't tell anyone I said that. Cole likes to look the part, but he's harmless." He put his arm around her shoulder. "And you don't have to worry, because I have your back. Cole would never hurt my girl."

Harmless? Cole scared her. He was fearless and erratic—a bad combination. If it wasn't for Michael's protection, she would stay far away.

She grabbed Michael's hand and led him into the house. She hoped Cole would find a corner and disappear. She couldn't handle his presence after dealing with her sister.

She walked through the house wondering where they could talk.

Music blared in the living room. Bodies were passed out in every corner. Trash littered the floor. They all used drugs to drown the pain. It wasn't any different for

Samantha. She came to Michael's to forget. She needed that tonight more than ever. But she couldn't find a quiet corner.

"Let's go to my room. We can talk if you want," Michael said.

Samantha nodded and followed.

He closed the door and sat on his bed. "I thought you were staying home tonight. Did something happen?"

Samantha bit her lip. She couldn't find the words to explain. He wouldn't understand anyway. "Just the same old crap from yesterday. Besides, it's boring at home."

"We don't have that problem here. Party's just getting started." He took a filled crack pipe off the dresser and lit it, passing it to Samantha.

She took a hit.

Michael grinned and pulled her onto his lap. "Better?"

She managed a half-smile and looked away. Was this her life now? She used to spend her Friday nights with Cassie and Lizzie and their infamous gossip-and-whine-fests. But she ruined their conversation tonight. Instead she surrounded herself with passed-out bodies, the smell of cat urine, and the occasional violent outburst from Cole. Did she prefer this to being with her twin?

An image of Lizzie with a tear streaking her face crossed Samantha's mind. She vacillated between wanting to be a good sister and wanting her next high. She needed to accept that she couldn't have both.

Michael paused and tilted his head. "Why so serious? Are you sure you're okay?"

Samantha nodded. It wasn't worth explaining. Whenever he had a problem, he'd cut and run. That's what he did when his family situation got rough. She wasn't ready to cut Lizzie and Cassie. But she didn't know how to make their relationship work. Somehow, she would figure this out. For now, she pushed the thoughts from her mind and focused on Michael.

She took another hit hoping everything would disappear.

***

The next morning came quickly. She woke next to Michael and a few of their closest friends sprawled across his bedroom. Everyone was still passed out from the party, but Samantha was wide awake. Her mind replayed the events from last night, and she wondered if she owed her sister an apology.

Once again, she had showed Lizzie her ugly side. Her problems weren't Lizzie's fault, but it was easier to blame her than solve them. Now Lizzie was engaged. Life would never be the same. Even though Samantha acted like she wanted Lizzie to go away, the thought of life without her twin frightened her. Cassie didn't have Lizzie's mothering instincts. She was certain Cassie would nag her to death once Lizzie moved out.

Beside her, Michael lay snoring, oblivious to her problems. She gazed at his muscular form, the sheet half covering his naked body and rising and falling with each breath. He was hers, and yet he wasn't. Lizzie had her happily-ever-after with Jeremy. Michael wasn't the happily-ever-after type.

She propped her chin on her hand and watched him sleep. Cassie and Lizzie didn't understand him, but

Samantha did. He feigned a bad-boy exterior, but deep down he had a heart of gold. His place was always open to his friends, and he didn't hold grudges. That's why the fight with Liam surprised her. Unless someone threatened those he loved, he didn't let arguments get violent and preferred to let a night spent partying solve everything. It was hard to be angry when one was high.

Cole, on the other hand, was different. Samantha always thought they made an unlikely pair. He was known for violence, always carrying his revolver and ready to fight for what was his. If Liam hadn't threatened Cole's business, last night would have ended differently. Michael would forgive easily enough, but Cole never forgot a betrayal.

Samantha smoothed back his black hair and sighed. She told Lizzie she didn't love Michael, and that was true. But Michael provided her with safety and comfort. Despite not being in love, he was always there when she needed him. Since he was best friends with Cole, the cocaine at parties would be endless. And it also offered protection from Cole's erratic outbursts, if she played the game.

Michael's eyes fluttered open. "Morning babe." He reached and pulled her close.

She nuzzled her head into his chest, wishing it felt more like home. Instead, she was hollow inside. She tried to love him, but the butterflies and tingling of romantic movies eluded her. Maybe she wasn't meant to fall in love. Maybe she didn't deserve to.

She ran her fingers down the small of his back. "I wish we were alone. It's been too long."

He kissed her nose as their foreheads touched. "Soon, I promise. Why don't you make us some breakfast? I'm hungry."

"What do I look like? You're personal chef?" Samantha threw a pillow at him and missed, hitting Cole in the face, who was asleep in the hammock across the room. Realizing her bad aim, she hid behind Michael before Cole realized what had happened.

He sat upright in the hammock, his face flush. "Which of you did that?"

Michael burst out laughing, his hand covering his mouth. "Wasn't me, man."

Cole glared at Samantha. The midday sun shone in his direction. Distracted, he shielded his eyes. "Why is it so bright in here? It's too early to be awake." He yawned and laid on the hammock, putting the pillow over his face.

Samantha glanced at her phone on the headboard. "It's called *the sun*. If you didn't waste so much time asleep, you'd recognize it. It's noon." Her face fell—Lizzie's engagement party. She promised Lizzie she would come, didn't she? "Mother is having a luncheon for Lizzie. I'm supposed to go."

"Food? I'm there. It's not like you're cooking anything." Michael hopped up, slipping on his pants.

"I didn't say I was going. Besides, you're not invited. My mother would have a heart attack if I come. If you show up, she'll keel over and die."

"What's the occasion anyway? I thought you didn't go to those things anymore."

"Lizzie got engaged. Everyone thinks it's a big deal."

"I take it you don't. To Jeremy, right? Not surprised. He always struck me as the proper kind—marriage, house, kids, white picket fence."

"You're not the proper kind then? Is that what you're saying?"

"That's an understatement. Michael, the marrying type? Why would he, when he has all this?" Cole threw off the pillow, motioning to the surrounding mess.

Michael shook his head, pushing Cole onto the hammock. "Don't listen to him. Look, I'm happy with what we have. No stress. Just each other and a good time." He wrapped his arms around her and pulled her close.

"It's just that Lizzie pays my rent. When she moves out, what then? She promised to support me, but can I accept that, for the rest of my life?" Hanging her head, she pulled away.

"Then you move in with me. Problem solved." Michael pulled his shirt over his head.

"I don't know. This engagement complicates everything." She sat on the bed, cradling her head in her hands. "Should I go or not?"

"Go. Don't go. Who cares? Do what you want," Michael said.

"It's not that simple. Lizzie wants me there but being around Mother is so hard. All we do is argue. I'm not emotionally prepared to handle this."

"Look. You know how I am about my family, but that doesn't mean you need to do the same. If you think you'll regret not going, then go. You must decide what you're willing to live with. Now, stop talking yourself out of it, and get ready for the fancy luncheon." Michael disappeared into the bathroom, leaving Samantha with her thoughts.

He was right. She wanted to go. Lizzie expected her. It was the right thing to do. Her decisions weren't stellar lately; maybe this would redeem her.

Cole sidled up beside her, eyes wild. He smelled of ammonia and rotten eggs.

She bristled at the closeness, wanting him to disappear.

"Take a few hits before you go. Then whatever the old bag says won't hurt."

"That's not a good idea." If she arrived at her mother's house high, it would reinforce Portia's bad opinion of her, not to mention ruin Lizzie's engagement party.

"It's a little bag. Less than an ounce. I'll give it to you for the bargain price of two hundred and fifty dollars, since you're Michael's girl and all." Cole jabbed her with his elbow.

She shook her head and approached the door.

Cole followed. "Trust me. This is your cure. Your miracle drug. With this, you're invincible." He waved the bag in her face.

Samantha paused. Her mother sent Samantha's emotions reeling whenever he saw her. She didn't need a hit before the luncheon. But she might need something afterward. What would it hurt? "I can't pay you now, and I don't know when I can."

Cole laughed. "You're going to your mother's, right? Everyone knows she's rich." He nudged her and winked. "I'm sure you'll find something of value. Bring it to my place tonight. But don't forget. You know what happens when I don't get paid."

He placed the bag in her hand and closed her fingers over it. Squeezing her fist, he grinned and walked away.

CHAPTER 3

Portia Barrett was a giant in the Bracken Point community. She had rescued the town when it experienced a decline in manufacturing jobs. Barrett Cosmetics had filled the void when it opened twenty-five years ago. Samantha and Elizabeth had grown up under the shadow of the company. Portia's image and business had come first—because it meant so much to the town. But Samantha thought otherwise. It wasn't because of the townspeople. Portia's own pride drove her and created a permanent distance between them.

The cosmetics company sat in the far section of Bracken Point, closest to the expressway to Kingston. It provided easy access for delivery trucks to ship products around the state, country and most recently, the world. As the primary employer of the town, Barrett Cosmetics prided itself on hiring its residents, affording them shorter commutes and comparable pay.

Portia's success allowed her to buy an expensive home in Bracken Point's premier community of Hillock. Only the wealthiest and most influential families lived there. It intimidated Samantha whenever she visited. The high hedges, meticulously maintained yards and gated driveways reminded her of prison. That's what her mother's house had become her teenage years—a prison she worked to escape. Why was she going back now?

At one o'clock, she arrived on her mother's doorstep. She changed from her T-shirt and jeans into a simple A-line dress, a pearl necklace, and matching white pumps. She hoped the outfit hid her recent activities and made her look more like a debutant. She didn't need Portia's harsh criticism today. She carried a clutch purse containing the bag Cole had slipped her. She didn't plan on using, but, knowing she had it helped her relax.

Steeling herself, she rang the doorbell. How would Mother react? Samantha didn't fit into Portia's high society world, a fact she was reminded of frequently. On her last visit, Portia had asked her to leave but couldn't deliver the news herself. Nora, her mother's assistant, delivered the news. It wasn't that Portia was afraid, but that she couldn't be bothered. The problems of her youngest daughter weren't interesting or concerning enough to take her time. Samantha wondered if Portia knew Lizzie had invited her. She dreaded her reaction if she didn't.

Sounds of giggling emerged from the massive entryway. She imagined people milling about, caterers serving sushi and champagne on silver platters, her mother orchestrating it from her perch in the living room.

She stepped off the porch, wondering if this was a good idea. Lizzie was the only reason she came. Was a civil afternoon with her mother possible, even for Lizzie's sake? She raised her gaze to the brick house, looming large with its white pillars, balcony, and picture windows.

She summoned her courage and climbed the few steps to the porch and rang again. Her mother's shrill voice and cackling laughter emanated through the door, leaving her frozen.

A wispy figure swung open the entrance. Eyes wide, the figure took in the unexpected sight.

Samantha smiled at her shocked expression. "Hello, Nora. Surprised?"

Nora's mouth fell open, her hazel eyes staring.

Samantha took partial delight in her reception, but that turned to dread when her mother appeared.

"Nora, who's there?" Portia, wine glass in hand, peered over her assistant's shoulder.

Samantha stared at her mother. The last year had been good to her. Her shoulder-length strawberry-blond hair had no sign of gray. Her face was free of wrinkles. For someone in their late forties, she had aged well.

"It's Ms. Barrett—I mean Samantha." Nora's gaze glued to Samantha as if she were a ghost. "We weren't expecting you." Nora turned toward Portia; her brow furrowed in confusion. "Should I set another plate for lunch?"

Nodding, Portia waved her hand, sending Nora toward the kitchen. "A little notice would have been nice, daughter. I suspect Elizabeth invited you. At least you cleaned up for the occasion. Come along. Everyone is in the living room."

Portia led past the spiraling staircase and into a gray room near the front of the house. Soft music played in the background while guests mingled. She didn't recognize most of the faces, and they made no move to acknowledge her.

She spotted Lizzie by the white grand piano listening to a young girl, not more than twenty, play. Her red hair cascaded over alabaster skin, highlighting her freckles. The music seemed to emanate from within, as if they were one. Samantha found herself mesmerized as the girl finished her song.

Samantha watched as the girl stood and gave a timid bow. When the girl's gaze darted to Lizzie, her face illuminated followed by a deep blush. Then she returned to the piano, poised for an encore.

Memories of her dad flooded back. It was his piano. He would play and sing every day as Samantha and Lizzie watched. She remembered his wavy blond hair and easy smile. Robert Barrett always smiled. When they had turned four, he taught them to play. Samantha grew misty-eyed, remembering their lessons. He had been a patient teacher and Samantha had blossomed as a pianist. But then he had been taken from her, and nothing was the same.

She jolted back to reality and prepared herself for her mother's formal introduction, but none came. Portia abandoned her without a word, positioning herself on the white chaise, like she was holding court.

Lizzie still focused on the young piano player.

Samantha tried to get her attention but failed. As she watched, a warm waft of air blew across her neck. She stiffened, concentrating on the music.

"She's talented, don't you think?" Jeremy whispered, the smell of whisky permeating the air. "That's my sister. She'll make Elizabeth a fine sibling. They already get along."

That was Jeremy's sister? She thought she would be much younger from Lizzie's description.

"I'm sure she's great, but Lizzie already has a sibling." Samantha moved to walk away.

Jeremy grabbed her elbow, holding her back.

"That she does. I guess that makes you my sibling too. Should we get to know each other?" He pulled her close, his breath bristling her skin.

She struggled under his grasp, trying to escape, but his grip grew stronger. "Let me go. You're hurting me."

Jeremy ignored her plea and pushed her against the living room wall. "Whether you like it or not, we will be a family. Might as well make the best of it. Elizabeth wants us to be friends." His lips grazed her ear as his hand traced the outline of her breast. "Think of all the family gatherings. Wouldn't want it to be awkward between us."

Samantha leveled her eyes at his. "Let me go, or I'll cause a scene."

Jeremy laughed. "Go ahead. No one would believe you. Even if they witnessed it, they would still think you're an evil, conniving, druggie bitch."

For a moment, his words hit home. Didn't most people believe that anyway? She was tired of people defining her by her failings.

Wrenching her hand from his grasp, she slapped him across the face. "That's a warning shot. Next time, I won't be so nice."

Jeremy rubbed his face and scanned the room. "I'm glad your sister knows her place. You need a strong hand to get you in line."

Identifying a chance to escape, Samantha ducked beneath his arm and grabbed a glass of champagne from a nearby tray. She ran into the hallway hoping he wouldn't follow.

She closed her eyes and tried to catch her breath. Who did he think he was, sneaking up on her and touching her like that? She was sorry for her twin, having to spend her life with an oily bastard like Jeremy. She took a sip of champagne and wandered into the library.

She placed her glass on the desk and perused the books on the shelves. Every wall was filled with books, from ceiling to floor, resting on brown wooden shelves. As a child, Samantha would hide in here to escape her mother's tirades. She never lived up to her mother's expectations, and Portia wasn't afraid to point that out.

Her fingers brushed a set of old books, her mind drifting to the past. Reading used to be her favorite pastime, her favorite way to connect with her dad and escape from reality. When her dad died, Lizzie rekindled her love for books. Lizzie had read to Samantha every night, resuming where Robert Barrett had stopped.

What was the book Lizzie had read to her? It was their favorite since before they could read. She ran her fingers over the titles until she saw it. *Little Women*. She slipped it off the shelf and cozied herself in the teal armchair in the corner. Confident no one would look for her, she kicked off her shoes and curled up, turning to the first page.

As she lost herself in the world of the March sisters, the door opened, followed by giggling.

Lizzie and the piano girl entered, laughing and teasing each other.

Samantha tried to hide beneath the book, content to be alone.

"This room is amazing. You must find a house with a library, or a room to make one. I'll come over and never leave." The young girl surveyed the room, eyes wide.

"You're always welcome. You'll be my sister. I'll make sure you have your own room, then you can sleep over." Lizzie smiled, but Samantha sensed something different about her reaction.

She stopped reading to concentrate on their conversation.

"Being your sister sounds strange. I mean, after we …" The young girl's voice trailed off, her face blushing.

Lizzie placed her hands on the young girl's face and raised it. "It might. But we can't tell anyone. It's our secret. Our families aren't ready to accept this."

Accept what? Her twin, her mirror image, the one who shared everything, kept a secret from her? A secret shared with Jeremy's sister but no one else? Jeremy was right. Amber was more of a sister to Lizzie. Jealousy seethed inside.

Closing the book, she rose, determined to reveal herself and figure out the secret. She cleared her throat when the door swung open again.

"There you are. You can't walk away without a word. This is your party. People are asking after you. And taking Amber too? Are you okay baby girl?" Jeremy approached Amber and placed his hands on her shoulders. "It isn't safe to wander about. I worry."

"I'm twenty years old, capable of taking care of myself. Besides, I was with Elizabeth. Don't you trust her?" Amber smoothed her dress, her eyes pleading with him to understand.

"I trust her. But tell me when you leave a room." He pulled Lizzie closer and placed his arms around both their hips. "I must have my girls close."

Samantha curled her lips. Jeremy triggered every alarm in her body. What did Lizzie see in him? Beyond his family and his money, what was the attraction?

She cleared her throat, drawing attention to her presence.

Elizabeth brightened. "Samantha. I lost hope. So glad you came. Does Mother know you're here?"

"Yes, she knows. I didn't want to cause a scene, so I hid in here."

Amber rushed forward. "This is your sister? I can see the resemblance. I've heard so much about you. Elizabeth says you're an expert photographer. Maybe you can take my picture?"

"My sister is mistaken. I gave up photography." Samantha approached the door, wanting to escape this circus.

"What a shame. Elizabeth says you're talented. You could start a business. I'm sure it would be successful." Amber's eyes grew wide. She sprinted toward Samantha and kneeled on the hardwood floor. "Your bracelet. It's just like Elizabeth's. How wonderful." She turned back and grinned. "Jeremy, did you see? They have the same bracelet. Diamonds, hearts—so cute. If I had a sister, we would have matching bracelets too. Or maybe matching necklaces." Amber droned on as Samantha tried to drown out the babbling.

"Yes, we've had them since high school. Lizzie, look what I found." She raised the book, showing her sister. "Memories from childhood."

Elizabeth rushed over and snatched it. She grabbed Samantha's arm and pulled her to the armchair, then squeezed over to share the space. "We read this every night. I'm surprised it's in such good shape."

"Let me see." Amber skipped, like a child of eight or nine, and looked over Lizzie's shoulder. "What's it called?"

"*Little Women*. Our dad read it to us every night when he was alive. After he passed, I took over. Samantha wouldn't sleep unless I read a chapter of this book. We read it hundreds of times."

"I've never read it." Amber sat on the arm, close to Lizzie, peeking. "Can I borrow it?"

Samantha glanced at her. She looked so lost and naïve despite her years. Her red hair and freckles made her look more like a Raggedy Ann doll than a twenty-year-old woman.

"I wanted to keep it for memories, but you can have it. You'd get more use anyway." She held the book toward Amber.

Jeremy pushed her aside and snatched it.

"What do you think you're doing? Amber, hallway. Now." Jeremy towered over his sister.

Without a word, Amber lowered her head and left.

Jeremy turned to the twins, his eyes softening. "Girls, I know you mean well, but Amber is impressionable. My job is to protect her, shelter her from the bad stuff. Please don't let her read anything unless you pass it by me. It's for her own good."

Elizabeth placed her hands on her hips. "It's *Little Women*. What's so wrong about that?"

Jeremy put his arms around her shoulders and pulled her close. "Let me read it. If I think it's appropriate, I'll give it to her. Please, let me have my way in this."

Elizabeth nodded and allowed Jeremy to guide her to the living room.

Samantha stared in awe. What did she witness? Her strong-willed sister, acting more like a Stepford Wife than the person she knew, seemed under a spell. Was she transported into the 1700s instead of living in the twenty-first century? It made little sense.

Determined to snap Lizzie from this nightmare, she chased after them. "Lizzie. Lizzie, wait. Can we talk?" Out of breath, Samantha tapped her twin on the shoulder. "In private." She glared at Jeremy.

"And the two shall become one flesh," Jeremy said.

"What does that mean?" Samantha narrowed her eyes.

"It means, soon we will be husband and wife. Whatever you say to Elizabeth, you say to me." Jeremy tightened his grip on Elizabeth's side. "I'm sure Elizabeth would agree."

Lizzie half-smiled, squirming under his embrace. "Jeremy, she's my twin. We've shared everything since the womb. Besides, we need to have some secrets for the wedding,"

Jeremy turned her toward him and kissed her forehead. "All right. If it's wedding related, I can do without you for a few minutes. But hurry back. I'm lost without you." He pecked her on the cheek and patted her behind.

"What's up? Everything okay?" Elizabeth said.

"Let's go upstairs. Too many eyes and ears here." Samantha looked into her twin's eyes, trying to find the connection they used to have.

"Why are you acting so strange? I invited you because I wanted you to bond with Jeremy and his sister. Yet, here you are, hiding in the library, wanting to talk to me alone. What gives?"

Samantha took a deep breath. It was better to get it out now instead of circling around her concerns. "Jeremy is an insufferable pig. He's controlling and condescending. If you marry him, you'll be miserable."

"Now you're giving me life advice? My drug-addict sister thinks she knows better than me? At least I found someone who loves me. I know where my life is leading. Every day I wake up, I worry I'll get a call you overdosed somewhere. Don't judge my decisions until you make better decisions for yourself."

Her words pierced Samantha like a dart. At one time, they were closer than sisters, sharing every thought. Lizzie had held her when their father passed, had stuck up for her when their mother put her down, and had loved her through her battles with depression. She thought it would last forever. But now her mind filled with anger and shame.

Needing an escape, she ran to the closest bathroom and slammed the door. She looked in the mirror, disgusted with what she saw. Had she sunk so low that her opinion didn't matter? Was she only the *drug-addict sister*? If that's what Lizzie thought, she would prove her right.

Fumbling with her purse, she removed the baggie Cole had given her earlier. Smoking this would make her indebted to him—a bill she couldn't afford. But she needed this. Without it, she was a ball of uncontrollable emotion.

She filled the pipe and lit it, puffing white clouds into the air. Her mind drifted to the sound of drums sounding a rhythm. She tapped her foot to the beat, humming along. The song changed, and shouts joined the thumping. After a moment, she realized the song called her name.

She stumbled to the door and opened it. "It's not locked. Can't you open a door? I'm high and I even know." Samantha chuckled.

"Samantha Jane Barrett. Doing drugs in my house." Portia, a hand on her hips, scolded Samantha as she did when Samantha was a teenager.

Elizabeth took a breath and entered. "Mother, leave. I'll take care of this." She pushed Portia aside and closed the door, locking them in. "Here, in Mother's house, at my engagement party? Cassie is right. You are selfish."

"You won't listen to me, so why should I listen to you?" She threw the pipe on the floor and inched close to Elizabeth's face.

"You're going home to sleep it off. We'll talk later. Cassie will drive you." Elizabeth stood, stone-faced.

"No need. I can drive myself. And I won't see you at home. I'm moving in with Michael."

"Like hell you are."

Samantha wrinkled her forehead in confusion. "Excuse me?"

"Moving in with Michael is the stupidest thing you've ever said."

"Michael gets me. He's the only one who understands."

"Michael is an ass."

Samantha clenched her fists, her cheeks turning red. "Stop judging people when you know nothing about what they've been through. Michael has a reason he uses, and so do I. Sorry we're not perfect like you. Go have your perfect life and let me live mine. I don't need you cleaning up my messes anymore."

"Someone has to. Michael won't. The minute you stop getting high, or worse yet, overdose and die, he'll move on the next girl. You're just a stop along the road."

Samantha's eyes bulged as she raised her hand.

Elizabeth grabbed both arms and held them at her sides. "I will fight for you, Samantha. If I must talk to your drug dealer myself, I will fight for you. I want my sister back, and nothing will stop me."

Why did Lizzie still care? Samantha did everything she could to push her away. But Lizzie kept interfering with her life. She should focus her attention on Amber, not her. She wasn't worth it.

"Your new sister is waiting for you. Leave me alone." Wrenching her arms from Lizzie's grasp, Samantha stomped on her sister's foot and pushed through the door.

CHAPTER 4

She never made it to Cole's house after the engagement party. In fact, she never made it to Michael's either. In her rush to leave her mother's house, she forgot to take anything of value. That meant she didn't have money to pay Cole. And when it came to money, even being his best-friend's girlfriend couldn't protect her. In the beginning, he sounded understanding, but, by the middle of the week, his messages became threatening. In hiding, Samantha declined dates with Michael and spent most of her time in her room. The baggie had a little left. Soon, she would run out. Going cold turkey was scary. But asking Cole for more, knowing she already owed him, was scarier.

To pass the time, she reread the Jane Austen books she had shared with Lizzie They were her favorite and helped her escape to a different world. She forgot about her argument with Lizzie. Instead, she immersed herself in *Emma*, her favorite of Austen's tomes.

Eventually, she would have to face her sister and discuss her behavior at the party. But she didn't know how to fix the argument from her latest stunt. She tried to contact her a few times, but she wasn't answering her phone. Samantha figured she needed space. Most likely, she was spending her time with Jeremy and Amber. Samantha had failed her as a sister.

As she got lost in the book, a knock on the door startled her.

Cassie stood on the other side, her eyes puffy. "Samantha, I don't know how to say this."

"Then don't." She closed the door and returned to her bed, retrieving the book.

Another knock came, more urgent than before. "Samantha. Please. It's important."

She trudged to the door and flung it open. "I'm trying to read." With her hands on her hips, she blocked the entrance, guarding her space.

"Let me in. Please."

"Whatever you have to say, say it. Make it quick." Samantha moved aside, crossed her arms and tapped her foot.

Cassie entered, holding a box of tissues and sat on the edge of the bed, patting the space next to her. "Sit. It's better if you sit."

She did as Cassie requested, a million thoughts running through her mind. She acted strangely. What was so important? Why were her eyes red and swollen? Something had happened. Cassie drew a breath. "We haven't heard from Elizabeth in days. Since her engagement party."

"She's with Jeremy and Amber." Samantha scooted herself backward, leaning against the pillow on the headboard.

"No, she's not. No one has heard from her since Saturday evening. Your mother issued a missing-person report yesterday."

Samantha froze. If she wasn't with Jeremy and Amber, why hadn't they said anything? Why didn't anyone tell her that Lizzie was missing?

She sprinted for her shoes and jacket. If Lizzie was missing, she would find her.

Cassie rose from the bed. "What are you doing?"

"Going to look for her. We know her better than the police. We can go to her favorite places, talk to people. We can find her." Samantha grabbed her car keys and headed toward the door.

Cassie stood in the entrance, barring her exit. "Samantha, no. We can't find her."

"Yes, we can. Why are you standing here, doing nothing? Lizzie is out there somewhere."

Cassie grabbed her shoulders and peered into her eyes. "Listen. We can't search for her." Tears streaked Cassie's cheek. Her hands shook as they jerked Samantha back and forth. "I'm trying to tell you. Your mother called. The police found her in an alley downtown. She was shot. She didn't survive." Cassie fell in a heap, sobbing.

Samantha's stomach churned. She struggled to stand. It couldn't be true. *Shot?* How was that possible? Everyone loved Lizzie. Samantha was the messed-up twin. If anyone deserved to die, it was her.

"Are you sure? What was she doing downtown? It doesn't sound like Lizzie. There must be a mistake."

When they were younger, she always sensed when Lizzie was upset or afraid, but she sensed nothing wrong this time. Cassie was right; she was selfish. Her tears poured out, plastering strands of blond hair to her face. Frantic, she ran to Lizzie's room. They were wrong. Lizzie wasn't dead. She was here, reading and snacking on cookies like she always did. And she would prove it.

Swinging open the door, she rushed inside. The room was dark. Shadows of Lizzie's pink unicorn and lava lamp danced on the walls. Her bed was made, the ruffles on each pillow perfectly positioned. She flicked the light switch, wishing Lizzie would appear. But her wish wasn't granted. She roamed around the room, taking in everything. It was as Lizzie had left it. Little trinkets placed on the dresser from beach vacations, books lined on a shelf, photographs of family and friends all remained the same.

Samantha gravitated toward a picture on the nightstand—a photograph of Lizzie and herself before the crack had consumed her. She gazed at the photograph, caressing the frame. Tears glistened in her eyes and trickled down her cheeks. Why? Was this her punishment? Lizzie didn't deserve this; she did.

She froze when she realized the truth. *Cole.* She told Michael he would shoot someone someday. He finally did it, except it was the wrong person. *She* owed him money, not Lizzie. This wouldn't have happened if Samantha was a better sister. It was her fault.

She traced the outline of Lizzie's face in the picture. She recoiled as the picture spoke to her. *You killed me. Murderer!* She lurched backward, dropping the frame and smashing the glass to pieces.

"Samantha. Are you okay?" Cassie burst in, glancing at the shards on the floor.

She glowered at Cassie, as if possessed. Without Lizzie, she didn't deserve to live. It was her fault Lizzie wouldn't have a wedding day. Her fault she died alone. She couldn't live with the guilt.

Eyeing the broken glass, she picked up a piece and raised it to her throat. "It's too late, Cass. I know the truth. I killed Lizzie." As her tears intensified, she inched the shard closer.

"No. This isn't the answer. Put down the glass."

Samantha's hand quivered. "Didn't you hear me? It's my fault. She tried to save me. Well, she didn't succeed, because I'm not worth saving."

Not seeing another option, Samantha attempted to jab the shard into her throat.

Cassie lunged forward, wrestling the shard from her hand before it caused damage. They fell backward on the bed, overcome with emotion.

"It's not your fault." Cassie held her as she shook, caressing her back.

"It is. You said she was downtown. There's only one reason. She confronted Cole. She said if I wouldn't get clean on my own, she would have to get involved."

"You think someone murdered her over a drug deal?" Cassie said.

"It makes sense. I owe Cole money. If Lizzie tried to talk to him, he could have mistaken her for me. It must be him. Nothing else makes sense."

Cassie pulled her close. "Your mother has the police hopping. They will solve this case. Until then, promise you won't do anything stupid. I promised Elizabeth I would look after you when she got engaged. I hold that promise. I won't let her or you down."

Samantha sniffed and wiped her face with the back of her hand. In an instant, her world turned upside down. She couldn't think of anything worse.

Then Cassie's phone rang.

"It's your mother." Cassie held out her phone.

CHAPTER 5

A week later, Samantha stood on the soggy grass, staring at her sister's freshly dug grave. It seemed like a dream. A week ago, they were drinking coffee and nibbling on cookies in their kitchen, sharing the latest gossip. Within a blink of an eye, everything had changed. Tragedy had severed their once inseparable connection. How could she continue without her?

Samantha had wanted to end it all when she found out, but Cassie had prevented her. All week, Cassie watched over her, scared she would try again. But Samantha didn't. Instead, she relied on Michael to sneak her crack. If she wanted to get past this, she needed something to dull the pain.

She pulled her hoodie to cover her head as the April rain mingled with her tears. Half the town attended the funeral, but she didn't know most of them. As the ceremony ended, the line of well-wishers trudged from the gravesite to their cars. They entered their fancy BMWs, limos and SUVs, ready to resume their lives, untouched. Instead of tears it surprised Samantha that everyone smiled and chatted as they walked, as if they were leaving a picnic, not a funeral.

The rain fell harder, but she didn't notice. While most cars left, two remained in the parking lot, waiting for their occupants.

"It's time." Cassie put her arms around Samantha's shoulders.

"She's gone, isn't she, Cass? Really gone? It's like a bad dream." Searching for her mother, Samantha turned toward the remaining cars. "Is Mother still here?"

"Yes. She's waiting for you." Cassie motioned to Portia. "The weather is getting worse. You'll be better at home. Some hot tea and a change of clothes will do you good."

"I can't leave her. I'm not ready. Not here, not now. What if she needs me?" She approached the casket and caressed the yellow roses on top.

Workers were folding the chairs and gathering items used for the ceremony.

Samantha stared at the casket, hoping they wouldn't lower it into the ground just yet. "Please Cass, I'll be fine."

"I can't leave you here by yourself. How will you get home? Let's go. Ride with me." Cassie tugged on Samantha's arm.

Sobbing, Samantha clung to Cassie for dear life.

"I know I should, but I can't leave her here all alone." She stood, paralyzed in fear. Her life had changed forever. Where should she go from here? Nothing made sense.

"Samantha, let's go." Portia cast an impatient look toward her now only daughter. "We have a crowd waiting at the house. They'll overwhelm poor Nora. Stop being so dramatic. Get in the car."

A herd of wild elephants wouldn't overwhelm poor Nora. She spent the last twenty years working for Portia, and Samantha was sure she could handle anything thrown her way.

"Go ahead, Mother. I'll drive back with Cassie." She shot Portia an annoyed look and sat on one of the remaining chairs. "Sit. There's no rush."

Cassie looked back and forth between Samantha and Portia and shrugged. Defeated, Portia threw up her hands and got in her car. Samantha had won the moment, but she wasn't sure she would win the war.

They sat in silence, pondering the events of the last few days. Cassie glanced at Samantha as if she wanted to say something but decided against it.

After about twenty minutes, Samantha broke the silence. "The roses were beautiful."

"Yes, they were. Elizabeth always loved yellow roses."

"She said yellow was a happy color, and she was always happy. No matter what happened."

Cassie smiled. "She loved you more than anything. She wanted you to be happy."

"I know." She patted Cassie's hand. "I think I'm ready now. Let's go home."

Cassie grabbed Samantha's hand and squeezed. They plodded to the car, half smiling, half crying.

They rode in silence. When they pulled up to the tree-lined, Samantha flinched, dreading the crowd inside. She sensed eyes on her all day, cutting her. They called her *the damaged twin* behind her back. At the church and the graveyard, people pointed and whispered. They blamed her, as she blamed herself.

Samantha entered the house with trepidation, wanting to lean on Cassie. But Cassie disappeared, looking for a friend. Desperate to escape the stares, she scanned the room, looking for a quiet place to hide. She remembered her favorite spot in the library and hoped it was empty. Sneaking into the room, she eyed the comfy teal armchair in the corner. Grabbing a book from a nearby shelf, she curled her feet underneath her and prayed no one would notice.

As she read, the door swung open. Jeremy and Amber entered, deep in conversation.

She sank deeper in the chair, willing it to swallow her. Holding the book closer to her face, she sat still, listening.

"Keep your eyes down and your answers short," Jeremy said.

Samantha peeked over her book. He had a firm grip on Amber's elbow. Her face was flush, her eyes red and swollen. Amber nodded, fixing her gaze to the ground.

"Chin up little one. Let me do all the talking. We'll pay our respects as expected Then you complain of dizziness, and we'll leave. Not a word otherwise, sister."

Distracted, Samantha dropped the book.

Jeremy and Amber startled and turned toward the noise.

"Sorry. How clumsy." She bent to pick it up, her fingers brushing Jeremy's hand.

"Here, dear sister." His gaze met hers, cold and calculating. "Even though the chance to marry Elizabeth was stolen from me, you will always be my sister. Elizabeth adored you."

Jeremy grabbed Samantha's hand and raised it to his lips. The invasion, slimy and cold, created a panic within her. Recoiling, she forced a smile and straightened herself. "Hello, Jeremy. It's so nice to see you pretending to care about my sister's passing." Samantha sauntered toward Amber. "Here. This was another of Lizzie's favorites. *Pride and Prejudice*. I want you to have it. She loved you like a sister."

Amber smiled and reached for the book then pushed it away. Crying, she ran from the room.

Samantha darted after her. When she reached the living room, Jeremy cornered her against the wall.

"Don't mind my sister. She's devastated. Elizabeth was her best friend. I'm being strong for her." He peered into her eyes, creating a panic inside. "Let me help you. For Elizabeth's sake. His eyes scanned her body, his gaze resting on her chest. Pinning her, he raised his hand, tracing the outline of her face. "So much like Elizabeth."

She cringed from his touch. She couldn't decide if he was grieving or was insane. Either way, something wasn't right.

"I'm not Elizabeth. Leave me alone."

She slipped from his grasp and ran. She kept running, past all the guests, until she reached the back yard.

Out of breath, she plopped onto the porch swing and listened to the squeaky sound as it swung back and forth. The rain, heavier now, splattered onto the porch. She hoped it would keep everyone inside. The solitude was nice. It was the first time since Lizzie died. Cassie had stuck by her side, even spending the night in her room in a sleeping bag on the floor. Samantha had stayed under

Cassie's watchful eye. She longed for a few moments of solitude, but Cassie interrupted her.

"Samantha. There you are. I've been looking everywhere for you. It's still pouring. Why don't you come inside?" Cassie peeked through the half-opened French doors with a concerned look. "I'm fine. The rain isn't bothering me. Lizzie always loved rainy days. Somehow, I'm closer to her out here."

Samantha approached the rose bushes lining the porch. They were Lizzie's roses. She had planted them here when they were teenagers and at Cassie's house when they had moved in. Gardening had been Lizzie's sanctuary and where Samantha remembered her the most.

"I know. But your mother has a houseful of guests, and she expects—" Cassie closed the door, easing toward Samantha.

"I know what she expects, Cass. I don't care. Today isn't about her, and I won't let her think it is." Samantha broke a rose from a bush and carried it across the yard.

"You're grieving—we're all grieving—but it isn't healthy to spend the whole day by yourself. Today is hard for everyone. Especially your mother. She lost a daughter. Can't you see it her way for once? She's grieving too."

Samantha smirked and twirled the rose, wishing her life were different. "She's grieving because the wrong child is dead."

"You know that's not true. Isn't that harsh?"

"It's not harsh enough. Trust me, Cass. You weren't there."

No one was there. They saw her masquerade but didn't know what she did behind closed doors. Only Samantha was privy to that, since she bore the brunt.

Cassie crossed to where Samantha stood. "I grew up with the two of you, remember? We had sleepovers all the time. Yes, your mother worked a lot, but it was all for you and Elizabeth. Hell, I was jealous of everything you had."

"It's not about the things, Cass. There's more to life than that."

Cassie took her by the arms and looked straight in her eyes. "We had a great childhood. Remember our favorite pastime? Playing dress up with your mother's clothes and the makeup samples she brought home. I still have pictures of our fashion shows. We were so cute in her skirts and dresses all dolled up. It was a good childhood. I don't know why you think it wasn't."

Samantha blinked back tears. Trying to make her understand was futile. "We were children. We didn't know what was beneath the surface. And whether you believe it or not, things weren't good."

"Things aren't good now. Instead of focusing on the past, can't you try to fix what's left? You still have your mother. Embrace that. Lean on each other."

"What about what *I* need? She was my twin. How am I supposed to move past this? No one asks how I feel. Hell, no one dares to talk about what happened around me—like, if they did, I might break or something. Know what? I'm already broken. So, you can go back inside and be the support you think my poor mother needs. Leave me alone."

"Let me help you. I know a guy. You can talk to him. He's good with things like this. He can help you process your emotions."

"I'm not talking to someone I don't know. I'll deal with this the way I always do."

"And how is that? Getting high with Michael? We can't ignore this forever. Eventually, you have to deal with your problem." Cassie glared at Samantha, her face bright red and her hand firmly on her hip.

"And what problem is that? My grief or is this a veiled attempt to get me drug counseling? I'm not interested in your psychiatrist friends from the clinic. You've brought enough of them home already."

"If you don't deal with your problem, it will kill you."

"The only problem I have is you." Samantha turned and met Cassie's glare. Cassie's face softened as she crossed the yard and enveloped her in a hug. Expecting a lecture instead, Samantha appreciated the kind gesture.

Maybe there was hope.

The two women rocked back and forth, releasing their pent-up emotions until someone interrupted them. The French doors swung open, and Portia stood on the porch, glowering.

"Hello Mother." Samantha approached the center of the back yard. Her mother was the last person she needed right now.

"Playing in the rain like you're twelve. Get in here. Nora will find you a change of clothes. Embarrassing me at Elizabeth's wake. You'll never change."

She ignored her mother and twirled in the center of the yard, her face pointing toward the sky. "Don't you feel her? She's here. The rain, she's watering her gardens. We should celebrate her life here, how I remember her, in her sanctuary. If we're celebrating her life, shouldn't it be where she was happiest?"

"Samantha, please. People will talk. Don't they have enough to gossip about?" Portia furrowed her brow.

"People are talking, huh? What are they saying? Because no one will say more than two words to me." Samantha charged toward where her mother and Cassie stood.

"Are they saying whose fault they think it is? Are they blaming you, Mother?"

The look on their faces let Samantha know she had gone too far, but she couldn't help herself. The guilt and grief took control.

"Don't worry, Mother. I don't blame you. I blame myself. It's all my fault someone shot her. It should have been me. Then you would still have your precious golden child." She stormed past them into the house.

She didn't get far before she broke down. How was she supposed to move on? Wasn't it enough to deal with Lizzie's death and her part in it? Why did her mother make everything more difficult?

Standing beside the door, she listened and heard Cassie say.

"Give her time. She'll come around."

"She's been a difficult child since birth. If she and my Elizabeth weren't identical twins, I'd swear the hospital gave me the wrong child," Portia said.

"Let me talk to her. I'm sure she will see it your way if you give her a chance."

"*Humph.* You can try, but you're wasting your time. She's been a disappointment her whole life." Portia waltzed into the house.

Samantha hung her head, feeling alone. Even with those comments, Cassie still didn't understand. Cassie admired Portia and refused to listen to Samantha's side of the relationship. Once again, Samantha carried her feelings toward her mother alone.

As she walked through the house, Samantha struggled to catch her breath. The walls closed in around her. Everywhere she looked, people were deep in conversation. They seemed to point and whisper. *There goes the addict. She killed her sister. Murderer!* The front door seemed miles away. If she reached it, the voices would stop. She shambled through the house, her head down.

When she reached the living room, something stopped her. Before she reacted, soda splashed on her and covered the floor.

"Are you okay? Let me …." Her obstacle grabbed a few napkins from a nearby tray and sopped up the liquid on her shirt.

Shock prevented her from moving. She didn't recognize him. He was probably one of her mother's friends. Still, he intrigued her. As he continued to apologize, she put out her hand to stop him. "I'm fine, thank you. Mother will freak if it ruins her floors." She moved to clean the spill on the hardwood but jolted away when the stranger's hand touched hers.

"I got it. You look like you've been through enough today. Besides, it was my fault."

She stared in disbelief as he cleaned the mess. What was it about him? His wavy brown hair had a tousled, almost bedhead look. He wasn't classically handsome, and normally not Samantha's type, but she couldn't stop looking. She couldn't explain it. He was calm and inviting, different from other men.

"I owe you a drink. It's the least I can do." He found a nearby couch and guided her toward the seats then returned with two cups of punch. "Here. This will help."

Samantha took a drink, still staring at the handsome stranger. Where had her mother hidden him? "Thank you. Were you one of my sister's friends? I don't think we've met."

He smiled. "No. I never had the pleasure of meeting your sister. You're Samantha, I presume? My deepest condolences for your loss."

"That's what I heard all day. Everyone is sorry for my loss, like that's supposed to make things better." Samantha looked into her cup, refusing to make eye contact.

"It's the safe thing to say. Most people are clueless at funerals and fumble for the right words. It's the thought that counts, I suppose. What would you rather they say?" The stranger's words were kind and measured.

Samantha relaxed and forgot about her escape. "I'm not sure. I wish people would stop telling me how to grieve. Maybe they should say nothing and give me space. I haven't been alone since I found out Lizzie died."

"Some people need alone time. But don't shut out the people you love. They will get you through the tough times."

The gorgeous stranger—she had to call him something other than this—smiled, and his deep brown eyes danced with care and amusement. He took her hand and she shook at his touch.

She blushed realizing the unexpected attraction. She had gathered the courage to ask his name when someone interrupted them.

"I see the two of you have already met …"

Samantha startled at the voice and retracted her hand.

Cassie leered over Samantha. "Don't you look cozy already. And you said you would never try counseling."

She gave Cassie a confused stare. "Is there something you aren't telling me? We were having a nice conversation."

"I'm sure you were. Samantha, this is Dr. Jonathan Green. He's the friend I told you about earlier. Jonathan is a psychiatrist. He specializes in grief counseling at the clinic downtown."

Psychiatrist. It all made sense. Cassie was at it again. That's why he understood, why he had such caring eyes. He talked to people for a living, making them comfortable, so they would spill all their problems. Well, that wouldn't happen.

"Let me guess. You work together? Cassie loves to psychoanalyze me, and you're not the first doctor she's brought by. No offense, Doc, but I'm not the therapy type. I'm not comfortable spilling my guts to strangers."

"I understand. It's too soon, anyway. But, if you ever want to talk, I'm here. Cassie and I have been friends for a while, and I know she's worried about you." Jonathan leaned back on the couch and peered over his glasses.

Part of her wanted to bare her soul and see what happened, but her head convinced her it wasn't a good idea.

"That's Cassie," Samantha said. "Always the mother hen. People deal with death all the time. I'm not a weakling. I think I've got this covered."

"You think counseling is for weak people? I disagree. It takes strength to admit you need help. I hope you realize that one day," Jonathan said.

Who did he think he was? Samantha fumed. She couldn't believe she found this guy attractive a moment ago. She was not weak. How dare he suggest such a thing?

"You know nothing about me. Are you making a professional diagnosis, Doctor? Shouldn't you get to know me before you decide I need help? Thanks, but no thanks."

"As for you." She stared down Cassie. "I can take care of myself. Why don't you worry about your own issues and leave mine alone?" She turned to walk away.

Cassie grabbed her arm. "Sam, can we talk? Somewhere private?"

"Save it, Cass. I don't need your help. I'll figure out everything on my own."

"No, you won't. I've watched you go downhill the past six months, before Elizabeth's death. What are you hiding? What's going on? Don't make me lose you too."

"Maybe you already have. It's time to move on. We're not kids anymore."

She turned and saw her mother headed toward them with an unsuspecting person in tow. "Samantha, this person says he knows you. Wherever from? You can't invite anyone. This is a private affair."

Samantha smiled as she recognized Michael. She threw herself into his arms and buried her face in his biceps. "You came. I wasn't sure."

"I told you I would be here." He gently wiped her cheek with his thumb. "Is there anything to eat? I'm starving," he whispered and gently nibbled her ear.

Michael wasn't her knight in shining armor, but he was consistent. She counted on him to be there when she needed him, and he never let her down.

"Not here." Samantha glanced at her mother and Cassie; she didn't need an audience. "Let's go outside." She grabbed Michael's hand and pulled him to the front porch.

"So, that's your mom, huh? You weren't kidding. Strung too tight. I can see why you need me to have fun." He pinched Samantha on the butt and pulled her in for a kiss. "Do we have to stay? I could show you a good time at my place."

She groaned, returning his kiss. Everything she had been feeling this entire day melted away in Michael's arms. Screw counseling; he was all the counseling she needed.

"I want to, but I can't leave yet."

Samantha trembled as Michael thrust his tongue into her waiting mouth, probing, longing. If only this could continue forever. She wanted all her memories, all her thoughts, to go away. Only Michael, he could be her cure. She wound her arms around his shoulders and ran her fingers through his thick black hair. Only passion, no thinking.

She jolted back to reality when someone shouted her name. Turning toward the house, she saw Cassie racing toward her, something in her hands.

"Samantha, this came for you." Cassie handed her a dozen yellow roses. "Is there a note?"

Yellow roses. Lizzie's favorite flower. Samantha's hands shook as she searched for the note. Her eyes grew wide as she read it. "I know what happened." She dropped the flowers and fainted.

CHAPTER 6

Her head throbbed. Disoriented, she propped herself on the pillows and surveyed the room—purple walls, a pile of stuffed animals, and a lone poster of Justin Timberlake stared back. Home. She tried to connect the dots, but everything was fuzzy. "How did I get here?" She attempted to stand, but her head wouldn't cooperate. "I'm dizzy."

"Well, you fainted." Michael sat on the edge of the bed, donning a smirk. "It was comical. I never saw someone faint."

"You would find it funny. The last thing I remember is arguing with Cassie." She eased herself up, dangling her feet off the bed. "Something about a handsome doctor."

Michael cocked his eyebrow. "Doctor, huh?"

She shot him a warning glance. "Jealousy doesn't suit you." Her hands pushed into the mattress as she found her footing. She grabbed Michael's arm for support. "Why did I faint?"

"You don't remember the flowers? They sure made a lot of commotion. I don't see the big deal. Aren't people supposed to get flowers at a wake?"

The flowers. Samantha covered her eyes and grimaced. It wasn't a dream. Someone sent flowers with a note. And not just ordinary flowers. Lizzie's favorite.

"Where are they?"

"In the kitchen. Cassie brought them home."

Michael steadied her on her feet as her excitement grew.

"Did she keep the note?" Not waiting for an answer, she darted to the kitchen. Hopefully, the note had evidence of Lizzie's murder or at least a way to contact the person who said they knew.

Michael followed her to the kitchen, like a forlorn puppy. "What's so important about the note? So someone claims to know what happened. It's probably some crazy person trying to get their fifteen minutes of fame."

She tracked down the roses, paying little attention to Michael. The vase sat in the middle of the island, next to the flowers Lizzie picked from her garden. Samantha paused, imagining her sister pouring coffee and grilling her about her recent activities. How she missed that. The note jolted her from her memory. She picked it up and scanned it for any information. Berkeley Street Florist. She recognized that name. Wasn't it around the corner from Cole's house? She could bring the flowers there and trace it to the sender. Deep in thought, she held the card to her mouth, wondering how much she should share with Michael.

"Oh no. That look. I've seen it before. You're going to play detective, aren't you?" Michael held up his hands and backed into the kitchen island.

"I need to know what happened. If this person witnessed something, I need to find them."

She raced to her room, searching for her phone. Hopefully, the florist had information on the delivery. It couldn't hurt to try.

"What if they can't share customer information? You're not the police. Why don't you hand the note to them, so they can investigate?" Michael hurried to keep pace.

Pausing in her bedroom, she stared at Michael. She couldn't keep this from him any longer. If he heard about Cole's involvement from the police first, it would affect their relationship. She drew a breath. "I don't want the police involved yet."

"Why? Getting a thrill from being Detective Barrett?"

"No. I don't want to tell them, because I know the murderer. It was Cole. I don't have any evidence yet, but I know it was him,"

Michael narrowed his eyes. "It wasn't him."

"I know you and Cole are close, that you want to defend him. But look at the evidence. Who else would have done this? Lizzie had no enemies."

"It was probably a freak accident. That part of town is dangerous. It could have been anyone."

"He carries that revolver. He almost shot Liam. Besides, I owed him money. They found Lizzie in the alley beside his house. She went there to confront him, to stop me from using. What if he mistook her for me? He left threatening messages, promising to hurt me if I didn't pay him. He did it. I'm certain."

"I've known Cole my whole life. He's not a murderer." Michael put his arms around Samantha and kissed the top of her head. "The police will handle it. No need for Detective Barrett. Besides, do you want to risk them investigating us, Cole, and everyone else? What if they search his house? It could implicate us. We need to lie low right now."

"My sister died, and you're more concerned about how this affects you and your precious druggie friends?" Samantha pulled away.

"They're your friends too. At least I thought they were. And until you have proof Cole did this, I won't let you destroy his life."

"Won't let me, huh? Well, at least I know where you stand." Samantha tried to push past Michael into the hallway.

He stepped in front of her and grabbed her shoulders. "Stop. You're not thinking. When you fainted, you hit your head hard. Sit. Let's talk this out."

"What do we have to talk about? I think it involves Cole, and you don't. What else is there to say?" Samantha struggled to get free, but his weight prevented her.

"Please hear me out. Sit."

Samantha relented. They settled on the bed, pushing the pillows and stuffed animals aside.

Angling himself to face her, he took her hands and rubbed them with his thumbs. "Lizzie's death hit you hard. Remember when I told you about my sister? When she was ten, I almost lost her. But you can't dwell on it. It isn't healthy to replay the events and try to figure it out. You'll drive yourself crazy. What happened, happened, and the sooner you put it behind you, the better you will be. Trust me."

Samantha lowered her gaze. Who was right? Cassie wanted her to talk about it. Michael wanted her to suppress it. Neither made her happy. If only it was all a dream. She could wake up, see Lizzie, hug her and tell her how much she loved her.

"Do you remember the day we met? You walked into Willy's Bar at one in the morning, dressed to the nines. Everyone stared at you. But you sat, ordered a cosmopolitan and ignored the stares and whispers. That's when I knew we would be friends. You have a strength about you. Don't let your current circumstances wear you down."

"It wasn't strength. I was too pissed at my mother to care what anyone else thought. This is different. I didn't almost lose my sister. She's gone, and she's not coming back. How do I deal with that, especially when I'm responsible?"

"You don't. I learned to compartmentalize it. Makes it so I don't think about it. Eventually, the hurt goes away. Sometimes you have to forget."

His way seemed easier— just forget. But how could she forget about her twin, the one she shared everything with since conception?

Was it strength to move on and forget her guilt and grief?

"I don't know. I suppose I can try. How do I turn it off? I can't stop thinking about it, about her, about everything."

Michael smiled and snagged a bag from his backpack. His eyes gleamed with a hint of mischief. Dangling it her direction, he winked. "This is how." He filled the pipe and lit it.

She blinked and stared. As if smoking crack would harm Lizzie's memory. Shouldn't she get clean for Lizzie's sake? Didn't she owe her that?

Michael offered the pipe as she struggled with her decision. Would getting clean bring back Lizzie? The damage was done. Why change now? Making her decision, she grabbed the pipe then dropped it when a bang startled her.

"It's Cassie! Michael, put that out." Samantha scrambled, picking the pillows and stuffed animals off the floor. She smoothed her hair and drug Michael into the living room.

To her surprise, Cassie wasn't there. Instead, Jonathan sat in the yellow room, sipping tea. He had an air of authority about him that she found comforting, yet dangerous. She stared, her stomach flipflopped, and she hoped Michael didn't notice.

"Breaking into homes now, are you, Doc? Or is Cassie behind this visit?"

"Hello, Samantha. I hoped you would be here. Cassie gave me a key. Care to introduce me to your friend?" Jonathan eyed Michael warily.

"I'm no friend. I'm her boyfriend. Samantha, who is this stiff?" Michael puffed

himself up, daring Jonathan to say something.

"Whoa, buddy. Settle down. I'm here professionally. I have no designs on your girl." Jonathan smiled and motioned toward the couch. "Please, both of you have a seat."

"If it's all the same to you, Doc, I'd rather stand." Samantha crossed her arms and leaned against the wall. Cassie was at it again, trying to orchestrate her life. At least she picked a handsome doctor this time. Handsome enough to get Michael jealous. She wasn't used to this side of him.

She glanced between them, intrigued by their interaction. They couldn't be more opposite. Jonathan looked serious in khakis and a brown sweater vest, his countenance emanating an aura of calm. While Michael, in his usual white T-shirt and jeans, shouted *irresponsible party boy*. She shouldn't be surprised the former excited her while the latter felt like an old shoe.

Jolted from her musings, she startled when Michael tugged her arm and pulled her into the hallway.

"What? And what was that nonsense out there? Since when did you become possessive? I didn't think we were that serious," Samantha said.

"Just because I don't want to marry you doesn't mean we're not serious. You know how I feel. Who is that guy anyway? And what did he mean, *professional basis*?"

"He's Dr. Green, one of Cassie's friends. He's a psychiatrist. Cassie thought he could help me deal with Lizzie's death. I turned him down, so I don't know what he's doing here."

"What? Like counseling? That's not a bad idea." Michael shrugged. "It might make you less crazy, to talk about it. You know?"

"Did you get counseling after what happened with your sister?"

"Hell, no. I didn't need any of that. How would sitting around talking about my feelings make me better?"

"Yet you think I should. Your logic doesn't add up,"

"Yeah, well, you're a girl. Don't girls love to talk about that stuff?"

Samantha jabbed him in the arm and returned to the living room. "Sorry, Doc. What did you want to talk about?"

"Cassie said you fainted. I wanted to check on you, see if you needed anything." Jonathan leaned back on the couch and took a sip of tea. "Are you feeling okay?"

"I'm not sick, if that's what you mean. That sounds like a trick question, Doc. I'm not falling for it. I don't need counseling." Samantha crossed her arms.

"You look tired. I'm sure you haven't been sleeping well." Jonathan leaned forward, his hands on his knees. "Your life turned upside down when your sister died. It'll take some time to feel normal again."

She glanced at Michael, but he wasn't much help. Instead of listening to the conversation, he was chuckling in the corner, his nose in a comic book.

Her attention redirected toward Jonathan. She stared, trying to decipher his motive. They hardly knew each other, yet he made a special trip to check on her wellbeing. His concern was condescending yet endearing. Cassie would be proud. She picked a persistent intermediary.

"I appreciate your kindness, but I'm fine." She approached the front door and held it open. "Thanks for coming, Doc. I'll tell Cassie you did your job."

Jonathan moaned and put his head in his hands. I'm doing it again, aren't I?" He scooted over, making room, and motioned to Samantha. "Please forgive me. Sit. I owe you an apology."

She ambled toward the couch, choosing instead to sit in the nearest armchair. She curled her legs underneath her and rested her chin in her palm. "I'm listening."

Jonathan drew a breath, moving closer. "It wasn't right for Cassie and me to corner you. We should have gotten your permission before we spoke about counseling."

"Yes, well, Cassie does what she thinks is best."

"I suppose she does. Just know, I won't push it, and I hope Cassie doesn't either. It isn't something to start unless you're ready. I hope you'll accept my apology."

This was unexpected. Samantha briefly met his gaze and felt a rush of relief. He understood. Perhaps he wasn't as bad as she originally thought. Perhaps she could talk to him.

She lifted her head and dropped her arms in her lap. "Thank you. No one has ever apologized before."

"I hope I'm not the last. Whatever is going on inside your head is your business only. When you're ready and willing to share, I can help you find someone. Until then, I won't pester you about it."

Jonathan placed his cup on the table, along with two brochures. "I've taken enough of your time. Remember what I said. The door is always open." Nodding at Michael, he strode through the front door.

Curious, Samantha peeked at the brochures. While Jonathan promised not to pester her about counseling, his parting gift told a different story. Picking them up, she outlined the titles with her fingers— "Overcoming Grief" and "Drug Abuse". Confused, she wondered what Cassie had shared with him. The Grief Counseling brochure made sense, but the drug-abuse information bothered her. Cassie must have told him she was a drug addict. How else would he know?

She took them to her bedroom, fully intending to ditch them. Once at the trash can, she relented. She placed them on her dresser and grabbed her worn copy of *Pride and Prejudice* and settled on the bed. She wasn't sure what to do about Cassie's meddling.

The rest of the evening passed in silence. Michael, engrossed in his comic book, sat on the purple beanbag chair tucked in the corner. While Samantha, nestled under the comforter, alternated between reading and thinking about Jonathan. She wanted to confront Cassie about the drug-abuse brochure, but she decided against it. She would get more honesty from Jonathan instead.

Distracted, she closed the book and meandered toward the dresser. She collected the brochures and shifted them in her hands. Was her drug use evident to everyone? And was it a problem? Lizzie thought so. Cassie and her mother did too. And now it seemed Jonathan, someone she had just met, agreed.

"Michael." Samantha joined him on the beanbag, pushing him to make room. "I need your opinion."

"Can it wait? Ironman is confronting Loki." He scooted over, fixated on the comic book.

"This is serious. I need to talk to you."

Michael groaned. "After this page."

"No." Samantha snatched the comic and threw it in the trash.

"Hey! That's a first edition." Michael moved toward the trash can, but Samantha stepped in front of him.

"Not until we talk." She held the brochures, hoping to spark his curiosity.

"Talk. I'm listening." Michael sat on the bed, brooding.

"Aren't you curious about these?" She waved them in front of his face.

"Should I be? What are they?"

"Jonathan left them. The grief-counseling brochure didn't surprise me, but he left this one about drug abuse too. Do you think Cassie told him?"

"Does it matter? Obviously, he thinks you need help. I agree. Let me get back to my comic."

"You think I need help? If I need drug counseling, you do too."

"I only agreed to get you to leave me alone. Do we have to talk about this?"

"Yes. Do we have a drug problem?"

"No." He pushed her aside and lunged for the trash. "Now can I read in silence?"

Samantha grabbed the comic and held it above her head. "If you want to read this again, sit and talk to me."

"Okay, okay. No, we don't have a drug problem. We can stop anytime we want. Haven't had any today, have we?"

Samantha shook her head.

"See? No problem."

"But I haven't had a day I didn't use. What if Lizzie was right?"

"Let's do an experiment." He picked the filled pipe off the headboard and lit it. "We'll smoke a little now. If you want to stop tomorrow, do it. No big deal."

He took a hit and passed it, blowing a puffy white cloud into the air.

Samantha took the pipe and held it for a moment. She could quit, right? One more night of fun and she could get clean. But did she want to?

***

She awoke the next morning to screams of panic. Michael was sound asleep next to her, the lit pipe on the blanket. Cassie screamed her name while holding a red cylinder. White foam covered the bed, and smoke filled the air. Not realizing what was happening, she wondered how Michael could sleep with all the noise. Samantha sat upright, the covers falling off while the foam slid to the floor.

"What are you doing?" Samantha covered her face and coughed, the combination of smoke and the smell of pool water making her gag.

"You could have died. Your bed was on fire. And he's—" Cassie jerked her head in Michael's direction— "still sleeping. What were you doing? The whole house could have burned down."

Samantha looked at the bed. The pipe had burned a hole through the mattress. What if Cassie hadn't been there? Michael didn't have rules about lit crack pipes. Maybe he should.

Cassie grabbed the culprit and held it in Samantha's face. "This. Is this worth your life? So many people care about you, but you would rather waste away in here, getting high."

Cassie was right, but Samantha didn't want to admit it. "Don't you think you're being melodramatic?" She lifted the blanket. "See? Hardly any damage."

Cassie pursed her lips and turned red. "I won't stand by while you kill yourself. You're more than this." She threw it on the bed, hitting Michael in the face.

"*Ow*. What the—" Michael sat up and stared at the unexpected visitor. "What happened and why am I wet?" He removed his T-shirt, revealing large biceps and the remnants of a six-pack.

Cassie wrinkled her nose and covered her eyes. "Put on some clothes, please. And leave. I have a mess to clean up thanks to your carelessness. Why would you fall asleep when that thing —" She motioned to the pipe— "was still lit?"

Michael furrowed his brow and glanced at Samantha. "What is she talking about?" Turning to Cassie, he stood and adjusted his pants. "You're the reason my favorite Marvel T-shirt is soaking wet? What did you spray on us, anyway?"

"I'm the reason you're still alive, dipshit. In case you don't understand, let me explain it real slow. You put a lit pipe on the blanket and fell asleep. Blankets are flammable. It ignited. Smoke went into the hallway and set off the fire alarm. I got a fire extinguisher and put out the fire. You slept through the whole thing. Thus, making you a dipshit. Any questions?"

Michael opened his mouth as Cassie stuffed the pipe, his clothes, and his comic book in his backpack. "Take your things and get out. Don't think about coming back. I can't believe someone can be so stupid." She threw the bag at him, prodding him down the hallway.

Samantha followed but kept her distance. Cassie had never been so animated. They continued into the living room, arguing like children.

"Samantha. She's crazy. It was just a little fire. Nothing was even damaged. Well, not much anyway. You need a new blanket. It's ruined." He pointed at Cassie. "Mainly because of her. Spraying a fire extinguisher on people, isn't that stuff toxic? Could be assault."

"*Assault?* Get out of here before you learn what assault really is." Cassie pushed him toward the door. "I don't care what Samantha says, you're no longer welcome. Now leave." With one push, she launched him through the doorway and slammed the door.

"Now to clean up. And don't think you're hiding something from me." She pointed a finger in Samantha's face. "Everything is going in the trash. Everything. And if I catch you smoking in this house again …"

"Yes, Mother Cassie."

Cassie shook her head and stormed off.

Following at a distance, Samantha steeled herself as she entered. Cassie was hard at work, holding two black trash bags and depositing whatever she found. She prepared herself for a fight, as she would have to defend her right to keep anything.

"Don't touch Justin," Samantha said, referring to her Justin Timberlake poster. "He didn't do anything."

Cassie rolled her eyes and seized Samantha's tattered stuffed bunny, proceeding to stuff it in the bag.

"Hey! That's Mr. Rabbit." Samantha snatched him away before he went into the abyss. "You can't get rid of him." She snuggled her bunny close and sat on the bed. "Don't I get a say? It's my stuff."

"But it's my house. I'm making sure you don't have a stash hidden in here. Does Mr. Rabbit have a secret hiding spot?" Cassie grabbed him, looking for a loose stitch.

"Mr. Rabbit isn't hiding anything. And I don't have a stash. Michael brings it. I don't need any here." Samantha snatched him back and curled up on the bed, hugging her stuffed friend.

"Get up. Everything on this bed is ruined, thanks to your boyfriend. I meant it when I told him that he isn't welcome."

"You don't understand him, Cass. He means well. Michael would never do anything to hurt me—something Lizzie never understood. I wish you gave him a chance."

"A chance to what? Burn down my house? Make you overdose? How you can put your trust in a crackhead amazes me."

Samantha shook her head. She would never understand. Cassie thought people should fall in love, get a house with a white picket fence and have plenty of children. She didn't understand people who lived outside the norm. And she made no attempt either. How she succeeded in psychiatry confused Samantha. She should have tolerance for people like Michael.

Frustrated, she held Mr. Rabbit tighter, glad Cassie hadn't looked inside. "You've done enough today. Go away. Let me sleep."

Cassie tugged on the sheets, trying to dislodge her. "These sheets are soaking wet. How is this comfortable? Get up, so I can see if the mattress is ruined too."

Samantha tumbled to the floor, clutching her knees.

Cassie filled the trash bags to the brim, sparing nothing.

A large object peeking from one bag caught Samantha's eye. She wandered over to inspect. It was her camera. Hesitant, she removed it and examined it, unsure what to think.

"You haven't touched that in months. I figured you didn't want it anymore." Cassie continued to clean the room, stuffing the ruined blanket and bedsheets into the trash bag. "You okay?" You understand why I'm doing this, right?" Cassie dropped the bag and put her arm around Samantha's shoulder.

"Before Lizzie died, she wanted me to take pictures again—open a photography business or something." Samantha clutched the camera and approached the window facing the backyard with a faraway look on her face.

"You tried that, and it didn't work, remember? You've never followed through on any hobby you had."

There was the word *hobby* again.

"What's the point?" Samantha squeezed her eyes shut and threw the camera into the trash bag. She crossed the room and paused at the door. "Leave my clothes, okay? I can't afford a new wardrobe."

CHAPTER 7

On Monday morning, Samantha woke before Cassie. Her mind filled with thoughts of Jonathan and Cole but for different reasons. Cole held secrets of Lizzie's murder, and she needed to find out what he knew. Jonathan was an enigma.

He was one in a long line of psychiatrists Cassie brought to the house. Each one tried to convince her that she was an addict and needed rehab. Each one left without reaching their goal. It shouldn't surprise her that Cassie shared her drug use with another. Yet somehow, Jonathan seemed different. The others treated her like damaged goods and acted like they were her savior. Jonathan treated her with respect despite her failings. If she confirmed his suspicions, would he treat her differently? She had to know.

As she got ready, she surveyed the contents of her room. Her beanbag chair, Justin Timberlake poster, and stuffed animals remained. Cassie also had allowed her to keep a few ceramic bunnies and her Jane Austen books, for which she was grateful.

She rifled through her closet, trying to find the perfect outfit. As she sorted through the hangers, something gleamed from the back corner. Her camera sat where she had it before Cassie's cleaning spree. Didn't Cassie throw it away with the rest of her things? She picked it up and ran her fingers over the slick surface. Sometimes she missed photography but reviving it now would be pointless. She wasn't sure why Cassie had put it back.

She inventoried the remaining articles. At least Cassie listened and left her clothes, which were mainly T-shirts and jeans. She evaluated her options, deciding which would make the best impression.

Jeans? No. Jonathan wouldn't take her seriously. She kept looking. A skirt? No, too professional. In the back of the closet, a gray and pink dress spoke to her. It was perfect. She grabbed it and held it up to the mirror. It was serious yet flirty.

She slipped it on and smoothed it out, admiring herself. The butterflies in her stomach caught her off guard. Was it anticipation of Jonathan or fear of Cole? She dismissed her thoughts, planning her approach. Her visit with Jonathan should be short. Cole's visit had higher stakes.

If she found evidence or tricked Cole into confessing, she could prove his guilt to Michael. But she knew her chances were low. Cole might be crazy, but he was smart. Proving his guilt would be difficult. First, she needed to bring his money. She wouldn't get through the front door without it. Desperate, she remembered Cassie's envelope system. She divided her paycheck into envelopes, each serving a different purpose.

Samantha tiptoed into the office and searched the desk drawers. The vacation envelope lay on top. Cassie wouldn't miss two hundred and fifty dollars. Besides, Samantha would replace the money. Returning to her room, she slipped it in her purse. She hoped she would survive both meetings unscathed.

She glanced in the mirror, grabbed the brochures and headed out the door. She had one stop to make. Gourmet coffee from Kirsch's would be the perfect entryway to her conversation with Jonathan.

Two coffees and two cherry Danishes later, she arrived at the clinic. Cassie tried to lure her here before, but never succeeded. Would she declare victory if she discovered her here? Samantha shook her head. She came on a mission, not because of Cassie's manipulation. She gathered her courage and gazed around.

The Bracken Point clinic was the only one in town. They shared therapists and doctors with the Kingston clinic which was an hour east. Cassie had interned at both clinics but raved about the Bracken Point community of doctors and patients. Samantha hoped arriving early in the morning would allow for a discreet meeting. She was pleased to see few cars in the tiny parking lot. She hoped Jonathan's car was among them. She grabbed her purse and reached for the coffee cups when her car door pushed against her, spilling the hot liquid.

"Shit. Watch what you're doing." She searched for napkins to clean the spill.

"So sorry. How clumsy. I didn't see you there. Let me help."

Samantha froze. That voice, it couldn't be Jonathan? Dropping the napkins, she turned around and grinned.

His brown hair was in disarray, his glasses crooked on his nose. She stifled a giggle.

"Good morning, Doc. I brought you coffee, if I can rescue it."

"An unexpected visit and coffee?" Jonathan closed his car door and approached her passenger side. "I can get it from here." As he reached across the seat, their heads bumped.

For a moment their eyes met, then Samantha pulled away, blushing.

Jonathan reached for the coffee containers as Samantha remembered the Danish. Reaching for the bag, she touched his hand. The smell of sandalwood and vanilla bedazzled her. She flinched, trying to regain her composure.

Jonathan grabbed the bag and examined it. "Danish and coffee from Kirsch's? I'm touched." He smiled and closed the car door. "I hope you can stay. It's been a while since I had a breakfast date." He winked, his eyes sparkling in the early morning sun.

"I don't want to disturb your work, but I'm not letting you keep the Danish to yourself." She shut her door and strolled toward the sidewalk, trying to avoid his gaze. She snuck sideways glances, her stomach flipflopping.

When they reached the clinic entrance, Jonathan fumbled with the key while trying to balance the coffee and Danish. Samantha caught herself giggling at the sight before offering help. "Before you make a mess of yourself, let me." She took both coffee cups from his hand and stepped aside while he unlocked the door.

"My office is down the hall. Last door on the right." He handed her the Danish. "I'll be there in a minute. Make yourself at home."

She meandered through the hallway, taking in the offices and meeting rooms. Each door had a sign telling the doctor's name or service provided—Divorce Care, Grief Counseling, Addiction Recovery, were a few. At the end of the hallway, a small office bore the sign Dr. Green and Ms. Roberts. So, Cassie shared an office with him. That makes it easier to spill secrets. She wondered about their working relationship. Was Jonathan her boss? She could report Cassie for conflict of interest.

She wandered into the room. Two desks faced each other. Two chairs sat in the corner. A couch squeezed against the back wall. There wasn't much room to walk. One desk had a vase of red flowers, pictures in ornate frames, and papers neatly organized. The other was a mess of papers and folders in different directions, an old coffee cup, and a single framed picture of a woman and young girl. It was easy to figure out which desk belonged to him.

She kneeled on the couch and admired Jonathan's certificates hanging on the wall. His undergraduate and doctoral certificates hung to either side. In the middle, a larger certificate overshadowed the rest. She ran her finger over the frame, reading its title. 'Patient Advocacy Award'.

"I received that last year. It's my highest achievement and greatest honor."

Samantha startled at the voice, not expecting his return so soon. "What's it for?"

"Helping patients with mental and substance-use disorders. It's my specialty." He squeezed into the tiny office and motioned to a corner seat. He passed her a coffee and Danish then sat at his desk. Twirling his seat to face her, he took a bite. "Delicious. Cherry is my favorite."

She took a tiny bite and managed a half smile. Cassie said he was a grief counselor. What a convenient lie. "Substance abuse. Cassie didn't tell me." Yet again, Cassie tried to force her into something she didn't want or need. "Is that what she's learning? How to counsel drug addicts?"

Jonathan took another bite and nodded. "She's my intern. This is her final internship before she takes her boards. Tell me why you're here. Since you live with Cassie, you didn't come to see her. Did you have a change of heart?"

She pulled the brochures from her purse. "You left these. I wanted to know why. Grief counseling makes sense, but the drug-abuse brochure … Did Cassie tell you?"

Jonathan leaned back in his chair and grinned. "I'm glad you read them. Wasn't sure if I was conspicuous enough. Did they help?"

"I didn't read them. Kind of passive aggressive, don't you think? Promising to give me space yet leaving these as a calling card?" Samantha narrowed her eyes.

"Take a deep breath and let me explain. I promised to leave you alone, give you space to decide for yourself. Leaving the brochures wasn't a push. I wanted you to see your options." He readjusted his glasses and folded his arms.

"Options for grief counseling, I understand. When Cassie told me Lizzie died, I was irrational. But isn't it normal?" She moved to the edge of the chair.

"Everyone reacts differently. There's not a normal when it comes to grief. Some can experience it and move on. Some turn to drugs and other chemical substances. Some get help. How are you dealing with it?"

She pursed her lips. "Some days are better than others. It's the not knowing that hurts."

"Not knowing who killed her? That's hard. According to the news, the trail is cold. No witnesses, no suspects."

"I know who killed Lizzie. I don't know if they'll ever catch him."

Jonathan jolted upright. "Have you shared this information with the police?"

"I don't have any evidence. Yet. You are avoiding my question. Did Cassie tell you about my drug use?"

"No. Cassie didn't need to tell me. Drug abuse is my specialty, remember? I can tell by looking at you. Dilated pupils, sudden irrational behavior— all signs of addiction. How long have you been using?"

She gritted her teeth. "Not long. It helps me deal with the pain."

Jonathan nodded. "Some of my patients started using after traumatic events, such as loss of a loved one. It's not uncommon. The problem is, what will you do about it?"

"Nothing. I have it under control. We have rules. It makes it safer. And I can stop anytime I want. In fact, I'm stopping today." Samantha stood to gather her things.

"It's not that easy. Stopping by yourself can be painful, even deadly. You need to be under the supervision of a doctor trained in substance abuse."

"I appreciate your concern, Doc. But I'm fine. I wanted to make sure Cassie didn't share my personal information, and now I know. Don't worry I'll see myself out." Flustered, she ran, trying to avoid any further conversation.

She wasn't an addict. And she wouldn't let him treat her like one. She rushed out the door as Cassie entered, giving Samantha a confused stare, and slid into her car. Perfect people like Jonathan and Cassie would never understand. She was better off without them.

***

The visit to Jonathan's office set her off balance. He was calm and measured, far different from her manic group of friends. And he said his piece without guilting or nagging, like Cassie and Portia were prone to do. It was a welcome change, and she was thankful. But the conversation still bothered her. He insisted she had a drug problem, like so many others in her life. But like the others, he didn't understand why she needed it. Crack was the leveler. It suppressed bad memories and lessened the pain. Without it, she was a bundle of mixed-up emotions. How was it different from a drug he would prescribe for anxiety or depression? She decided it wasn't different, and Jonathan wasn't able to lecture.

Frustrated, she tried to push her thoughts aside to concentrate on her next mission. She needed all her wits to outsmart Cole.

He lived downtown, two miles from the clinic. His brick house stood in a line of brick houses, all alike. At first glance, no one would suspect he sold drugs from his basement. Although a smell of ammonia sometimes permeated the air, his neighbors left him alone. Samantha figured they were too afraid to say anything.

She closed her car door and took a deep breath. Two cobblestone paths loomed in front of her—one to the front door and one to the basement. Multiple times a week she took the basement path with Michael, in search of their latest high. She was here for a different reason. Somewhere in Cole's house lay evidence about Lizzie's murder; she only had to find it.

She knocked on the front door, making it clear she was here for a casual visit. She hoped paying him what she owed would put him in a good mood.

The door cracked open. "Go around back."

"I'm not here for that. I need to talk to Cole."

The door widened, revealing a tall redheaded woman. She looked Samantha up and down. "You're that girl. The one who came last week. I never forget a face."

Lizzie had been here. Now she had proof. Michael couldn't deny Cole's involvement now.

"Tell Cole that Samantha Barrett is here."

"Everyone wants my brother's time. He's a busy man. Come back later." The woman pushed the door closed, but Samantha blocked it with her foot.

"I'm not leaving until I talk to him."

They struggled against the door until Samantha won, pushing the woman to the ground.

"Cole! One of your crazy girls is here. Says her name is Samantha." The redhead righted herself, rubbing her side.

"Does she have my money?" Cole bellowed from the next room.

"Yes, I have your money. Come and get it."

The woman shot Samantha a nasty look and disappeared down the hallway.

Cole appeared at the door a moment later, smelling of beer and rotten eggs. He leaned on the doorframe. "Well, well. Samantha Barrett. Wasn't expecting you, especially at the front door." He winked and shone a devilish smile. "All alone?"

Samantha steadied herself on the foyer table. Cole wasn't a stranger, but she didn't feel safe without Michael. She gathered her strength and stuck to her plan. "Cut the small talk, Cole. You know why I'm here." She clutched her purse by her side.

He outstretched his hand. "Pay me."

Samantha removed the money and handed it to him. "That's not why I came."

Cole furrowed his brow. "Why are you here? Didn't Michael warn you about being alone with me?"

Samantha fought to maintain her composure. What did murderers do when confronted? She took a deep breath and walked past him into the living room.

Cole followed close behind.

"Someone murdered my sister a week ago. They found her body in the alley down the street." Samantha faced him, her hands trembling.

"Your sister, identical twin, right?" Cole caressed a revolver lying on the fireplace mantle. "Her name was Elizabeth. Gorgeous girl. She came here last Saturday night. Pleading with me to stop selling you crack. I never met someone who cared so much. You were lucky."

A bell rang, disrupting their conversation. Cole excused himself and ran to the basement.

Samantha exhaled a deep breath and sat on the couch. Cole had confessed to seeing Lizzie before she died, further evidence of his guilt. The revolver he played with could be the murder weapon. Who played with a revolver in front of company anyway?

She looked, trying to find anything that would implicate him. A glint of silver shone from the hearth. She inched over and scooped it up. Tears formed in her eyes when she realized it was Lizzie's bracelet. This was the proof she needed. Michael couldn't deny the truth now.

The sound of whistling jolted her upright. She slipped the bracelet into her purse and returned to the couch.

Cole sauntered in, grinning. "Where were we? Ah, yes, your sister. Her death was unfortunate."

Samantha ignored his comment and stuck to her plan. "The police say someone killed her between Saturday night and Sunday evening. Do they know she was here?"

"First rule—don't talk to the police." He picked up the revolver and spun it in his hands. "They create more problems than they solve."

Samantha chortled. Of course, he had rules. Cole had rules for everything.

He aimed the revolver at the ceiling and pretended to take a shot.

Samantha flinched. She imagined Lizzie, possibly in this space. Had she been terrified?

She closed her eyes, forcing herself to ask. "Is there a second rule?"

"Yeah. Don't kill gorgeous ladies. I know you think I did it. Michael came by last night. I didn't think you'd have the nerve, but he thought you'd come." Cole pointed the revolver in the air. "Do you think I killed her with this? It would have been easy. One shot." He lowered it, stopping at her chest. Cocking the gun, he winked. *"Boom."*

Samantha jumped and ran out the door.

CHAPTER 8

She drove the five miles to Michael's in a panic, sorting out events in her head. Cole's actions proved he was dangerous, and she didn't plan to underestimate him. What was her next move? Unsure, her mind raced, vacillating between reporting her findings to the police or keeping quiet. If she kept quiet, would Lizzie forgive her?

She squeezed the wheel, her knuckles turning white. Michael had to believe her now. Lizzie's bracelet and Cole's erratic behavior were enough to condemn him, but Michael had a habit of defending Cole, regardless of his behavior. Even if she proved his guilt, there was no guarantee Michael would cross his best friend. There wasn't a perfect answer. Betray Lizzie or Michael—she must make a choice.

The turn into Michael's mobile park came too soon. As she struggled with her thoughts, she heard Lizzie's voice as if she were next to her. *You know what to do.* Samantha shuddered. It was the same voice she had heard the day she learned about Lizzie's death. Was this some sort of twin telepathy from the grave? What did Lizzie want? A waft of cold air crept down her back. *It's up to you. Only you can do it.* The voice grew louder. *Avenge me.*

Panicked, Samantha sped around the corner past several houses with kids playing in the yard. She aimed for the blue trailer in the back of the neighborhood. Cars were scattered about, a common sight after dark, but out of place for early afternoon. Confused, she swerved to miss a wayward squirrel and plowed into two blue trash cans, stopping short of the front porch.

As she approached the house, Lizzie's voice played in her head. *Avenge me.* What did she mean? She had already confronted Cole, and that solved nothing. Talking to Michael wasn't the answer, yet she didn't have many options. She gathered her courage and knocked on the door.

Loud music emanated from the living room. A scantily clad woman opened the door, beer in hand. She eyed Samantha with an air of caution, as if she were out of place. "Whatever you're peddling, Hun, we're not buying, and we don't need saving."

Two women dressed in bathing suits crept behind the greeter, shooting her with water guns. Squealing and joining the fight, she left Samantha standing in the doorway.

Leary, Samantha crept into the living room surveying the guests. This was not Michael's usual crowd. She expected a mixture of his high-school friends and Cole's clients, not the makings of an orgy. Michael sat on the couch, surrounded by girls leaning on his shoulders and whispering in his ear. Disgusted, Samantha grabbed a pitcher of beer from the coffee table.

"Care to explain yourself? Not that I'd believe you anyway." She narrowed her eyes and furrowed her brow.

Michael shoved the girls aside and stammered. "S-Samantha. I wasn't expecting—" He placed his hand near his mouth and whispered, "Did we have plans?"

Her eyes bulged as she doused him with beer and stepped backward. She strode to the radio and silenced the music. Climbing onto the coffee table, she cupped her hands to her lips. "Attention, hussies! This party is over." She pointed to several girls in the corner. "You too. Don't forget your clothes; your ass is hanging out."

Snickers and snide remarks directed toward Samantha didn't deter her mission. She kept her stern look and stared down anyone who tried to challenge her. Within five minutes, the crowd had cleared, leaving an angry Samantha and a dripping-wet Michael.

She surveyed the damage. She should leave the mess for him. He *did* deserve it. But the lost look on his face melted her anger. "I'd ask you why, but I don't want to know." Exasperated, she arranged the empty plastic cups into a pile on the coffee table.

Michael grabbed her chin. "Talk to me. Please." He dropped his hand to her side, entwining his fingers with hers. "Sit with me. I can explain."

She untangled her hand from his and slammed the cups on the table. "Explain what, Michael? How you invited strange girls to your house, how you partied without me, how you were having an orgy and were caught? You can't explain this away."

"You're right. I invited them, and I didn't tell you. But nothing happened beyond what you saw."

"And what if I hadn't come? What then? Are you saying you wouldn't have done anything?" Samantha squared herself and stared him down.

"I don't know. Can we talk about this later? I have a wicked headache. I promise I'll make this up to you." Michael led her to the couch and nuzzled her neck.

Samantha inched over and turned away. She felt his hands on her shoulders, creeping down her back. His hands went down her leg, hiking up her dress. She jumped and pushed him away. Unphased, he moved his hands to her chest, pulling and prodding. The smell of alcohol on his breath disgusted her. This was not what she wanted.

Grabbing his hands, she pushed harder. "No. We can't do this. It doesn't change anything."

"Let's not think right now. Just feel." He pushed her onto the couch, his lips rough on hers.

Samantha struggled underneath him. He was drunk, she reminded herself. Michael wasn't like this when he was sober. His hands covered her breasts, kneading them. This can't happen; she couldn't deal with this now. Her emotions were all jumbled.

"Michael, get off me," she whispered. Then her anger at all the recent events bubbled to the surface. She pushed him with all her might and slipped off the couch onto the floor.

"Want to play hard to get, huh? I didn't know you were in a playful mood." Michael reached for her on the floor.

Samantha jumped to her feet. "Don't take one more step. You're drunk."

"Maybe. That never stopped us from having fun before."

He reached out again.

Samantha slapped him across the face. "Don't touch me. Go sleep it off."

"*Ow!*" What was that for?" He stepped backward, rubbing his cheek.

"Go sleep it off. We'll talk when you're sober."

Michael nodded and stumbled to his room. Stopping at his door, he shouted, "You'll still be here when I wake up?"

"I'll be here." … until she figured out her next move.

Exhausted and numb she scanned the room, wondering how to spend the time. A strong cup of coffee would help. She walked to the kitchen and sighed. Dirty dishes covered every surface. She piled them into the sink and filled the coffee pot. Memories of Lizzie flooded back. Coffee was their vice. Whenever she came home late, Lizzie would make her a cup. They would stay up talking. How she missed that. She could use someone to talk to right now.

The chaotic events surrounding Lizzie's murder exhausted her. Sleep was infrequent since she learned of her death. Being alone in Michael's house helped her relax. She curled up on the bumpy couch. It wasn't the best place to sleep but at least no one bothered her. She turned on Netflix and found a mindless comedy routine to watch. Before she knew it, the stress of the last few weeks slipped away, and she fell asleep.

A few hours later, her phone chirped. She shrugged off the blanket. "I'm coming."

She stumbled half-awake through the house, knocking over the empty beer cans on the coffee table. Who was texting her? What could they want?

I know what really happened.

Her phone dropped from her hand and hit the counter. The person who sent the flowers. It had to be.

I was there when it happened. I know the truth.

Samantha shook. Each cryptic text confused and scared her. Did she dare text back? She was sure she knew what happened to Lizzie. Was this Cole playing tricks to throw her off?

Who are you? Samantha texted back.

I'm the one who knows the truth. I know who killed your sister.

She stared at the screen. Could she trust someone who refused to identify themselves?

Who are you? Samantha texted back. *How do I know I can trust you?*

I can't tell you who I am right now. You can trust me. I loved Elizabeth.

If you loved her you would tell me who you are.

If you loved her you would know who I am. She always listened to you but you never listened to her.

The words stung. Was this true? Lizzie always listened to Samantha's problems. But Lizzie's life was perfect. She never shared problems, because she had none.

How dare you, she thought. Her emotions welled up. It was too much. She threw her phone, not caring where it landed. Her mother was right. She was a worthless, spoiled brat who didn't care about anyone but herself, and now Lizzie was gone forever. She dropped to the kitchen floor, ignoring the impact.

Curling into a ball, she released all the pent-up feelings from the past weeks.

It was too late to fix anything between her and Lizzie. Why didn't she see Lizzie needed her? What did she miss?

A noise from the back of the house startled her. Michael was awake. She wiped her eyes and attempted to straighten her hair into a quick ponytail. Michael didn't have to know about the text messages. He would want her to ignore it. But she didn't want to. She needed to know.

"Sam? Are you still here? I found your phone." Michael yawned and entered the kitchen, his black hair sticking up in all directions. "Check your messages. It was buzzing like crazy out there."

"Thanks." Samantha grabbed the phone from him and headed to the living room. Her mind formed a plan. If Cole would not confess, she would confront him with the text messages. He couldn't run from that. Samantha folded the blanket and returned it to the closet.

"I'm sorry for what happened before. A few girls came over, and then it just grew. I didn't think. The last thing I want to do is hurt you."

Never intending to hurt her, was his normal response to events like these. The silly thing was, she believed him. Michael had a habit of poor decisions, mainly because his priority was having fun. But he never tried to hurt her. It wasn't his fault his feelings never crossed into love.

"It's getting dark. You can sleep in my bed. It's more comfortable than the couch."

Samantha kept moving like she hadn't heard him. Cleaning always helped her clear her mind, and she needed to think.

"Sam, stop. I'll pick up everything when I get to it. You need to sleep." Michael stepped in front of her, so she couldn't move.

"I need to find out what happened to my sister. Get out of my way. Things would be different without you."

"Different, how? I saved you from yourself, and you know it. You were taking everything too seriously, and I showed you how to have fun. That's what you need right now. Stop acting like a damn police detective and chill out."

"Chill out? I'm trying to figure out what happened to my sister, and you want me to chill out? You don't understand what Cole can do. You weren't there."

Michael tilted his head and scrunched his nose. "You went to Cole's without me? Why?"

"I needed to know. Lizzie was there." She pulled the bracelet from her dress's side pocket. "I found her bracelet underneath the hearth. She must have dropped it when they were struggling. There's enough evidence. You can't wish this away now."

Michael sat, cradling his head in his hands. "You have evidence she was there, but it doesn't prove Cole killed her."

"He had a revolver, Michael. I was in his living room, trying to have a civil conversation, and he twirled it around like a toy. He pointed it at me. You want to convince me that he's not a killer? His actions say otherwise."

"He was having a little fun. Stupid, yes. But it doesn't prove anything. You're wasting your time with Cole."

"How do you know?" Samantha struggled from his grasp and grabbed her purse.

"You're in no condition to leave." Michael stood in front of her. "I'm not letting you go."

"Like hell you're not. I will find out what happened, and you can't stop me. I know you're protecting Cole. I just don't understand why. I thought I meant something to you, but I was wrong—just like I was wrong about everything."

"I told you, Cole didn't do it." Michael towered over her. His face was red, and his anger matched hers. Samantha had never seen him like this, but she was too distraught to stop now.

Her fists beat on his chest. "How could you do this? How can you put him above us? My sister died, you idiot. She died. You're supposed to be on my side. Why isn't anyone on my side?" A tear streaked her face.

He grabbed her and pulled her close. "I'm on your side. I always will be. It'll be all right. Calm down. Just breathe." Grabbing a tissue, he wiped her eyes. "Better?"

Samantha nodded and burrowed her head in his shoulder.

"If it makes you feel better, I can help you find out the truth. I still don't think it was Cole, but I can ask around. Maybe someone saw something?"

It wasn't part of her plan, but it would have to do. It wasn't safe to go snooping in that part of town after dark. "Okay. Thank you."

"I know what you need." Michael kissed her forehead then kissed both of her eyelids. "You need to forget. We'll start fresh in the morning." Michael crossed the room and put on his favorite Kenny G CD.

Samantha avoided his gaze and tugged on her ear. Kenny G meant one thing, and she wasn't sure if she was interested. Part of her wondered why she stayed with him. His behavior today showed he wasn't serious about their relationship, but she couldn't bring herself to break up with him. Who would she have then? And did she deserve better than Michael? After everything she had put Lizzie through, she doubted it. Michael was familiar, the only constant she had anymore. It was easier to stay with him than not.

He extended his hand and helped her off the couch. Wrapping his arms around the small of her back, he swayed to the beat.

Samantha laid her head against his chest, taking in his smell. The familiarity of cigarette smoke, vanilla spice, and beer calmed her senses. As they swayed, her worries about Cole and Lizzie faded. She lifted her head and gazed in his eyes.

Michael leaned forward, his lips grazing on hers. His urgency grew as he lowered his hands down her back, squeezing her butt. Samantha answered back, her body starving for more than Michael usually gave.

When the song ended, he lifted her and carried her to the bedroom. Placing her on the bed, he removed his clothes. He was comfortable, safe, but she felt no excitement when they had sex. It was a one-sided affair, concentrated on his release. Samantha thought he might change if she said something, but she didn't want to hurt him with her complaints. Instead, she sat and waited for him to take the lead, hoping things would change.

"What are you waiting for?" He stared at her in bewilderment. "Take off your clothes." He sat next to her on the bed, his hand on her thigh. "Need help?" His lips settled on her neck as his hands slid up her thigh and parted her legs. "This won't do." He reached for a condom in the bedside dresser. Turning, he hiked up her dress and peeled off her underwear. Without speaking, he slipped himself inside.

Samantha froze as he entered, deflated but not surprised. His strides were short and rough—enough for his release but not hers. As he finished, her mind drifted. She pictured Jonathan and his tousled brown hair. What would it be like to run her fingers through it and gaze into his dreamy brown eyes? Would it be different from how it was with Michael?

He rolled over on his back, out of breath.

Samantha laid there, trying to piece everything together. Her life had once made sense. Now, she wasn't sure. She pulled on her underwear and rolled onto her side on the edge of the bed.

Michael was already snoring.

Samantha cried, wondering what the heck she should do now.

CHAPTER 9

S amantha sat and shielded her eyes from the blaring sun. It was morning already.

Michael was asleep next to her, snoring like a freight train.

She sat on the edge of the bed and pulled on a pair of Michael's shorts and a white T-shirt. Something about last night bothered her, and it wasn't just the text messages. Sex with Michael was always quick, and, in the past, they were both satisfied. This time, it was different. But she couldn't figure out why. Thoughts of Jonathan dominated her brain. She wasn't sure what she wanted anymore.

She grabbed Lizzie's bracelet from her purse and put it in her pocket. She wanted to keep it close until she figured out what to do.

Coffee. That's what I need. The perfect way to start the morning. Maybe then I won't be so numb.

She walked to the kitchen and brewed a pot. The sound and smell relaxed her mind. She carried her mug to the window and stared into the front yard.

As she stood, watching the mobile park come to life, a Ford Focus arrived. Curious, she tiptoed to the front door. She peeked through the window as two well-dressed men approached the porch.

A firm knock startled her. She froze, hoping they would leave.

"Michael Grant, this is the police. Please open the door."

They knew! Her hand went into her pocket, caressing Lizzie's bracelet. This was her chance. Tell the police and avenge her sister. Lizzie wanted her to, right?

As she wrestled with her decision, the knock came louder. "Grant. It's Detectives Logan and Patrick. We have questions for you. Make this easy on yourself. Open the door now."

Hesitant, she waited for Lizzie's voice to dictate her move, but it never came. She considered Michael's words from last night. What if she was wrong? She needed guidance, but Lizzie wasn't cooperating. Was it a sign?

Without a clear direction, she kept quiet. They wanted to talk to Michael, not her. She placed her mug on the counter and walked to the back room.

Michael was sprawled on the bed, still snoring.

"Hey, wake up. We have visitors."

A noise came from under the blankets. He pulled the sheets over his head and ignored her.

Samantha peeled the blankets back and stooped to look him in the eye. "It's the police. And I didn't call them. They have questions about something."

Michael half opened his eyes. "Huh? What are you talking about?"

"Two detectives are outside asking for you. Get up and see what they want."

"I don't have to talk to them." Michael closed his eyes and pulled the covers over his head.

"I want to. Maybe they have information that could help us figure out what happened."

"No. I'm not playing detective, and I'm not talking to the police. Just like Cole taught me—no warrant, no talking."

"Michael, please. Talk to them for me? I promise to keep quiet."

A pillow flew across the room. "You won't let me sleep unless I talk to them? Fine. But I'm not doing this because of those puppy-dog eyes. I'm doing this so I can sleep." He pulled on his pants and stumbled to the door. "You owe me for this, Detective Barrett. After this, I'm done."

Samantha followed him to the door.

He opened it a crack and sniped at the detectives. "Yeah, what do you want?"

They looked amused as they took in Michael's disheveled appearance. "Rough night, Grant? Promise we won't keep you too long. We have a few questions about the Barrett case. We got a tip that says you might know something." Detective Patrick peeked his head around the door, glancing inside. "Mind if we come in?"

"Yes, I mind. What kind of tip, Patrick? Are you suspecting me now?"

"Calm down, Grant. It's nothing, really. Must follow every lead. Is Ms. Barrett with you? Her mother told us she may be here."

Samantha observed from inside the door. They wore suits and carried small notebooks with pencils. Michael seemed familiar with them, and she wondered why. Detective Patrick seemed to do all the talking while the redhead wrote.

She pushed past Michael and onto the front porch. "I'm here, Detective."

Michael shot her a quick glance, as if telling her to be quiet.

Samantha paid it no attention and smiled at Detective Logan.

"Good morning, Ms. Barrett. We came from your mother's house. We have a few questions about your sister, Elizabeth Barrett. We can ask them here or at the station, wherever you're more comfortable." Detective Logan smiled.

"I can answer whatever questions you need. Here. Outside." Michael closed the door and stepped in front of Samantha. "I'm sure you have all the information you need from Sam."

"Actually, we don't. If you insist on staying outside, Grant, we can talk here. Is there somewhere else Logan can take Ms. Barrett?"

"By the tree." She pointed a few feet away. "There are lawn chairs. We can speak there, if you would like, Detective Logan." Samantha gave her biggest smile.

Michael balled his fists. He would give her an earful when this was over.

Samantha led the detective to the lawn chairs and sat.

"Thank you for speaking to me, Ms. Barrett." Detective Logan stared at his notebook, trying to find his question. "Do you know a Cole Weston?"

Just the facts, she reminded herself. If they came from her mother's house, there was no telling what combination of truth and conjecture Portia shared with them.

"Yes. I've met him a few times. He's Michael's friend." She glanced in Michael's direction, wondering what Detective Patrick was asking him. He paced back and forth, his hand on his forehead. She could tell Michael didn't trust them, but she didn't understand why.

Detective Logan flipped through his notebook, searching for his next question. "Other than Michael's friend, do you know anything else about him? What he does for a living, his hobbies?"

He was fishing for something. Samantha didn't want to share her information. Cole would know who tipped them off, and Michael would never forgive her. She looked at the ground.

"Ms. Barrett, you're keeping something from us. We will find out. We've been tracking Mr. Weston's and Mr. Grant's activities for months. If you know something, it's your obligation to tell us." Detective Logan put his hands on his knees and leaned close.

Samantha took a deep breath. "My sister went to see Cole that Saturday night. She told me she was going, and Cole confirmed it." She fiddled with Lizzie's bracelet in her pocket. "Beyond that, I don't know."

"You've spoken to Cole since the murder?"

"Yesterday. At his place. I know Lizzie was there. I wish I could tell you more." She caught Michael's eye and froze. How would he react if he knew what she had just shared? She turned back, wishing this was over. "Any more questions, Detective?"

He closed his notebook and crossed his arms. "I've been chasing drug dealers for the past ten years. Weston and Grant are at the top of my list. They're bad news. When I see a beautiful young woman like you hanging around trash like them, I get mad. If I can help you get away—"

"Detective Logan, is everything okay?" Detective Patrick approached them with a disturbed look on his face.

Michael came up behind Samantha and put his arms around her.

Detective Logan closed his notebook and looked at his shoes. "I have no further questions." He moved to walk away then stopped. "Wait. Ms. Barrett, did you get a flower delivery the day of your sister's wake?"

The flowers. Her mind drifted to the text messages. They were related, she was certain. Should she mention them? Could you go to jail for withholding evidence? She swallowed hard and pushed her thoughts aside. "Yes. I'm sure my mother already gave you the flowers and the note. What else did she tell you?"

"We can't reveal what she told us. Is there anyone at your mother's company who had problems with Elizabeth? A disgruntled employee, a jilted lover?"

"Everyone loved Lizzie. I can't imagine anyone had a problem with her. Why would you ask?"

"We traced the flowers to your mother's office. Someone who works with her had ordered them with the company's credit card." The detectives looked at Samantha, gauging her response.

"Are you saying someone at Mother's office knows what happened and said nothing? Could that person be involved?"

Detective Logan closed his notebook. "We're not saying anything. We're collecting information. If we have more questions, we'll be in touch." He retrieved a business card and handed it to Samantha, leaning in to whisper in her ear. "If you ever need help, please call me. You're too nice of a girl to be hanging out with garbage."

She took the card and placed it in her pocket, hoping Michael didn't notice.

The detectives walked a few yards and huddled in a corner beside the house, comparing notes.

Michael lit a cigarette and puffed smoke near her face. "What the hell was that?"

"What do you mean? He was asking questions. What did the other one ask you? Did you learn anything?"

"Don't change the subject. Did you tell him about Cole? He slipped something in your hand. What was it? This isn't the first time I've dealt with this pair."

Samantha looked him in the eye. "I had to tell him something. Lizzie was in Cole's house before she was murdered. They needed to know, so they can investigate. Now it's in their hands. If they find evidence against him, then I was right. If not, Cole will be exonerated. I don't understand the big deal."

"You don't understand, because you haven't been under the microscope. Logan has it out for us. I wouldn't put it past him to frame Cole, and your evidence might be enough to do it. He's a dirty cop." Michael kept glancing back and forth between Logan and Samantha, looking ready to pounce.

She ignored his paranoia. The detective seemed genuine and professional to her. Michael would search for any excuse to discount her theory about Cole. "Can we get back to my questions? Does Patrick suspect Cole? What did my mother tell him?"

Michael extinguished the cigarette and plopped in a chair. "After your conversation with Logan, I'm sure he does. Patrick wasn't informative."

Samantha sat next to him, feeling defeated. Someone at her mother's office claimed to know something about Lizzie's death, but she hoped to get more from Michael. If he knew these detectives, why wasn't he willing to do some digging to get information from them?

The detectives finished their conversation and returned to Samantha and Michael. "Thank you both for your time. We have the information we need here." They headed to their car, and Detective Patrick turned to meet Michael's eyes.

"Oh, and Mr. Grant. Stay away from Mr. Weston and don't think about leaving town."

Once they were out of earshot, Michael mimicked, "Stay away from Mr. Weston, and don't leave town." He turned to Samantha, his face red. "Why did I agree to talk to them again? This is screwing up my life."

"Screwing up *your* life? You're so selfish. All you can think about is partying and getting high. Who cares about what I want? Who cares about what I need? It's all about you, isn't it?"

Michael grabbed a lawn chair and threw it at the house. "I always do what you want. I always think about your needs. Hell, Samantha, I even considered Cole's involvement, because you were so sure he was. Never tell me that I don't care about you. But I'm more concerned about Cole. Thanks to your wild imagination and your mother's big mouth, the cops are looking into him. I have to warn him."

"Warn him? You know I still think he's involved somehow. What happened to letting the police figure everything out?"

"Using my words against me, *hmm?* I told you those guys are crooked. They have a grudge against Cole, and this is giving them what they need. Give me a chance to prove you're wrong. If you are, everyone is wasting time, and the real killer is getting away."

"So, what do you propose? Are you playing *detective* now? That's not your thing, remember?"

"Go to your mother's office and see what you can find out. I'll snoop around Cole's house and the old neighborhood. I'll text you if I uncover anything and we can meet for lunch.

That could work. She wasn't sure what they would discover, but she hoped it would solidify her decision.

***

After leaving Michael's, she stopped by her house to shower and find suitable clothes. Portia had standards for appearance. No one made it past the front desk unless they looked the part. She chose a simple outfit—a pale blue silk shirt and navy-blue pencil skirt. A white clutch completed the look. She put Lizzie's bracelet in the purse for safekeeping and drove to Portia's office. They hadn't spoken since Lizzie's wake, and Samantha thought it was better that way. Conversations between them never ended well, but this was too important to ignore.

The detectives hadn't spoken to her mother since this morning, so she hoped she would be the first to tell her the news. With any luck, she was having a slow morning, so they could talk.

When she arrived, the front desk buzzed her in. The secretaries had known her since she was little. They usually greeted her with a smile. This time no one smiled. Only a look of pity, as if she was a child who had lost her dog. She ignored them and kept going. The elevator ride to the executive offices gave her time to think. How could she make Portia listen? She took a deep breath as the elevator neared the top floor.

Nora stood guard to her mother's office. No one saw Portia unless they made it through her. Undeterred, Samantha breezed past, paying her no attention.

"Samantha, this isn't a good time. Your mother is busy. Can I make an appointment? Maybe later this week." Nora rushed to keep pace with her, trying to match her stride.

"No thank you, Nora. She will see me now. It's important." Samantha continued, ignoring the pleas from her mother's lackey.

Portia's office comprised of many parts. To one side was a staging area where they prepared products and presentations for clients. In the middle was a conference room and several smaller offices for her close associates.

To the right side stood Portia's corner office, complete with floor-to-ceiling windows.

Nora was right; it was busy. People bustled around, like little ants. Samantha stood close to the wall, trying not to get trampled. She searched for the orchestrator of the chaos, spying her mother shouting orders from the far end of the hallway.

"One hour, people. Any mistake on this presentation will result in a pink slip." This proclamation would scare away most people, but Samantha smiled, shook her head and beelined for her mother.

"I see you're using scare tactics as motivational tools again, Mother. Is that effective?" Her hands rested on her hips as she gave Portia a disapproving look. "I suppose you have a moment to talk?"

"I'm in the middle of a huge deal with a new client, and you want to talk?" Portia handed papers to a passing employee and approached her corner office.

Samantha hurried after her. "It's important, Mother. The police came to Michael's house this morning. They were asking questions."

"So, that's where you've been hiding. I told them I thought you'd be holed up with that degenerate. Did they arrest him? They should."

"No, Mother. They didn't arrest him. Why would they?"

Portia snorted and sorted through papers on her desk. "What a shame. Well, whatever were they asking then? I told them everything they need to know. Everything." Portia's eyes fixed on Samantha's, cold and emotionless.

"I'm sure. But they did some digging about the flower delivery. They have a lead on who sent them. You need to know this, Mother."

"Does it matter? If it leads to an arrest, I don't care about the details. I have a business to run. They do their job, and I do mine." Portia turned and rushed out the door.

Samantha stood in the office doorway and shouted, making sure everyone in the office heard. "But if it implicates someone here at your company? Wouldn't that concern you?"

Portia turned and stared at Samantha. She walked back down the hallway and pulled Samantha into her office. "This isn't the place to talk. You want everyone knowing our business?"

"I want you to listen. And since this place is the only one that matters, where else can we talk? Someone here knows what happened. It wouldn't surprise me if the detectives showed up soon."

"What are you implying? Everyone loved Elizabeth."

"Someone here knows something, Mother. Whether or not they did it, someone knows what happened. We can find out who it was. The police are trying, but we can help too. Ask around."

"I don't have time right now. We're getting ready to launch a new product line. Amber! Where is that girl? Get in here and help me." Portia scurried around the room, shouting orders and pushing Samantha aside.

"I'm not going away, Mother. This is too important. Anything here can wait. I'm sure your client would understand."

"You're the one who never understood. This is a business. Whatever you are babbling about can wait until this evening. I'm on a deadline. Amber! She's never around when I need her." Portia flitted around the room, chaos surrounding her as people rushed to implement her orders.

"Since you insist on staying, make yourself useful. Here, set up this display. The vendors will be here soon. Amber!" Portia shoved a box of cosmetics at Samantha and stormed down the hallway.

As if on cue, a petite girl carrying a large box entered and stumbled in front of Samantha. She couldn't help but stare as the box fell to the floor. Boxes of lipstick, blush and mascara scattered everywhere.

"Oh, no." The girl bent to scoop up the cosmetics.

"Here, let me help you." Samantha caught her eye as they cleaned the rest of the mess. She looked familiar. "Do I know you?"

The girl turned toward the display and stacked the boxes. "You're Elizabeth's sister. I forgot you looked so much alike. What are you doing here?"

How could she forget? Jeremy's timid little sister and Lizzie's shadow. "Amber. It's good to see you again. You work for my mother? How brave. She's looking for you."

"I'm sure she is. The warehouse was busy." Amber went straight to work, putting each item in their own little rows on the display.

Samantha watched her small frame and delicate hands work, making the display come alive with product. Amber's red hair complimented her freckles, and her natural smile made her seem friendly. But there was something about her. Something that screamed, *Proceed with caution.*

Samantha bent to collect a box of lipstick and handed it to her. She tried to meet her eyes, but Amber looked away.

"I learned some interesting news from the police about Lizzie. I hoped to talk to Mother and the people in the office," Samantha said.

"About what? I'm sure if the police have a tip, they'd come here themselves."

"Oh, they probably will. A delivery came from this office. Something about some flowers. Someone ordered a bouquet of yellow roses from this office with a cryptic note. Something about knowing what happened to Lizzie." Samantha paused and judged Amber's reaction. Could the girl know something? She had access to the top floor.

Amber froze. "I'm sure multiple people ordered flowers for Elizabeth's wake. Why would that be surprising?"

"Ah, but I didn't say they were for her wake. Just that someone ordered flowers from this office. Someone knows about Lizzie's murder. What do you know, Amber? Is there something you're not telling?"

Amber turned bright red and stammered. Samantha was on to something. She sensed it.

Jeremy poked his head around the corner.

Samantha forgot he worked here. She caught his eyes and continued. "The detectives traced the flower delivery here. They tied it to a corporate credit card."

Jeremy rushed in, face flushed. "Amber. Portia's been looking for you everywhere. Stop socializing, and get work done for a change?" He barged between them, casting a side eye at Samantha. "You know better. If I don't see hustle, you're on your own for dinner tonight."

"Yes, Jeremy. Everything will be ready. I promise." Amber lowered her gaze to the floor and returned to making her little rows of cosmetics.

He strolled up to Samantha, a sly look on his face. "I never thought you'd show your face here. Any reason you graced us with your presence?"

"Not really. I had news about Lizzie's case I wanted to share with Mother. I was asking Amber if she knew anything about it."

"News from who? Watch where you get your information."

"I think it's credible. Detective Logan is gathering evidence before he makes an arrest."

"Interesting. Samantha, can I have a word with you? Let's go in your mother's office. It's more private."

Remembering his aggressive behavior at the wake, she stood her ground. "Whatever you need to tell me, you can tell me here."

Jeremy grabbed her arm and pulled her close. "I'm not sure why you're nosing around here asking questions. Playing detective? You know what happened to your sister. No one here was involved. That all hangs on you and your friends."

"Get off me, Jeremy. Let me go." Samantha tried to free herself from his grip.

"After I make this clear. Wherever you go, trouble follows. Stop snooping around here, and stay away from my sister. She's young and doesn't need your influence."

His hand wrapped around her wrist and twisted. "If you don't, I'll make sure you stay away from her. Permanently."

Samantha trembled. Jeremy always struck her as unstable. And what did he mean by *permanently*? This situation grew more complicated every day.

Lunch. That's what she needed. She strode to the elevator and breathed a sigh of relief when she was finally alone. Jeremy and Amber were grieving, but they made her uneasy. Something wasn't right. But she didn't know what.

Her phone buzzed as she reached the bottom floor. Michael. Hopefully, he had good news.

Meet me at Plato's Pizza for lunch. They arrested Cole.

CHAPTER 10

Plato's Pizza was packed. Every night, college kids and twentysomethings hung out after partying. But Samantha didn't expect a crowd at lunch. She surveyed the dining room ready to pounce on the first available seat. With all the families and businesspeople on lunch break, it would be difficult to find a quiet place to chat. She hoped for a spot in the back for privacy, in case Michael's mood was explosive.

She had little to share. Portia wasn't cooperative, and no one in the office was talking. She thought about the strange encounter with Jeremy and Amber but pushed it from her mind. Grief brought out the worst in people, and they were no exception. She decided to give them the benefit of doubt, for now.

She eyed a family leaving a booth in the far corner. Determined, she zoned in and raced to claim it. As she reached it, someone stepped in front of her. They crashed, his soda spilled on the floor, and her phone went flying.

"So sorry. Here, let me help you." Her gaze went from the soda on the floor to the man standing in front of her, and she laughed. "You have to stop meeting girls this way, Jonathan. This whole coming-to-the-rescue stuff doesn't fly these days."

Jonathan smiled. "Samantha Barrett. Are you telling me I don't have to spill soda all over you to get you to have lunch with me?"

"Lunch, huh? Well, I'm supposed to meet Michael, but I don't know what's holding him up. I suppose we could share this booth, since it's so crowded. I need to figure out where my phone went."

Jonathan looked behind him and saw a phone lying under another table. "Excuse me." He picked it up and turned to face her. "I suppose rescuing your phone is looked down on too?"

"I'll allow it. Thank you."

He glanced at the screen and held it out. "Kingsbrook Lake. Haven't been there since I was a kid. Do you go often?"

They settled across from each other. Samantha placed her phone in front of her and glanced at him. "I used to. Lizzie and I loved to hike the trails and picnic. Haven't been in almost a year. What are you doing here anyway?"

"Psychiatrists have to eat too. I love pizza, and this is the best in town. Have you ever been here before?"

"Michael and I come here sometimes. I've never been during the day. I didn't realize it got so crowded."

"Oh yeah. This place is always hopping. Their deep-dish Chicago-style is fantastic. Want to split one?" Jonathan motioned for a waitress. "The usual, please. Oh, and two Cokes."

"The usual? You must come here a lot." Samantha glanced at her phone then looked toward the front door. She hoped Michael wouldn't show up.

"At least once a week. Most times I bring it back to the clinic. I used to eat dinner here every Friday night. When Rachel was around." His brown eyes clouded over.

"Let me guess, an ex-girlfriend?"

"No. Rachel was my daughter."

He had a daughter; did that mean he had a wife? She glanced at his hand and didn't see a wedding ring. She wanted to ask but decided it would be too bold.

"Did something happen to her?"

Jonathan lowered his head, his eyes misting. "I lost her two years ago to a drunk driver."

No wonder he understood grief; he had experienced it himself.

"I'm sorry. I can't imagine. Losing Lizzie was hard but losing a daughter must have been horrible. I mean, I'm so sorry, Jonathan. How old was she?"

"Five. It was horrible, but, like all things, you deal with it and move on." He blinked back a tear. "Enough about me. What's the deal with you and Michael? According to him, you two are a thing. Are you serious?"

Samantha blushed. She wasn't used to a guy being so forward. They would flirt and hint at an attraction, but they would never ask about Michael. The question stumped her. She wasn't even sure what they were anymore.

"We've been dating for the last six months. We've never defined it. Michael isn't the serious type." She couldn't believe she said those words. But Michael wasn't serious, and she wasn't sure he ever would be.

"So, you're saying I have a chance?" His eyes danced, making her blush.

She looked at the table. "Are you flirting with me, Doc?" She wasn't sure if he was flirting or teasing. Either way, it had an impact.

"Ah, back to *Doc* now, are we? That's okay. I'll leave it alone."

Samantha fiddled with her napkin, trying to avoid his gaze. The silence broke when the waitress arrived with a steaming hot pizza topped with mushrooms and peppers, her favorite. How did he know?

"Is it against the rules to serve you a piece? Or is that not allowable these days?"

Samantha smiled, her gaze meeting his. "I suppose it's okay. It smells delicious."

The piping-hot pizza dripped with sauce and cheese. Either it was the time of day or the company, but she never remembered Plato's tasting this good.

Jonathan wrestled with a long piece of string cheese as he took a bite.

Samantha laughed as he struggled to eat the gooey mess.

"It's good, huh? I told you it was the best in town." He put down his pizza and stared. "You have something. Right on your cheek." He reached across the table with a napkin. "Let me …"

She froze as his hand touched her face. She caught a whiff of vanilla mixed with garlic from the pizza crust. It smelled nice—like comfort, like peace, like home. As he removed his hand, she grabbed it, not wanting the feeling to end.

"Thank you. You didn't have to do this. You don't know me. Just because I'm Cassie's friend and a complete wreck doesn't mean you have to—"

He squeezed her hand sending shockwaves through her. "This isn't out of obligation. Cassie's friend or not, I want to get to know you. Is that so hard to believe?"

"When you grew up the way I did, it is. No one liked me for me. There was always a catch." She snatched away her hand and looked at the ceiling, trying to repress her memories and tears.

"I didn't mean to bring up the past. But I want you to believe you have worth just the way you are. No strings."

"No strings? You've met my mother. Love and attention were always full of strings."

"Yes, your mother ..." Jonathan sat back and adjusted his glasses. "Was she always so demanding?"

"Pretty much. I have a few memories before my dad died. She was softer, more present in our lives. That's why it hit me so hard when she changed. Lizzie said she had to change. She had to be tough. I don't know. Lizzie dealt with it much better than I ever did."

"Change is hard. Especially when it's sudden. I'm sure she thought she was doing everything she could to provide for you."

"That. Right there. That's Cassie. She always took Mother's side, finding an excuse for her behavior. I could believe it if she tried to listen. But she never did." Samantha sipped her soda. "I know you mean well, but, like I told Cassie, you don't understand unless you were there. Even the fleet of psychiatrists Mother hired when I was a teen couldn't decipher our relationship.

"Now I know why you hate us psychiatrists so much. Saw some real doozies, huh? Not all of us are whack jobs." Jonathan winked.

"How do I know you're not a whack job?" She tilted her head and gave him a coy smile. "I'll have to complete a full investigation to make sure you're not trying to manipulate me with soda and pizza."

"Oh yes, because that's how we psychiatrists work. Ply them with comfort food in a crowded restaurant."

They both laughed. She felt like a real person. No manic episodes, no desire to get high. Only a comfortable conversation with a friend. She wished the feeling would linger. "This is nice. I haven't felt this relaxed in forever. Thank you."

"We're two people hanging out, eating pizza. Nothing special. It will all return in time. You're still grieving. Give yourself the time you need. You'll feel normal again."

"Normal? I'm not sure what that means. Even before Lizzie, normal wasn't something I was used to. I'm sorry, Doc. You don't want to hear about my baggage." Samantha looked at her phone. She had only told Jonathan some of her past. How would he react if he knew the whole story?

"We all have baggage. It's how we deal with it that defines us. Let me speak as one survivor to another. Grief takes time to overcome. You can't run from it; you must confront it, let it run its course. Otherwise, it will consume you, and you will never recover."

"How did you deal with Rachel's death? I mean, how did you get to this point? Looking at you, people wouldn't realize something happened. But you experienced something dreadful. How do you recover from that?"

"Honestly? It was hard. It's still hard. It doesn't go away. But you learn ways to get better. When it first happened, I didn't go to work and barely ate for weeks. I was mad at the world. How could someone take the life of my beautiful daughter because of their selfishness? I was livid, and I turned that hatred inward and hated myself."

Samantha lowered her gaze. "That's how I feel. I keep telling myself that Lizzie would still be here if I was a better sister, better friend, better person. I blame myself more than the person who did it."

"It's a stage of grief. You must go through it. But don't get stuck there. It's not my fault a drunk driver killed Rachel, and it's not your fault someone murdered Lizzie. You have to free yourself from the guilt. It's the only way to keep healing."

"But aren't you still mad at the person who killed her?"

"Of course, I am. But my anger toward him has decreased. They convicted him. He'll be in jail for several years. Being mad at him won't help me heal faster. What I can do is find ways to end addiction. Alcohol and drugs are the problems. If I can combat that, I'm doing something for Rachel."

That's why he helped people dealing with addiction. It was his way of coping. If he felt this way about drug abuse though, why was he spending his time flirting with her? He knew she had a problem. Yet he flirted like he was interested. It was an act. It had to be. He wanted to tear down her defenses, so she would agree to get help. She reminded herself to guard her heart. This wasn't the real thing.

Samantha's phone buzzed, jolting her back to reality. "It's Michael. I should see what he wants. I had a great lunch. Next time, you don't have to spill a drink to get a date." She smiled and looked at her phone.

"If our paths should cross again, I would be delighted." Jonathan made an exaggerated bow and reached for the check.

As she readied herself to leave, she eyed Jeremy approaching their table, Amber tagging behind. What did they want? Were they stalking her? She rolled her eyes and sunk into the booth.

"Isn't this cozy? Who's your friend? He's not your usual type, is he? Does Michael know?" Jeremy saddled up to the booth and sat. "Crackheads like Michael are more her type. Going up in the world, huh Sam?"

Amber stood to the side and looked at her feet, not making eye contact.

"Jeremy, if you're interrupting our lunch, the least you can do is allow Amber to sit with us too."

"Unnecessary. Just got word the police arrested your drug-dealer friend, Cole, for Elizabeth's murder. You need to find another supplier." Jeremy leaned over as he left and whispered to Jonathan as he left. "Good luck with this one. She's wild."

Samantha blushed as they walked away. "I apologize. Jeremy was Lizzie's fiancé. We never got along."

"No explanation needed." His expression changed.

Jonathan knew she used, but he acted like it was new information. She wondered what he thought but didn't dare ask.

They left the table in silence.

Samantha followed behind him to the parking lot. She stopped on the sidewalk and touched his arm. "Thank you again for lunch. You were right. It *is* the best pizza in town."

She searched for a smile, a piece of the guy she had lunch with, but he was nowhere to be found.

"No problem. Tell Cassie I said *hello*." And off he rushed, crushing her heart as he walked down the street.

Now what? She was more confused than ever. But she didn't have time to think. Her phone buzzed with another text from Michael.

Meet me at your house.

She hopped in her car, reminding herself Michael was a better match.

Chapter 11

Samantha expected an extra car in the driveway, but she didn't expect her mother's silver BMW parked next to Cassie's Jeep. Michael's car was nowhere in sight—a godsend since dealing with both would be a nightmare. Whatever Portia wanted, she hoped it was quick. Michael's mood was unpredictable lately. How he would behave around Portia after learning about Cole's arrest would be anyone's guess. She compartmentalized her thoughts about Cole, Jonathan, and the mystery of Lizzie's death. She needed her wits to deal with her mother.

Hoping to go unnoticed, she turned the door handle and cracked it open. Two women occupied the front living room, coexisting in awkward silence. Cassie paced the length of the space, her brow furrowed. Portia, stoic as usual, sat upright with her legs crossed. A pained expression covered her face, something beyond her grief for Lizzie.

Samantha lowered her head and tiptoed toward her bedroom. Anything that brought Cassie and Portia together was ominous. As she crossed the hallway from the living room toward her haven, a voice caught her off guard.

"Hey. Have a minute? You didn't come home yesterday. Is everything okay?"

Cassie stood in the hallway, her eyes warm and inviting.

"Yep. Just need a shower." Samantha continued toward her room when a hand grabbed her elbow.

"Before you go, can I get your opinion? I was thinking of painting the living room. I have a few options. We can decide together."

Samantha turned and narrowed her eyes. "I know Mother is here." She wrested away her arm and took two steps.

Cassie rushed in front of her and stood, arms crossed. "I called her, because I'm worried. You almost set the house on fire, then you make a mysterious trip to the clinic and brush me off. Then you disappear for a whole day. What did you expect me to do?"

"Mind your own business?" Samantha pursed her lips and narrowed her eyes. "Your loyalty is lacking, Cass."

"My loyalty is to Elizabeth's memory. I promised to look after you, and I keep my promises. Come into the living room and talk to us, so we know you're okay." Cassie's eyes softened. "Do it for Elizabeth."

Lizzie's memory. That's an interesting way to gain cooperation. Portia was the queen of guilt trips and used them to get obedience throughout Samantha's entire life. Now Cassie was guilting her over her sister's death. She had two options. Get over it or lock herself in her room. She decided it was better to talk. Experience with Cassie proved she would wait her out if she chose the latter.

Samantha curled her lip. "Fine."

She shambled into the living room and plopped on the armchair closest to the hallway. If things turned south, she could make a quick escape. Curling her feet underneath her, she turned away from Portia, refusing eye contact.

Cassie sat in the armchair facing Samantha and glanced between her and Portia. "We're here because we're worried. Jonathan said you spoke to him about drug counseling, but he won't tell me anything else. You're safe here. Tell us what's going on."

"Nothing. I'm fine. May I please be dismissed for a shower? Mother obviously doesn't want to be here."

Portia pursed her lips, staring straight ahead. "I left an important meeting with a client for this. Cassie asked you a question, and you better answer."

Samantha turned to face her mother. "You want me to talk now? How about this afternoon when I tried to get your attention at your office? You didn't have time for me then, but Cassie calls, and you drop everything?"

"Don't be impertinent. I had no idea you almost burned down the house. Cassie paints a disturbing picture, one I cannot tolerate. I should have put my foot down much earlier, but Elizabeth was certain it was a phase."

"Put your foot down? I make my own decisions, Mother. You have no business here. Kindly leave." Samantha jumped to her feet and motioned toward the door.

"Ladies, this is not helping," Cassie said. "Please sit."

Both women ignored her and concentrated on each other.

Portia stood and met Samantha's gaze. "They arrested Cole Weston today. It's only a matter of time before your connection to him is made public. Then what? Do you want to be known as the drug addict who killed her sister? Because that's exactly what the media will say. Elizabeth went to his house because of you. She died because of you. And every time you look in the mirror and see her face staring back, she will haunt you."

A tear crept down Samantha's face. Lizzie was already haunting her. The voices had stopped since yesterday, but Samantha knew they would return. She took a shallow breath and rocked back and forth. Her mother deserved a retort to her hurtful comments, but she was right. Defeated, she covered her face and fled to the hallway bathroom.

She stood by the door, eavesdropping. She wondered if Cassie would finally understand why she didn't have a relationship with her mother.

The muffled sounds grew louder as Cassie's voice screeched her frustration. "That was not the plan! I told you what to say. Accusing her of involvement in Elizabeth's death will not convince her to get help! Your misplaced anger made our intervention impossible now."

"She's beyond helping, and it's past time you realized it. Don't call me again," she heard Portia shout, followed by the sound of a door slamming.

Her mother's dismissiveness and hurtful comments cut to the core. Was she beyond help? Portia thought so. But Portia never had an encouraging word. Once again, Portia reminded her of her failings. She didn't understand why she expected different.

Don't let her win. She jolted up. *Stand up. Fight for us.* Lizzie's voice was as clear as if she were there.

Samantha struggled to her feet and looked in the mirror. Lizzie *did* haunt her. How could she make her stop? She saw Lizzie's face staring back. But what if she didn't? Would Lizzie leave her alone?

Tears flooded her face as she stared at the ghostlike reflection. Her grief was almost unbearable. It tore at her gut, and a strangled sound escaped her throat as she attempted to keep the wrenching pain inside. She had to quell her grief.

She retrieved a box of hair dye she had bought months ago from the cabinet. This wasn't the first time she wanted to change her appearance. But she never had the guts. Now nothing held her back. She spent the next few hours in the bathroom, changing her blond hair to black.

After a warm shower, she meandered to her bedroom. With a towel wrapped around her head, she put on her comfiest pajamas. The soft purple fabric enveloped her and relieved the tension from earlier in the day. With trepidation, she unfurled the towel and let her hair fall down her back. Glancing in the mirror, she flinched at the reflection. Her face stayed the same, but the once-sunny blond hair she shared with Lizzie was gone. As she stared, another image appeared next to her—the same face but with blond hair.

Why? Avenge me. Don't forget me. The voice was stronger.

Samantha trembled. Dyeing her hair hadn't made Lizzie go away. What did she expect? They arrested Cole, that should be the end of it. Why was Lizzie still invading her thoughts? Desperate, she grabbed a pair of scissors from the top dresser drawer. Dyeing her hair wasn't enough. It needed something more, then she could look in the mirror without crying. Then the voice would go away.

She raised the scissors. How bad could it be? A straight cut across, nothing more. Her hands trembled and tears flowed. Visions of Lizzie scolding her stopped her. *Lizzie. I'm so sorry. It's all my fault, all my fault.* Samantha sobbed to herself. The scissors fell on the floor with a clatter as Samantha crumpled in a sobbing heap.

A knock at the door startled her. "Go away, Cass. Not now." She peeled herself off the floor and threw herself on her bed. All her pent-up emotions flooded out. She threw her pillow against the wall, knocking down the nightstand lamp with a satisfying *clang* on the wood floor. *Fitting,* she thought. She felt like that broken lamp; her light was gone and her world shattered.

"Samantha. What was that? Are you all right?" Cassie sounded panicked in the hallway and banged harder on the door. "Let me in, or I'll break down the door."

"I'd like to see you try." Samantha curled into a ball on the bed. "I'm fine. The lamp fell, no big deal."

"It *is* a big deal. You can't stay in there forever. You need help. Please, let me call Jonathan. If you're not comfortable talking to him, I'm sure he has other people he can recommend."

Jonathan. Samantha pictured him as she had seen him at Plato's. His eyes danced, even when speaking of his daughter—until Jeremy ruined it. He already thought she was damaged. Talking about her issues would make it worse. She didn't want him to see her that way.

"I already told you, no counseling. If you can't respect my feelings about it, then I can crash at Michael's for a while."

"If I promise not to talk about it, can I come in?"

"After what you pulled with my mother this afternoon, you expect me to trust you? Go save someone else. You heard my mother. I'm not worth it."

"I admit inviting Portia wasn't my best idea. But her opinion isn't mine. You are worth it. Please let me in."

Samantha sighed. Cassie pushed because she worried. She wished Cassie trusted her enough to let her figure things out her way. "Okay, but just for a little bit. I didn't sleep well last night, and I'm tired." Samantha unlocked the door.

"What did you do to your hair?" Cassie stared at Samantha with a look of disdain. She caressed Samantha's now-jet-black locks. "A drastic change, don't you think?"

Samantha jerked away and sat on the beanbag chair against the far wall. "I needed drastic." She drummed her fingers on her thigh. "What do you want?"

Cassie set to righting the room, collecting the pillow and lamp fragments. "Why are the scissors on the floor?"

Samantha snatched the scissors from Cassie's hands. "Can you stop for one second? I don't need you to take care of me every minute of the day. Leave everything where it is. It's fine."

Cassie sighed. "Okay. I'll leave it for now. But I can't stand by and watch you do this to yourself. It's like you don't even want to live anymore."

"What do I have to live for? Lizzie's gone. She was the only one who cared. I must live with that for the rest of my life. What kind of life is that?"

"I care. And Jonathan cares. He can help you overcome your grief."

Jonathan cared? Where did Cassie get that information? He was kind during lunch, but it was only a ploy, wasn't it? Both were playing games, trying to get her to commit to rehab. She decided it was easier to play the game than call them out.

"You promised. Even Jonathan thinks I need space. Please, let me do this my way."

"I know I promised. But your way isn't working. Instead of healing, you're killing yourself."

Cassie was right. But she saw no other way.

"I had lunch with Jonathan today." She shot Cassie a warning glance. "And we didn't talk about counseling. He told me about his daughter. Does he have a wife?"

Cassie tilted her head. "Why are you asking?"

"No reason. I didn't see a wedding ring, so I wondered. Does he?" Samantha fumbled with her bracelet.

"He did, but she left him when Rachel was three."

Why would anyone leave a guy like Jonathan? He knew pain, yet he dedicated his life to help others. The more she learned about him, the more she was interested. "He's been through so much. How does he keep calm?"

Cassie's eyes shined. "Interested in the doctor, are you, Sam?"

Samantha looked away. "No. Intrigued, maybe."

Cassie chuckled. "That's a start. Anyone's better than Michael."

Samantha smirked and plopped on the beanbag, refusing to acknowledge the comment.

After a moment of silence, Cassie spoke. "Do you ever think of happier times? High school, college. Back when it was simpler?"

Samantha smiled. "Sometimes. We had fun. Our road trips to the beach, staying up all night talking—we made an interesting threesome."

"I miss those days. We were close then, you and me. I miss that."

Samantha smiled. "I miss it too."

But things are different now, she thought. Life happened, and she had drawn the short stick.

Samantha stood and wandered to the window, her mind replaying the past. She stifled a laugh. "Remember when Lizzie wanted to be a chef?"

Cassie put her arm around Samantha's shoulders and smiled. "The half-cooked chicken, right? We all laughed about that one. I think we ate takeout for weeks after that." They chuckled. "We need to talk about her, Sam. Keep her memory alive. It will help both of us."

"I'm not trying to forget her. It just hurts so much. How do I move past this, knowing I'm the reason she was downtown to begin with?"

Samantha fingered her bracelet, rubbing it between her thumb and forefinger. Cassie didn't know about her visit to Cole's house or her discoveries. Without them, Cole was still sitting in jail, accused of Lizzie's murder. The need for evidence was inconsequential now.

A knock at the door interrupted her thoughts. She jolted up, realizing it was Michael. Even though he was late, at least he arrived after Portia and Cassie's failed stunt. She pushed her thoughts of Jonathan from her mind, focusing on what Michael had discovered about Cole. Samantha stood in the hallway, leaning against the wall, while Cassie opened the door.

Michael stood on the opposite side, shifting his weight from foot to foot.

"Oh, no." Cassie shook her head and closed the door. Turning around, she met Samantha's gaze. "He's not coming in."

"He has information about Cole. Let him in, Cass. We'll stay in the living room. I promise." Samantha crossed her heart and stuck out her bottom lip.

Cassie clenched her jaw and spoke through her teeth. "Fine." She swung open the door, glaring at the unwanted guest. "Thirty minutes, no more. And I'm watching you."

Michael glanced at Samantha then followed Cassie into the front room. "Thank you, Cassie. I'm sorry about last time. Won't happen again."

"Of course, it won't. I'm not letting you out of my sight. Sit," Cassie barked as Michael hurried to obey. "Talk. You have twenty-nine minutes left." Cassie glanced at her watch then stared him down.

Samantha joined Michael on the couch, her hands trembling as she spoke. "Are you okay? Your text was so matter of fact. I wasn't sure how you were feeling."

Michael rubbed his chin and tilted his head. "You dyed your hair. Nice look. Something dark and dangerous going on." He inched closer and put his arm around her shoulder.

She ducked under his arm and pulled away. "We're talking about Cole. Why didn't you come to Plato's, and what took you so long to get here? Have they charged him? Were you there?"

"Whoa. So many questions. I couldn't make it to Plato's, because I was trying to post bail. I was at his house when it happened. They arrested him, but he's not charged with your sister's murder. They say he's a person of interest, whatever that means. He's facing felony drug charges. The whole time, Logan grinned from ear to ear. He can't wait to get him on murder charges. I hate that guy."

Samantha pursed her lips and lowered her face. A person of interest meant they didn't have enough evidence to convict. She had evidence and knowledge that could help. Conflicted, she stood and paced the room. "Is he professing his innocence, and do you believe him?"

"You know how I feel. Cole is many things, but not a murderer." Michael fixated on Cassie. "With no evidence, they must let him go. If they pursue the drug charge, he'll get ten years at best. And he's not blaming you, Samantha. Although he could."

"Why would he blame Samantha?" Cassie crossed her legs and fidgeted with her necklace.

"Because I went to his house and questioned him about Lizzie's murder. She was there the night of her death. I found her bracelet in Cole's living room."

Cassie rose and stood in front of her. "Did you share this with the police?"

"Some of it. I told Logan that Lizzie was at Cole's house, but I didn't tell him about the bracelet." Samantha approached the bay window in the front of the room. "Lizzie talks to me. She wants me to avenge her. She's trying to tell me something, but I don't know what."

Cassie tossed up her arms. "Were you planning on telling me any of this? And what do you mean, *talking to you*? Like a ghost? Can you see her?"

"I hear her voice in my head. It's like she's still here, trapped until we solve this. I don't expect you to believe me, but it's the truth."

"I believe you think it's the truth. Were you high at the time? Regardless, you need to tell the police everything. I have Detective Logan's card somewhere." Cassie disappeared down the hallway, as if on a mission.

Michael crossed his arms. "Samantha, you can't give Detective Logan the bracelet. He's looking for any reason to lock up Cole. He's innocent. I bet my life on it."

"I'm not planning on it." She tapped her foot, wondering how to make Cassie understand. A moment later, Cassie breezed back into the room, card and phone in hand. "I'll dial, but you're talking to him. If this Cole person is guilty, you owe this to Elizabeth."

Samantha snatched the phone from her hands and threw it on the couch. "I'm not telling him anything else unless I'm ready. I told you I'm not sure if I'm supposed to tell them. Lizzie will tell me what to do."

Cassie bit her tongue, glaring at Samantha. "You're letting a drug-induced voice decide whether you talk to the police about your sister's death? I thought Elizabeth was important to you. Guess I was wrong." She pushed past Samantha and grabbed her phone. "If you're not calling, I am. Someone has to be the adult."

Michael grabbed Cassie's hand and squeezed. "Don't. Detective Logan isn't as nice as you think. He'd do anything to lock away Cole—and me. Besides, if Cole is innocent—and he *is*—the real killer is getting away. Let that sink in. Give us some time. Please."

Cassie looked into Michael's eyes and lowered her arms. Her stubborn face signaled the end of discussion. "Your time is up."

Samantha stared at Cassie. "Please, Cass. Even if you call, I'm not talking to him. Without my information, your call is useless. I'm not relinquishing Lizzie's bracelet. He has to find his evidence another way."

Cassie took a breath and put her phone on the table. "You're unbelievable. I'm glad Elizabeth isn't alive to see what you've become."

Frustrated, Samantha scowled at Cassie, clutched Michael's hand and drug him out the door. "Take me somewhere fun. I need a distraction."

CHAPTER 12

Willy's Bar teemed with activity. Couples peppered the dance floor, swaying to "Tequila" by Dan and Shay. Others crowded the bar, drinking and sharing the latest gossip. Round tables sat on the edge of the dance floor full of the usual crowd. For a Tuesday night, seats were scarce.

Amidst the commotion, Samantha stood in the doorway, fidgeting with her bracelet. She squeezed Michael's hand and gulped, wondering if this was a good idea. Willy's was a staple in their partying agenda; they would have a few beers here then go to Michael's to party.

She thought a familiar place would calm her spirit, but thoughts of the past few days plagued her instead. She recognized most of the faces, yet something was different. Her stomach churned as she scanned the room. She asked for a distraction, and this usually fit the bill. But something felt amiss.

She spied two seats at the far end of the bar next to the dance floor. Dragging Michael behind her, she dodged the people and tables, settling into the high-backed chairs.

"Let's dance," Michael whispered. "I want to hold you so close you can't think of anything but me."

Samantha reluctantly followed him onto the dance floor, but her mind was elsewhere, stuck on Cassie and their argument.

"I know when something's not right. What's going on? We're supposed to be having a good time."

"I know. But Cassie's in my head again, and I can't get her out."

"Did you ever think it's time to move on? You don't have to live with her. I've asked you to move in with me multiple times, and you keep saying *no*. I think that will solve your problem. No more mother hen judging your every move."

Samantha sighed. "I don't think it's the right time, is all. Buy me a drink." She grabbed Michael's hand and led him to the bar.

"Two bottles of Guinness, please." She faced Michael. "I don't know what's wrong with me, but I'm off tonight. Like, I can't relax." She surveyed the room and raised the bottle. "Hopefully this will do the trick, but I think I need something stronger tonight."

"How about we finish up here and go to my place? We can watch some trashy TV and forget about the rest of the world."

Samantha downed the drink and spun around. "Liam's here." She stood and cupped her hands to her mouth. "*Liam!*"

Michael sighed. "I don't think this is a good idea."

She patted him on the arm. "You're good friends. Just because Cole thinks he's dangerous doesn't mean we have to."

Liam caught her gaze and nodded. Parting ways with the bevy of beauties around him, he sauntered over, a drink in one hand and a half-dressed girl in the other. "Didn't expect to see you here." He nodded at Michael and scooted into the empty chair next to Samantha. "This is Clara. Go get us another round, honey." He slapped her butt as she sashayed to the other end of the bar.

"Flavor of the week?" Michael winked.

Liam laughed and fist-bumped Michael. "You know it. Until I find something like this sweet thing"—He winked at Samantha and flashed a wide smile—"I'll enjoy myself with the honeys."

Michael shook his head and shuffled his feet. "Man, you'll get in trouble one of these days. Try to straighten him up while I'm in the bathroom, Sam." He headed to the back of the bar.

Liam shimmied his chair closer to Samantha. "I heard about your sister. How are you coping? Need anything?"

Samantha stared at the bar top and fumbled with the napkin under her drink. "I'm fine. At least, I will be. Time heals, right?"

"Yeah, but it must be hard." Liam looked around then leaned in. "I heard they arrested Cole. Rumor has it, he's involved. That puts you in an awkward position, with Cole being best friends with Michael and all." Liam eyed her up and down, licking his lips.

Samantha closed her eyes and inhaled a deep breath. "We're taking it one day at a time. Cole hasn't been charged. He's a person of interest or something like that. As for me and Michael, that's none of your business."

"I didn't mean to offend. Here, take this as a peace offering." Liam slipped her a bag of liquid packets and a syringe. "If it gets tough, take these."

Samantha crinkled her forehead and held the bag eye level. "What're these?"

He grabbed her arm and lowered the bag into her lap. His gaze flitted around, assuring no one was watching. "Don't flash it around. You know better. Put it in your pocket. It's your rescue plan."

"I can't pay for these." She handed it back to him, but he wouldn't take it.

"It's on the house. Just don't tell Michael or Cole. They're still mad about last time."

Samantha bit her lip. Liam was still working against Cole. Was this a ploy? She wasn't sure it was wise to get in the middle of this game.

Before she could protest, Clara came behind him with two drinks.

Liam smiled and put his arm around Clara, sauntering to the other end of the bar.

She looked toward the bathroom door then slipped it in her pocket. Whatever Liam had given her, she would figure it out later. Right now, she was concerned with finding out what happened to Michael. His trip to the bathroom lasted longer than normal. She scanned the room for her wayward boyfriend. Her gaze stopped at a table near the back of the bar. Michael sat, talking to one of the girls from the party she had interrupted the previous day.

Clenching her jaw, she marched in his direction, pushing people aside. Michael took *irresponsible party boy* to a whole new level. And she was determined to straighten him out.

As she passed, someone else caught her eye. Two tables from Michael sat a man, slouched over a pitcher of beer. She looked closely. He seemed familiar, but she couldn't readily place him.

As if he sensed her presence, he lifted his head and stared. For a moment, he said nothing. Then he smiled, as if he had deciphered a riddle. "Samantha Barrett. Thought the black hair could fool me, huh? Sit. Drink to your sister."

Jeremy. He was the last person she expected here. This wasn't his usual place. Were things so bad he had to come here? Remembering their last encounter, she girded herself and sat across from him.

Jeremy's hands trembled as he poured her a glass. Short stubble covered his chin, and his eyes looked puffy and glassy.

"You look horrible."

Jeremy laughed. "Do I? Wouldn't know. Haven't slept. Tell me, does she haunt you too?"

Samantha jolted up. Did he know? She didn't doubt his words. The circles under his eyes, his messy hair and disheveled clothes hinted at something. "Does she talk to you?"

"I wish she did. I see her image everywhere, staring at me. She's trying to tell me something, but nothing comes out—only her spirit floating around, not leaving me alone."

Samantha squirmed, adjusting herself in the chair. "What do you think she wants?"

"No idea. I can't sleep until I get her out of my mind." He downed another glass and sneered. "They're not charging Cole with her murder yet. Idiotic police force can't find any evidence." He slammed the glass on the table and lifted the empty pitcher. "Bartender! Another round."

"They don't do that here. This isn't one of your fancy nightclubs. Why are you here anyway?"

"Beats me. I just drove, and this is where I ended up. Wasn't expecting you. Pure coincidence. Is your brute of a boyfriend here?"

Samantha glanced behind her shoulder. "Yes. Somewhere."

This side of Jeremy was new. He acted like a grieving fiancé, not a slimy bastard. Had she misjudged him?

Jeremy leaned closer and whispered, "I like the new look—a naughty version of your sister."

"You like it?" Samantha's lip curled as she ran her fingers through her hair. "It's not too much? I wanted to cut it."

As if a switch flipped, Jeremy stood and pushed the chair backward. "No." His eyes opened wide and seemed to spit fire. He pounded his fist on the table and glared at Samantha.

His reaction shook her. Glares from bystanders burned into her as she realized they had an audience. "Jeremy, sit. People are watching."

"You will not cut your hair. Black, I can tolerate. Obey me in this, Elizabeth." Jeremy loomed over her, his voice growing louder.

"Jeremy, please. I'm not Elizabeth." Samantha rocked back and forth, trying to contain her feelings. "Please, Jeremy. I promise I won't cut it."

He took a breath and sat. "Good." He reached across the table and took her hands. "It's for the best, Elizabeth. I know what's good for you. Trust me."

His touch confused and revolted her. How could he flip so quick? Something wasn't right, but she didn't know if it was the grief talking.

He raised her hand to his lips and placed a slimy kiss, meeting her gaze.

She wanted to run but was afraid of his reaction. She managed a half smile and shrunk inside.

Without warning, he sprung to his feet, his face red. "Back away, druggie. She's mine, and no one can have her." Jeremy knocked over the table, erasing the distance between him and his foe.

Who was he talking to?

Samantha turned and saw Michael, his face red but his voice calm.

"Easy now." Michael held a hand toward Jeremy while placing the other on Samantha's shoulder. "Samantha, Liam's three tables behind you. Go." He pushed her backward.

Refusing to budge, she stood behind him, bracing herself behind a chair.

Michael crossed the divide and faced Jeremy head on. "Leave her alone. Go home. Get a shower, and sober up. If I see you near my girlfriend again—"

Jeremy's fist slammed into Michael's face, pushing him back a few paces.

Chants of *"Fight! Fight!"* filled the place as a crowd formed.

Michael rubbed his cheek and looked at Jeremy, eyes bulging. As the crowd closed around them, Michael launched his fist, landing Jeremy on the bar floor. He shook his hand and winced. "I won't warn you again." Turning around, he grabbed Samantha's hand and headed out the door. "What was that about? I always thought he was odd, but that was creepy."

"He's crazy with grief. He said Elizabeth is haunting him, then he called me Elizabeth and yelled at me about my hair." She shook as she recounted the incident.

"Don't go near him unless I'm with you. He's unbalanced. There's no telling what he will do." Michael led her to the car and turned the ignition. "That's not the distraction I wanted to give you. Should have gone to my place instead."

Samantha tried to center herself as he drove, but she couldn't control her thoughts. Everyone's voice spoke at once, until she couldn't handle it. Her hand felt the bag in her pants pocket—Liam's rescue plan. If nothing else worked, maybe these would. She removed it and opened it.

"What are those?" Michael asked. "Where did you get them? Did Liam give them to you?"

"Are we playing twenty questions? Relax. He gave them to me as a rescue, and I need something right now after what Jeremy pulled."

"Those are speedballs. They're dangerous. I know people who died taking that stuff."

"But I'm not *people*. I know what I'm doing, and I'm perfectly fine. Besides, you don't get to tell me what to do. Liam promised these would help. He's a friend. He wouldn't give me something dangerous." Samantha poked the syringe into a packet and filled it, then she injected herself. "It chases away all the ghosts. *Now* we can have a good time. You do want to have a good time, don't you, Michael?"

"A good time? Yes. But I want you alive. Since your sister's engagement and death, you've been different, taking too many risks doing stupid shit. I'm worried about you. If anything happened—"

"Worried about me? Why? I'm in complete control. Don't be such a wet blanket. You've been listening to Cassie too much."

Michael swallowed hard, focusing on the road.

Samantha put the bag in her purse and stared out the window. What was Michael's problem? Was there a difference between cocaine and speedballs? Didn't speedballs contain cocaine anyway? What difference would it make to mix it with heroin? Besides, she needed it.

Within minutes, she relaxed. Her mind cleared, and a feeling of euphoria replaced her pain. This was what she needed.

They drove in silence until they pulled in front of his mobile home. When he parked, Samantha jumped out and ran to the front door.

"Home sweet home. If you play your cards right, I might take you up on your offer and move in." Samantha winked at Michael as he closed his car door and joined her.

"Samantha, we have to talk."

"No talking. Only this." She wrapped her arms around him and kissed him, her tongue probing.

"Not here." Michael looked around to assure none of his neighbors were watching. "Inside."

They floundered into the house.

Samantha wasted no time before crushing him into the nearest wall. "Don't you want this, Mikey? C'mon, I know you do. You're all I want to feel right now." Her hands reached to his butt and squeezed.

He kissed her neck, gently at first, then nibbled as her groans increased. He pushed her against the wall and fumbled with her bra strap, then he heard a crash.

The bag and syringe spilled onto the floor.

Michael's attention went to the drugs, and he retracted. "Sam, I can't." He entered the living room and stared through the back window.

"*Can't?* Why can't you? Am I not good enough for you? I'm good enough to hang out with but not to fuck?"

"This isn't you, Sam. It's the grief and the drugs talking. You're never like this on crack."

"I can't be that person anymore. You know that. More than anyone, you know how Lizzie, how that day … Screw it." Samantha righted her clothing and collected her belongings. "I'm going. I can't do this right now."

"Where are you going? You can't drive like this."

"What happened to you? I thought you understood me. I thought you supported whatever I needed. You were my rock, Michael. Now what do I have?" Samantha stormed from the house, grabbed Michael's keys and sped off in his car.

CHAPTER 13

The sound of mumbled voices woke Samantha from a deep sleep. Her arms hung beside her, numb and tingling. With her legs heavy and mind fuzzy, she attempted to sit up and determine her surroundings. She lifted her neck a few inches and dropped it onto the pillow as an immense pain bore through her temples. She remembered little from the previous night. While the times she got high with Michael proved harmless, she feared this time was serious.

Surveying the room, she saw Portia sitting in the corner chair. Cassie huddled by the door with a familiar person, their backs turned. She analyzed each clue, wondering where she was. The bed felt hard and uncomfortable. No longer in her outfit from the previous night, she shivered in a light gown. A machine beeped to her side, connected to something attached to her arm. What had happened, and why was she here?

Portia approached her bedside, eyes narrowed. "She's awake. Now can I tell her how stupid she acted?"

Samantha tilted her head and regarded Portia's appearance. Her clothes looked slept in, her makeup gone. A lone tear gathered in one eye. For the first time in her life, Samantha wondered if Portia cared.

Cassie and the man turned around, rushing to her bedside. "Sam. You gave us a scare. Don't do that again. I hope you don't mind, but I called Jonathan. He can help."

Jonathan. He was the last person she wanted to see. She shrunk. "I don't need help. Thanks for coming, Doc, but I have all the help I need."

"I don't think you understand the gravity of the situation, daughter. If we are to move past this, Dr. Green is our best hope," Portia said.

"Move past what? Can someone explain what happened?"

Jonathan moved forward, but Portia pushed him aside. "According to the police, you crashed into a tree. At least you weren't going fast enough to kill yourself. When they admitted you to the hospital, they ran some tests. You had cocaine and heroin in your system. They called it a *speedball.* The news is full of overdoses and deaths on that combination of drug. What were you thinking?"

"Guess I wasn't thinking, Mother. Nothing new, right? Ever the disappointment. Didn't want to let you down. You made your obligatory visit. Now you can leave." Samantha glowered at the gathered audience. "All of you."

"Ms. Barrett, please, allow me." Jonathan guided Portia to her seat in the corner and approached the bed. He smoothed out a section of the blanket and sat next to Samantha.

She lowered her gaze and rubbed the sheet between her forefinger and thumb. Her heart beat faster at the closeness, but her mind sent warnings to suppress any emotion. She swallowed hard and raised her gaze, meeting his for a fleeting moment. She remembered why Jonathan stirred such turmoil inside her. His eyes bored into her soul, threatening to take everything she once knew and turn it inside out.

"Hi, Samantha. I hope you don't mind, but Cassie thought I could help. When they admitted you last night, they found cocaine and heroin in your system. Do you remember taking those?"

Samantha turned away, a tear starting down her cheek. Scenes from the bar replayed in her mind—Liam, Michael, the crazy incident with Jeremy. Now the hospital. How much lower did she plan to sink before she sought help? Closing her eyes, she tried to block the thoughts plaguing her.

One voice carved its way through. *Trust him.* It was Lizzie. Where was she last night? *Listen to him.* Maybe it was time. She wasn't sure she wanted to get clean. She wasn't even sure it was possible. But maybe she owed it to herself, to Lizzie, to try. Samantha gulped back her remaining tears and turned toward Jonathan.

Grabbing her hand, he squeezed then rubbed it with his thumb. "It's okay. We don't have to talk about this now."

"Like hell. If this doesn't bring her to her senses, then nothing will. She's lucky we're here and not at her funeral." Portia stood and leered over Jonathan and Samantha.

"Ms. Barrett, I sense your concern, but I must insist you sit." Jonathan loomed over Portia, arms crossed.

Portia stammered and returned to her seat, pouting like a punished child.

Samantha stifled a giggle and worked to regain her composure. No one stood up to her mother, especially a geeky psychiatrist like Jonathan. He intrigued her more every time they met.

He returned to her bedside with a wide smile. "I want you to concentrate on getting better physically. However, you need to know the consequences. Because you tested positive for illicit drugs, they are charging you with driving under the influence. They could increase the charges, but your mother intervened. She got them to agree to drug court."

Her face fell. Being indebted to her mother didn't sound like a good alternative. There had to be another option. "And if I don't agree to this drug court?"

"Samantha, we all talked." Cassie stood on the opposite side of the bed, her hands pressing on the mattress. "And this is the best option. You avoid jail time and finally get the help Elizabeth and I have been trying to get you. Not agreeing wouldn't be wise."

"Everyone is deciding for me then? Good to know. Why don't I stop thinking for myself? You can tell me when to shower, when to piss. I'll just be a vegetable the rest of my life."

Cassie's face reddened. She pursed her lips and puffed.

Jonathan raised his hand and opened his eyes wide. "Cassie, remember what we talked about?"

She nodded and retreated to the door.

He returned his attention to Samantha, grabbing her hand once more. "If you don't agree to drug court, it could mean jail time. The case would go to trial. It could leave you susceptible to additional charges. Drug court is a better option. Of course, the final decision is yours."

Samantha dropped his hand and propped herself on the pillows. "What's involved? I need to know what I'm promising."

"It's a program to help you get clean. You go to court, admit you're using and want to work toward sobriety. Typically, you have a therapist trained in drug abuse stand up with you, someone you commit to work with. Then the court tracks your progress with regular check-ins. The goal is to become sober and healthy, both emotionally and physically."

"And who is willing to stand up with me? I don't have a good history with counseling, if you remember."

Jonathan tilted his head and winked. "I would be honored to stand up with you. I have space in my group counseling sessions at the clinic. We can try that and then explore other options, if needed."

Samantha stared straight ahead. Jonathan with the dancing brown eyes wanted to stand up in drug court with her, vouch for her, help her get clean. Knowing how she reacted to counseling, how difficult she was with her friends and family, he still wanted to help her? If she had to pick a therapist, Jonathan would be her first choice. Seeing no other option, she relented. "If you promise to stand by my side, I guess I can try it."

He gazed into her eyes and placed his hand over hers. Everyone else in the room disappeared. It was only her and Jonathan, and he would make everything right.

As she got lost in his brown eyes, the door pushed open, bumping Cassie into the edge of the bed. Samantha broke their gaze and pushed herself upright, surprised to see her newest visitor.

"Sam, you're okay. I was worried. I told you not to take that speedball. The next time I see Liam, I'm giving him a piece of my mind." Michael ran to her side, opposite Jonathan, and sat.

"You knew she took that speedball, and you still let her drive?" Cassie moved within an inch of Michael's face and wagged her finger. "You are stupid and irresponsible. She could have died. Of course, you're always too busy getting high to think about that."

Michael looked down and fumbled with the zipper on his jacket. "You're right. I told her not to take it, but I could've done more." He turned to Samantha and took her face in his hands. Brushing back her hair, his eyes welled with tears.

"Your car. I'm sorry." She looked at the bed. "I broke your rule."

"No, I'm sorry. I should have stopped you. What can I do to help?"

Jonathan slapped Michael's back. "I'm glad you came. She will need all the support she can get. Mainly from you."

"She has it. Whatever I need to do." Michael turned to Samantha and brushed her cheek with his hand. "Whatever you need, say the word."

Samantha put her hand over his and stared into his eyes. She needed everyone to leave her alone. But now she had little choice. "We have to get clean. I need to do this for Lizzie. And you need to do this for me. Jonathan is going to drug court with me. I'll start counseling with him."

"Drug court and counseling, huh?" Michael sniffed. "Not a bad idea." He pulled away toward the edge of the bed.

Samantha grabbed his jacket and pulled him back to face her. "We can do it together. You said whatever I need. This is what I need."

"Don't press him into something he's not ready for," Jonathan said. "Drug counseling is not an easy thing to commit to. Give him time."

"It's okay, Doctor." Michael took her hands. "Sam, I promise to be clean around you. I won't invite you to my parties or do drugs in your presence. Don't know if I'm ready for anything else. Will that be enough for now?"

Samantha lowered her gaze. At least Michael was here and trying. He could have cut and run, like he did with his family, but he was here instead. She couldn't force him to get clean, but she hoped her accident scared him enough to consider it.

"I suppose." She yawned and stretched her arms over her head. "I appreciate the visit everyone, but can I get some sleep? I have a wicked headache."

Everyone made their goodbyes and shuffled out the door.

Jonathan paused in the doorway. "I'm glad you're okay. I promise, we will get through this. I will help you find peace."

Samantha smiled and closed her eyes. Jonathan with the dancing brown eyes, her personal guardian and savior.

As she slept, a voice played in her mind. *Chase peace, find it, hold on to it.* Perhaps she was finally on the right path.

***

The day after she went home from the hospital, she appeared in drug court. She still had some bumps and bruises from the accident and needed help getting around. Cassie took off a few days from the clinic and stayed by her side, helping her heal from the crash.

The day of the hearing, Cassie drove her to the courthouse in awkward silence. They would label her a drug addict and order her to get sober. The accident convinced her that she had a problem, but she wasn't ready to say it was the crack. Taking the speedball was a poor decision—one she vowed never to repeat. But cocaine by itself had never hurt her. She could play the game for a while then return to her old habits. After the court deemed her clean, who would know if she used again?

Samantha closed the car door and gazed at the limestone building. It sat high above ground with steps climbing forever. She smiled when Jonathan caught her eye, waiting for them near the entrance. As she took one step at a time, she thought about Lizzie. This would please her. For an instant, she considered getting clean for Lizzie, as a tribute. Then she pushed the thought from her mind.

When she reached the top, Jonathan wrapped his arm around her, supporting her into the building. Cassie hung back, walking behind them with Portia. The four entered the courtroom, Jonathan sticking close throughout the entire procedure.

Cassie and Portia showed quiet support throughout the hearing. Neither dared to raise their voice or protest. Whenever one of them raised an eyebrow at Samantha, Jonathan's stern look set them aright.

She was partially disappointed Michael didn't come but understood he wasn't ready to quit using. She wasn't sure if she was ready either, but she had few choices.

The court revoked her license for a year, making her a captive in her own house. Now she had to depend on Cassie for everything, and she wasn't sure how far Cassie would go to keep her from using.

Afterword, they stood on the courthouse steps, breathing a sigh of relief. She would attend counseling regularly and check in with the court once a week. She also had to submit to random drug tests and receive visits from a drug court officer. This would continue for a year or until the court deemed her clean.

Jonathan handed her a piece of paper. "This is the schedule. First group starts tomorrow. We meet twice a week at the clinic. Come early so you can meet everyone before the session begins."

Samantha sighed. Groups were not her thing. "Can't I observe the first time? Talking about my problems in front of strangers makes my stomach turn."

Portia opened her mouth and promptly closed it after a look from Jonathan.

"You're safe in the group. I'll be there to help you." He took both her hands in his and peered into her eyes. "The hardest part is admitting you need help. I'm your biggest advocate. I won't let you down." He squeezed her hand, turned and walked toward his car.

CHAPTER 14

You killed me. Murderer. The voice came louder. Samantha covered her ears, trying to drown out the sound. Still wearing her hospital gown, she stood in the alleyway behind Cole's house. A blood-curdling scream startled her. She saw Lizzie struggling with someone, his arms wrapped around her neck. The bang of a pistol resounded, and she crumpled. The man ran down the street, leaving Lizzie alone. Samantha ran to help her, but Lizzie was no longer there. A commotion sounded behind her. Turning, she saw Lizzie, Jeremy, and Amber approaching her and chanting, *"Murderer,"* as they grew closer. Samantha crouched by the brick wall and screamed.

"It's okay. I'm here." Michael put his arms around her and squeezed. "Deep breaths. It was a dream." He stroked her hair and whispered in her ear, "You're safe."

Samantha sniffed, trying to dam her tears. "I saw Lizzie. In the alleyway. They were struggling, and he shot her. It was my fault. If I wasn't using, if she hadn't gone to Cole's—it's my fault."

"That's not true. Dr. Green said you would have nightmares. That's all it is. Your mind is playing tricks on you. Relax and go back to sleep."

"I can't. My mind is racing. I've been sober for three days, but I can't do it anymore. Why can't things return to normal? I'd do anything for a hit."

"I thought you wanted to get clean. That's why I'm sacrificing my time, right? I could be at a party right now. We could be at a party."

"You're supposed to be helping me, remember? Not reminding me what I'm missing. Don't make Cassie kick you out again."

Michael hung his head. "She doesn't want me here to begin with. She lets me stay because she doesn't want you to be alone. But I know she's spying on me." He threw a stuffed animal at the nanny-cam Cassie had installed in the corner and waved. "Hi, Cassie! Just following orders. Nothing to see here." He faced Samantha. "You know, if you moved in with me, you wouldn't have to put up with her."

"She means well. Besides, I'm court-ordered to get clean. Trust me. It wasn't my decision. If I'm to do this, I need your help. You have to distract me when I get a craving." She rolled over and looked at her phone. "Holy shit. It's eight-thirty." She threw off the covers and rummaged through her closet. "Why didn't you wake me?"

"You didn't sleep well last night. I figured you could use a few more hours. What's the hurry?" Michael pulled on his white T-shirt and sat on the edge of the bed.

"My first counseling session with Jonathan is in half an hour. I can't be late. I don't even know what to wear." She tossed aside clothes as she dismissed them in her mind.

"Who cares? It's only a counseling session. No one is judging your outfit." Michael tilted his head and scrutinized her urgency. "Or are you worried about what Dr. Green might think?"

"Don't be silly. Why would I care what he thought? He's Cassie's boss, and he's been nice. Nothing more." She grabbed a sweater dress from the back of the closet. "Too conservative?"

"You have a crush on the doctor, don't you? It's all over your face. I should have seen it at the hospital. Is it the glasses? I hope it's not the glasses."

She blushed.

"It's his eyes, isn't it? It's always the eyes. Damn, Samantha. I can't compete with that." Michael flopped onto the bed, feigning anger.

She punched him in the arm and returned to her search. "Stop. I spent the night with you, didn't I? Besides, Jonathan isn't my type." Except he was, a realization that surprised her. Jonathan woke feelings she didn't know she had. But he was her therapist, and that was off limits. She shook away the thought and refocused on her closet.

She retrieved a yellow sundress and held it next to the blue sweater dress. "Which one? The yellow is more comfortable, but the blue is professional." She bit her lip, deciding.

Michael grabbed both dresses and threw them onto the bed. "In all seriousness, do you have a crush on Dr. Green or not?" His eyes narrowed, demanding an answer.

"Don't be an idiot." She brushed past him toward the bed. "I'm going with the yellow sundress." She shrugged off her pajamas and slipped the sundress over her head. "Will you drive me?"

"No." Michael plopped into the beanbag, his head in his hands. "Things are changing between us, aren't they? It's not the same anymore. Like, I'm competing with your new life."

"Feel free to cut and run, like you did with your family. If this is too hard, you don't need to stay."

"I'm not leaving you. I don't like how everything is changing, but I'm not going anywhere."

Samantha smoothed out her dress and combed her hair. "Life is full of changes. Can't expect things to stay the same forever." She paused and stared at Michael's reflection in the mirror. "You can come with me. We can do it together. It might make you feel better." She approached the beanbag. "It will do you good."

A knock interrupted them.

Cassie pushed open the door, her eyes shining as she beheld Samantha's outfit. "You look gorgeous. That outfit will blow away Jonathan." She glanced at Michael and smiled.

Michael chortled. "Hello! Boyfriend here."

As the two women continued, he tossed up his arms and pulled himself to his feet. "If you want to set up my girlfriend with some fancy doctor, at least wait until I'm gone." He wagged his finger in Cassie's face. "It's called *respect*."

Cassie licked her lips and regarded him. "That's what it is, respect, huh? And having a party full of girls without your girlfriend is what again?"

Michael's nostrils flared. "Nothing happened." His face reddened; his breathing shallowed. "You're planning my replacement right in front of me. Not cool."

Cassie smirked and raised her eyebrows. "Don't worry, sweetie. Someone will want you someday. Some women value brawn over brain. Think blonde, dumb and desperate."

She turned her head in Samantha's direction. "Meet me outside in five minutes. I'll drive you to the clinic."

Samantha crept behind Michael and encircled his waist, raising her arms to stroke his biceps "Ignore her. She likes to give you a hard time." She nuzzled her face in his back. "And as far as Doc is concerned, you needn't worry. He's my friend at most. Besides, I love your brawn, and I'm not dumb or desperate."

Michael scooted her in front of him and engulfed her with a hug. "And you're not blonde anymore either." He kissed the top of her head. "I trust you. If you say there's nothing between you and the doctor, I believe you." He patted her bottom and flashed a toothy smile. "Go, before Cassie throws another of her zingers. I'll be here when you get back."

Samantha stood on her tiptoes and planted a kiss on his mouth. "Thank you."

Taking one more look in the mirror, she ran to join Cassie outside. As they drove, she smiled, lost in a dream about Jonathan and his dancing brown eyes.

***

Samantha paced the hallway of the clinic, waiting for Jonathan. One by one, people filled the meeting room next to his office. A young woman approximately her age, several men in their late twenties, and a few teenagers rounded out the group. Trying to gather her courage, she closed her eyes and took a deep breath. As she turned to enter, she ran into an older man in the doorway, looking like he'd come from a Grateful Dead concert.

"Watch where you're walking." His blue eyes shone underneath his biker hat, and a white beard covered his face. His wide girth filled the door, making it difficult to pass.

Samantha bit her lip. This wasn't a good idea. Sharing her problems with Jonathan proved hard enough. Telling her story to strangers like this crotchety man asked too much. Seeking relief, she closed her eyes and spun, banging into Jonathan as he entered.

Jonathan adjusted his glasses and straightened himself. "Ms. Barrett. It's nice to see you. Have you met Gus?" He motioned toward the older man standing in the doorway.

Samantha balked at the formal greeting. Something seemed different. This wasn't the person from the pizza place or the hospital or drug court. This was someone she hadn't met. Jonathan with the dancing brown eyes was there in body but not in soul. The spark behind his eyes was gone and, in its place, stood a wooden, sterile Dr. Green.

She took a deep breath and donned her best smile. "Good morning, Doc." Turning toward the older man, she outstretched her hand. "Hello, Gus. I'm Samantha." Shooting Jonathan a sly grin, she sauntered into the room and found a seat by the door.

Gus and Jonathan followed, closing the door behind them.

Jonathan settled in front of the room, straddling a chair. All gazes centered on him, ready to follow his lead.

Samantha stared, memorizing the waves in his hair, the way his forehead crinkled when he spoke and the way his mouth curled into a smile when he greeted each person. He wore khakis as usual but complemented them with a red sweater-vest and tie. Despite the awkward greeting, Samantha found herself captivated.

The brief exchange of pleasantries ended, and Jonathan called the meeting to order. "We have a new member. Samantha Barrett, please stand and introduce yourself. Tell us why you're here." Jonathan looked in her direction, his face solemn and serious.

Samantha struggled to her feet, formulating the words in her mind. She stared at the floor and mumbled, "Hello. I'm Samantha."

"Speak up, young lady," Gus bellowed from across the room.

"My name is Samantha. I don't know why I'm here." She raised her voice, glaring in his direction.

"You're here because you have an addiction. We all have addictions. Can't get clean unless you admit your problem," Gus said.

Samantha sucked in a breath and shot Jonathan a nasty look. Who was this guy, and why was he harassing her? "Does it matter? This is my first day. Can't I get a break?"

"Young lady, I've been in recovery for five years," Gus replied, "and I fight it every day. If you want to get well, Dr. Green is the one to help you. But you must help yourself. This group is all about honesty. We hold each other accountable. We're a family. If you aren't willing to commit to getting better, you won't."

"You want honesty, Gus? I'm here because I have to be. I crashed into a tree after taking a speedball. I only took it once, but I've been on cocaine for the past six months. Do I want to help myself? I don't know. They never gave me the chance to figure that out. Guess that means I don't fit in here." Samantha walked out the door and ran down the hallway. When she reached Cassie and Jonathan's office, she collapsed on the small couch and sobbed.

Somehow, she had to figure this out. How could she sit in the same room with Jonathan, her insides tingling, while he treated her like any other patient? Why did it bother her so much? Didn't she assure Michael he was her true love? And yet Jonathan's presence made her stomach flipflop and her legs turn to jelly. She needed another therapist, but who would stand up with her as Jonathan did?

The door creaked open.

Samantha raised her head, her brow wrinkled, as Gus entered the office. "What do you want?" She lowered her gaze and rubbed her dress's fabric between her fingers.

Gus cleared his throat and sat at Jonathan's desk. "You're me." He took a deep breath and drummed his fingers on his knee. "Five years ago, they caught me with an ounce of cocaine. It was my first offense, and our overzealous police force was ready to prosecute to the fullest. Dr. Green tried to convince the town to implement a drug court. Then he asked me to try it—vouched for me and everything. But I didn't want help. My sister forced me to take part, and I'm thankful she did. I took a while to own my part in my addiction, to voice my failings, especially to strangers. But it works. I'm proof. And Dr. Green, he's good people."

Samantha crossed her arms and leaned forward. "If you understand, why were you so harsh? Didn't you need time before you admitted your sins to the group?"

"Did I want time? Yes. Would more time help? Nope. Procrastination helps no one. Face your issue head on. Admit your failings. We don't judge. We've all been there. But it starts with honesty and freely admitting your addiction." Gus placed his hands on his knees and pushed himself up. "I've said my piece. Hope to see you again, young lady."

Samantha tucked her legs underneath her and curled into a ball. She raised her head to watch Gus leave then lowered it to her knees. She wasn't special. Jonathan showed the same kindness to Gus and countless others. Had she mistaken compassion for attraction? She rocked herself back and forth as the tears flowed. Jail time seemed preferable than the emptiness eating her insides.

Sometime later, the door swung open. Jonathan entered, closing the door behind him.

Samantha sank into the couch, hoping it would swallow her. The small office couldn't hide her, even though she wished it would make her invisible.

Jonathan whistled while he organized papers on his desk.

She watched his eyes dart around the room, wondering when he would notice. She pulled her knees closer to her chest, holding back a sniffle.

As if he sensed something amiss, he spun his chair around, facing the couch. Samantha inched up her head and caught his gaze. He leaned back in the chair, crossing his arms, donning an amused grin. They sat in silence for a moment, neither acknowledging the other.

Unable to stand the silence, Samantha broke. "Hello, Doc. I'm waiting for Cassie to pick me up." She straightened herself, turning to meet his gaze.

"Gus said you went to my office. I'm glad you stayed. How are you feeling?" He readjusted his glasses and leaned forward.

Embarrassed and *stupid* were the first words to cross her mind. Michael was right. She *did* have a crush on Jonathan. And now she had to deal with it. She couldn't stop attending group, and getting another counselor approved could take weeks. This was her only way right now. She had to make the best of it.

"I'm sorry. I behaved like a brat. Gus explained how you helped him recover. I understand now. Please let me continue." She fidgeted with the edge of her dress, trying to avoid his eyes.

"The first meeting is the hardest. I'm glad you want to continue. It'll be easier next time." Jonathan reached across and grasped her hands. "I meant it when I said I would help you. Addiction isn't the real you. I see something inside, something bright and wonderful. One day, the addiction will be gone, and the true you will shine. I'm waiting for that day." Jonathan dropped her hands and reached for his phone. "Let me drive you home. I'll call Cassie."

Samantha wished he had come off distant, like he had earlier, instead of warm and caring. When they were alone, she felt special and important. But Jonathan made everyone feel that way, didn't he?

They exchanged few words as he drove. Samantha stared straight ahead, trying to avoid his glance. She spent the ride replacing thoughts of Jonathan with memories of Michael. Although Michael didn't cause her stomach to flipflop he didn't toy with her emotions. She hoped Jonathan would be out of her system by Thursday. If he wasn't, counseling would be painful.

CHAPTER 15

ichael stood on the porch as they pulled up. Jonathan nodded in his direction and turned off the ignition. "I see he's sticking close. I'm glad you have support. It's essential for recovery."

She stared at Michael and smiled. Since the hospital, Michael rarely left her side. She was lucky to have him and Cassie, even though they struggled to get along. "He's a great help. Thanks for the ride, Doc."

She clutched the door handle but felt a jerk.

Jonathan grabbed her arm and turned her to face him. Their eyes locked in silence. He raised his hand and brushed back a layer of wayward hair cascading down her face.

She flinched at his touch as her mind raced with questions.

Jonathan took a deep breath and drummed his fingers on the steering wheel. "Samantha, I need to tell you something. I've been trying to find the right time, since we met at Plato's, to tell you."

Samantha flinched. He wanted to give the friend speech. He sensed her attraction and wanted to shut her down. "It's okay, Doc. I know. We're meant to be friends, nothing more. Besides, I have Michael, and you have your patients at the clinic. It would never work." She slid closer to the door. Her heart beat faster as she wished for escape.

Jonathan's face fell. "Yes. You have Michael. He's taking good care of you?" Jonathan tilted his head and cocked his brow.

"Cassie takes him to task if he doesn't. Thanks for being a good friend, Doc. I appreciate your kindness. But I'm fine. I'll see you Thursday, and I promise to behave." Samantha exited the car and bolted up the hill.

Screw recovery. Without crack, she couldn't handle the emotions any longer. She panicked as the craving hit, wondering if telling Jonathan was wise.

As she approached the porch, Michael grasped her shoulders, pulling her close.

They watched as Jonathan drove away.

"What were you talking about? I watched. It didn't look platonic to me. I don't trust him."

Samantha approached the front door. It had been three days without cocaine. The cravings consumed her, but she didn't want to admit it. Why was stopping so hard?

She turned to Michael and pulled on his hand. "Don't be crazy. We're just friends. I need something to relax."

Michael followed her to the bedroom and watched as Samantha rummaged through her dresser drawers. "What are you looking for?"

"I don't know. Anything."

She spied Michael's backpack in the corner. Thoughts of group and Jonathan made her emotions spiral. She didn't know if she should scream, cry, or laugh. Desperate, she snatched the bag and dumped its contents onto the bed. He had to have crack hidden somewhere. She rifled through clothes, body deodorant, gum, and change, searching for her fix. "You didn't bring any?"

In a panic, she unzipped each pouch until she emptied it. She threw the backpack against the wall and sank into the beanbag chair, holding her head in her hands. "Why didn't you bring any? I need a safety net, Michael." Her eyebrows knitted together as she glared at him. "Go get some crack. And don't come back without it."

Michael took a deep breath and crossed his arms. "No. Dr. Green said you would have cravings. I can get you through this. How about some pizza? I'll order your favorite from Plato's—mushrooms and peppers."

"You don't trust him, remember? And I don't want pizza. I want to dull the pain. Go get some crack, and let's party." She sauntered to him and ran her hand down his side. "It'll be like before. Isn't that what you wanted this morning? Show me a good time."

He grabbed her wrists and held them in front of her. "I said *no*, and I meant it. Do you want to risk getting caught? A probation officer could show up anytime, demanding a urine sample." Michael eased her on the bed. "Sit and relax. I'll light some candles, play some soft music and get you something for lunch."

Cassie got to him. She had no other explanation. Samantha's face contorted, and her nose wrinkled with disgust. She kicked him in the nuts and ran from the room.

Michael grimaced but regained his composure. He ran after her and tackled her. Samantha kicked and screamed as he dragged her back to the bedroom. Throwing her on the bed, he guarded the door to prevent another escape.

"This is kidnapping. I can go where I want, and you can't stop me." She stomped her foot and eyed the door for an opening.

"You can try. Now I know why Cassie reversed the locks. I'm locking you in until she gets home. I'll be back with lunch." Michael backed out the door.

As he left, Samantha grabbed a ceramic bunny from her headboard and launched it in his direction.

He ducked as it shattered around him. "I'll bring a broom and dustpan too." He closed the door and locked it, leaving her alone with her thoughts.

Samantha paced the room, frustration growing. She jiggled the door handle. When that didn't work, she picked up any item she saw—her lamp, the book ends from her headboard, the beanbag chair—and chucked them at the door.

She felt like a caged animal. Since she'd come home from the hospital, Cassie searched her belongings every day and spied on her through the nanny-cam. She didn't have any privacy anymore. She sat on her bed and rocked. This had to end.

Cassie had put the nanny-cam in the corner. If she could reach it, she could regain control. She climbed on the dresser, trying to knock it down, but slipped. Undeterred, she grabbed several hardcover books and threw them until the camera dislodged from the wall. She crumpled onto the floor, exhausted, and sobbed until she fell asleep.

A few hours later, voices in the hallway shook her awake. She lay on the floor, her dress wrinkled and her hair a mess. The room looked like a war zone, with shards of glass and ceramic pieces scattered everywhere. She propped herself up and surveyed the mess. Smoothing her hair back, she grimaced, remembering her tirade.

Gus was right. She had a problem. If the accident wasn't enough to convince her, the disaster surrounding her did the trick. She eased herself to her feet and straightened her dress. By now, Cassie would be home, and Michael would brief her on her tantrum. She waited for Cassie to enter, expecting disapproval and condescension on her face. As the voices grew louder, Samantha girded herself for the onslaught. Whatever Cassie dished, she deserved.

"Locking her in was the only choice. What did you want me to do? Allow her to run out of the house, steal my car again and find a way to get her fix? You gave me a job, and I did it. Don't question my tactics." Michael's voice came through the door, ripe with frustration.

"Next time call me. If she's raging, someone needs to be here. Leaving her by herself is dangerous," Cassie said as the door handle jiggled.

When they entered, Cassie's eyes narrowed, and her mouth opened wide. "What is this mess?" Her eyes shot flames at Michael as he avoided her glance.

Samantha stood in the middle of the room, sobbing. She shifted her gaze from Cassie, to Michael, to the mess on the floor. She was devoid of explanation. Averting her gaze from Cassie's, she stammered. "I don't know what happened. The group session … Jonathan … I was embarrassed. The craving came so quick. I—" Samantha wiped her tears with the back of her hand.

Cassie's eyes softened. She wrapped her arms around Samantha and patted her back. "It's okay."

Guiding Samantha to the bed, Cassie held her hand, stroking it with her own. Cassie lifted Samantha's chin and looked in her eyes. "Jonathan said this would happen. It's a part of the process. You will have cravings. Your emotions will spiral, but we are here."

Samantha sniffed back her remaining tears and wrapped her arms about Cassie. No one had said recovery was easy. Gus had warned her it would be hard. The next time she saw him, she could say she understood.

***

Thursday came quick. Michael woke her at eight with a breakfast of pancakes, strawberries, and orange juice. He presented the meal on a tray adorned with a single purple lilac, her favorite color. As he placed it on her lap, he gave a deep bow and smiled. "Your breakfast, my lady."

Samantha covered her mouth and giggled. "Your cooking or Cassie's?"

Michael sat on the bed and popped a strawberry into his mouth. "Who do you think? Have you ever seen me cook?"

Samantha smiled. With Michael and Cassie's help, she had survived the past forty-eight hours with little craving. Her emotions settled as they provided a distraction from her thoughts—distractions she needed to fill in the time. She focused on recovery and let the investigation go. The police could handle it. The text messages had stopped once Cole's investigation began. They seemed focused on him, like Michael said they would. It wasn't worth her time to get involved. Cassie and Michael did everything they could to keep her mood light and happy, something that didn't go unnoticed.

She smiled at Michael as she ate, but her mind raced elsewhere. Her second counseling session was in an hour, and it terrified her. She prepared a speech this time, hoping it would help calm her nerves. But seeing Jonathan was another matter. His behavior confused and excited her. She didn't understand why he treated her one way when they were alone and another in front of the group. Today, she planned on maintaining a professional relationship, no matter what his eyes did to entice her.

After breakfast, Michael drove her to the clinic. He walked her to the meeting room and paused in the hallway. "I'm waiting here. Don't leave with anyone else." He smiled then plopped himself on the nearest bench.

Samantha strolled into the room, keeping an eye on Michael.

Gus approached her from behind, offering a cup of juice and a donut. "Glad to see you, young lady. Wasn't sure if I'd scared you." He smiled wide, revealing a mouthful of teeth.

"I don't scare easy. Thanks for the treats." She took the offering and glanced to the hallway. Michael had disappeared from his place on the bench. Curious, she peeked out the door toward Jonathan's office.

Gus looked over her shoulder at two men talking. "Boyfriend?"

Samantha turned her head. "Yes. He's supposed to wait for me, not talk to Dr. Green." She proceeded down the hallway, determined to break up the pair.

Jonathan looked up as she approached and grinned. "Samantha. I'm glad you came." He turned toward Michael and shook his hand. "Thank you for the information. And remember what I said." He put his hand on Samantha's shoulder and steered her toward the meeting room. "Shall we?"

She trembled at his touch and hoped Michael didn't notice. When they reached the room, Samantha broke free and found a seat next to Gus. She hoped looking into Gus's blue eyes would help her forget about Jonathan's.

The meeting began with introductions. She breathed a sigh of relief when Jonathan started on the opposite side of the room. One woman shared about her addiction to prescription drugs and how it had destroyed her marriage. A teenager shared his addiction to meth. Another shared how his parents kicked him out of the house for using heroin. One by one, they shared their stories, and Samantha took it in. Jonathan listened intently to each person, asking questions where appropriate and guiding their thinking. He thanked them for their bravery and encouraged a supportive atmosphere. She marveled at his ability to show compassion yet hold them accountable.

"Samantha. Would you like to share?" Jonathan turned in her direction.

This is where everything had gone wrong last time. In anticipation for this moment, she had memorized her speech, hoping it would lessen her embarrassment. She took a breath and glanced at Gus, expecting him to speak. Instead, he nodded in approval and mouthed, *You got this.*

She stood and looked straight ahead. If she met Jonathan's eyes, she would chicken out. Gathering her strength, she closed her eyes and clenched her fists at her sides. "I'm Samantha, and I'm addicted to cocaine. It started six months ago at a party. I had a terrible relationship with my mother and smoked coke to escape the pain. Then someone murdered my sister. I was so upset I took a speedball one night and crashed into a tree. That's when Dr. Green intervened. I think I'm ready—I *hope* I'm ready—to get clean."

She sat to sounds of clapping.

Gus slapped his meaty fingers together and flashed a satisfied smile. "Welcome to the group, young lady. You'll do fine."

The rest of the meeting passed in a breeze. Jonathan mixed compassion with direct accountability, giving each person tips and a game plan for the coming week. Samantha took notes, hoping to apply his guidance for the tough times ahead. For the first time, recovery seemed possible, and she intended to grab it.

Jonathan concluded the meeting at ten o'clock, wishing everyone a successful weekend. They wouldn't meet again until Tuesday. Samantha's lips curled, and her gaze fell. Waiting until Tuesday to see Jonathan again would be pure torture.

"Young lady, Tuesday will come soon enough. In the meantime, take this." Gus handed her a card. "If you need anything, call me."

Samantha took the card and watched as he walked out the door. She gathered her notebook and pen and moved toward the hallway. Michael should be on the bench waiting.

As she walked, a voice stopped her. "Samantha, wait," Jonathan called from his seat in the room. "Please. Sit for a moment?"

She turned around, staring at the ground. "Michael is waiting."

"He'll wait. This is important." He motioned to a seat in front of him. "I won't take too much of your time. Please."

Samantha sighed and trudged to the seat, refusing eye contact. "Did I do something wrong, Doc? I thought everything was better this time."

"Yes, it was. I'm glad you and Gus are getting along. He's a good ally. He'll help you if you let him." Jonathan adjusted his glasses. "Michael told me about the incident on Tuesday. You shouldn't be ashamed. It's a part of the process. He told me distracting you from emotional issues is helping."

Samantha stared at the floor, counting the tile squares as he talked.

"That has me worried, though. True healing will come if you confront your emotional issues, not ignore them. Michael isn't trained in this, and Cassie is too close, but I would like to help you more." Jonathan leaned close.

"And how could you help me more, Doc? Isn't this enough?" Samantha lifted her head and met his gaze.

"I can tell you're hurting. The pain behind your eyes is more than an addiction. I want to help you heal completely. If you let me."

"Why? You confuse me, Doc. Why are you so interested in me? Because I'm Cassie's friend? Because my mother has money? What is it?" Samantha rose, her face flushed.

"No, none of those reasons. I can't explain it. But something is there, something beyond your pain, beyond your addiction. I can help you find that person I know you can be." He extended his hand, his eyes warm and inviting. "Let me?"

Samantha glued her hands to her side. Stone-faced, she looked in his eyes. "You want to delve into my soul, Doc? It's not a fun place to be."

"I'm prepared. I'll pick you up tomorrow around three o'clock? We can get coffee."

Samantha nodded in agreement then rushed out the door. Whatever she agreed to, she hoped it didn't lead to disaster.

Chapter 16

Samantha stood barefoot on the gravel road. A river of blood flowed toward her, barely touching her feet. She spun around, trying to run, but her feet turned to stone. Cackling voices surrounded her, taunting her. *Why Samantha? Why did you kill me?*

She called out, "I'm sorry. I didn't mean to. Please forgive me, Lizzie."

The shadows circled her, reaching for her, clawing her face and arms. *You could have saved me. You let me down.*

The ground shook beneath her feet, freeing them from their prison. She ran toward the main road, batting at the shadows. A woman waited at the end of the road, her hair flowing in the wind. As Samantha approached, a faceless man grabbed the woman's neck and threw her on the ground. Samantha screamed as he withdrew a revolver. Pointing it at the woman's head, he pulled the trigger. Samantha shrieked and jolted upright in bed.

She tried to catch her breath as sweat formed on her brow. The nightmares came frequently. Michael had stayed the past few nights and helped her through them, but last night she was alone. When left to herself, the cravings intensified. And the nightmares made it worse.

She climbed from bed and threw on a pair of pants and a shirt from the pile on the floor. No one was home, and Jonathan wouldn't be here until three o'clock. One hit wouldn't hurt. Then the nightmares wouldn't bother her. She searched her phone for a number, someone who wouldn't tell Michael.

Her fingers stopped on Liam's name. He was still on the outs with Cole and Michael, so he wouldn't tell. Her heart beat faster as she tried to convince herself to dial. She pushed it—then hung up.

Everyone was afraid she would relapse. But was it a relapse if she only used it when she had nightmares? She squeezed her eyes shut and grimaced as she pushed the dial button again. This time she let it ring. She took deep breaths, waiting for Liam to answer.

"I'm trying to sleep. Make it quick," Liam said.

"It's Samantha. Sorry to wake you. I'm out. Could you bring me some crack? I'll pay you."

Liam's voice changed. "Samantha. Where have you been? Haven't seen you around for a while. Everything okay"

"Yes, but can you please help me? Come over this morning. No one is home."

"Can't you get something from Cole or Michael?" His voice quivered. Michael must have followed through on his promise.

"I don't think Cole is talking to me, and I don't want Michael to know. Please, Liam. I need this."

Liam sighed. "Okay. I'll be there in a few hours."

Samantha hung up and stretched on the bed, drumming her fingers on her knees. What could she do in the meantime? She needed something to distract herself.

A hot shower, that would help. She walked to the bathroom and turned on the hot water. Standing under the showerhead, she closed her eyes as the stream trickled down her face. *Samantha. Don't do it.* She jumped backward and bumped her head on the shower wall. *Fight. Fight for peace.* Samantha grabbed her head and crumpled on the shower floor. The nightmares, voices, and visions of Lizzie still plagued her. She didn't know how to stop them.

She peeled herself off the floor and crawled from the shower. Her hair dripped, forming a puddle. She wrapped a towel around herself and stood at the mirror, brushing the tangles from her hair. She flinched when an image of Lizzie appeared.

"Go away. I can't deal with this. It's too much." Distraught, she pulled her hair until a clump fell out. Something had to change.

A pair of scissors lying on the sink caught her eye. Jeremy thought she looked like Lizzie, even with black hair. If she cut it, the resemblance would end and so might the nightmares and visions. Samantha sniffed back a tear and grabbed them. She wouldn't think about it this time. Lizzie wouldn't stop her. She grabbed a handful of hair and cut right below her chin. Her hands trembled as she made quick work of her hair. The jagged edges stuck out, much different from the flowing locks she'd had. She dropped the scissors in the sink and stroked the remains.

A knock on the door shook her back to reality. *Liam.*

She threw on an oversized shirt and leggings and ran to the door. "Just in time."

Liam rested his arm on the doorframe and cocked an eyebrow. "New look. I like."

"Give me the bag."

"Not so fast. Where's my money?"

"Bag first."

Liam handed her a bag of liquid packets and a syringe.

"Speedballs? I thought you were bringing crack."

Liam tilted his head and laughed. "You don't need that baby stuff anymore. You graduated, darling. This will make everything feel good."

Samantha stared at the bag. This is what had caused the problems in the first place. She bit the inside of her cheek and glanced at Liam. This would take care of her nightmares, but at what cost? Desperate for a solution, she caved. "How much?"

"Let's make it an even thousand."

Samantha froze. A thousand. It would take the rest of Cassie's vacation money to cover it. But it was worth it. "I'll get it. Wait here." Samantha turned toward Cassie's office.

"Wait a second. I'm intrigued. You can pay in other ways." Liam licked his lips and beheld her.

Samantha rolled her eyes and continued toward the office. "I won't tell Michael you said that." She returned a moment later with the money. "Here. Keep this between us, okay? Or I'll tell Michael you tried to seduce me."

Liam raised his hands and backpedaled toward the door. "I figured it was worth a try. If you change your mind, you know where to find me. And if you need more, call. Just don't tell Michael you got this from me, okay?" He winked and walked toward his car.

Samantha closed the door and rushed to her room. She sat cross-legged on her bed, Mr. Rabbit in her lap. She removed the syringe and laid it on the bed then smoothed out the bag next to it.

The negative voices came. *Druggie. Addict.* She covered her ears to drown them out. If she could go a week without using, she wasn't an addict. She had proved that, right? Did it matter if she needed it now and then? It would be different if she used every day. She clasped her hands and held them in front of her face, rocking back and forth.

She sat like that for the next few hours. Her mind clouded with thoughts of Jonathan and Gus. What was wrong with her? Why did she let others' thoughts affect her? She never considered Lizzie's feelings, even smoked in front of her when she had asked her to stop. Yet it concerned her what Jonathan and Gus would say.

It wouldn't be wise to take one before Jonathan came. But at least she had a rescue plan. She undid the stitch in Mr. Rabbit's back and slid the bag and syringe inside. They would be safe for now. She placed Mr. Rabbit on her headboard and approached the closet. Choosing a red sundress and matching pumps, she headed to the bathroom.

Her hair protruded in every direction. She tried to make sense of the mess, brushing it to no avail. The jagged cut created uneven lines, making it impossible to tame. Desperate, she grabbed Cassie's sculpting gel and smoothed the rough edges. After some experimentation, she made the pixie-cut work.

As she finished, she heard a knock on the door. *Jonathan*—just in time.

She adjusted her dress and slipped on her pumps. Opening the door, she flashed Jonathan a wide grin. "Good afternoon, Doc."

Jonathan gaped at her new look. "Red suits you. Ready?"

Samantha pouted. "Notice anything else?"

"My stomach is growling. How about some lunch with that coffee?"

Samantha huffed. "Let's go." Either he was obtuse or was deliberately ignoring her haircut.

"Where are we going?" Samantha asked.

"A little place called Ruby's Diner on the edge of town. Great service, wonderful atmosphere, and the best chicken-fried steak." Jonathan's eyes shone, and his smile widened.

"Sounds yummy. I haven't eaten."

They rode in awkward silence until they pulled into the diner parking lot. It was a throwback to the 1950s, complete with a jukebox, terrazzo floor, and neon signs. Jonathan approached her door but retreated when she shot him a disparaging look. He would learn.

Samantha joined him on the sidewalk, smiling at his choice. "Nice. I love fifties-style diners. Do they make malts or milkshakes? Extra points if they make both." Her eyes sparkled as she flashed him a coy smile.

"Both, but the malts are better." He slipped his arm around her shoulders and escorted her inside.

Patrons filled the counter area and most booths. Jonathan grasped her hand and pulled her through the restaurant toward an empty booth in the back.

They scooted in on either side, their feet touching. Samantha blushed and looked away. The proximity erased her mind and made her heart flutter. All thoughts of Liam and the speedballs left her mind. Who needed drugs when she had Jonathan? Except, she didn't.

A plump older woman set two menus in front of them. "What'll you have?"

"Two coffees, two chicken-fried steaks and two pieces of peach cobbler, please," Jonathan said.

Samantha cocked an eyebrow. "Hungry and thirsty?"

He paused. "I ordered for you, didn't I? Habit, I suppose. But you will *love* the cobbler."

She smiled and folded her hands on the table. "I pegged you for the observant type, Doc. But you haven't noticed." She smoothed her hair and leaned forward. "Or have you?"

Jonathan cleared his throat and averted her gaze. "Yes, well, I didn't think it appropriate to share my feelings."

He had feelings? That meant he cared. The possibility thrilled her. She reached across the table and laced her hand with his. "Tell me about it. I'm listening."

Jonathan released her hands and chuckled. "You'd make a great therapist." He lowered his gaze and whispered, "But I don't think my feelings are professional, so I'll keep them to myself."

What did that mean? Did he love it or hate it? She needed to know. "I thought we were friends. Friends share everything. I won't tell."

Jonathan scanned the diner before he leaned close. "Between you and me, short hair is sexy."

She didn't expect those words. He found her sexy. The thought shocked her. She pulled back and settled into the far end of the booth. They sat in silence, both averting the other's gaze, until Samantha mustered the courage to speak.

"Why did you become a therapist? Were you like Cassie, psychoanalyzing all your friends in high school?"

Jonathan laughed. "Not quite. I kept to myself. Not many people wanted to hang out with a chess champion."

"Chess, huh? Never played. You'll have to teach me." Samantha smiled. "Then what made you become a psychiatrist? I can't imagine a chess geek choosing psychiatry as a profession."

"It wasn't a popular decision. My parents wanted me to be a doctor, but I don't think this is what they had in mind." He tapped his fingers on the table. "I like helping people. In college, I was the one people sought for advice. They liked that I listened and never judged them. I got involved in the Peer Educator Program, and I was hooked. I wanted to help people dealing with addiction the rest of my life."

She always wondered how people knew what they wanted and went after it so easily. Why couldn't she do that?

Jonathan leaned forward. "What about you? Tell me something I don't know."

Samantha froze. *Something he didn't know.* What could she share that would interest him? She looked at the table and fumbled with her dress. "I know every Jane Austen book by heart."

"Closet romantic?"

Samantha blushed. "I suppose. It's nice to hope a true love exists, someone who understands you despite your flaws."

He smiled and leaned his elbow on the table. "Do you have a favorite? *Pride and Prejudice* perhaps? I hear that's the most popular."

"*Emma*. She's headstrong and makes mistakes, but Mr. Knightley still loves her."

"Good choice. I don't think I've read that one. I should add it to my reading list."

He wanted to read her favorite book. No one was interested in her likes before. Michael never read anything beyond a comic book. Jonathan was something from a romance novel—almost too good to be true.

"One day, I want to go to the Jane Austen Centre in Bath, England. Lizzie and I wanted to go together, but plans changed."

He leaned across the table and looked in her eyes. "I hope you get there one day. When you do, I know Lizzie will be there with you, in spirit."

Samantha managed a smile.

The waitress appeared with their drinks and food, breaking the mood.

They exchanged glances as they ate but maintained an awkward silence.

Samantha moved the steak around with her fork but didn't take a bite. "Do you think it's possible to find peace?

Before Lizzie died, she said I wasn't at peace. With all my mess, do you think I can find it?"

Jonathan choked back a piece of steak. "That's a loaded question. Peace is subjective. No one views it the same." He sipped his coffee. "I'm at peace when I'm able to help my patients. It's tied to desires and passions. Find something that excites you. Peace is bound to follow."

"I don't have a passion."

"That's not true." He leaned close. "I still see a spark. Something excited you, before the cocaine. What was it?"

She shrunk in the seat. Lizzie was the only one who believed in her passion. Her stomach churned, wondering how Jonathan would respond. It wasn't a serious career, as his and Cassie's. It wasn't lucrative, like her mother's business. He would dismiss it like the rest, as a time-consuming hobby.

"Photography. But it wasn't serious. Can't make a living taking pictures."

Jonathan flashed a wide smile. "Sure, you can. Many people make a living taking pictures. Have you considered your own photography studio?"

"Lizzie wanted to do that. We tried once, but Mother shut it down. She isn't the supportive type." Samantha stirred her coffee, remembering Portia's outburst. "I haven't touched my camera in months."

"Perhaps you should. I would love to see your pictures. You could share them with the group. Pursuing your passions is a great help in recovery. It gives you something to replace your cravings, something to work toward."

"I appreciate your confidence, Doc, but I gave up a while ago."

"Give me two months. If you're not taking pictures by then, I owe you a malt."

Samantha brightened. "A malt *and* a milkshake."

Jonathan proffered his hand. "Deal."

CHAPTER 17

Samantha woke early the next morning, pondering their bet. Jonathan hoped to succeed where Lizzie hadn't. But she was sure of her victory. Photography used to be her passion. How did he plan to revive it? She could taste the malt on her lips, knowing he had low odds.

She grabbed a bowl of popcorn from the kitchen and curled up on the couch. Saturdays meant Netflix, and she planned to binge *The Umbrella Academy*. The solitude calmed her—no Michael demanding attention, no Cassie lecturing about her hair. It was blissful.

A knock threatened to thwart her plans. She wasn't expecting anyone until later. Cassie was working extra hours at the clinic, and Michael wouldn't be over until the afternoon. She put down the popcorn, trudged to the door and swung it open.

No one was there. Instead, a box sat on the doorstep with a note attached. She picked up the box and ran her fingers over it.

> *Samantha,*
>
> *You have passions. I see it in your eyes. I hope this camera will ignite your passion. I look forward to seeing what you*

do with it.
Jonathan

She placed the box on the coffee table and opened it, shocked at what she saw—a Nikon D850, her dream camera. Her eyes widened. Why did he send such an expensive gift? Was he determined to win the bet? She couldn't accept this.

Or could she? Photography used to be her obsession. She would go to the lake as the sun rose and take pictures of landscapes. Whatever emotion she had been dealing with would melt behind the camera. It was her and nature, a perfect escape.

Until her mother broke her spirit. She shuddered recalling Portia's tirade about photography. It was a trash hobby and not worth her time. Then she met Michael, and the crack replaced her first passion, like Lizzie had said. Was she ready to revive it?

Even if she was ready, should she accept such a gift from Jonathan? Therapists don't send their patients three thousand-dollar cameras. And friends don't either.

Her mind raced as the TV-show episodes continued playing. She couldn't focus, wondering about Jonathan's true motive. As the sixth episode ended, she heard sounds of arguing from outside the room. She rolled her eyes. *Great. Cassie and Michael.* She turned off the television and prepared herself for the onslaught.

"I told you to park beside me, not behind me," Cassie said. "Move your car. If I get a call from the clinic, I have to leave. I'm not chasing you down."

"I didn't know you were that kind of doctor. Psychiatrists get emergency calls too? Like, someone needs to talk to you, because they can't decide where to go for dinner?"

Cassie's eyes bulged. "Do not make fun of mental health. My client's mental well-being is often a matter of life and death. Don't belittle their struggle."

Michael raised his hands and backed away. "Sorry. Didn't mean to offend."

Cassie groaned. "And to think, I was starting to tolerate you." She put her purse on the armchair and sat.

Michael smiled and sat next to Samantha. "Hey, babe. Did you miss me?" He grabbed a handful of popcorn and settled into the cushion.

Samantha managed a half smile but didn't move.

"What's this?" Cassie looked in the box and pulled out the camera, her eyes wide with excitement. "Isn't this the one you wanted? How did you afford it?"

"I didn't. Read the note."

Cassie pulled the note off the box, her eyes and smile widening. "Jonathan, huh? Interesting."

"He's buying you expensive presents?" Michael stood and snatched the note from Cassie. "What is this about passions? Is something going on between you?"

Cassie hit him on the arm. "He means passions—like things you love to do. Samantha loves photography. He wants her to take pictures again."

Michael faced Samantha, crinkling his brow. "Is this true? He wants you to take pictures. Is this part of therapy?"

Samantha grabbed the camera and placed it in the box. "It's going back. He shouldn't have sent it." She stormed to her bedroom, box in hand. This was causing more problems than she could handle.

Exhaling, she threw the box on her bed and dove into the beanbag. This non-relationship with Jonathan plagued her. She was partly to blame. Her flirting got out of hand. But he flirted too, even called her *sexy*. It had to stop, and she would say as much the next time she saw him.

The camera had to go too. She approached the bed and removed it from the box. She twirled it in her hand and thought about Lizzie. She would want Samantha to keep it, but she couldn't. This represented her old life. She didn't deserve it in her new.

She placed it back in the box and sat next to it. If life was different, she would pick someone like Jonathan. He was kind and calm, not to mention handsome in a geeky way. But her life wasn't different, and he wasn't available. Michael was the best she could hope for, and he wasn't all bad. At least he tried. She would end this on Tuesday, then Jonathan wouldn't make her melt inside.

She left the box on the bed and joined Michael in the living room. Four more episodes of *The Umbrella Academy* would make everything right.

***

Samantha spent the weekend smoothing things out with Michael and rehearsing her conversation with Jonathan. By Tuesday, Michael believed nothing was transpiring between them, but he still insisted on driving her to counseling. They brought the camera along, intending to return it.

"Do you want me to go with you?" Michael turned off the ignition and turned to face her." I can talk to Dr. Green, if you want."

"That's not a good idea. It's my problem, and I'll solve it." Samantha reached for the box in the back seat and exited the car.

"If you need me, I'll be here. Oh, and don't make him cry. He seems like the type."

Samantha shook her head and traipsed inside. She hoped it was early enough, so they could talk before group. She didn't need this hanging over her head for the next hour.

Jonathan stood in the meeting room, reviewing his notes. The room was empty. Good, she had beat everyone else here.

She gathered her courage and approached him, camera in hand. "Good morning, Doc. I hoped we could talk."

Jonathan looked up and smiled. "Of course. I see you got my present. They rated it high, so I thought it would do the trick. Do you like it?"

"Thank you. Yes, I've wanted this exact camera for a while."

"Good." He returned to his notes, his pen hanging from his mouth.

"I can't accept it."

"Why? It's the one you wanted. Did it help you think about photography?"

"Yes, but I can't accept it. Do you know what a Nikon costs?"

He winked. "Pretty sure I do. I bought it."

She put the camera on a chair next to him as her gaze flitted around the room. He wasn't listening. She had to make him understand. She glanced toward the door as Gus entered.

He waved and settled into a seat on the opposite side.

"Doc, Jonathan, please." She lowered her voice so Gus wouldn't hear. "Don't you think this is a conflict of interest? You're my therapist. I admit, I was flirting with you the last few times we met, but this is too much. It's gone too far. Please, take it back."

Jonathan dropped his notebook and pen and pursed his lips. "Alright. I'm sorry it made you uncomfortable. That wasn't my intent." He took the camera and left the room.

Samantha composed herself and sat several seats from Gus. She avoided his eyes, hoping he wouldn't ask questions. They sat in silence for a moment, waiting for the room to fill and for Jonathan to return. She felt Gus's gaze on her as the rest of the group entered and found seats.

One empty seat remained next to her, and Gus moved to occupy it. "Everything okay, young lady? It looked intense—you and Dr. Green."

"It's nothing. He thinks I have a passion, and I think I don't."

"Everyone has passions. It's what keeps us going. My passion helped me recover, and it still helps me stay on the right path."

"You have a passion?" Samantha raised her eyebrows. "What is it?"

"Not unless you tell me yours."

"I told you. I don't have one."

"Same stubborn girl from the first day. I thought you learned." Gus stood and walked away.

"Wait. I want to hear yours. So, I'll tell you what Dr. Green thinks my passion is."

Gus turned and stood in front of her.

"Photography. I used to take pictures. Dr. Green thinks I should start again."

"But you don't. Why? If you once loved it, chances are you will love it again."

"Because it never got me anywhere. It's a stupid hobby."

"There are no stupid hobbies. Except grass collecting. That's a stupid hobby."

Samantha smiled. Gus made a good point. She could love it again. But not now. Things were unsettled. If her life calmed down, she would consider it. Right now, she was too busy putting one foot in front of the other to try.

Jonathan returned to the group, refusing to meet her gaze. The meeting was cold and awkward. Samantha squirmed in her seat, eager for its end. She didn't make him cry, as Michael had warned, but a distance existed between them.

He settled into his chair in the front of the room and greeted the group as normal. Instead of introductions, he went straight to the session.

Samantha grimaced as he lectured about passions. He was determined to rub this in. She slouched in her seat, wishing she had stayed home.

Each group member shared their passion, but none of them interested her until Gus. Samantha perked up when his deep voice filled the room.

"As you said, Dr. Green, passions are important. Mine helped me recover, and it gives me direction, something to strive for. Most people don't believe me, but my passion is painting. Getting a fresh canvas and covering it with paint, creating a whole new world for people to enjoy, that's what charges me up. One day, I want to put my work in a gallery show in Kingston. It's good to have dreams."

Samantha stared. *Painting*, she wouldn't have guessed. And he was brave enough to try for a gallery show. She respected his courage, but she didn't have that drive in her. Everything seemed pointless. She wasn't capable of change, so why did they keep pushing?

Beads of sweat formed on her brow as she realized she was next. Jonathan met her gaze, but the warmth she loved was gone. This was a disaster. Why didn't he skip her? He knew how she felt about photography, and things were awkward enough. Making her share would be humiliating.

Frustrated, she stood and walked out the door, not knowing if she would return.

***

One day in-between counseling sessions left little time for reflection. Her mind replayed Tuesday's meeting, trying to sort out what went wrong. She knew trouble was abound when his eyes went cold. Once again, he was no longer Jonathan with the dancing brown eyes. Every time he pulled back, her heart sank.

Between Cassie's meddling, her burgeoning feelings, and Jonathan's mixed messages, she felt like a yo-yo. Did he realize what he was doing to her?

She sighed, hoping she didn't ruin their friendship. It wasn't right, but the thought of losing him shook her.

She plopped onto her bed and hugged a pillow to her chest. Mr. Rabbit fell from his place on the headboard. His floppy ears and half smile taunted her. She caressed the stuffed rabbit's fur. Everything she had worked toward the past two weeks faded. She wasn't like Gus. Change wasn't an option. This was who she was, and it was time to embrace it.

She ran her fingers over his backside stitching. Liam had sold her plenty for the next few days. Her eyes misted as she undid the stitch. She would never be more than a druggie. At least she knew her place.

A knock interrupted her. Not knowing if it was Michael or Cassie, she closed the stitch and hid Mr. Rabbit underneath the pillow. "Come in."

The door opened, but it wasn't Michael or Cassie. Jonathan stood in the doorway, a forlorn look on his face. "May I?"

Samantha's eyes grew round. What was he doing here? "Doc, I wasn't expecting you. Especially here, in my bedroom." She stood and kicked a bra and underwear underneath the bed.

"I didn't want to wait until tomorrow." He approached the bed, his hands shaking. "May I sit?"

She nodded then moved to the beanbag chair. His presence unnerved her, spiraling her emotions further.

He ran his hands through his hair, concentrating his gaze on the floor. "About yesterday. I owe you an apology. I'm afraid I was overzealous. My desire to prove you wrong overruled my better judgment. If you misconstrued anything I've said or done, that's on me."

Samantha took a breath and looked away. This was the breakup speech. Except they weren't dating. So why did her heart hurt?

"It's common to have an attraction between therapist and patient. Our sessions can evoke pent-up emotions, making us susceptible to misplaced feelings. It's called *transference*. But it's not real."

Her eyes welled as he spoke. It made sense. But her feelings had begun before he was her therapist. Didn't that count for anything? She stared straight ahead as he continued.

"I'm invested in your recovery. Now that we are aware, we can be more careful. I don't want you to quit the group, and I still want our Friday coffee sessions." He stood and knelt beside her. "I hope to win back your trust. Can we try again?"

She turned and looked into his eyes. They were back. Jonathan with the dancing brown eyes had returned. She took his hands and stood. "We can try, Doc."

He squeezed and flashed a smile. Why was she so upset when she had Michael? She couldn't shake Jonathan from her mind. Her insides tumbled as she thought about his words. She would tread lightly from now on. As much as her heart wanted, she couldn't allow herself to fall in love.

CHAPTER 18

Samantha struggled through dinner, trying to compartmentalize her feelings. Jonathan wasn't an option, but she couldn't shake her attraction. His words made sense, and she was happy his cold stare was gone, but a piece of her was missing. Transference was the only answer. It explained why her feelings had grown so quick. But what if it was more? What if something between them, beyond the doctor-patient relationship, existed?

She moved around her chicken with her fork and sighed.

"Where's Michael?" Cassie asked. "He's usually by your side, lapping like a puppy dog."

Samantha shrugged. "Not here. He has a life."

Cassie put down her fork and propped her elbows on the table. "What's wrong? You don't look like yourself. Did you have a fallout?"

Samantha knew she meant *Michael*, but she could only think of Jonathan. "You could say that."

Cassie's gaze bore into her.

"I gave Jonathan the camera back."

"Why? It was a thoughtful gift. Plus, it could help you recover. Focusing on something you love can take your mind off any cravings."

"It was inappropriate. I'm trying to maintain a professional relationship, but none of the professionals are cooperating."

"This is a unique situation. Jonathan is the most ethical therapist I know. He had a reason behind the camera."

Samantha smirked. "In his mind, I'm sure he did. But it doesn't make it right. He keeps telling me how inappropriate a relationship would be, how anything we may be feeling isn't real, but then he buys me an expensive gift. He can't have it both ways, Cass."

"You don't know him like I do. I wish you'd give him a chance, be more open to the possibility."

"The possibility of what? He made it clear he's only interested in my recovery. Besides, aren't there rules against it?"

Cassie sighed. "There are. But I care about both of you. I saw a spark the first day you met. That's why I kept pushing his involvement. You both need something. I hoped you could heal each other."

Samantha wrinkled her brow. "Are you talking about his daughter's death? He's healing fine without me."

"It's more than that. I told you about his ex-wife."

Samantha shook her head. "If you're so concerned about him, *you* date him. Forget it. I'm done." Samantha threw her fork on the plate and stomped down the hallway.

"We're not done talking." Cassie chased after her, grabbing Samantha's shoulder. "I'm worried. You did so well those first two weeks. I hoped the extra session with Jonathan would help, but it's driven you further away. You're not using again, are you?"

Samantha's mind drifted to Mr. Rabbit and her secret. "No. I haven't touched it in two weeks. Care to search my room?" She put her hands on her hips and folded her arms.

Cassie sighed and backed away. "That's okay. I trust you." She turned to walk away then spun back. "By the way, do you know what happened to my vacation money? The envelope is empty."

Samantha sucked in a breath and froze. "No idea."

Cassie shot her a knowing glance but backed off. "I'll ask Michael the next time he comes over." Cassie walked toward the kitchen.

Samantha bowed her head and closed the door. If she had kept Jonathan's present, she could have sold it to replace Cassie's money. But she had already returned it. Asking Jonathan to give it back seemed counterproductive. She would think of something.

***

Cassie drove Samantha to the clinic the next morning.

She shook , recalling her reaction and abrupt exit on Tuesday. Gus had given her an earful when she acted rash. She expected today to be no different.

The car ride was silent. Her mind wavered between logic and love. Or was it lust? A platonic friendship was all she could hope for, but she couldn't shake her feelings. Being stuck in limbo sucked.

Cassie parked and got out. "I'll be in my office. Come get me when you're done. Oh, and be nice."

Samantha saluted her and walked to the meeting room. She was the last to arrive. Jonathan stood in the middle of the room, readying his notes. She spied a seat next to Gus and slid in, flashing him a smile.

"Good to see you, young lady. Take any pictures recently?"

"No. Paint anything recently?"

"Yep. A nice bowl of cherries." Gus winked and gave a hearty laugh.

Samantha suppressed a chuckle as Jonathan cleared his throat to begin. "Good morning, group. Today I want to talk about something we all have, something that plagues us, that possibly led to our addictions—something interfering with your recovery today."

Samantha leaned forward. What did everyone in the room have in common? She didn't believe they experienced the same issues. Who else had a sister haunting them and a mother berating them? Curious, she fixated on him as he continued.

"It may present itself differently for each one of you. I'm talking about the feeling that haunts you. The one that says you're not good enough. The one that won't leave you alone. I want to talk about that feeling this morning and how you can combat it. I like to call them your *demons*. Think for a few minutes. What are your demons? Then meet with your partner and discuss. Remember, this is a safe zone."

Demons. What were hers? She wasn't sure. Over the past few sessions, Gus had become her accountability partner, and she was grateful for his help. Since he was more experienced, she looked to him for guidance. She turned, hoping he would share first, but he motioned for her to begin. "I don't know. Go ahead. Tell me I say that too often, but I don't know what my demons are."

"Do you remember the first time you used? What were you feeling? That's a good place to start."

Samantha tilted her head. "No harsh words? I'm not used to this side. You could replace Dr. Green, talking like that."

Gus chuckled. "I'm not that good. This is a difficult topic. I figured you needed some extra care. Besides, it took me a while to come to terms with my demons."

"How did you?"

"Doing what we're doing now. Talking. The only way to find them is to talk about them. They'll make themselves known. Now, answer the question. What were you feeling?"

Samantha closed her eyes, remembering her first party with Michael and the fight that drove her there. "Guilt, loneliness—the usual."

"Keep going. What else?"

A tear crept down her face. She searched for the words but couldn't find them. "I don't want to talk about it."

"It's okay. It's just me. You're safe."

"No one understands. They think I'm exaggerating, but they weren't there. She made sure of that."

Gus took her hands and leaned close. "I'll do my best to understand. Tell me."

Samantha scrunched her eyes, trying to hold back. "It doesn't matter. She'll never change. What's the use?"

"This isn't about her. It's about you. Tell me what she did. Getting it out will help."

Samantha scanned the room. Everyone was in deep conversation with their partner. Jonathan circulated, offering his support. She hoped he wouldn't come near them. She wasn't ready to lose it in front of him.

"You have to let it out. That's why it's called a *demon*. It's eating you alive. Unless you confront this, you'll never recover."

She squeezed her eyes shut as the memories flooded her. "I never told anyone what happened. My mother did it all behind closed doors. Lizzie didn't even know."

Gus put his arms around her shoulders. "Then it's time you let it out. Keeping it inside won't help."

Her mind replayed the incidents as she told Gus the truth—Portia screaming when she stained her dress; slapping her when she talked at parties; locking her in the bathroom when she refused to stop crying over her father's death. It got worse over time. When she was a teenager, Portia's abuse intensified. She favored Lizzie, while Samantha got scraps. Lizzie got the newest clothes, technology, and cars. Samantha had to work for anything she wanted. Lizzie tried to stick up for her, but it backfired in ways Lizzie never knew. Portia would visit her room at night with a list of things she had done wrong. Whenever Samantha spoke to defend herself, Portia slapped her across the face. She worked hard to keep it from Lizzie, covering the bruises as best she could with makeup. But the physical abuse was nothing next to the verbal. That cut her down more than the slaps and bruises ever could.

The night before Michael's party, she had dinner with her mother. They were in Portia's kitchen, putting the dishes in the sink, when Samantha told her she had quit her job to pursue photography. Portia was irate. She smashed a plate at Samantha's feet and wagged her finger in her face.

Samantha shuddered as she remembered the words. *You will never be good enough. Look at you, playing with your camera instead of getting a real job, like your sister. You're irresponsible and an ungrateful little bitch. Your actions reflect on me, and you're nothing but a piece of trash.*

As she convulsed in a sea of tears, an arm embraced her from behind. She turned around, her eyes clouded, and broke down in his arms. He patted her back and whispered soothing words in her ears. She beheld his smell—sandalwood and vanilla. Since when did Gus smell so good?

She wrapped her arms around him and clung. He was much taller than Gus, and thinner.

Confused, she opened her eyes. It was Jonathan. Blinking back tears, she let go and stumbled to her seat. She had lost it, in front of him. She blushed as she covered her face with her hands. It was too much, but she didn't want to run like last time.

Jonathan pulled a chair in front of her and sat. "This is good. You need to face it in order to conquer it. Great progress." He sat for a moment, letting her cry, then turned toward Gus. "You've been here. You know the drill. Next meeting, share your tips for dealing with demons. Help her through."

Gus nodded and pushed his chair closer. He put his arm around her as Jonathan closed the meeting. She appreciated Gus's kind gesture and fatherly advice. It was needed.

"Good group. We will continue this discussion next week. And remember, if you need anything, contact your partner first, then contact me."

Samantha fumbled with her bracelet and turned to Gus. "Can I ask you a question?"

He leaned forward, his hands in his lap. "Sure."

"Do you still have cravings? Does it ever completely go away?"

Gus took a breath and clasped his hands together. "Sometimes. But I know my triggers. When they strike, I implement Dr. Green's strategies. They help."

"You're saying I'll always feel this way? I was hoping for a different answer."

Gus took her hands. "You have to put in the work. Know your triggers and find ways to handle them. But it won't magically disappear. Once you let down your guard, it could creep up on you. Just keep working. You'll get there."

She looked down and shook her head. She knew her triggers. Whenever her emotions spiked, the cravings hit. Today's session was no different. She thought about Mr. Rabbit and Liam's speedballs. She would need one of Jonathan's strategies tonight.

Gus helped Samantha to her feet and embraced her. "I believe in you, young lady. You'll tame this demon yet.

Remember, I'm a phone call away. I got you." He smiled and walked toward the hallway.

Samantha took her time gathering her things, hoping her face would not show her emotion. She had carried these secrets for so long, not even sharing them with Lizzie. She didn't want Cassie to pry.

"Samantha, one second?" Jonathan rushed over, stopping her from leaving. "I'm glad Gus was there for you today. I didn't expect such a reaction to that exercise. But when you open a wound, things pour out. It was bad, wasn't it? Much worse than you let on."

She stared at the ground, counting the tiles. If she relived it, she wouldn't be able to face Cassie.

"Yes, well, no one believes me, so who cares? I've gotten good at carrying it."

"You don't have to. Can I pick you up for lunch tomorrow? I'll buy you that malt you wanted. We can talk, start the healing process, so you don't have to carry it alone."

"I don't know why you spend so much time trying to heal me. I'm damaged. We all know that. Why are you wasting your time?"

Jonathan pulled up a seat and straddled it. "I've been counseling addicts for ten years. Most don't have a support system, so I try to provide that for them. I know you only have Cassie and Michael and that you are dealing with a lot of hurt right now. If I can be there for you, help you through this, I want to try—not just as your therapist but as your friend."

Jonathan confused her every time they spoke. She wished he would decide if he wanted to be her therapist or something more. The not knowing tore her apart. "Do you think we can be friends?"

Jonathan smiled. "Yes. I think we can. Are we on for tomorrow?"

Against her better judgement, she nodded. Her emotions were too raw to argue.

***

Ruby's Diner was empty. Samantha wondered if Jonathan had arranged it, so they could talk in private. They sat in the same booth at the back of the diner. Jonathan ordered malts and grilled-cheese sandwiches, reminding her of childhood.

She slid into the far end of the booth, distancing herself. Until Jonathan decided about her, she wanted to guard her heart.

"How are things with Michael? I worry he'll hinder your recovery. Any sign he's ready for rehab?" Jonathan leaned back and adjusted his glasses.

She picked at her sandwich. "He comes by a couple times a week. He tries, but he isn't ready. It'll take a lot to tear him away from Cole."

"May I ask what you see in him? Nothing against Michael, but you don't seem compatible."

"You're not the first to say that. And I don't have an answer. Except that he's familiar, and he didn't abandon me. He could have walked away after the accident, but he didn't. That counts for something. I can't walk away from him now."

Jonathan nodded. "I admire your loyalty. He's lucky to have you."

Samantha smirked. "Loyalty? Is that what it is? Cassie calls it *stupidity*, but there's no love lost between her and Michael. Maybe someday she'll see him like I do."

Jonathan smiled. "Cassie is hard to impress."

"Yes, she is. What about you? Have you ever been with someone who wasn't right for you?"

He coughed and rubbed the back of his neck. "Payback, huh? I'll bite." He pushed aside his drink and clasped his hands on the table. "My ex-wife."

Cassie had mentioned an ex-wife, but Jonathan had never talked about her.

"What was she like?"

"Cold, self-absorbed—everything I said I didn't want."

"Why did you marry her, then?"

"False sense of love, I suppose. We met in college. She turned to me when her boyfriend ran off with another girl. I thought it was true love, but I was just a filler. When her boyfriend came back years later, they had an affair. Then she decided the life I gave her wasn't exciting enough, so she left Rachel and me and took off with him."

Samantha reached across and touched his hands. "I'm sorry. I can't imagine thinking you're in love and someone leaves you like that."

Their gazes met for a moment before he looked away.

"Yes, well, that's in the past." He picked up his sandwich.

They ate in silence, not knowing what to say next.

After Jonathan finished his sandwich, he leaned back in the booth. "Did you tell Cassie about your last group session? She's too close to counsel you, but, as a friend, she would be a great support."

Samantha shook her head. "No. And I don't plan to. If I need help, I'll call Gus. That's what he's for, isn't he?"

"Yes. I'm glad I chose him for your accountability partner. It's good that you opened up to him yesterday. But I still think Cassie would make a great ally." His hair fell into his eye as he sipped his malt.

"Cassie doesn't know what happened, and Lizzie barely knew."

"When did it start?" Jonathan propped his elbow on the table, staring intently ahead.

"After my dad died, something in her snapped. And I got the brunt of it." She avoided his glance, stirring the malt with her straw.

"Why didn't you tell Lizzie? She had to know something was wrong."

"It wasn't Lizzie's fault. I shielded her from Mother as much as I could. If she found out what Mother was doing, she would have said something. I didn't know how Mother would react to it, so I didn't tell her."

"It takes strength to protect your sister. But you don't have to carry it alone anymore. You have Cassie and Gus." He paused and took her hands. "And me."

She blushed and looked away. "Thank you, Doc, but I can't tell Cassie."

"Why? It would help her understand. She loves you like a sister."

Samantha shook her head. "What good would that do? She's close to my mother. It would cause drama. It's better this way."

"It's eating you up. Someday you must come to terms with it, talk to Cassie and your mother. Otherwise, it will keep haunting you."

Samantha smirked. "I'm used to things haunting me. Between my memories, the nightmares and Lizzie, I don't sleep much anyway."

Jonathan cocked his head. "Nightmares? When did they start?"

"After drug court. Michael says it's a withdrawal symptom. Every time I have one, I'm manic the next day. That's why I cut my hair last week."

Jonathan leaned back, rubbing his chin with his hand. "Why didn't you say something? Aren't nightmares something you would share with your therapist?" He leaned forward. "Or your friend?"

"If it's a withdrawal symptom, what could you do? I figured it would pass with time."

Jonathan adjusted his glasses and tapped his head. "Could be. What other symptoms have you had? Cravings, hallucinations?"

Samantha bit into her grilled cheese, buying time to think. He knew too much already. She wasn't prepared to tell him about the voices or Mr. Rabbit's secrets. Some things were better kept to herself.

"Not really. Two weeks clean and counting." She managed a half smile and slurped the remainder of her malt.

CHAPTER 19

After the emotional upheaval of the last few weeks, Samantha needed a break. Michael proposed a movie night, and she was shocked Cassie agreed. They settled in front of the television, Cassie in the armchair and Michael and Samantha snuggling on the couch.

"*Thor: Ragnarök* is still on Netflix." Michael picked up the remote and searched.

Cassie jumped and snatched it. "Not another Marvel movie. I had enough after *Thor: Dark World* yesterday."

Samantha raised her eyebrows. "Watching movies without me? I thought you hated each other."

Cassie and Michael cast furtive glances at each other and looked down. "It's not what you think. He's still an annoying idiot. We had to do something when you were with Jonathan."

Samantha chuckled. She was happy they were getting along. Michael grew on people once they got to know him, so she wasn't surprised Cassie came around.

"*Ragnarök* is better than *Dark World*, I promise." Michael leaned forward and reached for the remote.

Cassie held it in the air, out of reach. "No Marvel. Let's watch something a little more civilized." She scrolled through the options, landing on a drama Samantha didn't know. "This is about Diane Arbus, the famous photographer." Cassie pushed Play before anyone could object.

Michael groaned and sank into the cushion. "We have to sit through this boring crap?" He grabbed a handful of popcorn and shoved it in his mouth.

Cassie ignored him and looked toward Samantha. "Have you thought about taking pictures again? You still have your old camera. The weather is perfect for photography."

Samantha sighed. She had thought about photography, especially after Gus had shared his passion. If he could set his sights on a gallery show, she could pick up her camera and take a few pictures. "Maybe. Let's watch the movie."

For the next two hours, they watched in silence. Samantha marveled at Diane's use of photography to show everyday issues with humanity. It put a face on the struggles people wrestled with—made them human. She could do that. She could use photography to affect change, bring awareness to drug issues. Her eyes grew wide with excitement as ideas ran through her head. She didn't want to share with Michael and Cassie right now, but she couldn't wait to share her ideas with Gus.

Michael snored by the end, sending them into fits of laughter. Cassie threw popcorn, trying to get it in his open mouth. Samantha laughed so hard all her worries melted away. If only every night ended this way.

Michael snorted and shook awake when the next piece of popcorn hit him. He sat, a disoriented look on his face. "Movie over?" He stood and stretched, bellowing a loud yawn.

"We should turn in. Thanks for the good time, Cass. We should make this a regular thing." Samantha took Michael's hand and led him to her room.

Michael settled on the bed while Samantha rifled through her closet. "What are you looking for?"

"My camera. If Diane Arbus can become a famous photographer, I can take pictures again."

"Pictures of what? Flowers? Puppies? Perhaps pictures of tacos. That sounds like a good idea. I'm always interested in tacos."

Samantha threw a pillow at him. "Be serious. I want to take pictures of people, like Diane Arbus does. Ordinary people doing ordinary things. A commentary on the state of our town."

Michael yawned. "Sounds boring. Can we talk about this tomorrow? I'm exhausted." He drew the blanket to his chin and fell asleep.

Samantha put the camera on her headboard and stared. For the first time, she felt energized. Photography did give her a high. Lizzie was right all along.

***

During the next few weeks, Samantha and Jonathan fell into a pattern. They had group sessions Tuesdays and Thursdays and lunch every Friday. Samantha enjoyed the predictability of their non-relationship. It gave her something to look forward to, especially when she craved cocaine.

A month sober was cause for celebration. They made plans at their usual Friday place to indulge in malts and peach cobbler. Samantha crossed off the days on her calendar, anxious for Friday. But, by Wednesday, her mood had changed.

"Friday is the big day, right?" Cassie plopped onto the bed.

"Not anymore. Mother summoned me to dinner." Samantha played with the blanket's frayed ends.

"That's good, right? You can make up. I've never understood the rift between you."

Samantha stood and approached the window. "It doesn't matter. I've been summoned, so I cancelled with Jonathan. He sounded disappointed, but we can always celebrate next week."

Cassie joined her at the window, putting her arm around her shoulders. "You're keeping something from me."

She turned to face her. "I've tried to tell you, Cass. Many times. But you brush me off, because you don't believe me. Why keep trying?"

"Tried to tell me what? If I haven't listened to you, tell me. I'll do better."

"Will you? You're trained to listen to people's problems, but that never applied to me. You always thought you knew better. But I told you. You weren't there. No one was."

Cassie sat on the edge of the bed, her hands in her lap. "I'll listen."

Samantha paced the floor as she told Cassie what she had shared with Gus. Cassie listened and didn't interrupt.

When Samantha recounted the last interaction with Portia, Cassie rushed over and embraced her.

"I'm such a fool. Why didn't I know? Why didn't Lizzie know? Hell, Samantha, you should have told us."

"I didn't want to burden Lizzie. She tried to stick up for me, but she didn't know what Mother did behind closed doors. No one did."

"Is that why you started using?"

"That's the consensus from the group. I never connected the two, except that I was mad at her. I never qualified it as abuse. But now I know."

"You can't go Friday night."

"I don't think I have a choice. I can't avoid her forever."

"That may be true, but you can't go alone. I'm going with you. And this time, I have your back." Cassie pulled her close and squeezed.

Relief swept over Samantha. Finally, she felt like Cassie was a friend, even a sister. Together, they could conquer the world. Or conquer Portia's abuse, whatever was easier.

***

They stood in front of Portia's door, arm in arm, poised to brave whatever she dished.

Cassie gave Samantha an encouraging smile and rang the doorbell. After reliving Portia's abuse multiple times the past week, Samantha was fearful of her reaction. But Cassie's presence and support gave her courage to conquer this demon.

Portia answered the door, out of character for her. Samantha staggered at the change. Instead of her normal cavalier reception, she welcomed Samantha with open arms. "Daughter. What a gorgeous dress. And your hair, I love what you've done with it. Très chic." Portia grabbed her by the shoulders and kissed both cheeks.

Caught off-guard, Samantha flinched at her embrace. What was she up to?

"Hello, Mother. I hope you don't mind, but I invited Cassie."

"Cassie is like a daughter to me." She turned and grasped Cassie's hand. "You are always welcome. The others are waiting in the living room. Shall we?"

Samantha and Cassie shot each other confused glances as they followed Portia. *Others?* She never said it was a dinner party. What was her motive? She put herself on high alert, ready for whatever Portia had in mind.

They reached the living room, expecting a crowd. Instead, two men waited, both making Samantha's stomach churn but for different reasons. Jeremy sat on one couch, drinking a scotch and looking rough. He'd cleaned up since they last met, but the dark circles under his eyes and wrinkles in his forehead showed he had seen better days. Samantha thought he looked older, as if the past month had aged him.

She switched her gaze to the far corner and froze. Her mother invited Jonathan. Why? Her heart skipped a beat as their gazes locked. He knew about the abuse; he knew her emotions were raw, yet here he was, in the lion's den. Why didn't he say anything?

Portia commanded attention in the center of the room. "I'm glad you came, Cassie. It will even things out. Jeremy, you can sit next to Cassie at dinner. Samantha, you can sit next to Dr. Green." Portia flitted about as if on a mission. "I'll check on dinner. Be back."

Cassie approached Jeremy, giving Samantha a clear line to Jonathan. For a moment, she stared, as if she saw a mirage. Then they moved toward each other, meeting in the center of the room.

"Why didn't you tell me Mother invited you?"

"I didn't get a chance. She called me today."

"You could have given me a heads up or something."

"Then you would have told me not to come. I didn't want you to be alone with her."

"Cassie came. I told her everything."

"I'm glad. You need as much support as possible. Despite everything, she loves you."

Samantha nodded. "I know." Samantha startled when Portia entered the room.

"Dinner is ready. If you will follow me." Portia led the group to the dining room, ensuring everyone sat in their assigned seat. Taking her place at the head of the table, she rang for service. "I'm afraid I'm short on help tonight. Only have Margaret." Turning to her maid, she cooed, "Thank you, dear Margaret. I would be lost without you."

Had Portia gone mad? She never treated people this way, let alone hired help. Samantha raised her glass to her lips, casting Portia a wary look. She hoped Jonathan and Cassie weren't falling for her masquerade.

Margaret delivered the meals on china plates featuring little bluebirds. Samantha had admired the plates as a child but never ate off them. They were for special occasions, and Samantha wasn't considered special enough. She wondered why her mother changed that now. Throughout dinner, Portia was animated, sharing stories about Samantha and Lizzie. She acted like a proud mother, and Samantha wondered where she'd been her whole life. Could Portia change? Samantha was afraid to hope.

"Dr. Green, tell me. How is my wayward daughter doing in therapy? Is she cooperating?" Portia sat back and twirled her wine glass. "I hope she's not giving you any problems. She was the difficult twin."

There she was. It was only a matter of time before the real Portia revealed herself. She kicked Jonathan with her foot, warning him.

"I'm afraid it's confidential. I can say I'm pleased with her progress." Jonathan raised a piece of chicken to his mouth with one hand and squeezed Samantha's thigh with the other.

She flashed him a half smile and concentrated on her food.

"Is there anything I can do to help? Offer employment maybe? A regular job could help her stay in line."

Jonathan sipped his wine. "We don't want to rush things. When Samantha is ready, a job will come. Right now, her energy needs to be focused on recovery."

Samantha breathed a sigh of relief. Working for her mother spelled disaster. Confinement in a desk job, listening to her shrill voice bark orders every day—the thought of it made her shudder.

"Don't you think the leadership of a strong man would help her, Doctor?" Jeremy spoke from across the table. His eyes scanned over her, stopping at her chest. He licked his lips and winked.

This was Jonathan's first encounter with Jeremy, and Samantha was anxious to see how he'd handle it. Michael was prone to fist fights when pushed, but the doctor was different.

"The goal is to create a strong, healthy woman, not one dependent on others. I'm encouraging Samantha to pursue her passions, discover what makes her heart race, and embrace that. Directing her time and energy toward something she enjoys is the best way to recover."

Samantha blushed as she considered his words. Did he know he was talking about himself? Nothing made her heart race like him. She looked at her plate as his hand touched hers under the table. Jonathan grabbed it and squeezed. She squeezed back and smiled, hoping he wouldn't let go.

"Passions? Isn't that shortsighted? You can't build a career from a passion. I've tried telling her that, and now you're encouraging it?"

Jonathan stroked Samantha's hand with his thumb and faced Portia. "With all due respect, Ms. Barrett, passions make the best careers. Cassie and I are passionate about helping people, and we have successful careers. Samantha loves photography. I'm hoping she will take it up again. There are many ways to make a living."

"Ha. So you say, Doctor." Portia put down her fork and leaned toward Jonathan. "You think photography will cure her? Tell me, are you sure she's been clean for a month? She can be tricky, you know. Perhaps dear Jeremy is right. A strong hand, like yours, Doctor, is what she needs. What say you, Jeremy?" Portia raised her eyebrow and shot Jeremy a taunting glance.

Jeremy stood and slammed his fists on the table. "You promised her to me Portia." He met Jonathan's eyes. "Portia promised her to me."

"Now, Jeremy. Don't make a scene. Go to the living room and have another scotch." Portia touched his arm and led him away.

"I know he's grieving, but that was spooky," Cassie said.

Jonathan continued eating, seemingly unfazed by Jeremy's outburst.

Samantha glanced at him from the corner of her eye. What was he thinking? By now she knew Jeremy was insane, but this latest display was worse than anything he had done before. Michael would have leapt to action, but Jonathan sat as if nothing happened.

When Portia returned, Jonathan pulled back Samantha's chair and helped her stand. "Ma'am, I can't stand by while you berate your daughter and sell her to the highest bidder. She's much more than you give her credit for. Thank you for a lovely meal, but we must be going."

Portia stared. "I don't know what she's filling your head with, Doctor, but I gave her a good life. Don't be fooled by her tales of woe. Perhaps it's best if you go. Could you escort Cassie home, so I can have time with my daughter?"

Jonathan steadied Samantha as she shook. "I'm afraid I can't." He turned toward Cassie. "Please make sure Samantha arrives home safely." He squeezed her hand one more time then strode to the door.

Cassie took over and guided Samantha behind him, but Portia prevented their leaving. "Before you go, daughter, I want to know something. Is there anything between you and the doctor?"

"No, Mother. He's my therapist."

"He *is* attractive, and he seems smitten with you. Tread lightly, daughter. While I approve based on his profession alone, you could get hurt. I don't see him wanting someone as damaged as you long-term."

Cassie's eyes narrowed, her mouth poised to speak, but Samantha tugged on her arm, pulling her out the door. "It's not worth it, Cass. I knew she wouldn't change."

CHAPTER 20

The following Friday, Cassie drove Samantha to the clinic to meet Jonathan. He was working late and wouldn't be able to pick her up in time for their regular lunch date. Cassie grinned from ear to ear as she drove, not hiding her joy.

"How many lunch dates is this? Six? Last Friday at your mother's counts."

Samantha sighed. It was enough for her to struggle with the idea, but now Cassie had to push the issue. Once again, she was trying to orchestrate her life.

"You do know I'm still dating Michael." Samantha hung her arm out the Jeep's window, the breeze blowing past her.

"That's a technicality. Anyone not willing to get clean for you isn't worth your time. Jonathan is a better match." Cassie pulled into the clinic's parking lot and parked.

"You keep pushing this. Do you think it's wise to push a romantic relationship with my therapist, especially when I'm trying to balance all the other emotional messes of my life? And don't give me that line about us healing each other. We both know that's stupid." Samantha faced Cassie. If only she knew the struggle. Keeping things platonic with Jonathan ripped her apart, but it was necessary. Besides, he made his feelings clear multiple times. Wanting more was foolish.

"Elizabeth wanted you to find peace. Jonathan is your best chance. He can put Portia in her place, and Jeremy doesn't faze him. The fact he went to Portia's house for dinner last week gives him extra points. Would Michael stick up for you like that?"

"Michael doesn't know what happened. And he's too oblivious to suspect anything."

"Point proven. He'll show his true colors soon enough, and you'll see. Besides, I believe love cures all. So, if you fall in love with Jonathan, the rest will come."

Samantha shook her head at that logic. She had a degree in psychology, and she believed this mumbo jumbo? Hopefully she didn't fill her patients heads with this nonsense.

"Jonathan wants to help me heal. That's what you wished for. Stop pushing me into something else. Besides, he's not interested."

"I wouldn't be so sure. He doesn't offer personal counseling to his other patients." Cassie winked then opened the Jeep door.

Samantha hopped out. "Because that would be unprofessional. How did you get your degree? It seems I know more about medical ethics than you do."

Cassie stopped on the sidewalk, her hands on her hips. "I see the way you look at him. He looks at you the same way. Deny if you must, but something is there, and I think it's marvelous." Cassie breezed past her into the clinic.

Samantha shook her head and followed, hoping Cassie would come to her senses.

Jonathan's head was bent over his desk, his glasses perched crookedly on his nose. Samantha wanted to adjust them but resisted the urge. He wore his signature brown sweater-vest accompanied by tan khakis. She smirked at the messy desk and his ink-stained fingers, wanting to organize his chaos into something manageable.

"Hello, Doc. Ready for lunch?" She flashed a smile, a glint of mischief in her eyes.

"Samantha. Oh, yes. Let me finish this report." He propped his elbow on the desk, causing papers to slide on the floor. "Crap. Sorry, it's been a stressful day."

Samantha collected the papers and handed them to him. "You need a secretary. I'm surprised Cassie puts up with this."

Jonathan laughed. "She voices her opinion, but I'm afraid I'm beyond help. Whenever she's tried to organize my side of the office, it goes back to this within a day. I think she's given up." Jonathan finished writing and threw the pen on the desk. "Finished. Shall we?"

Samantha followed him outside to his car and slid into the passenger seat, fastening her seat belt. Glancing toward the driver side, she crinkled her brow.

He stood outside the driver's door, his hands searching his pockets. "Oh no. I don't have my wallet."

"That's okay, Doc. I have money." Samantha patted her purse.

"No need. We'll swing by my apartment on the way to the diner."

His apartment? Samantha's stomach flipflopped. This didn't seem like a good idea anymore. It seemed more like a move from Cassie's playbook. She took several breaths and devised a plan. Jonathan would get his wallet while she waited in the car. She rehearsed the scene as they drove, avoiding conversation.

"Here we are. Let me help you out." Jonathan rushed to her side of the car and opened the door. "It'll take a few minutes. My apartment is like my office, so my apologies."

Stay in the car. Don't take his hand. Stay in the car. Samantha chanted to herself, but one look into his eyes and her will evaporated.

Jonathan proffered his hand, smiling wide.

She placed her hand in his and followed him up the steps.

"I'm on the second floor. It's not much, and I can't vouch for its cleanliness. The life of a bachelor, you know."

He led her up a flight of stairs and down a dark hallway. Five apartments lined up on either side. When they reached the third on the left, he stopped and unlocked the door.

A small kitchen was attached to a similar-sized living room. In the back, a hallway led to two bedrooms and a bathroom. Samantha turned into the living room and sat on a black leather couch.

Jonathan stood between the kitchen and living room, his hands on his hips. "It's not much, but it's home. Can I get you anything?"

"No. It's nice. Perfect." She surveyed the room and saw something shaped like a football and a striped shirt on a corner chair. She picked it up. "Rugby, right? Never took you for the type."

Jonathan grinned. "I play, when it's in season. I was on a rugby team in college, and it stuck."

Sports. That was a revelation. She tried to picture him on the rugby field, sweat dripping down his face. That was something she had to see. She knew so little about him, but, with every revelation, she liked him more. He was different than the guys she dated—calm yet surprising. Jonathan embodied everything she wanted in a relationship; except he wasn't available.

"Would you care to have a seat? We can talk a bit. It's more private than Ruby's."

They settled on the couch, exchanging furtive glances. Being alone with him confused her. He ignited a passion and put her at ease. It was a dangerous combination she never experienced before.

"I wanted to thank you for last Friday. I never got to tell you how much it meant to me, going to my mother's and sticking up for me."

"Someone had to. I don't think you should see her again without Cassie. She's not likely to change."

"I know. Part of me wants to cut her off. That's what Michael did with his family. But I'm not sure if it's the right thing."

"That's a decision only you can make. Whatever you decide, you don't have to put up with her abuse. Tell her how it makes you feel. Otherwise, it'll continue."

Samantha smiled. Jonathan had answers for everything. He was comforting and safe, things her chaotic life lacked. She adjusted herself on the couch, brushing her hand against his. Her stomach fluttered as she remembered why this wasn't a good idea.

She wasn't Jonathan's type anyway. He needed someone put together, like him, not someone struggling to survive. She had too much baggage to interest him long term. Her mother made that clear last week.

"Why are you wasting time with me? You're a handsome doctor, and it's Friday night. You should be on a date, not stuck with a crazy like me."

"Would it surprise you if I said I'd rather be with you?"

Samantha jolted up. "Why?"

"Because I see something in you. I told you that yesterday, and I meant it. If I had met you sooner, it would be different. Who were you six months ago, Samantha? I could have fallen in love with that girl."

She gazed into his eyes, longing for his embrace. She bit her lip and blushed, wishing things were different. She was supposed to be in love with Michael, but that wasn't true. Jonathan made her heart flutter. Falling in love wasn't in her game plan, but resisting Jonathan was becoming impossible.

He eased closer, their legs touching. Her body shook at the proximity. Leaning forward, he traced the outline of her face, stopping at her chin. His mouth trembled as he lowered it onto hers. Awkward at first, his lips grew more demanding.

She briefly retreated then leaned in, devouring the taste she longed for. As the kiss deepened, she wound her arms around him, her hands teasing his hair. Even the smell of him excited her. This was a momentary interlude not to be repeated. But she wanted to enjoy it while she could.

Jonathan slid his hand down her back, tugging her dress. He lowered her onto the couch, his lips on her face, her neck, traveling down her chest.

Her breathing quickened as she tried to compose herself. Somehow, she was losing control in a way she never experienced with Michael. This side of Jonathan surprised her. He was a safe place and a dangerous storm at the same time.

He slid his arm down her leg, hiking her dress. His hand felt warm as it caressed her inner thigh.

She withheld a scream, releasing a small squeak instead.

Jonathan paused, searching her eyes for permission.

Inside, Samantha repressed her fears. Since meeting Jonathan, she wanted this, wanted him. Her body came alive at his touch, but her mind shamed her. Diverting her gaze from his, she hugged her knees to her chest.

Jonathan moved to the opposite side of the couch. He folded his hands and tapped his thumbs. "I'm sorry. I didn't plan on this, believe me." He stood and paced the length of the room. "I've never done this before. If you want another therapist, I'll contact the court."

"There were two of us, Jonathan. Don't think I wasn't willing."

He bit his lip and knitted his brow. "You are my patient and in a vulnerable situation. I took advantage. Let me make this right."

"It was a momentary weakness. Nothing more. Can we forget about it and move on?"

"I broke your trust."

"You didn't. And now it's forgotten." But it wasn't. His kiss, his touch was forever burned into her brain. Whatever else happened between them, she wouldn't forget this night.

Looking for any distraction to change the subject, Samantha walked to the other side of the room. Her long tapered fingers rested on a picture of a young girl sitting on the coffee table.

"Rachel?" Samantha asked, already knowing the answer.

Jonathan sighed and took the picture from Samantha's hands. "Yes. This was the last picture I had of her before . . ."

"Before the accident." Samantha finished, feeling a sudden flush of sadness and confusion. Despite losing his daughter, he had it all together. He had every right to give up and hide in his apartment the rest of his life. Instead, he continued to help others as if the unthinkable had never happened. "How—" Samantha tried to find the words to ask.

"How do I keep going? Easy. There's no alternative. Either you keep going, or your grief monopolizes your life. I wasn't willing to let my pain win. I owed Rachel that much. I had to keep living, so her memory would still be alive, in me. It isn't natural, and some days I do struggle, but I fight, because Rachel would want me to be happy."

Samantha's eyes welled with tears, both for Jonathan and herself. She put her arms around him and squeezed. They hung on to each other, each trying to fill the hole death caused.

After what seemed like hours, Jonathan pulled away, holding her at arm's length. "How about dinner? There's a Chinese place down the street that I swear has the best egg rolls in town."

Dinner. That didn't sound too hard. She had to eat. Besides, being in public would help them keep their hands off each other.

"Okay. But I get to choose what we talk about. Let's stick to the weather and food. I've had enough deep conversation for one day."

CHAPTER 21

Samantha woke to smells of bacon wafting through the house. Sounds of laughter and banging pots came from the kitchen. She threw off the blanket and stretched, hoping Cassie was making her famous Saturday morning breakfast. For the first time, Samantha woke without a craving. Instead, she found a smile plastered on her face. A smile because of Jonathan.

Her mind turned briefly to Michael, wondering how she should break the news. By now, he knew something was different. He had sensed it when she came home from the hospital. But after last night, she had to tell him. He deserved the truth.

Jonathan had surprised her last night. After the awkward incident at his place, they ate dinner at a Chinese restaurant downtown. The conversation had come easily, and her worries faded. Jonathan had listened to her hopes and dreams, making her want to try. All these years, she blamed her mother for her failures. Jonathan helped her see her own fears stood in the way, not her mother's actions and opinions.

The entire evening had been magical. Although they didn't verbalize it, he dropped his objections to their relationship. Jonathan had stuck close all evening, holding her hand, caressing her cheeks and kissing her lips. It was everything she had hoped and more.

They didn't mention the camera again, but Samantha had mentioned photography. She still had her old camera and decided to give it a chance. Jonathan had proposed a trip to the lake, so she could practice in a quiet setting.

Anxious, she scooped it off the headboard, knocking over Mr. Rabbit. She picked him up and stroked his ears. He served a purpose, but she didn't need him today.

She placed her camera on the bed and chose a pair of shorts and a tank top. She brushed her hair and checked herself in the mirror. Only one person stared back. At least Lizzie wasn't making an unexpected appearance today. She wanted to enjoy every minute with Jonathan, with no interference.

Samantha strolled down the hallway into the kitchen. Stunned, she hung back and watched the scene unfold. Cassie and Michael were hard at work making breakfast. Instead of arguing, they were teasing and laughing. It made her news about Jonathan a little easier to break.

"Put the bacon on the paper towel to drain the grease." Cassie stood next to the island, directing Michael's every move.

His eyes sparkled, and his smile widened. "Like this?"

Cassie nodded then sprinted toward the stove. "The gravy …" She grabbed a spoon and scraped the bottom of the pan, stirring repeatedly. "You have to keep stirring, otherwise it'll burn."

"How do you expect me to do multiple things at once?" He jumped in, bumping into Cassie as he grabbed the spoon from her hand.

Their heads touched briefly as they erupted in a fit of giggles. Although unexpected, Samantha found the scene heartwarming and a promising hope for the future.

"Aren't you cozy?" Samantha said from the entryway. "When did this happen? Thought you hated each other."

Cassie's face reddened as she dropped the spoon into the pan. "Good morning. We're making breakfast— bacon, pancakes, biscuits and sausage gravy. Want some?"

Michael fished out the spoon and continued to stir, avoiding Samantha's gaze. "Sorry I wasn't here last night. I heard Dr. Green kept you company."

"Yes. That's what I wanted to talk to you about. After breakfast?"

Cassie looked back and forth between them. She grabbed the spoon and pushed them together. "I can handle this. Go talk."

Michael wiped his hands on his pants and followed Samantha to the living room. They sat on the couch, looking straight ahead. "You look nice. I mean, you always look nice, but something's different about you today."

"Thank you. What's going on with you and Cassie? You look chummy lately."

Michael crossed his arms and leaned back. "She's not all bad. She's teaching me to cook. Never thought you'd see that, did you?"

Samantha laughed. "No. Cooking isn't your thing. Maybe you won't burn down the house now."

Michael grinned and leaned closer. "You wanted to talk about Dr. Green? Everything okay?"

She took a deep breath and turned to face him. This would be difficult. Michael had his issues, but he never left her, even when he should have. "I don't know how to say this. Since the accident, you've been by my side and helped me through the worst of it. You've been my rock for so long, I wouldn't be here without you."

He grabbed her hand and patted it. "It's Jonathan, isn't it? I'm not surprised. I lost you to him weeks ago. I was waiting for both of you realize it. Besides, you don't need someone like me holding you back. You're strong, and you're getting stronger. Hanging out with me is asking for a relapse."

Her eyes grew misty. "I wish you would get help too. There's more to you than partying and getting high. I saw you with Cassie. She's a great girl."

Michael laughed. "With Cassie? She's all right, I guess. But I'm not the settling-down type. You know that." He placed his hands on her shoulder and looked into her eyes. "There's no future with me, but Jonathan is the real deal. Go for it."

Samantha encircled him with a hug. "Thank you for understanding. I know it sounds trite, but I hope we can still be friends."

Michael grinned and his eyes clouded. "Best friends." He returned her embrace, rubbing her back and stroking her hair.

"Ahem." A sound from behind Samantha made them jump.

She turned and saw Jonathan, a bouquet of wildflowers in hand. Bouncing from one pair of arms to another didn't seem right. She flashed Jonathan a smile and looked to Michael for approval.

"Take care of her, Dr. Green. She's a heck of a woman." Michael shook Jonathan's hand then disappeared into the kitchen.

"You told him." Jonathan sat in the chair, his hands trembling. "These are for you. I hope you like wildflowers. They seemed to suit you."

"They're beautiful. Thanks." She placed them on the coffee table then sat on the couch and drummed her fingers on her thigh. "Cassie and Michael made breakfast. The bacon smell woke me up. Want some?"

"If it's okay with you, I'll pass." Jonathan shifted his eyes, avoiding her gaze.

She plopped on the coffee table and leaned toward him. "About yesterday, it was freeing. Even Michael noticed a change." She grabbed his hands and gazed into his eyes. "And don't worry about him. We had a talk. He understands."

Jonathan let go and ran his fingers through his hair. "Michael may no longer be an issue, but we're in dangerous waters." He pushed her aside and paced the floor, his eyebrows furrowed. "In the eyes of the court, I'm still your therapist. I shouldn't have told you my feelings last night, and I shouldn't have kissed you. I take responsibility for that."

Samantha leapt to her feet, narrowing her eyes. Why does he keep second guessing himself? The back and forth was maddening. "Can't take back what happened, Doc."

"Please, not *Doc*." Jonathan's eyes clouded. "This is difficult enough."

She puffed up herself to meet his eyes. "We have feelings for each other. I haven't felt this alive in years. Do you think toying with my emotions is wise in my state?"

"I'm not toying with your emotions. Everything I said last night was true. That doesn't change the ethicality of the situation. If we were outed, it could jeopardize your court case, my license, and your recovery. I can't live with that on my conscience. At some point, we must think practically before it gets out of hand."

Samantha placed her hands on her hips and crinkled her nose. "What are you saying? Are you breaking up with me before we even began?"

"I don't know what I'm saying. I want to be with you, but I don't want to risk everything we're trying to build. You're turning a corner. Getting involved will cloud your recovery, possibly lead to a relapse. I would be taking advantage of your heightened emotions."

"I don't mind playing with fire if you don't. What if this thing is the best we'll ever have? Are you willing to walk away without trying, or are you willing to take a chance?"

Jonathan's brow glistened with beads of sweat. "Someone has to be the adult."

Samantha inched closer and wound her arms around his neck. "Oh, I plan on being adult-like." She ran her fingers through his hair.

He quivered under her touch as she raised her lips to his. At first, he pulled back. But as she deepened the kiss, he relinquished, toppling her onto the couch.

"You make a good point, Ms. Barrett. But I'm not convinced."

"I think I can work on my persuasion skills, if you give me a chance."

Jonathan smiled. "I'm intrigued." He straightened himself next to her, his wide eyes piercing hers. "This is against my better judgement. I promised myself I wouldn't do this." He took a breath. "If we try this, we have to keep it under wraps. No one at the clinic can know, not even Gus."

"I promise. But can we still go to the lake? That is, if you can keep your hands off me in public." Samantha's eyes twinkled.

Jonathan kissed her nose. "Only if you bring your camera. I'm anxious to see those photography skills you bragged about last night."

Samantha squealed and ran to her room. She grabbed her camera and peeked in the kitchen. Cassie stood over Michael, teaching him how to flip pancakes. Samantha giggled when Michael flipped one to the ceiling. Cassie shot him a disapproving look and called him an idiot. At least she left them in good company. Smiling, she snuck to the living room.

"Got my camera." She winked. "Ready?"

They locked arms and headed out the door.

***

As they drove, Samantha replayed the morning conversation. Logically, Jonathan was right. It was the same argument she used on Cassie yesterday. Yet the thought of losing him when he brought equilibrium to her life frightened her. Was that love or transference? She shook the thought from her mind. Jonathan wasn't professing love, but neither did Michael. She reminded herself to take one step at a time, and everything would fall in place.

Kingsbrook Lake glistened in the mid-morning light. Samantha hadn't been here in a year, but it hadn't change. She remembered her time with Lizzie—hiking, canoeing, picnicking. This used to be their happy place.

Jonathan retrieved a blanket from the back seat and approached the grassy edge.

Samantha followed, her eyes round, beholding the scenery.

"Is it as you remembered? You said you haven't been here since you were little. Has it changed?"

Jonathan looked around, his hand on his hip. "No. Some places freeze in time. This place is one of them." He pointed to the far end of the lake. "That's where my dad taught me to fish. I wasn't any good, but it was fun."

"You fished?" Never would have guessed. What made you stop coming?"

"Life, I suppose. Once I hit high school, we were too busy with chess tournaments and studying. This place fell to the wayside. I'm glad I came back with you."

"I'm glad we came too." She stopped by a tall oak tree. "This is the perfect backdrop." She snapped a few shots then ran toward the water. "Put the blanket here. The sun's angle is just right. I want to photograph you."

Jonathan chuckled and extended a hand. "Oh, no. I'm not photogenic. I'll sit and watch."

Samantha frowned. "Please? I want you to see yourself like I do."

He mustered a half smile and looked toward the ground. "Okay. Where do you want me?"

Samantha helped him lay out the blanket and positioned him. For the next hour, she toyed with the backdrop, angling him to make best use of the morning sun and taking an untold number of pictures. Her joy returned, like Lizzie said it would. Was it the photography or Jonathan? Perhaps a combination of both. A new person welled inside, a mixture of who she was and who she hoped to be.

"That was fun." She settled on the blanket next to him.

He pulled her close, nuzzling her hair.

"Aren't you afraid someone will see us?"

"No one is here. Besides, I enjoy the smell of you."

She snuggled closer and shut her eyes. The smell of dew mingled with vanilla hung in the air. Her body relaxed, taking in the sounds of nature. "Have I told you about my dream? I haven't had one in a while, but now it's clear."

"No, but I'd love to hear it." He adjusted himself so her head lay in his lap.

"Cassie and I watched a movie about Diane Arbus. Have you heard of her?"

Jonathan shook his head. "Is she a photographer?"

She smiled. "Yes. She's famous for taking pictures of people in unusual situations. She captured the plight of people living on the edge of society. It put a face on the issues of her day. I want to do that. Put a face on people struggling with addiction, show they are real people who need compassion and help, not people to be shunned."

Jonathan traced the outline of her face. "That's an admirable dream. I'm glad you're dreaming again. It's a sign of recovery."

"It's because of you. You give me strength to find dreams. Lizzie tried, but you showed me a new way to think and feel. I'm grateful."

Jonathan leaned down and kissed her. The world seemed brighter in his arms. Everything Lizzie tried to tell her finally made sense. She didn't need her mother's approval to reach her dreams. She could chase them and achieve them through her own hard work. She straightened herself and met Jonathan's gaze.

"Someday I want to have a gallery show, like Gus wants. Maybe we could do it together. People flocking to see my work gives me a rush. Do you think it's possible?"

"Anything is possible, if you work for it. I think it's a great idea. If I can do anything to help, let me know. I can't wait to see what you do with your talent."

Samantha smiled. Everything was falling into place. No more cravings, a wonderful boyfriend, and plans for a future—was this the peace Lizzie had wanted her to find?

Jonathan ran his fingers across her forehead. "I want to know everything about you. What was your life like before your addiction? Why did you abandon photography? I understand your issues with your mother, but you said Lizzie was supportive."

His question jolted her, broaching the past. Why did he ruin their moment with therapy talk? She wanted to spend the day with her boyfriend, not recount her failings. She sat and bit her lower lip, not wanting to answer. "You won't understand. Cassie didn't, Lizzie didn't. It's all in my head."

Jonathan smirked. "Well, that's usually the case. What went on in your head? People see the same events differently based on their experiences and personalities. If it was true to you, then no one can say otherwise."

"Can you share that with Cassie? You're not training her well."

"I'll put it on my to-do list." He reached for her hands and drew them to his heart. "Feel that? It beats for you. You're safe. No judging. Tell me how you felt."

Samantha sighed. They were going to do this. Jonathan was at his best when he put on his psychiatrist hat. Every time she tried to distract him, he returned to this, as if he didn't know how to manage a relationship outside his job. She relented, hoping to get back to where they were last night. "You know how my mother feels. And you know how she treated me. I guess I didn't have the confidence to make it work, even with Lizzie."

"But the day you started using, you told her you wanted to do photography full time."

Samantha chortled. "And we know how that went. That's the night I met Michael. Sometimes I think dating him was on purpose." She tilted her head and smirked. "It became a game; how can I make Portia angrier this time? Photography pushed her so far, but Michael, that would push her over the edge."

"So, you upped the ante with cocaine?"

"You could say that. But don't blame this on Michael. He has his own demons."

"No judging, remember?" Jonathan cocked his head. "What about Lizzie? What did she think?"

Samantha sighed. "She hated it. Lizzie was my protector, but she couldn't protect me from using. Oh, she tried, but I didn't listen. The last time I saw her, she threatened to talk to my drug dealer if I didn't quit."

"And did she?"

"That's how she died. She went to Cole's house and confronted him."

"The police told you that?"

"No. Cole told me. I went to his house and told him I knew he killed her. He told me Lizzie was there. Besides that, I found her bracelet beneath his hearth."

"And you shared this with the police?"

"Some of it." Samantha pushed herself up and wringed her hands. "I didn't tell them about the bracelet or the revolver. When I went to his house, he pulled a gun on me. It wasn't loaded, but he pointed at my chest and pulled the trigger."

Jonathan bolted up. "Samantha, you have to tell the police. They are building a case against Cole right now. This is vital information."

"I know, but what if he comes after me? He's not a person to trifle with."

Jonathan wrapped himself around her and kissed the top of her head. "Do you want me to go with you?"

Samantha nodded. She hoped with Jonathan's strength she could finally do the right thing.

***

On the way home, they stopped by the police station. For a moment, she wondered what Michael would say. He still believed Detective Logan was a dirty cop and didn't trust him. Was she right to tell him what she knew? Jonathan believed it was the responsible thing to do, but was it what Lizzie would want?

Jonathan held her hand as the desk sergeant escorted them to Detective Logan's office. Samantha paused before they entered, trying to hear Lizzie's voice for direction. Nothing came. As the detective greeted them, Jonathan squeezed her hand and flashed an encouraging smile.

Samantha let go and took one step forward. She held out Lizzie's bracelet, her hands trembling. "Detective Logan, I have something to tell you."

CHAPTER 22

The lake trip solidified it. Samantha needed photography. While Jonathan gave her life calmness and joy, photography gave her excitement and direction. She spent the next week taking pictures of landscapes and the few random people who agreed. The nightmares and voices stopped, and her cravings disappeared. For the first time, she felt centered and alive.

Excited to see her work, she dusted off her printer and pulled up the pictures on her computer. Photographs of the lake filled her screen along with candid shots of Jonathan. He proved the perfect model to ease her back in and help regain her confidence. She smiled at the pictures as she chose the ones to print. Within minutes, they covered her bed.

Jonathan's face adorned every photograph. She perused them, trying to find the right one. It would be a thank-you gift—a framed picture to hang in his apartment, thanking him for his help.

A knock on the door came as she narrowed her choices. Pictures of Jonathan lounging on the blanket, donning a lopsided grin and leaning on a tree with his arms crossed made the cut. She went back and forth between the five remaining pictures as Cassie opened the door.

"Everything okay?" Cassie strolled in and glanced at the bed. "If someone saw this, they might think you were obsessed. Why all the pictures?"

"I'm picking one as a gift. What do you think? I like this one." Samantha held a close-up of Jonathan that accentuated his eyes and smile.

"Good choice." Cassie moved some pictures aside and sat on the edge of the bed. "I have news. Detective Logan called. He wanted to thank you for turning in your evidence on Cole. They formally charged him this morning."

Samantha dropped the pictures on the bed. Her stomach turned. This was good news, wasn't it? What would Lizzie say about Cole's arrest? Her voice had remained silent since her last nightmare. *I did it, Lizzie. My evidence got him indicted. Can you rest now?*

But what about Michael? It was Monday, and she hadn't seen him since she broke up with him last week. How was he taking the news? Did he know?

She turned to face Cassie. "So, they had enough evidence to charge him? Did his revolver match?"

"Don't know. They had enough for a grand jury to indict. He's being held for one million dollars."

"Does Michael know? I haven't seen him in a week." Samantha ran her finger over the picture. Cole's arrest and indictment for Lizzie's murder was something she wanted. So why did it feel anticlimactic?

"I called him after I talked to Detective Logan. I figured he deserved to know. He's struggling. Maybe you can visit him sometime? If you're strong enough."

Samantha knew what she meant. If she was strong enough to avoid temptation. Six weeks sober was something to celebrate, but she wasn't out of the danger zone yet. It would take years to call herself *clean*. Gus was still in counseling after five years. She was in for the long haul.

"I've thought about it. Is he mad at me?"

"Because of Jonathan or Cole? He understands about Jonathan, but we didn't talk much about Cole. It's strange. He's becoming a pesky little brother instead of an annoying idiot. A step up, I think."

Samantha chuckled. "I'm glad you're getting along. And I'm glad Cole will pay for what he did to Lizzie. It's what I wanted." Samantha collected the pictures and stored them in her top dresser drawer. She flashed Cassie a half smile and sat on the beanbag chair.

"When do you start at Through the Lens?" Cassie asked.

"Thursday evening."

Samantha recently landed a job at a portrait studio in town, taking pictures of little kids, families, and anyone else who came in. It wasn't her dream of being the next Diane Arbus, but it was photography, and it would do.

"Are we still on for dinner? Jonathan said something about Yancy's. Sounds like the perfect spot for a celebration."

Samantha rubbed the edge of her shirt between her forefinger and thumb. "I don't know why we're celebrating. Through the Lens isn't much of a job. I take pictures of kids all day. Big deal."

Cassie joined her on the beanbag, squeezing her to one side. "It *is* a big deal. Everything is coming together. Cole's indicted for Elizabeth's murder, you haven't used cocaine for six weeks, you have a photography job and you have Jonathan. Sounds like everything is great to me"

Samantha managed a smile. Cassie was right. Everything was great. She couldn't ask for a better outcome. "You're right. Thank you, Cass. Should we get ready? Jonathan's picking us up soon."

Cassie stood and slipped something from her pocket. "Here. I have a feeling you might need these tonight." She pressed two condoms in her hand and winked.

Samantha grinned. "Are you trying to tell me something?"

"Trust me." Cassie turned and walked out the door.

She grabbed her camera and put it on the headboard next to Mr. Rabbit. The stuffed animal fell on her bed, its lopsided grin staring at her. She ran her fingers over the stitch. She flinched, thinking of what he hid. Her fingers pulled at the stitch—then pulled it tight. Mr. Rabbit didn't fit into her life anymore. She smoothed back his ears and put him in the back of her closet.

Ever since their first kiss, she longed for tonight. She slipped the condoms into her purse, wondering if Jonathan had similar thoughts. Until this point, they had only kissed. Jonathan had been careful each time, and she could tell he fought to keep control. She wondered what it would be like to make him lose control. Was it possible? The idea excited her.

She refocused onto the evening's celebration. Jonathan was proud of her new job and promised a fancy dinner at Yancy's to celebrate. She chose her sexiest black dress and did her hair. Jonathan wouldn't be able to resist. Everything was coming together, and she wanted to enjoy it. She closed her bedroom door and joined Cassie in the living room, anxious to enjoy her new life.

✳✳✳

After leaving Yancy's, they dropped off Cassie at home. She gave Samantha a wink before exiting the car. When they entered Jonathan's apartment, he unlocked the door and motioned for Samantha to enter.

"Can I get you anything?"

"I'm stuffed. Yancy's was amazing, but I don't think I can eat for a whole week." Samantha laced her fingers with his and guided him to the living room. "I don't have work tomorrow, so I don't have a curfew." She flashed him a smile and led him to the couch.

They sat, meeting each other's gaze then looking away. Samantha blushed whenever their eyes met.

"Have you spoken to Michael about Cole's arrest?" Jonathan angled his body, so their knees touched.

Why did he mention Michael now? Samantha loved him, but sometimes he was so obtuse. Wait … She loved him? Her heart beat faster at the realization.

"I don't want to talk about Michael." She moved closer and covered his hand with hers. Should she tell him? What if he didn't return her feelings? She gazed into his eyes, searching for an answer.

Jonathan gave her a nervous smile and stood, approaching the kitchen. "How about some coffee? Or maybe a glass of wine?"

Samantha sunk into the couch. "I'm fine."

Why was he acting this way? True, they hadn't had much alone time, but that wasn't an issue tonight. They should be taking advantage of it, not worrying about coffee and wine.

He returned with two wine glasses. "In case you change your mind." He set them on the coffee table and sat at the far end of the couch.

Samantha fumbled with her bracelet and frowned. "Why am I here if you're sitting over there? Is everything okay?"

He exhaled a breath and gulped. "I'm sorry if you had expectations, but I'm not sure this is a good idea."

Samantha fumed. "We've been over this multiple times. I thought we agreed. I'm not willing to give up on us."

"I think we need to slow down. You've made so much progress the last six weeks. If we have sex, it will complicate things."

"How can it complicate things if I love you?"

Jonathan's eyes grew round. "What did you say?"

"I said, I love you. You don't have to say it, but I did. And I meant it. It's not because you're my therapist. It's not because you saved me. I love you, and I think I did from the moment we met."

He crossed the room and took her in his arms. "I love you too. That's why I'm so careful. If I hurt you, I wouldn't be able to live with myself."

"You won't hurt me. I just want to be with you."

He didn't need a further invitation. As if consumed with hunger, he leaned in, devouring her lips. He wasn't the calm, staid doctor she came to love but a person possessed with desire. It surprised and aroused her.

She returned his kiss with a sense of urgency, releasing the tension she'd held for weeks. Her hand roamed down his back. She stopped at his butt and squeezed.

He pulled away to catch his breath. "Are you sure?"

Samantha nodded. She licked her lips and kicked off her shoes.

He drew her in, his lips as urgent as before. She ran her fingers through his hair and tore off his glasses. He tugged at her dress as she made short work of his sweater-vest and shirt. Her hands explored his back, tracing the indentation of his shoulder blades. Then they roamed down and circled above his waist. Jonathan trembled as she unbuttoned his pants.

He unzipped her dress and stood back as it fell to the ground. "I've dreamed of this." He cupped her face and kissed her as he lowered her to the couch. Stepping aside, he removed his pants, standing in nothing but his underwear.

Samantha stared. His arms were more muscular than she imagined. Her eyes moved toward his chest. She wanted to run her hands over it and play with the tufts of hair. Her heart beat faster knowing he was hers, and she couldn't wait to possess every inch. She reached for him, but he paused and sat on the couch.

"Wait. I want this to be right. Before we do this, you need to know. I haven't had sex since my wife left when Rachel was three. I don't have protection. I wasn't planning on this."

Samantha smiled. He hadn't had sex in four years, and here they were. She wasn't sure if his words were a compliment or not. "It's okay. Cassie slipped a condom in my purse." She retrieved it and waved it.

Jonathan chuckled. "So now my intern knows about my sex life?"

"She made a good guess."

He blushed and looked down, a wisp of hair falling over his eyes.

She smoothed it back and took his hand, outlining his palm with her fingers.

His breathing deepened as he grabbed her chin and pulled her close. His lips grazed across her face, kissing her forehead, her eyes, her nose before settling on her mouth. He teased her with his tongue, flicking it in and out, before sliding it in.

Every sensor in her body activated, giving into ecstasy. She caught her breath when he pushed her back and traced the outline of her breasts. She longed for his hands to roam her body—wanting, needing his warmth. It was never like this with Michael. She didn't know until now what she'd been missing.

His breathing quickened as he unclasped her bra and watched it fall away. He cupped each breast and stroked them. "Gorgeous." He lowered his mouth to her nipple and teased it with his tongue.

She released a gasp, pulling on his hair. As his mouth traveled down her stomach and rested above her navel, she arched her back, begging for more.

He splayed his fingers up her thighs and slipped them into her clitoris, massaging it with his thumb.

She closed her eyes and took a deep breath. Where did this feeling come from?

They shed their underwear and gazed at each other. Samantha ran her fingers across his penis and helped slip on the condom. He eased her onto the couch and kissed her—first on the lips, then on the neck. He inserted his finger once more, teasing her until she climaxed. This was more than she expected and so unlike any other sexual experience she'd had. Jonathan was electric, and she became alive under his touch.

"No more. I want you." She reached for his shoulders and pulled him down.

He entered her with slow strides. As she raised her hips to meet his, the strides deepened, filling her. Their bodies moved together until they both climaxed. Jonathan finished then lay beside her, a silly grin on his face.

Was that how it was supposed to feel? She had never orgasmed before. Jonathan made her body respond in ways Michael never could.

"You were amazing, Doctor. You can examine me anytime."

He flashed a wide smile. "Happy to oblige." He stood and approached the bathroom. "Now you have to stay the night. I have a shirt you can wear."

Samantha collected her clothes and folded them on the table. She sat on the couch as Jonathan threw her one of his old t-shirts. It smelled like him—vanilla and sandalwood.

Jonathan put on his glasses and settled next to her, wrapping his arm around her shoulders.

She snuggled on his chest and closed her eyes. Finally, everything was right in her world.

CHAPTER 23

Samantha woke the next morning with a smile. Last night was a revelation. She never knew her body would react in such ways. Something about Jonathan—his kiss, his touch—ignited fireworks within her.

She sat and beheld the room. Instead of Michael's chaotic mobile home, she was in Jonathan's serene bedroom. That's not to say it was organized. Shoes littered the floor next to his dresser. Papers covered an armchair in the corner. Books lay scattered across the floor. But if it was clear of trash and bodies, Samantha was pleased.

He lay next to her, his chest rising with each breath. She rolled to her side and ran her fingers over his chest. He stirred as she traced his navel, stopping below his belly button. She moved to her knees, positioning herself between his legs. He opened his eyes as she peeled off his underwear. Samantha put her finger to his mouth then replaced it with her lips. He attempted to sit, but she pushed him onto the pillow. She flashed him a mischievous grin and returned to her position. Her hand wandered to his penis. She stroked it, causing him to groan. She covered the tip with her mouth, teasing it with her tongue.

Jonathan squeezed her shoulders, pushing her farther. He tangled his fingers in her hair and pulled. As she closed her mouth around him, he moaned. "Did Cassie slip you an extra condom? Because I can't take anymore."

Samantha smiled. She reached next to the bed and pulled one from her purse. "Thank goodness for Cassie."

He slipped it on then flipped her onto her back. She guided him inside of her, her hands clawing at his shoulders. His strides came longer and harder, until her entire body shook. Now that she knew it could be like this, she didn't want it to end.

He collapsed next to her, his brow beading with sweat. "That's one way to wake up."

If only she could wake up with him every day. She brushed back a wayward hair. "Do we have to? I wish we could stay here all day."

Jonathan rolled over and kissed her nose. "Unfortunately, yes. We have group today." He climbed from bed and hummed a tune on his way to the bathroom.

She watched him leave, fixating on his butt. He was sexier than most girls knew, and she reveled in that secret. As he ran the shower, she put on her dress from the prior evening and perused the room.

His white buttoned-down shirts hung neatly in the closet next to his tan khakis, a pleasant surprise from what she saw in the rest of the room. His sweater-vests were folded on a shelf next to an old shoebox. Curious, she lifted the lid. Her fingers glided over old pictures and letters. She opened one and read it.

> *Dear Jonathan,*
> *I can't live this life anymore. Tell*

*Rachel I'm sorry. You were right. I didn't
love you enough to stay.
Hannah*

He had kept her good-bye note. Last night was the second time he had mentioned his ex-wife. She figured it was old news and didn't bother him anymore. Why did he keep it?

She returned the letter and closed the lid. Jonathan never ceased to amaze her. He acted calm and serious, but he came alive in the bedroom. He counseled people to deal with their demons and move on, yet he had a box of old letters in his closet. There was more to him than she knew.

She meandered around the bedroom, trying to learn about the guy she came to love. What made him tick? How could he present one way but have so many hidden secrets and emotions? She stopped at the dresser. His wedding ring sat in front of a picture of Rachel and another woman. It was the same picture she'd seen in his office. She picked it up and examined it.

Jonathan stepped from the bathroom, a towel around his waist, and stood behind her. "That's Hannah, Rachel's mom."

Samantha placed the picture on the dresser. "Your ex-wife. She was gorgeous."

Jonathan took off the towel and pulled on a pair of underwear and khakis. "Most thought so. But looks don't replace what's in the heart. That's where true beauty lies."

Samantha watched as he buttoned his shirt and donned his sweater-vest. She never understood how Hannah could leave him or Rachel. It boggled her mind.

"I lost my dad when I was six, but it wasn't his choice. I can't imagine what Rachel felt like when her mom chose to leave her." She sat on the edge of the bed and smoothed out the covers.

Jonathan moved the papers and sat on the armchair. "It was hard, but I think it was worse on me. Children are resilient, and Rachel was only three. Somehow, that softened the blow."

"Do you still have feelings for her?"

Jonathan adjusted his glasses and looked down. "We were married for five years and had a child." He rubbed his eyes. "I can't help but have feelings toward her, but it's not love anymore."

That sounded reasonable. She couldn't ask him to forget about someone who meant so much at one point. He seemed to be handling it in a healthy, realistic way.

"Well, I don't understand why she left you in the first place; although, I'm glad she did." Samantha flashed him a devilish grin.

Jonathan lowered his head and managed a smile. "It was partly my fault. I was a workaholic. My patients at the clinic came first, and she was jealous."

"But your work is important. Gus told me what you did to set up drug court in Bracken Point. Your work has saved so many lives. I'm proof."

"Yes, but when you're only concerned about yourself, no one else matters."

Samantha ran her bracelet between her thumb and forefinger. She was guilty of selfishness, like his ex-wife. Lizzie would still be here if she had looked outside herself. But Jonathan taught her selflessness. He dedicated his life to help others. She wanted to do that too, as a tribute to Lizzie. Jonathan deserved someone who could work beside him. Someone who understood his need to reach people. She hoped she could be that person.

"Did she come to Rachel's funeral?"

"She did." Jonathan gulped. "She was drunk, and she spent the whole time yelling at me, blaming me for what had happened." He stood and wiped a tear with his thumb. "But that's in the past. I haven't seen her since, and I don't expect to."

He put his wallet in his pocket and opened the door. "Should we stop by your place, so you can get changed? Might look strange attending group in that dress."

Samantha nodded and reminded herself to bring a change of clothes next time.

***

Jonathan drove to the clinic with one hand on the wheel and one hand on Samantha's thigh, sporting a lopsided grin. She placed her hand over his and beamed. For the first time in years, she felt loved and wanted. Nothing would bring her down today.

When they arrived, Jonathan paused. He surveyed the parking lot then put his arm around the driver's seat and faced Samantha. "Ready? Remember, we can't let anyone know what's going on between us."

"Are you sure you can keep your hands off me, Doc?" Samantha winked.

"As tempting as you are, Ms. Barrett, I'm all business today." Jonathan flashed a wide grin and exited the car.

They walked to his office in silence. Samantha wanted to grab his hand, but she knew that would cause suspicion. Hiding their love affair wouldn't be easy. She wondered if he thought the same thing.

They exchanged glances down the hallway while trying to stifle their true feelings. Today's meeting would be a test of their relationship. If they survived unscathed, they stood a chance. Samantha investigated each room as they passed, hoping they were alone before they had to face the group.

Jonathan put his briefcase on his desk and closed the door. "Well, Ms. Barrett. Seems we have some time before group." He sat in his chair and pulled her on his lap.

Samantha giggled. "Are you sure it's wise, Doc? I thought we were being careful?"

"I closed the door. I think that's careful enough." Jonathan lowered her head to his and kissed her.

Samantha wrapped her arms around him and ran her fingers through his hair. How could they get through group if they couldn't stop touching each other?

Jonathan picked her up and moved her to the couch. "When I'm with you, I feel like a teenager again. Why is it I can't keep my hands off you?"

She flashed him a mischievous grin. "Would you say you're suffering from an addiction, Doctor? Because we have a group to deal with that."

He smiled then leaned down, taking her mouth in his. His hand moved up her leg, hiking her sundress above her thigh. Samantha tugged on his shirt, untucking it from his pants. As he loosened his tie, they heard a knock.

Jonathan paused and looked toward the door. "In a minute." His face turned white as he attempted to right his clothes.

Samantha froze on the couch. Jonathan's shirt was half untucked, his tie lopsided. She took a breath and hoped the knock was from Cassie. She saw a smudge of lipstick on his cheek and made a move to wipe it off. Before she could, the door swung open.

"Sorry to disturb you, Dr. Green." Gus stood in the doorway accompanied by someone Samantha didn't know. Whoever he was, his presence startled Jonathan. Samantha watched his countenance change. His playful smile left, leaving a frightened look in its place. Gus stood aside, allowing the stranger to take the lead.

Jonathan stared at him and stammered. "Dr. Boyd. I wasn't expecting you. Ms. Barrett and I were concluding a private session." He tapped his fingers on the back of his chair, his eyes shifting around the room.

Dr. Boyd cleared his throat and sat at Cassie's desk. "Dr. Green. I came to observe your group session. Seems my plans have changed."

"Lee, before you say anything, please." Jonathan jerked his head in Samantha's direction, his eyes pleading.

Lee nodded and motioned to Gus.

"Let's go, young lady," Gus said. "Dr. Boyd and Dr. Green need to talk in private."

Samantha pushed Gus aside and turned toward Jonathan, grabbing his hands. "Jonathan, I'm not leaving. This concerns both of us. We need to face this together." She attempted to meet his gaze, but he avoided her.

He released her hands and looked at the ceiling. "I'm sorry. I'm so sorry."

Beads of sweat formed on his brow. He swallowed hard and sat in his chair.

Gus put his hand on the small of Samantha's back and escorted her from the room. She turned around and tried to get Jonathan's attention, but he wasn't watching. Instead, he rocked back and forth in his chair, his head in his hands.

Gus led her down the hallway and guided her to a bench. "Would you like me to drive you home?"

Samantha crinkled her brow. "No. I'm waiting for Jonathan."

Gus shook his head. "I don't think he's coming out anytime soon. And when he does, he won't be able to drive you home. You do know who Dr. Boyd is, don't you?"

Samantha shook her head and looked toward the ground.

"He's Dr. Green's therapist. Didn't know he had one, did you? Even doctors have issues, and Dr. Green has plenty."

Samantha closed her eyes and thought about Hannah and Rachel. He had baggage too. "I know about his ex-wife and daughter. I didn't know he had a therapist. I thought he knew how to deal with it all." But did he? She thought about the shoebox and his wedding rings. Did he know how to deal with it, if he held onto those things?

"You thought he was perfect? He's far from perfect, but he's a great doctor. I'm glad Dr. Boyd and I walked in on you. He'll give Dr. Green a good talking to, but I doubt he'll report him. I don't want Dr. Green's reputation destroyed over this fling."

Samantha's nostrils flared. "It's not a fling. We're in love."

Gus shook his head. "I'm sorry to tell you, but it's not love. I bet you haven't had any cravings since being with him, that you're dependent on him for emotional support. Can you stand on your own two feet without him? You can't love someone else until you love yourself. And I don't think you're there yet."

Gus didn't understand. Had he ever been in love before?

She jumped when a door slammed down the hallway. Dr. Boyd exited, but Jonathan was nowhere in sight. She rushed, trying to open the door, but was stopped.

"Ms. Barrett, I'm sorry. But it's over. Dr. Green needs his space. Gus, please drive her home," Dr. Boyd said.

Samantha's eyes flamed. "No. It's not over until Jonathan tells me it's over." She banged on the door with her fists. "Jonathan! We need to talk. Please let me in." Why wasn't he fighting for us? Was last night a lie? She couldn't understand how he changed so fast. One minute they were in love, the next he shut her out.

Dr. Boyd touched her shoulder and met her gaze. "This isn't your fault. You'll get past this, but it'll take time. Dr. Green and I will talk about your next steps. For now, go home and rest."

"Rest? You destroyed my life, and you want me to rest?" Samantha clenched her fists at her side as her face reddened.

Dr. Boyd took a deep breath. "I understand your feelings. But we both know this relationship was wrong. It interfered with your recovery, and Dr. Green's. Two broken people don't make a whole one."

Gus and Dr. Boyd didn't understand. Jonathan wasn't broken. He was the most put-together person she'd ever met.

Dr. Boyd guided her down the hallway. "It's for the best. Whatever went on between the two of you wasn't healthy."

How could he say it wasn't healthy? When she was with Jonathan, everything was easy—no cravings, no nightmares—she was happy and peaceful. And now that was snatched from her.

She balled her fists as they walked toward Gus's car. Was she mad at Dr. Boyd for interfering or mad at Jonathan for surrendering so easily?

Both. She was mad at both. But mainly at herself for thinking she deserved to be happy.

CHAPTER 24

Samantha woke on Thursday morning with renewed hope. It was group day and the first time she would see Jonathan since they had been discovered. All Wednesday, she replayed the events in her mind. Gus and Dr. Boyd had said he was broken. How could that be true? How can a broken person counsel others so well? And if he was broken, why couldn't they heal each other, like Cassie said she wanted? More importantly, why didn't Jonathan stick up for them?

She tried to call him multiple times since Tuesday morning, but he wasn't answering his phone. She knew consequences were unavoidable if someone had discovered them, but she didn't expect him to shut down and disappear. She expected better from someone trained in human relationships. Didn't she deserve an explanation?

She searched her closet for the perfect outfit, wanting to remind him what he had squandered. He might be serious about ending things, but she wasn't ceding without a fight. Determined, she slipped on a tight black dress that accentuated her curves.

"Hey. You all right?" Cassie leaned on the doorframe, a concerned look on her face.

"Sure. What do you think of this outfit? Too much? Jonathan won't be able to resist."

"About Jonathan ..." Cassie gulped. "This is my fault. I should've known better. You weren't ready for a relationship, and I don't think he was either."

"What are you talking about? Pushing us together was the best thing you did. We're in love, Cass. I just have to remind him."

"I don't know. Dr. Boyd told me it's a false sense of love. You replaced your addiction with Jonathan. But you're not cured."

"Screw Dr. Boyd. It wasn't his business. Everything was perfect until he stuck his nose in it." Samantha glared at Cassie. "Why are you on his side, anyway?"

"Believe it or not, I'm on your side. And I take full responsibility for what happened. Somehow, I thought you and Jonathan could heal each other. Instead, it looks like I made everything worse. Dr. Boyd is recommending I have one more internship before I take my boards. He doesn't think I'm ready."

Samantha softened. "I'm sorry, Cass. But I don't agree with Dr. Boyd. What I have with Jonathan is real. And no one can convince me otherwise." She looked in the mirror and checked her hair. "Do you think this will do the trick? Or is it too obvious?"

"I think you should stay home today. Let's have a movie marathon. Michael wants me to watch another Marvel movie. It would be more fun with you."

Samantha shot Cassie a confused look. "Michael? That's new. You guys a *thing* now?"

Cassie wrinkled her nose. "*Ew*, no. He's tolerable, that's all. It would be nice if you hung out with us. Michael asks about you. He's concerned."

"There's nothing to be concerned about. Once I see Jonathan, everything will return to where it was Tuesday morning, before Dr. Boyd got involved."

Cassie swallowed and looked at the ground. "I don't want you to get your hopes up. You must realize it's over between you and Jonathan. You have to move on."

Samantha pursed her lips and looked in Cassie's eyes. "It's not over. We love each other. You don't give up on love. You convinced me to give him a chance—you don't get to talk me out of it."

"I take responsibility for pushing you, but I'm trying to do right. I should have discouraged this from the beginning, but I thought I could fix things for both of you. You don't understand the extent of Jonathan's struggles."

"I keep hearing that. Dr. Boyd used the word *broken*. So, his wife left him, and he lost his daughter. We all have baggage. That doesn't make him broken. How can he win awards and gain the confidence of the court and counsel so well if he's broken?"

"I don't have an answer to that. But that doesn't mean he's perfect."

"Gus said the same thing. I know he's not perfect." *But he's perfect for me.* "I hope you have fun, but I'm going to group. If you won't drive me, I'll call Gus." Samantha grabbed her phone from the headboard.

"Okay, I'll drive you. But please put on a more conservative outfit."

Samantha grinned and hugged her. "Thank you, Cass."

Samantha arrived at group half an hour early. She hoped Jonathan would be there, so they could talk in private. Cassie agreed to postpone the movie with Michael and wait in her office; although Samantha was convinced she wouldn't need her. After she set Jonathan aright, she planned on an early lunch, preferably at his apartment.

She took a deep breath and smoothed out her dress. At Cassie's request, she changed into a purple modest sundress instead of the black cocktail dress she had chosen. It was subtle, but it accomplished the same thing. She walked the length of the hallway and stopped at the meeting room.

She turned into the meeting space, surprised by what she saw. It was empty except for Dr. Boyd, who sat in a chair in the middle of the room, reading a book. Was he observing the session? Confused, she entered and stopped next to him.

"Dr. Boyd. Didn't expect to see you here. Are you observing Dr. Green today?"

He looked up and smiled. "Ms. Barrett. Nice to see you. I wasn't sure you'd be here, but I'm glad you came."

"You didn't answer my question. Is Dr. Green here? Are you observing him?"

Dr. Boyd rested his hand on his chin. "Cassie didn't tell you, did she? Just as well that it comes from me. Dr. Green is on leave. He will not be returning to group."

Samantha knitted her brow. "Leave? For how long?" She couldn't believe it. He wasn't coming back to group. How could he go on leave without a word to her? Did she mean that little?

"Six months. And don't think about calling or seeing him. He's heading out of town in a few days. He needs to get his head straight." Dr. Boyd leveled his eyes at her. "And you need to concentrate on your recovery. I'm petitioning the court on your behalf. Your case will be moved under my name. Dr. Green insisted." He returned to his book and left Samantha alone to absorb the news.

She paced the room, trying to piece everything together. Something must be wrong with her. Everyone she loved abandoned her—her dad, her sister, now Jonathan. Why wasn't she enough to make them stay? She tried to choke back tears as she ran into the hallway. As she turned toward Cassie's office, she collided into Gus, almost knocking the larger man to the floor.

Gus grabbed her shoulders, preventing her from moving. "Young lady, are you okay?"

Samantha narrowed her eyes but refused to answer.

Gus removed his hands but blocked her escape with his body. "Young lady, Samantha, care to talk about it? There's an empty room across the hallway."

Samantha softened when he used her name. Gus never called her *Samantha*. "I don't think it will help. No one can make this right."

Gus put his arm around her and led her to the empty room. He turned on a light and closed the door. Guiding her to a chair, he sat across from her and took a breath. "You expected Dr. Green, didn't you? Dr. Boyd should have told you before group."

"What does it matter? Jonathan left without a word. No explanation. You can't tell someone you love them one day and disappear the next." She crossed her arms and huffed.

"You can if it's the right thing to do."

"How do you know it's the right thing? Everything in my life was finally perfect. I was sober, got a job, had a wonderful boyfriend, and now it's all falling apart. If Jonathan had stayed and fought for us, I wouldn't feel this way."

Gus leaned forward and narrowed his eyes. "So, it's all about your feelings. I see. No concern for Dr. Green's career or *his* demons, huh? And yes, he has demons just like we do. Before you judge him and his decisions, why don't you consider his reasons? If you loved him, you would know his struggles."

A tear started in her eye. The text messages had read that if she loved Lizzie, she would have listened to her, known her problems. Was it the same with Jonathan? Was she being selfish again? No. It couldn't be that. Jonathan and Lizzie would have told her if something was wrong. She would have listened, wouldn't she?

She looked at Gus then stared at the floor. This was too much. She couldn't handle it anymore. She pushed the chair aside and ran to the hallway. It was time to go home. Only Mr. Rabbit could help her now.

***

Cassie drove in silence. Samantha tried to process everything Dr. Boyd and Gus shared, but it didn't make sense. Jonathan never hinted at issues. He told her how to cope with Lizzie's death, how to manage her cravings and how to deal with her mother. He had everything figured out. She was the damaged one, wasn't she?

How could she miss so much about the people she claimed she loved? She loved Lizzie, and yet she didn't know everything about her. Now Jonathan. Why did everyone else know about Jonathan's struggles but her? Cassie knew, Gus knew, and yet she never suspected anything was wrong. Her heart raced, and her palms grew sweaty.

Her thoughts concentrated on Mr. Rabbit. She still had the speedballs Liam sold her. They would help her forget. Cassie and Michael planned on watching movies all day. She could give an excuse and hide in her room. They wouldn't suspect anything. Besides, Michael should understand. He told her drugs were the cure for runaway emotions.

Michael was in the living room when they arrived. He engulfed her in a hug and kissed her head. Samantha was surprised with the sense of comfort and familiarity. He still held a special place in her heart.

"Cassie told me what happened. I'm sorry. I thought better of Dr. Green. He didn't leave you an explanation?"

Samantha let go and sat on the couch. "No. Thank you, but you don't have to be so understanding. I left you for him, remember? Stupid decision."

Michael glanced at Cassie then sat next to Samantha. "Not stupid. You were in love with him. Were you ever in love with me?"

Samantha looked away. "Do you want me to answer?"

Michael grinned. "I know the answer. We were comfortable together. I think we love each other, but we weren't *in love*, if you know what I mean. But the doctor … I know you believed that was real."

"It was real. It *is* real. But now it's over."

"You have us. We're not going anywhere. We're watching a Marvel marathon. Why don't you join? The distraction could help," Michael said.

"Why are you being so nice to me? I broke up with you, I got your best friend indicted for murder, and I'm a damaged basket case. You're both better off without me."

"Because you're *Samantha*, and you wouldn't hurt someone on purpose. You had reasons for everything. Even if I don't agree with you half the time, I know you're doing what you think best. And I don't know what I'd do if you weren't in my life."

Samantha choked back a tear. Michael was the one who drove her crazy, the one who never listened and did stupid things to make her mad. Now he acted nice and understanding. How did he change without her noticing?

Cassie squeezed next to Samantha and put her arm around her. "If you would rather take a nap, we understand. But if you need company, we're here."

Samantha gave her a hug and stood. "I think a nap is what I need. Thanks."

She walked to her bedroom hoping they wouldn't know what she was thinking. While Michael and Cassie tried to convince her they cared, she didn't deserve their love. She closed the door and sat on her bed, cradling Mr. Rabbit. If she took a speedball, she would disappoint everyone rooting for her. But who did she have in her corner again? Michael and Cassie. Everyone else had disappeared. Gus thought she was selfish. Dr. Boyd lacked compassion, and Jonathan had run away. She pulled the stitch and removed the bag and syringe.

The last time she took a speedball she ended up in the hospital, but that was because she had chosen to drive. If she took this in her room, by herself, there shouldn't be a problem. She stuck the syringe into the bag and filled it. This would erase Jonathan from her mind. Everything would be like it was before he entered her life.

As she raised the syringe, the door swung open. "Samantha! What are you doing?"

CHAPTER 25

Michael stood in the doorway, his eyes wide. "Where did you get those? If it was Liam, he's a dead man." His face reddened as he snatched the bag off the bed. "The syringe too. We're not going back to the hospital today."

Samantha closed her eyes and handed him the syringe. "Can I at least have some crack? Of all people, you should understand. Just enough to get through this."

Michael settled himself on the bed, propping up against a pillow. His long legs stretched next to hers, reminding her of their past. "That bad, huh? Dr. Green didn't realize how good he had it with you."

Samantha chortled. "He's too much of a coward to face me. And now I'm stuck with Dr. Boyd. He's an emotionless amoeba of a man. There's no point in continuing. Everyone will blame me for Jonathan's disappearance. Gus already does. I'm sure Cassie will too, in time. I can't handle this on my own."

"You're not on your own, remember? Cassie and I aren't going anywhere. And you can't do anything to make us leave."

"Are you sure about that? Because I'm pretty good at making people go away—my dad, Lizzie, Jonathan." Samantha scrunched her eyes and turned away.

"Your dad and Lizzie weren't your fault. And Jonathan wasn't either. He has his own issues, from what Cassie tells me. You need to focus on yourself and forget what anyone else says or does. You need to love yourself."

"When did you get so wise?" Samantha tilted her head and smiled.

"Hanging out with Cassie, I suppose." Michael tapped his hand on his thigh. "She's growing on me."

"I'm glad you had her. I didn't do a good job breaking up with you, did I? I'm sorry if I hurt you. It seems I'm good at that."

"Don't talk that way. It was mutual, remember? I couldn't compete with Jonathan. He's a much better guy than me anyway. I'm sure he'll come around if you give him space. It doesn't have to be over forever."

"Thank you, but it's done. He's going on leave for six months. I doubt I'll see him again. Dr. Boyd is making sure of it." Samantha rubbed the blanket between her fingers. "And now I have to finish counseling with Dr. Boyd. How can I do that when all I want to do is punch him?"

"Whoa! A little violent, don't you think? I wouldn't have expected that from you." Michael laughed. "Can you find another counselor? I'm sure Cassie can help."

"I'm not sure how it works. Mother arranged all this. I hope she doesn't have to get involved again. You see why I need something? How can I handle my feelings when I don't have something to numb myself? I need it."

"No, you don't. It's your crutch, so you think you need it, but you'll do fine without it."

"How do you know? You still use. Is it a crutch for you?"

"I've been clean for a week, with Cassie's help. And yes, it is a crutch, but I'm learning to work through it."

Clean for a week? How did that happen? She begged him to get clean with her, and he had refused. But he hangs around Cassie for a few weeks, and then he's ready? Why didn't anyone listen to her?

"I didn't know. Did you just quit? Jonathan said that's dangerous."

"It's okay. Cassie is helping me. And she can help you too. If Dr. Boyd is a bad fit, she will find a better fit, and you can petition the court yourself. Whatever it takes to get better."

Samantha approached the window. "I can't do it, Michael. I thought I could, but I can't. With Jonathan, it was easy, but now, the cravings are too much. All I can think of is getting high, so I won't have to think of him anymore."

"Getting high isn't the answer. After you come down, you'll still have to deal with it. I know. It didn't help me deal with my parents. We're still not talking. Drugs are a temporary help not a long-term solution."

Samantha leaned on the windowsill and stared. Had she been so preoccupied with Jonathan that she didn't see how Michael had changed? This wasn't the guy she had dated. "When did you get so serious?"

Michael laughed. "Serious? Can you tell Cassie that? She still thinks I'm an irresponsible goofball. But I guess that's better than what she thought before."

"Seriously, though. You weren't like this when we were together. Is it because of Cole?"

"Cole's indictment made me think, yes. But it's not just because of that. I saw how happy you were with the doctor, how you got back into photography and started thinking of the future. I guess I wanted some of that. You know, a future."

"And, do you have a future? Something with Cassie, maybe?" Samantha shot him a sly smile.

"Heck, no! She's more like a sister. Besides, I'm doing this the right way. I need to take care of myself first, figure out what I want. Cassie found a rehab place a couple of hours away. I'm going next week."

She never thought she'd hear those words. Why did they bother her so much? She wanted him to get help. At least she thought she did. Samantha clenched her fists and took a deep breath. This wasn't what she pictured. She should be with Jonathan, and Michael should be partying. That was the correct balance of the world. But in this messed up reality, she was alone, and Michael was thinking about his future. It didn't make sense.

She managed a half smile. "I'm happy for you. I hope it works out."

"You can come too. I think it will help more than Dr. Boyd or Dr. Green. It's intensive counseling, but they get great results."

"How long will you be gone?"

"Six months." Michael grabbed her hands and gazed in her eyes. "Please consider coming."

She dropped his hands and turned back to the window. "I'll think about it. Right now, I just need to sleep. Can we talk later?"

Michael gathered the speedballs and the syringe and stood by the door. "Okay. But remember, sleep only. No more drugs."

"No more drugs." Samantha laid on the bed and pulled the covers to her chin. She watched as Michael closed the door. He was going to rehab. She couldn't believe it. What kind of magic did Cassie work? Nothing made sense. While Michael thought of a future, she struggled to maintain her present. Where did that leave her?

She had two choices—Go with Michael or slide back into her addiction. Jonathan would push rehab. Although he thought he could help her through everything. And he had tried. He got her to realize the truth about her mother, and he had helped her rediscover her passion. She couldn't decide if she loved him for how he had helped her or hated him for disappearing. Did he even think about her?

She remembered their night of passion that carried over to the next day, the last day they had spent together. She missed his smell and his touch. And his eyes. His dancing brown eyes. She had to decide before the court intervened. But not now. She wasn't in a good place.

She rolled over and pulled the covers over her head. Then she cried herself to sleep, unsure of what to do next.

A few hours later, her phone buzzed. She jumped, hoping Jonathan had decided to talk to her. She reached for her phone on the headboard, disappointed when she didn't recognize the number.

Why didn't you listen to me?

Samantha froze. Listen to who?

Why did you frame an innocent man? It's your fault he's in jail.

Who was texting her? One of Cole's girlfriends? Or maybe his sister. Her hands trembled as she read the text.

He didn't do it.

Samantha shook her head and texted back, *He didn't do what? And who is* he?

He didn't kill your sister. I told you I know who killed her. But like always, you didn't listen.

It wasn't one of Cole's girls. The texter was at it again. But why? The grand jury had indicted Cole for Lizzie's murder. If Cole didn't do it, why didn't this person go to the police with their information?

Who are you? I need your name. Samantha was through playing games.

No. I can't tell you who I am now. Too dangerous.

If it's too dangerous, go to the police.

I can't tell the police. I'll give you the information tomorrow. Meet me in the alley by Willy's Bar at 8 a.m. And come by yourself. People are watching.

She put down her phone and scratched her head. Why did the person say people were watching? This mystery solidified her belief that she had missed so much with Lizzie. Could Cole be innocent? Michael would never forgive her if he was. Regardless, the person wanted to meet at Willy's in the morning. How could she get there?

And should she go in the first place? She wasn't sure. When she thought it was Cole, she wanted answers. Now that it might not be him, she was afraid to discover the truth. Who else could have killed Lizzie? Everything hit her at once.

She grabbed Mr. Rabbit and smoothed back his ears. Michael had taken everything she had gotten from Liam. She would have to deal with her emotions another way. She closed her eyes and tried to process the past twenty-four hours, but it was impossible. She saw Cole's face accusing her of framing him, Gus and Dr. Boyd accusing her of being selfish, Michael and Cassie scolding her for using again. Lizzie's voice sent her over the edge. *You are selfish. It's your fault. I want my sister back.* Samantha curled into a ball on the bed. Nothing she did was right. She was worthless, damaged, and not capable of change. It was time she admitted the truth. There was one way out, and she intended to use it. She shook as she picked up the phone and dialed.

A voice at the other end answered, "Hello, beautiful! What's the occasion?"

"Liam? You said to call if I changed my mind. Come pick me up. I need a good time."

The only person who could make her forget was Liam. He wouldn't shield her from herself. She could have a good time and chase away all the ghosts.

"I'll be there in a bit. Put on your tightest dress. I'll show you the night of your life."

Samantha regretted her decision as she disconnected the call, but it was too late. Liam would be here in a few minutes, and she knew what he wanted. But did it matter anymore? Michael had moved on; Jonathan had disappeared. She had to find a way to take care of herself. It worked before Jonathan, why wouldn't it work now? She picked a tight red dress and planned her escape. Michael and Cassie were watching movies in the living room. They wouldn't notice if she slipped out the back door. Then she could wait for Liam outside. They would never know she had left.

Liam arrived a few minutes later and honked his horn.

She glared at him and glanced at the house. "Quiet! Michael and Cassie are in there. You don't want him to know you're here, do you?"

"He's still your keeper? Why call me, when you have him?"

"I don't *have* him. We're just friends. But he'll still kick your butt if he sees you here."

Liam laughed. "Get in the car. I have a fun night planned. Guaranteed to make you forget everything and everyone but me."

Samantha got in the car.

Liam put his hand on her lap and squeezed. His touch revolted her, but there was no way out now. She glanced at the house before they left and saw Michael peeking from the living room window.

Liam moved his hand under her dress and sped away.

CHAPTER 26

Samantha held her body rigid in the seat as Liam's hand crept up her leg. She flashed him a half smile, but inside, she was dying. Why did she think this was a good idea? Once again, her decisions stunk. *But what choice did I have?* It was all Jonathan's fault. This wouldn't have happened if he had faced her like a man instead of hiding like a child.

She jerked toward the door when Liam took a right turn too fast. He grinned at her, his blue eyes shining. "I thought we'd start the night at Willy's then back to my place. We'll have plenty of time for you to pay for these." He removed his hand and raised a bag of speedballs.

That's why she had called him, right?

As they neared Willy's, Samantha's stomach churned. This wasn't like before. Michael never treated her this way. She glanced out the window. Michael saw them pull away. She closed her eyes and wished he was following them.

Liam pulled into the parking lot and turned off the ignition. He leaned over, inches from her face. "How about a little taste to start things off?"

Samantha froze. Liam smelled of cigarettes and Axe body spray, a gross combination. She wondered why women flocked to him. He wasn't even handsome. His blond hair stuck up in all directions, as if he didn't take time to brush it. His T-shirt hung loosely over his thin frame, accentuating the lack of muscle. His wiry arms reminded her of an octopus, not a man. Were the drugs worth this?

Liam crushed her against the door, his lips dry and rough. Samantha's eyes grew round as she tried to push him off. He grabbed her arms and held them in her lap. "Remember what you promised, sweetheart. A bit of fun for you"—he waved the bag—"and a bit of fun for me." He traced her breast with his hand. "Perhaps you need something to help you relax."

Liam moved back and retrieved a liquid pack and a syringe. He filled it and handed it to her, a sly smile on his face. "This will do the trick. Go ahead. Then we can have fun."

Samantha swallowed hard. She wanted the drug. It would help her forget. And being with Liam would help her forget too. She took it from him and injected it into her arm. She handed the syringe to Liam with a tentative smile, hoping the drug would take effect soon.

Liam pushed down the strap of her dress and traced the outline of her chest. "I like to see what I'm getting." He lowered her dress, revealing her breasts. His hand grazed them, his thumb running across her nipple. "Nice. But this will have to wait. Get yourself together, and let's go dance." Liam slammed the car door and lit a cigarette.

Samantha readjusted her dress as a tear streaked her face. What was she doing here? She took a deep breath and exited the car, steadying herself against the door.

Liam grabbed her hand and pulled her into Willy's, not noticing her tears.

Willy's was packed, normal for a Thursday night. Liam pulled her through the crowd to the dance floor and held her close. "Dancing with a Stranger" by Normani and Sam Smith played from the jukebox. *Fitting.* She should be with Jonathan, but he drove her to this.

Liam rested his head on her shoulder and nibbled her ear. His hands roamed down her back and rested on her butt.

As they danced, everything blurred. The dance floor swirled around her as her head felt heavy. Everywhere she looked, she saw Jonathan's face. This wasn't helping her forget.

Liam raised his head and kissed her, his tongue invading her mouth. She wanted to push him away, but she couldn't find the strength. His mouth traveled down her neck and across her chest.

She closed her eyes and froze, not knowing what to do next. The drugs had done their trick. She was immobilized, left for Liam's desires. But, like Michael had told her, the problems with Jonathan remained. It dulled her emotions, but it didn't remove the hurt.

She opened her eyes and glanced toward the door. *Michael.* He had followed her. She shuddered, wondering what he would do to Liam.

Liam tickled her ear with his tongue and whispered, "Having fun?"

Her eyes darted to Michael. He stood next to the bar, watching, but made no attempt to stop Liam. He glanced toward the right and nodded at someone inches from the dance floor. She blinked, trying to make him out, but her eyes blurred.

Without warning, someone pulled her backward. Her eyes widened when she saw a fist smash into Liam's face, landing him on the ground. Who did she have to thank? She expected Michael to knock out Liam, not this stranger. She rubbed her eyes, trying to place him.

As she struggled to focus through the haze of the speedball, Michael's arms wrapped around her. His eyes shot flames at Liam. He moved forward but stopped when a hand rested on his shoulder.

"Leave him." The man turned toward Liam. "Only scumbags manipulate women with drugs. He's not worth our time. Take Samantha home, and make sure she's okay. Cassie will know how to help."

Jonathan. He hit Liam? What was he doing here anyway? Samantha stared as tears soaked her face. Seeing him rekindled memories of what they were. She wanted that back, that magical evening at his apartment, not this mess at a bar. What would he think, seeing her with someone like Liam? He wouldn't want her now; she'd sunk too low.

Michael sat her in a chair and approached Jonathan. She tried to catch Jonathan's eyes, but he wouldn't look in her direction. Was he mad at her? She tried to hear their conversation but couldn't over the loud music and her own sobbing. Michael's eyes narrowed as he talked, and his voice grew insistent. Jonathan shook his head at first, then he glanced at Samantha and sighed. What were they talking about, and why did her stomach churn as she looked at them?

After a few more minutes, Michael returned. Jonathan left without saying a word, leaving her confused and depressed. "Let's get you home. Cassie is worried."

They were silent for most of the ride, until Samantha gathered her courage to speak. "Are you mad at me? You have the right. But are you?"

Michael sighed. "Mad at you? A little. I'm madder at Liam and Dr. Green. Liam took advantage of you, and Dr. Green … well, if he'd talk to you, we wouldn't be in this situation."

"Why was he there anyway?"

"When I saw you leave, I told Cassie to call him. He must answer to his part in this. I followed you and had him meet us when I knew where Liam took you. He wanted to confront Liam. Trust me, I've wanted to take out Liam since the first time he gave you a speedball, but Dr. Green insisted it was his fight."

"I've never seen him like that before. To see him knock out someone like that was surprising."

"Everyone has anger in them when pushed far enough."

Samantha pondered Michael's words. Seeing her with Liam made him angry. Was it out of guilt, or did he still have feelings for her? She shook her head. He was doing it again, sending mixed signals and confusing her. She couldn't handle these thoughts right now.

Michael pulled into the driveway and helped her from the car. "The next time you get in trouble, text me. I like being your rock, and I don't plan on stopping."

Samantha hugged him then ran to meet Cassie on the porch. She didn't say a word but wrapped Samantha in a hug and guided her inside. After a warm cup of milk, Cassie tucked her in bed. Maybe she did need help. Going to rehab with Michael sounded like a possibility.

Nothing else was working.

***

Samantha slept until morning. Michael and Cassie guarded her door and made sure she didn't leave. Not that she wanted to. Last night showed her the ugly side of drug use. One she didn't want to revisit again.

Her head swirled with questions about Jonathan. He'd arrived, knocked out Liam then disappeared without a word. Why didn't he let Michael deal with it? And why did he leave so quick? She knew answers weren't coming. He was leaving soon for six months. She would have to figure this out on her own.

She chose a pair of jeans and an oversized T-shirt from her closet. It was Friday, the day of her standing lunch date with Jonathan. She got dressed and stared out the window, thinking of him. Even when he had punched Liam, he was in control. Calm, measured, even when angry. The only time she saw him lose control was in the bedroom. And she longed for that moment again.

She wiped back a tear with her thumb when Cassie appeared at the door. "How are you feeling? Sleep well?"

Samantha turned to her, eyes puffy. "Yes. About last night. I'm so sorry, Cass. I don't know what I was thinking."

Cassie grabbed her hands and led her to the bed. "It's okay. Michael and I talked. I understand why you did it. We should have been more helpful. I know losing

Jonathan shattered you, but I didn't think you'd turn to Liam for comfort."

Samantha snorted. "Comfort? No, I turned to him for escape. And it was stupid. I regretted it after it happened, but I didn't know how to get out of it. At least Michael followed me. He's pretty terrific, don't you think?"

Cassie smiled. "He'll do. He's grown on me."

"What did Jonathan say when you called him? Did he come because he wanted to or did you make him?"

"I told him it would be a good idea if he came. He's more stubborn than I thought. When I told him that you went off with Liam though, he stopped making excuses."

"Why is he so confusing? All I get is mixed messages. For once, I want him to tell me the truth. I need to know, Cass."

"I know." She stood and pulled her to the door. "Michael has a surprise for you in the living room. I think it will help."

Samantha crinkled her nose, wondering what surprise Michael could have for her. She walked behind Cassie through the hallway, stopping by the entryway.

Michael stood, clasping his hands in front of him. He took a deep breath before he spoke. "Hey. I know things are tough right now, and you need answers. I hope you will sit and listen. Someone has to talk to you. I hope it will help."

Michael moved aside to reveal Jonathan sitting on the couch. Samantha caught her breath in her throat and looked toward the floor. He came. She had so many questions. Now they could talk and work out things. But was that possible? Embarrassment from last night swept over her. He'd seen her at her lowest. He knew she'd relapsed. He wouldn't want her now.

She lifted her head and met his gaze, trying to figure out his thoughts. His eyes looked tired and no longer held the spark she came to love. She looked at Cassie, her lips quivering.

Cassie grabbed her hand and squeezed then guided her to the armchair.

Samantha curled her legs underneath her and hung her head. It hurt too much to look at him.

Michael nodded at Jonathan and followed Cassie to the kitchen.

They were alone, something she had longed for over the past forty-eight hours. And it was thanks to Michael, not because Jonathan wanted to be here. She bit her lip and fidgeted with her shirt.

Jonathan took a deep breath. "I'm sorry."

"You said that Tuesday morning. In fact, that's all you said. You're sorry. What does that mean?" Samantha raised her eyes to meet his, her cheeks reddening. Tears streaked her face as she beheld his appearance. His hair was tangled, his clothes looked slept in, and dark circles outlined his eyes. For a moment, she softened, realizing this affected him too. But then she remembered his cowardly way of handling the situation, and her anger returned. He was distraught. Good. He deserved it. She stood and paced.

"Since Tuesday, I've wanted to talk to you. To hear your side of the story. To know why you walked away without a word. But now, it doesn't matter. If all you can say is you're sorry, you can leave. I don't need a coward."

Jonathan gulped and leaned back on the couch. "That's fair. I suppose I deserved that. But I had my reasons. A clean split was the best way to handle this. If we talked it out, our emotions would cloud our thinking, making it impossible to do what was necessary."

Ever the therapist. Didn't he ever let go and allow his emotions to take over? She shook her head. Only in the bedroom. Everywhere else, he was serious and staid. She remembered his face the first time they made love, full of passion and feeling. But every other time, he disengaged whenever his emotions showed, resulting to questioning her like a patient instead of talking to her like a boyfriend.

She choked back a tear. "What's so bad about emotions? That's where love comes from. And I thought we were in love. Was it all a lie?"

"I told you from the beginning our involvement was a bad idea, and yet, I let it get out of control anyway. I let our emotions rule, and that had consequences. We have to face those and do what's best for our mental health."

Samantha shook her head. "You sound so clinical, like we were a trial in an experiment. What happened to you? Hannah broke you, didn't she? It's more than Rachel's death. It was Hannah. She destroyed your ability to love."

Tears formed in Jonathan's eyes. She'd nailed it. That's why he was in therapy. That's why he was broken. He was still reeling from his divorce. How could she have missed it?

"You asked if everything between us was a lie. It wasn't. When I said I loved you, I meant it. You were the first person I said that to since Hannah. Did Hannah break me?" He swallowed hard. "Yes. But that doesn't diminish how I felt." He paused and met her gaze. "How I feel about you."

"What are you trying to say? I'm tired of the games. I'm tired of the mixed messages. Tell me what you mean. Don't leave me guessing."

Jonathan stood and crossed the room, grabbing her hands. "Fair enough. No more mixed messages." He caressed her hand with his thumb. "Sit next to me?"

Samantha nodded and followed his lead to the couch. She angled herself to face him, her hands in her lap. He looked like a lost puppy, confused about his next move. She wanted to reach for his hand but decided against it.

"When I met you, I didn't intend to fall in love. I was doing Cassie a favor. But that lunch at Plato's changed things, then you had your accident, and I wanted to do everything I could to help you, to shield you from pain. I think I was in love with you from the start."

Samantha's stomach flipflopped. He *was* in love with her. Her heart raced when he reached for her hand. She squeezed it as he continued.

"I fought it for a while, but every time I saw you, it got harder. I was your therapist, and dating you was not only against the rules, it was unethical. Until you, I prided myself on ethical behavior. When we were caught, I felt guilt and shame. I not only failed my profession, I failed you."

"If I get another therapist, like Dr. Boyd, we can make it work, right? That's the objection?" Her eyes pleaded with him.

Jonathan released her hands and shook his head. "I don't think it's wise. Hear me out. You just relapsed. You need time to recover, without a relationship. Intensive counseling like a rehab center will help you more than group counseling will. I should have pushed for that in the beginning. You need to find yourself, love yourself, and be comfortable in your own skin before you have a relationship with anybody."

"I don't want to lose you. Everyone I love disappears from my life. I don't want to lose you too."

"Let's make a date. When you find that peace Lizzie was talking about, when you can stand on your own two feet, call me. I'll still be here, waiting."

Samantha leaned on her elbow and gazed into his eyes. A tiny spark appeared, reminding her of the man she loved. He was right. She needed rehab, but the thought of going away for six months scared her. She needed time to think.

Jonathan kissed her forehead. A tear fell as he walked out the door. He said he would wait, but did he mean it? If she went to rehab, would he still be here, or was that a ploy to get her to go?

She curled up on the couch and hung her head. Nothing about this was easy.

CHAPTER 27

After Jonathan left, Samantha sat on the couch and sobbed. Her life had turned upside down, once again, and she was left trying to pick up the pieces. Jonathan said she had to find peace, like Lizzie had told her. She had to find herself and stand on her own two feet. But was that possible? Even before the cocaine, Lizzie had taken care of her. She wasn't sure she knew how to stand on her own.

After what seemed like hours, Cassie joined her on the couch. She gathered her in her arms and let her cry. Every emotion she'd felt since childhood came out. Grief over her dad's death, Portia's abuse, Lizzie's death, and her break up with Jonathan poured out like rain. Cassie patted her back and held her while she rocked back and forth.

"What did he say? Did he explain himself?" Cassie said.

Samantha nodded. "He did. But it doesn't make it better. Hannah left him four years ago, and he still isn't over her."

"Are you sure it's Hannah? He has a lot of guilt about Rachel that he's still working through."

"It's Hannah. And I'm so stupid that I missed it. He has a picture of her and Rachel on his desk. I found a box of old letters in his closet, and his wedding ring was still on his dresser. How could I be so blind?"

"He said he's still in love with Hannah?"

"No. But he did say she broke him, and he's not over it. He said I was the first person he loved since her, but he doesn't think I'm ready for a relationship."

"That's promising though. It sounds like the door is open. Give him time and focus on yourself. He's just a distraction right now. In the meantime, you have us." Cassie smiled at a person standing between the living room and kitchen.

Samantha looked up. *Michael*. He was still her rock. After everything she'd done, he was still here. She let Cassie go and approached him, engulfing him in a hug. "Thank you. It didn't fix anything. But thank you. At least now I know."

Michael kissed the top of her head and held her close. "I wish it could be different. I hoped he would come to his senses."

"It's okay. It's better this way. I'm fine." Samantha returned to the couch, hugging her knees to her chest.

Michael glanced at Cassie and back at Samantha. "What do I do? I can't leave her like this."

"Go. I got her. A little girl talk will do her good."

Michael nodded and walked toward the door. "Call me if you need anything."

Cassie smiled and turned her attention to Samantha. She stroked her hair then lifted her chin to meet her eyes. "Want to talk? I'll only listen, promise."

Samantha managed a smile. "I'd like to see that. You're not the silent type." She rested her head against the couch. "It's not fair. I never had a chance. Dad died too soon, and Mother"—she pursed her lips—"never allowed me to grieve. Since Dad, I never felt loved, until Jonathan."

"Elizabeth loved you."

Samantha smirked. "She did, in her way. But she never understood me. We argued so much the last few years. I didn't know her, Cass. I didn't know her problems, her secrets. I didn't know anything. All I could think of was the next thing to set off Portia and then my next high. And it was the same with Jonathan. I thought both were perfect, but they weren't."

"No one is perfect. And that includes you. Don't be so hard on yourself. Nothing that happened was your fault. Elizabeth would never blame you for what happened, because you did nothing wrong. She loved you, failings and all."

Samantha wiped her cheek with the back of her hand. "But did I love her enough? I wasn't a good sister. You even said that. I was selfish and childish. There's no excuse for how I treated her. And now I can't even apologize." Samantha buried her face in her arms.

"We can move past this. You have me and Michael. We're not much, but we're here. You'll get through this."

"Michael's going to rehab for six months. And you're still trying to finish an internship for your boards. I'm just a burden."

Cassie put her hands on Samantha's shoulders and straightened her. "You're not a burden. Besides, you couldn't get rid of me if you tried. You know how stubborn I am."

Samantha stood and paced. "What do I do now, Cass? I'm pretty sure I lost my job before I started, since I didn't show up yesterday. So, I'm back to being an unemployed drug addict, depending on others. I'm not letting you support me for the rest of my life."

"I won't. We'll figure this out, get you clean and on your own two feet. I believe in you, and I'm not giving up. And you can't give up either."

Samantha crossed her arms and sat in the armchair. At least one person was in her corner. Two if you counted Michael. She still wasn't sure of her next step, but at least she had someone willing to help her find it.

A phone buzzed on the coffee table, making them startle. Cassie grabbed it, her eyes crinkling as she read. "Have you gotten strange texts before?"

"What do you mean?" Samantha moved and looked at her phone.

Why weren't you there? You were supposed to meet me this morning.

"Please tell me this isn't from Liam," Cassie said.

Samantha snatched the phone. "It's not Liam. I don't know who it is, but I think it's the same person who sent the flowers."

"The flowers from Elizabeth's wake?"

"Yes. This person texted me soon afterward, saying they knew who had killed Lizzie. I thought it was a sick joke. But now they want to meet me."

"And you planned on going by yourself?"

Samantha sighed. "I didn't think I had a choice. Last night they texted that Cole was innocent. If he is, it's my fault he's in jail."

"They have evidence Cole is innocent, and they haven't gone to the police?"

"They don't want to involve the police. I thought I should go."

"It's not safe. What if it's a trap? If Cole is innocent, it could be Lizzie's murderer. Did you think of that?"

She hadn't considered that. Why would Lizzie's murderer be interested in her? She had to find out who sent those messages. "I have a chance to do right by Lizzie, to discover what happened. I need to go."

"I understand your need to make things up to Elizabeth. But are you making it up to her if you end up dead? Think this through."

"I have thought it through, Cass. I need to do this."

Cassie took a breath. "If I can't talk you out of it, we at least need a plan. If you get in a bind, you'll need a way out—like a way to get help. You know, your own personal bat signal or something."

"Bat signal? You *have* been hanging around Michael too much."

Cassie smiled. "Maybe, but I'm serious. Is there a way you can send a text or something to let Michael know, something he'd understand? C'mon, all the good spy movies have them."

Samantha paused. She had a point. Having an escape plan, a way to signal for help, did make sense. "How would I let him know it was a signal without telling him what I was doing?"

"Easy." Cassie grabbed her phone.

Samantha wants to make a bat signal in case she gets in trouble again.

"So, what's your bat signal?"

Samantha thought. Michael was always her rock. Including that made the most sense. "Tell him he's my rock. If I text that, I'm in trouble."

Cassie texted then put down the phone. "Done. Now for the next thing." She stood and got her purse. "I'm coming with you."

"This isn't your battle, Cass. It's mine. It's time I stop being selfish and do something for Lizzie. I have to see what this person knows."

Cassie nodded. "I understand, but you're not going by yourself. Either I go with you or we tell Michael."

Samantha relented. Involving Michael was a bad idea. He had changed, but he was still rough around the edges. There was no telling how he would act if he was agitated.

"Okay. We go together."

Samantha looked at her phone and texted, *I'll be there in an hour. Best I can do.*

The person texted replied, *Don't be late. I'm waiting.*

Samantha turned to Cassie and grasped her hands. She still hadn't decided about rehab, but at least she was doing something for Lizzie.

***

They arrived at Willy's bar an hour later. Samantha was glad the meeting was in the daytime. This wasn't a place to hang around after dark. She closed the car door and clutched her phone in case she received another text message. Her hands shook as she beheld the scene, trying to figure out where the person hid.

Cassie exited the car and stood next to Samantha, clasping her hand. "Are you sure you want to do this? We can call the police. Or Michael. It might be safer."

Samantha shook her head. "I have to do this, Cass. If you don't want to stay here, I understand. But I have to follow through."

"If you're going, I'm going. We're a team, and I won't abandon you." Cassie squeezed her hand. "Where do you think this mystery person is?"

"They said in the alley. I don't know how they'll react seeing you. They said to come alone."

Cassie squinted pointed to the side of the bar. "There. I think someone's waiting."

Samantha glanced to the alley next to the bar. Someone was there, but Samantha couldn't make them out. Hand in hand, both women approached the figure, determined to solve this mystery once and for all.

Samantha's stomach fluttered as they neared the alley. Whoever waited better have the information she wanted. Clearing Cole's name after she had gotten him indicted would be the perfect gift for Michael after all his help. And finding out who murdered her sister would give her the closure she needed.

They reached the alley and stood facing someone leaning against a wall. Samantha stared, surprised at the sight. She unclasped Cassie's hand and ran toward the person. "Amber? What are you doing here?"

Amber moved forward, her red hair waving in the wind. "Hello, Samantha. I hoped you'd come alone, but I see you brought a friend."

Samantha lifted her hand and cradled the young girl's face. Her left eye was swollen, and it wasn't from crying. She had black and blue marks on her cheek, reminding Samantha of her experience with Portia. Samantha's eyes filled with tears as she realized what had happened. "Did Jeremy do this to you? I knew something wasn't right with him. Come with us. We'll get you help."

"No. I'm beyond help. You can't do anything."

"Listen to me. I know what it's like. I went through abuse with my mother. I can get you help. It's never too late."

"I'm sorry, Samantha, but it is."

Samantha crinkled her brow trying to figure her out when it all went dark.

CHAPTER 28

She awoke in a strange place, unable to move. Her head throbbed as she rolled onto her side and tried to sit. Cars honked outside the window, and music blared from the room next door. She was downtown, that much she knew. Although the curtains were opened, the lack of penetrating light told her it was nighttime. She had been here several hours. But where was *here*?

The walls were dingy, covered in an off-white, almost dirty gray. The carpet was threadbare and smelled of cigarette smoke and mold. This had to be an old motel. She tried to move, but rope tied her legs together. She tried to raise her hands to check for injuries, but a cloth-like material pinned them behind her back. At least she wasn't gagged. She could scream, and someone could rescue her. But was that wise?

She surveyed the room, trying to see who else was there. Cassie and Amber were nowhere in sight. Instead, she saw a wild-eyed crazed man with disheveled clothes standing in the middle of the room. Who was he, and what did he want? She squinted, trying to identify him.

"Good, you're awake. Took you long enough. No worries, we can stay the night and be off in the morning."

Off in the morning? What was he talking about? She had to escape before he took her farther from Bracken Point. Samantha scanned the room as she devised a plan.

"Looking for your friend? Don't worry. She'll be okay. I left her on your boyfriend's doorstep as a gift."

As he stepped closer, Samantha's eyes widened. *Jeremy.* She should have known better. It was all a trap. Cassie had warned her, but she walked right into it.

She listened as he continued, hoping he would allude to their location. "What boyfriend, you might ask? You have so many, don't you? I'm sure the good doctor will take fine care of her. They'll make a great couple too, since you won't be seeing them again." Jeremy put one foot on a chair in the middle of the room and leered.

He had left Cassie on Jonathan's doorstep. To what end? Didn't he know they wouldn't rest until they found her? By now, Jonathan would have the police searching every building in town. But what if Jeremy had taken her to a different city, a different state? Could they find her then? If she could keep Jeremy talking, she might be able to buy some time.

"Where's Amber? I saw what you did to her. I told Lizzie you were an insufferable pig, but that doesn't begin to cover it. Tell me the truth, you bastard."

"Amber is doing penance for texting you. That wasn't part of my plan, but it fell together nicely once I decided to use it."

So, he was behind the last text message. That's why it sounded more demanding than the first ones. Amber's messages sounded sad and depressed, while Jeremy's were forceful and demanding. She needed to work on her detective skills.

"I told you at your mother's dinner you belonged to me. She tried to pawn you off to the doctor, but she promised you as a replacement to Elizabeth. At first, I thought she was joking. Who would want a druggie bitch for a wife? Then I decided you would be perfect. You'd do anything for a fix. What a brilliant way to control a wife."

He wanted her to replace Elizabeth. He was mad. "I don't belong to anyone, especially a slimy bastard like you. I'm not sure what kind of hold you had over my sister, but you don't have a hold over me."

Jeremy pulled a bag from his back pocket. "I wouldn't be so sure. I got this for you. Cocaine, right? Do you snort or smoke?" He tilted his head and laughed. "Not that it matters. Drugs are drugs." He threw the bag at her. "You'll have to work to use it. If you do as I say, I'll untie your hands. For a little bit."

Samantha shuddered. She stared at the bag, resisting a craving. Jonathan was right; she wasn't sober yet. But she couldn't let Jeremy use that to control her. She tried to bat away the bag with her knees but failed.

Jeremy knelt beside her and held the bag close. He ran his fingers up her side, stopping at her breast. Samantha flinched. Liam had demanded similar in exchange for drugs, making her feel dirty. Jonathan and Michael had saved her from that mistake. Who would save her now? She mustered up her courage. Resisting the cocaine was the only way to combat Jeremy. He wouldn't expect her resolve. She closed her eyes and thought of Jonathan and the strategies he had taught in group. As she refocused her thoughts on the lake and photography, her cravings lessened.

Jeremy massaged her breasts through her shirt. "Does my touch excite you?" He opened the bag and waved it by her nose. "Will this help? Be a good girl, and you can have all you want." He raised his hand to her face and caressed her cheek. When his hand neared her mouth, she bit, sending him reeling on the floor. "*Ow!* You Barrett girls are a feisty lot, aren't you?" He shook his hand and sneered. "Don't try that again, bitch." He slapped her across the face, causing her head to hit the floor.

"I'm used to that game, Jeremy. It was Mother's favorite way to discipline. You'll have to do better to break me."

Jeremy laughed. "I'll break you. Just like I broke Amber. If I have to kill you like I did your sister, so be it."

He killed Lizzie. It wasn't Cole; it was Jeremy. That's why he said she was haunting him at the bar that night. It wasn't grief; it was guilt. She should have known. Something didn't feel right about him. She tried to warn Lizzie, but she wouldn't listen. Mainly because she wasn't worth listening to. Tears welled in her eyes as guilt and shame consumed her. If only she had made Lizzie listen. If only she hadn't gone into that bathroom to get high. If only she could return to that day and do it over. Then she would have her sister.

"You thought it was Cole, didn't you? That's what we wanted you to think. Logan and I planned the whole thing, after I convinced him it was self-defense. I told him Elizabeth was the crazy one, came at me with a meat cleaver. I had to defend myself and Amber. Convincing story." He paced the room. "Logan would do anything to get a murder rap on Cole, so I used it to my advantage. Think it was your evidence that got him indicted? It was mine. I planted the murder weapon at his house. That's what convinced the grand jury, not some stupid story about a bracelet. It's amazing what some sweet talking with that sister of his can do."

Logan was a dirty cop. Michael was right. She reminded herself to never doubt him again. If he had helped Jeremy frame Cole, the police wouldn't be a great ally right now. There was no telling who else was involved. Determined to escape, she let Jeremy ramble as she studied the room, planning her route.

Without warning, Jeremy picked her up and threw her onto the bed. "Crying over your sister? Did you believe she loved you? Did you think she would love a drug-addict bitch like you?" He knelt beside her on the bed. "She despised you. And your mother feels the same. As for Cassie and the good doctor, well, they are better off without you too. It's not like the good doctor loved you. If your own twin hated you, why would someone as accomplished as him give a fuck?"

Samantha tried to drown out his words. He was trying to tear her down, to make her think nobody cared. But that wasn't true. Lizzie had loved her. She might not have understood her, but she had loved her. Michael and Cassie loved her too, they proved as much the last few days. And Jonathan. She smiled thinking about him. He said he would wait until she was clean and stable. That meant something, didn't it?

"Why did you kill Lizzie? I saw you at the engagement party. You had her under some spell. From what I saw, she did everything you said. So, why kill her?"

Jeremy laughed. "You don't know much about your sister, do you? You don't know what she did that night, how I caught her." His eyes grew sinister.

"Caught her with what?"

"Not what. *Who.*"

Samantha stared. Lizzie was with someone else the night of her engagement party? That didn't sound like her. "Liar. I don't know what Lizzie saw in you, but she was loyal. She wouldn't cheat on you, even if you deserved it."

Jeremy cackled. "You'd like to believe that, wouldn't you? Elizabeth never wanted to marry me. She was after someone else. Someone young and naïve who she could manipulate. She thought she was smart, doing it right under my nose. But she couldn't hide it for long."

Samantha tried to piece together his insane rant, but it wasn't making sense. Who was he talking about? Someone at the office? No one Samantha knew fit his description. "You're not making sense. Elizabeth wouldn't do something like that."

"She wouldn't? But she did. Saturday night after the engagement party, I went to Amber's room to check on her. That's when I saw it. Elizabeth was there, naked with her lover, hoping I wouldn't discover them. But I did."

Everything Jeremy said didn't match what she knew about her sister. Elizabeth never mentioned a lover. She told Samantha she was happy with Jeremy. Like Jonathan, she kept secrets from her, but why?

Samantha shook her head, trying to understand. "It has to be a mistake. Who was she with?"

The door opened behind Jeremy. "Me."

CHAPTER 29

Samantha's eyes widened. *Amber?* She knew something was different between Lizzie and Amber the night of the engagement party, but she never guessed they were involved. "You? You and Lizzie had a fling?"

"It wasn't a fling. We loved each other." Amber's face reddened.

They loved each other. It reminded her of Jonathan. Gus had called their relationship a fling, and it disgusted her. Jonathan meant so much and to have that reduced to nothing destroyed her. Had she done the same to Amber? She knew how it felt to have love torn from her. She stared at Amber, trying to guess her thoughts.

Jeremy turned around and backhanded Amber across the face. "Enough! I told you not to talk about it." Amber rubbed her cheek, a tear forming in her eyes. "Look what you made me do. Next time, obey the rules, and that won't happen."

Amber rubbed her jaw and stared at the ground. Had Jeremy treated Lizzie this way too? Samantha didn't understand why Lizzie agreed to marry him.

Jeremy glanced at Amber. "I have to prepare for our trip. Please watch our guest, and make sure she doesn't try to escape." He walked to the other side of the room, rummaging through a backpack.

Samantha stared at Amber, piecing together the puzzle. She wanted to believe she loved her sister but was hesitant. She didn't know her well enough. What if she was part of Jeremy's plan?

Samantha watched Amber sit in the corner chair, holding her jaw from Jeremy's slap. Her eyes were cold, as if she were protecting herself from feeling.

Samantha knocked a pillow off the bed in Amber's direction. "Hey."

She looked up and crinkled her brow. "What?"

"Come over here and talk to me."

Amber looked around. "Are you crazy? Jeremy would never allow it."

"He won't let you talk to me? What kind of hold does he have over you anyway? I can't figure out if you're a victim or an accomplice."

Amber glanced at Jeremy. "I don't owe you an explanation. Hush before he comes back and catches us talking."

She had to get Amber alone. She would never answer all her questions in front of her brother. Was it fear or misguided loyalty?

Jeremy zippered the bag and sat on the bed next to Samantha. "Better settle in for the night. Amber, you get the floor." He curled his body around Samantha on the bed. "I've waited for this. You're mine tonight."

She froze as his breath tingled her neck. Where were the police? Jonathan and Cassie should have contacted them by now. She concentrated on the outside sounds, trying to hear police sirens, but all she heard was loud music and yelling. How would she get away from him?

"I like it this way, you tied up. I can do whatever I want." His fingers trailed along her side, settling on her navel. He made a circle with his fingers then let them wander down her pants. Was he doing this in front of Amber?

She cringed as his fingers probed her vagina through her clothes.

"I thought Elizabeth would be the perfect wife, but she betrayed me." His mouth neared her ear, licking and biting. "You'll make the perfect substitute. Especially since you're of no value to anyone. They won't miss you. The three of us will have the perfect life together."

Jeremy turned her on her back and lifted her shirt. She shook as his fingers caressed her chest. He unclasped her bra and lowered his mouth, sucking each nipple.

She choked back tears, trying to imagine Jonathan. Did Amber know what was transpiring? How could she lie on the floor, knowing what her brother was doing, and allow it to happen? It was up to her to end this.

Jeremy moved toward her feet and untied her legs. "Be good, and you'll get you're fix."

Now was her chance. She calculated her move. With enough force, she could kick him in the balls, incapacitating him for a moment. Then she could make a run for it. She sucked in a breath, enduring Jeremy's touch until the time was right.

He positioned himself between her legs, grinding against her clothes. When he raised himself to remove his pants, she lifted her knee, leaving him sprawled back on the bed.

"Motherfucker! You bitch!"

Samantha made a move to run but stopped when she saw Amber on the floor. Could she live with herself if she left her here? Would Lizzie want her to rescue Amber? She stood over her, wrestling with her decision when she felt something hard strike her head.

***

The next morning, Samantha woke with a headache worse than the previous day. She opened her eyes, disappointed in what she saw. No one had rescued her during the night. She was still with Jeremy, her hands and legs tied together. Were they having trouble finding her, or did they not care, like Jeremy had said?

The room was dark, with only the light from the early morning sun shining on the walls. Amber sat in a chair in the corner, a faraway look on her face. She glanced toward the door where Jeremy stood. He was organizing a pile of supplies for their trip—to where, Samantha didn't know. She closed her eyes, hoping they wouldn't realize she was awake.

"Amber, I'm running some errands. You're in charge. Remember what happens if you disappoint me." Jeremy walked out the door, leaving the two women alone.

"Amber, he's gone. Can we talk now?"

Amber knitted her brow. "What do we have to talk about? How you made Jeremy angry last night? How he took it out on me after he knocked you out? You should have taken it. You won't be able to fight him forever."

"What did he do to you?"

"It doesn't matter. I should be used to it."

"What did he do to you? Tell me."

Amber wiped away a tear. "What he wanted to do to you."

Samantha's eyes widened. "He raped you?"

"Jeremy doesn't call it rape. He loves me, and that's how he shows it."

"Amber, that's not love."

"I know that, after Elizabeth. We were in love. But Jeremy is all I have left."

"That doesn't mean you have to stay. He's abusing you, and you deserve better."

"I had better." Amber approached window and sobbed.

Samantha lowered her gaze. She didn't have better; she had the best. And Samantha knew nothing about it.

"Tell me about you and Lizzie."

Amber sat on the edge of the bed. "What do you want to know? You want to tell me how wrong it was? How I shouldn't have loved her?"

"No. Tell me the good things. I missed this part of her. I need to know how happy you made her."

Amber shook her head and gave a half-smile. "We were happy. At least we tried. Jeremy didn't make it easy. I think I got a thrill sneaking behind his back."

"Did Lizzie know what Jeremy was doing to you?"

"No. She knew he was controlling and abusive, but she didn't know he forced me to have sex with him. I didn't want to tell her, to protect her."

That sounded familiar. It was the same reason Samantha didn't tell Lizzie about Portia's abuse. Except Jeremy's abuse was far worse.

"If she knew Jeremy was abusive, why did she agree to marry him?"

"I convinced her. If she married him, we could be together. Then I could withstand Jeremy's assaults. I didn't see another way. But I was stupid."

"You did what you could to be with the one you loved and survive."

"I should have told Elizabeth what was happening. We could have gone somewhere Jeremy wouldn't find us."

"But you didn't, and that's okay. When you're being abused, you can't think straight. Don't blame yourself for what happened. You didn't make Jeremy do that stuff to you. And you didn't make him kill Lizzie."

Amber smirked. "You're good. You almost had me convinced. But I know what you're really like. I know how you made Elizabeth cry, how you broke her heart for months. Don't think a few kind words will change anything."

Samantha sighed. "You want to revisit all my failings now? Jeremy is gone. We could plan that escape you wanted. You can get away."

Amber laughed. "You think so? I can't run away. He'll track me down. There's no escaping him."

"But there could be. Untie me."

"No." Amber sobbed and looked toward the wall.

"Please, untie me. We're on the same side."

"How do you figure that?"

"We both loved Lizzie, right? That makes us on the same side."

"I loved Elizabeth. The jury's still out on you."

Samantha sighed. This again? Same thing as the text messages.

"Lizzie was my twin. I wasn't always the best sister, but I loved her. And she loved me, despite what Jeremy wants me to believe."

Amber bit her bottom lip. "She did love you. That's why she never told you about us. She said you were dealing with enough, that you didn't need our problems."

There was the common thread. Samantha was too busy with her own issues to even see that Lizzie had problems. If she asked her questions, talked to her and acted like a real sister instead of a drug addict, she would have known. It was too late now, but she could help Amber.

"I admit, I was selfish. I regret that. But that's not why Lizzie died. She died because of your brother. The guilt lies solely on Jeremy, not on us."

Amber turned to face Samantha. "You think I don't know that? I was there when he did it. I held her when she died. Then I was forced to clean up the scene and plant her body in the alley. You think you have problems? You have no idea what Jeremy has put me through my entire life."

"Then let me help you. I can get you away from him, give you a place to live. If you let me, I can help you through this."

Amber chortled. "You want me to believe you, after the way you treated Elizabeth? She was so busy cleaning up your messes and trying to save you that she couldn't save herself. We were careless that night, because she was distraught over you. She couldn't convince your drug dealer to stop selling you cocaine, and she didn't know what to do next. She came to my room in tears and forgot to lock the door. That's when Jeremy came in." Amber broke down sobbing.

Samantha's eyes welled. Lizzie had lived a whole life she didn't know about. While Samantha was busy partying and getting high, Lizzie was falling in love with someone but too afraid to say anything. That's why she said Jeremy's sister needed someone to look after her. That's why she was marrying him in the first place. It was all because of Amber. And Samantha's selfishness had ruined Lizzie's chance at happiness.

"It doesn't change anything, but I'm sorry. I didn't know. We can sit here all day and talk about what an awful sister I was, but that won't bring back Lizzie. Right now, we must concentrate on the one who caused this. We must get away from Jeremy. I want to help you Amber, and not just because my sister loved you. I want to help you be safe. No one should live in fear. Lizzie deserved better. You deserve better. Please. Let's work together."

CHAPTER 30

Amber approached her, wiping back tears. "How? Jeremy could be back anytime. If you escape, he'll kill us both."

"Untie me first. I need to figure out where we are, plan the best route."

"If I untie you, how do I know you won't leave me here?"

"You have to trust me."

Amber paused. "Are you sure you know what you're doing? Two unarmed women escaping a madman doesn't seem like it has the best odds."

"We're smarter than him. We can do it. Trust me?" Samantha tilted her head.

"Okay. But this better work." Amber untied Samantha's arms and legs then looked in her eyes. "Don't underestimate my brother. He's not stupid. Even if we get out of this building, we might not get far."

Samantha rubbed her wrists and surveyed the room. "He's insane, which is worse than smart. We must plan our every move, in case he returns before we're far enough away." She pulled back the curtain and peeked out the window. "What floor are we on?"

"Fourth. Why?"

"I need to know how long it will take to get downstairs." She opened the door and scanned the hallway. "We're in the middle of the hallway, so we have a long walk to the staircase." She bit her lip and tapped her foot. "I think we can make it downstairs in two minutes. Less if we make it down before Jeremy comes back."

"And what then? Where do we go?"

"Do you have a cellphone?"

"Yes, but Jeremy tracks my calls and text messages."

"We'll have to chance it. What's the nearest restaurant?"

"Star-Crossed Diner is across the street."

"Give me the phone."

Amber took her phone from her back pocket and handed it to her.

Samantha was glad Cassie thought of the bat signal. Now to see if it worked. Cassie knew she was kidnapped, so Michael was already on high alert. He would be expecting the text.

You are my rock. SCD downtown. Two packages waiting.

"He won't recognize Michael's number, and it will take him some time to figure this out. By then, we should be at Cassie's. We'll decide what to do from there."

Amber regarded the room and nodded. "When he comes back and we're not here, he'll rage. Like he did the night he killed Lizzie. This better work."

"It will. Michael's not the sharpest person I know, but he'll understand. Now let's get to that diner."

Samantha headed for the door but stopped and turned around. Amber stood in the middle of the room, her eyes closed, shaking. Samantha put her arms around her and patted her back. "It's okay. We can do this. Be strong."

Amber shook her head. "I'm not strong. I couldn't stop him. Not when he touched me when I was eleven. Not when he raped me when I was fourteen. And not when he killed the only person who ever loved me." Tears fell from her eyes. "I can't do this."

Samantha raised her chin and met her gaze. "Yes, you can. You were strong enough to be with Lizzie behind Jeremy's back because you loved her. Now it's time to love yourself and break free. You can do this. We can do this."

Amber gulped back a tear and nodded. She entwined her fingers with Samantha's and crept into the hallway. Samantha squeezed her hand, reassuring her of her presence.

Samantha monitored each room as they passed. Most doors were closed, but some were cracked open, waiting for maid service. She took count of which ones in case they had to hide. They tiptoed past five closed doors when they heard footsteps. Samantha pulled Amber into the next open room, hoping a guest wasn't occupying it.

"Is it Jeremy?"

Samantha peeked out the door. "No. But we learned something. If we hear any noise, we hide in the nearest open room."

"What if someone is already in there?"

"We take that chance. We have to keep going. Three flights of stairs down. Are you ready?"

Amber looked toward the ground and nodded. They tiptoed toward the staircase, hoping for a quick exit.

The first flight down was easy. They took one step at a time, making sure they didn't make a noise. When they reached the next flight of stairs, they panicked. Samantha pulled Amber into the second-floor hallway as three men brushed by them.

Amber's body shook as they waited for them to pass. "I can't do this. I can't do this."

Samantha put her hands on her shoulders. "Breathe. You're hyperventilating. It's okay. We're almost there."

Amber's face turned white as she stared into the stairwell. "Jeremy." She pushed Samantha into an open room and closed the door. "Why did I let you talk me into this? He'll kill us."

"Be quiet." Samantha put her ear to the door and listened. "I think he's gone."

"If he went to the room and finds we're gone, he'll return, looking for us. This is a mistake. We need to go back." Amber's voice quivered.

"No. You have to be strong. We can't let him win. Downstairs and across the street, that's all we need to do. Michael will be there waiting for us."

"How do you know? What if he doesn't come?"

"He'll come. Some people are worth depending on, and Michael is one of them. He's never let me down, and he won't today."

"Isn't he your drug-addict boyfriend? Why didn't you text the doctor instead? I'm trusting my life on a drug addict. Great."

Samantha sighed. "Michael is the best person to rescue us. Besides, he's been clean for a week. He's up to the job. You can't judge people by their failings alone. He'll be there."

Amber shook her head. "This isn't right. I'm going back up. You go to the diner. I'll try to buy you some time."

"No. I'm not letting you go back to him. We're going down the last flight of stairs and across to the diner. No excuses, no turning back." Samantha grabbed Amber's hand and opened the door. She looked both ways down the hallway then ran to the stairwell, dragging Amber behind.

They reached the final floor and looked behind them. If Jeremy knew they had escaped, he hadn't discovered them yet. Samantha tugged Amber toward the entrance. "Almost there. Which way is the diner?"

"To the left. About a block down," Amber huffed, out of breath. "Can we rest?"

"No time." Samantha looked behind them then ran across the street. She kept running, Amber lagging behind, until they reached the diner. They paused on the sidewalk outside, looking for Michael's car.

"Is he here? I knew he wouldn't be. Why did I trust you?"

"He'll be here." Samantha tapped her foot and looked back and forth. Michael better hurry. Jeremy would be along any minute. As she scanned the street for her captor, a horn honked on the side of the diner. "See? I knew he'd figure it out." She yanked Amber's hand and jumped in the car.

"Thank God! Cassie's going crazy. What happened? She doesn't remember much."

"I'll explain later. Drive." Samantha glanced toward the motel and saw Jeremy running toward them. They had to figure out a plan, quick. It wouldn't take Jeremy long to find them.

CHAPTER 31

I just want to know one thing. Did that bastard rape you? If he even touched you—"

Samantha bit her lip. Michael didn't need to know the extent of her nightmare, and she didn't want him to know what Jeremy had done to Amber. "No. He didn't rape me."

"Good. Now what's the plan?"

"Until we figure it out, drive. I'll keep an eye to see if he's following us." Samantha sat turned toward the back seat.

Michael glanced at her, his eyes misting. "Thank God Cassie thought of a way to let me know where you were. When you didn't come home last night, we were terrified. Cassie wanted to call the police, but Jonathan wouldn't let her."

Jonathan. He was there. But why wouldn't he call the police? It didn't sound like him. He was the one who had convinced her to go to the police about Cole. Structure, law and order, that was his go-to. She wondered about his reasoning but focused her attention to the information she learned instead.

"Cole didn't do it."

"What?" Michael shot her a confused glance as he turned a corner.

"It wasn't Cole. I was wrong. Jeremy killed Lizzie. He admitted it and threatened to do the same to me. He's insane, and Amber's in danger. We have to get her to safety."

"I'm more worried about you. If he killed your sister and he wants to kill you too, we have to stop him."

Samantha put her hand on Michael's thigh. "I'm sorry I didn't listen to you. Jeremy bought Logan off; although I'm sure he didn't need much convincing. They planted evidence to frame Cole. You were right. This time, I promise I will listen."

Michael placed a hand over hers and smiled. "It's okay. I understand. We'll get past this. Now, we need a plan. I can't keep driving forever. Where are we going, so I can tell Cassie where to meet us?"

Samantha tapped her forehead. "Amber, do you still have that cellphone?"

Amber sat in the backseat, her face turning ashen. "Yeah, why?"

"You said he tracks your calls and texts. Could he track your location too?"

Amber's eyes widened. "I think so. What do we do?"

"Give it to me." Samantha snatched the phone from her hands and threw it out the car window. "That helps. What do you think his next move is?"

"I don't know. He's unpredictable. He'll stop at nothing to get what he wants."

"What does he want? I don't understand why he kidnapped me and dumped Cassie on Jonathan's doorstep. It doesn't make sense. Why would he want me to replace Elizabeth?"

"He wants control. And he wants to make sure Cole takes the fall for him. I can't say he's logical. He's been unstable his whole life."

Samantha believed that. Jeremy never seemed in touch with reality. Looking back, his actions were more than creepy; they were disturbing, hinting at a deeper problem.

"We have to get a step ahead of him. Control the situation. But I'm not sure how," Samantha said.

"Your house is out of the question. He'll check there first," Michael said.

"Good point." Samantha tapped her fingers on her thigh. "We have to go somewhere public, where he wouldn't suspect." Her eyes lit up. "I got it. Michael, give me your phone. I'll call Cassie and tell her where to meet us."

They pulled into the parking lot a few minutes later. Cassie waited for them outside.

"A diner? This might work. I doubt Jeremy would check here," Amber said.

"Even if he does, it's public enough that he won't do anything. He'll wait until we're alone. But we won't give him the chance."

Cassie hugged Samantha. "I'm so glad you're okay." She turned toward Amber and Michael, grabbing Amber's hand. "The four of us will come up with something. I promise."

"Four? I thought five would be a better number." Jonathan appeared from inside the diner. "I have a table in the back." His gaze rested on Samantha, warm and caring. "Shall we?"

He never stopped surprising her. Whenever she thought he was gone, he appeared again. Although Jeremy had gotten him in this mess by dumping Cassie at his place, he could have left everything to Michael. But instead, he came. Tears welled as she stared, beholding him.

Michael put his arm around her shoulders and led her to the sidewalk in front of the diner. "Are you okay? If you want him to leave, say the word."

Samantha shook her head. "No. Thank you though. We could use all the help we can get. Besides, Jonathan might have some insight, being a psychiatrist and all."

"I know we're not together anymore, but I still worry about you. If he does anything to make you upset or spiral, he will answer to me."

Samantha smiled and hugged him. "I meant what I texted you. You are my rock, and I'm lucky to have you. Let's go in." Samantha clasped his hand and led him to the back booth she shared with Jonathan every time they came.

They filed in, Jonathan and Michael on one side, Samantha, Amber and Cassie on the other. She stared at the two men who meant so much. One always had her back and the other, her heart.

Cassie turned toward Samantha and Amber. "What happened? The last thing I remember was Samantha trying to convince you to come with us. Then everything went dark, and I woke up outside Jonathan's apartment. I don't even know who knocked me out."

"Jeremy said he dumped you on Jonathan's doorstep. Why didn't you call the police then?" Samantha asked.

"Believe me, I wanted to. But Jonathan said it could put you in danger. If they figured out where you were and surrounded the place, whoever had you could've decided to kill you."

"So, you waited. How did you know I would figure a way out?"

"Because you're you. If there was a safe way to get out, you would find it. And I was right," Jonathan said.

Samantha met his gaze, then looked away.

"I'm sorry. Jeremy set up the whole thing. When he found out I had texted Samantha, he devised a plan to kidnap her. He wasn't expecting you," Amber said.

"But why dump me outside of Jonathan's? Why not kill me?"

"He figured you didn't know it was him. Believe it or not, Jeremy doesn't kill someone lightly. Unless you disrespect him or make him angry, he has no desire to hurt you. He probably figured Jonathan's was the safest place," Amber said.

"Plus, he was able to rub it in. He told me Jonathan didn't love me and would make a life with you. He tried to hurt me anyway he could." Samantha avoided Jonathan's gaze as she spoke, afraid of his response.

Jonathan's voice, soft at first, grew bolder as he talked. "I know you don't like it when I say it, but I'm sorry. I'm sorry I left you when you were vulnerable. I'm sorry I didn't know what was happening with Jeremy. And I'm sorry I didn't realize the threat he posed when I saw him at your mother's. I should have known something wasn't right."

Samantha turned to him and fumbled with her bracelet, still refusing to look him in the eyes. "It's not your fault. You didn't know. I didn't even know. We need to put that aside and figure out how to stop him."

"Easy. Call the police." Cassie retrieved her phone, poised to dial.

"Now you want to call the police." Samantha shook her head. "I don't think it's a good idea. I didn't believe Michael when he said Cole was innocent, but I believe him now. Plus, Logan co-conspired with framing Cole. I don't know how deep it goes, but I don't trust the police. This is up to us. When we corner Jeremy and get a confession on your cellphone, then we can call the police. I owe it to Michael, and Cole."

"We can report this to other detectives. They can't all be as bad as Logan," Cassie said.

"I'm not taking the chance. This is up to us. Lizzie wanted me to avenge her death, and this is how I'm doing it, whether you're with me or not."

Cassie touched her hand. "Of course, I'm with you. I might not agree, and I might be scared out of my mind, but I'm with you."

"We need to know more—what makes Jeremy tick, why he's like this in the first place. We can use it to our advantage to make a trap that causes him to confess." Jonathan looked at Amber. "You need to tell us your story. How long has Jeremy abused you?"

Amber looked at the table. "It started in fifth grade. Jeremy's always been off-balanced, but it's more than that. It wasn't always violence. He didn't hit me until recently, when I got in the way of his plans. Before that, he abused me in other ways."

Jonathan leaned over and met her gaze. "You're safe here, among friends. What other ways? We need to know what he's capable of, what drives him. What did he do to you?"

Samantha looked at Amber and nodded. Samantha grabbed her hand and squeezed, not letting go until Amber finished her story. Amber needed to get this out, and Jonathan was an excellent therapist. He knew how to put people at ease, so they weren't afraid, and it was working with Amber. If only he had his personal life figured out like his professional one.

Amber swallowed hard as a tear crept down her face. "He was controlling. I wasn't allowed to have friends. He told me what to watch, what to wear, what to believe, all under the guise of helping me fit in with the other girls. But he didn't want me to be around the other girls. He was grooming me."

"Weren't your parents suspicious? How did they not see what he was doing to you?" Cassie asked.

"They were too busy working. Jeremy was responsible, smart. They trusted him," Amber said.

"Amber, you said he was grooming you. You know what that usually means, don't you?" Jonathan said.

"Yes. Jeremy claimed me for himself. It started with touches. He would touch me through my clothes then ask me to touch him. As we got older, he progressed, until he raped me when I was fourteen. After that, it was a regular thing. I was his, and no one else could have me. Until Elizabeth."

Samantha wrapped her arms around her. "I wish you told Lizzie. She would have helped you. We would have helped you."

"Elizabeth was my first, besides Jeremy. She made me feel loved and wanted. I didn't want to ruin that. I didn't want her to be disgusted and leave."

"She wouldn't have been disgusted. It wasn't your fault," Samantha said.

"Wait. Am I missing something? Elizabeth and *you*? Why didn't she say anything?" Cassie said.

"We couldn't risk Jeremy finding out. But he did anyway, and that was when he killed her."

Cassie let out a deep breath. "We have to kill that bastard."

Michael laughed. "I've never heard such language from you. Intriguing."

Cassie kicked him under the table and scowled. "Get serious. We have to do something about Jeremy."

"We'll deal with Jeremy when it's time." Jonathan grabbed Amber's hands. "You need to know it wasn't your fault. When this is over, I want to offer you free counseling at the clinic. You can work past this. We won't let him destroy you."

Amber smiled. "Thank you."

"Let's get focused. How can we pull this off? He's armed. I'm not risking your life. Or anyone's at this table," Michael said.

"If we set the trap, then we take away his control. We have the element of surprise." Samantha felt Jonathan's gaze burn into her head but focused her attention on Michael.

"We can't underestimate Jeremy. From what you shared, Amber, he's unstable at best. That means he's unpredictable." Jonathan folded his hands on the table and tapped his thumbs. "We need to be prepared for anything."

As they pondered Jonathan's words, a waitress appeared with four cups of coffee, a malt, and five cobblers.

"I took the liberty of ordering for everyone." Jonathan lowered his head, trying to meet Samantha's eyes. "Samantha can attest to the cobbler."

The waitress set the malt in front of Samantha, and she froze. He ordered her favorite drink. Was this a peace offering or did it mean more? She sniffed back a tear and raised her head, wishing they were alone. Their eyes met for a moment. Instead of the dancing brown eyes she fell in love with, she only saw longing, sadness, and fear. Unable to hold the gaze, she looked toward her malt and twirled her straw.

"I thought a malt would help," Jonathan said.

He always knew how to make her smile. "It does. Thank you."

"We still don't have a plan. Where can we lure him? It must be somewhere safe, where we can record his confession—somewhere he would go but would afford us protection," Cassie said.

"The office. The top floor is large with few hiding spaces. Samantha and I know that place by heart. It's perfect," Amber said.

"We're not going in without ammunition," Michael said.

"And where are you planning on getting that? I'm not comfortable with you carrying a gun," Cassie said.

Michael reached and grabbed Cassie's hands. "I know how to shoot. I'm not a complete buffoon."

"That's not what I mean. I just don't want you to—" Cassie swallowed, her eyes tearing. "This whole thing scares me. I understand why you don't want to call the police, but this doesn't feel right. I don't want you"—she squeezed Michael's hand—"or anyone else to get hurt."

Samantha looked at them and smiled. They fought it, almost as much as Jonathan fought their relationship, but she saw something in them. She hoped they would act on it, before it was too late. "No one will get hurt if we plan this right. Amber and I should be the bait. If he knows we're there, he'll come."

"No." Jonathan's voice bellowed. "I don't want you involved. Michael and I will handle this."

Samantha's eyes narrowed. "You can't prevent me from coming. This concerns me, not you. He killed my sister. He kidnapped me, and he's been abusing Amber. We're going, and we will be a part of this, whether you want us to or not."

Jonathan took a breath and glanced toward Michael.

Taking the cue, Michael stood. "Cassie, Amber, let's go back to my place and finalize plans. I have what we need there." He turned toward Jonathan. "We'll meet you at Portia's office in an hour. I'll text, if we need anything."

Samantha watched them leave then sank into the seat. They were alone, something she wished for earlier. Her stomach flipflopped as memories of their Friday lunch dates danced in her head. She fought back tears as Jonathan reached for her hand.

"Look at me, please. When I found Cassie outside my door and she told me what happened, my heart stopped. Seeing you with Liam was bad enough, but knowing you were kidnapped destroyed me. If anything ever happened to you—"

"I'm fine, Doc. I got us out of there, and I can get through this situation too."

Jonathan flinched and released her hands. "So, I'm just *Doc* now, huh? Okay. I get it."

Samantha watched his eyes well and regretted what she said. But how else was she supposed to deal with him? He explained himself, but it wasn't enough. She still thought him a coward.

"Do you know why I'm seeing Dr. Boyd? It isn't unusual for a psychiatrist to see another therapist for support, but it's more than that." He folded his hands on the table and took a breath. "It's my fault for keeping my emotions hidden. Since Hannah, I've kept my feelings inside. That's one of the reasons I struggled with our relationship. Even when I decided to give it a chance, I wasn't ready to open up, and that's on me."

Samantha crinkled her brow. "So, the person I fell in love with isn't real? He's someone putting on an act, making me think he's got it together?"

"It wasn't an act. I kept things hidden, yes, but everything I told you was real. It took a while, but my professional life isn't a problem anymore. It's relationships. That's why I never dated after Hannah. She didn't destroy my ability to love but my ability to trust."

Samantha pursed her lips. "You don't trust me? That's something you could have shared."

"It's not that easy. Hannah broke my trust when she cheated on me and left. I didn't know how to recover from that. Therapy helped, but, when we were caught, I questioned everything. Dr. Boyd made me think. You were clean for two months, but that's not long enough to ensure sobriety. It was possible you didn't love me but used me as a replacement for cocaine. I couldn't go through that again, being with someone who didn't love me for myself."

"So, you decided for me. Instead of involving me in the discussion, you decided I wasn't worth the risk."

Jonathan rested his elbow on the table and rubbed his eye. "You're not understanding. Walking away from you killed me. Those days away, not able to talk or see you, were torture. And now, being this close to you and not able to take you in my arms … hell, Samantha." Tears flowed from his eyes as he spoke. "This tears me apart more than Hannah ever did."

"Then why are we putting ourselves through this? Do you think I don't love you? Every time I see you, I want to touch you, to run my fingers through your hair and tell you how much I love you. I can't imagine life without you. But if you can't trust that, I don't know where that leaves us."

"I'm not saying I don't trust you. Please understand. But you're not in a place where you can tell the difference. I need to know this is the real thing. I need to know you love me for me. Please see it from my perspective. If I lose anymore of myself to you and this doesn't work out, it will devastate me worse than Hannah."

Losing her would hurt more than losing Hannah? Yet he had pushed her away. She struggled to understand his logic but saw it was tearing him apart. She softened, realizing being mad at him wasn't solving anything. What would? She grabbed his hand and squeezed.

"Where do we go from here? Do we throw away everything? I can't handle anymore back and forth. Either we're together or we're not."

Jonathan gulped. "I told you I would wait for you. Isn't that enough?"

"No. I don't know what that means. I go to rehab, and you wait around for me to get out? What if you're not ready then? What if you meet someone else? So much can happen. We're either together or we're not, none of this half-and-half stuff."

"I want you to go to rehab. I want you to find yourself again, without any interference from me. But I'm not going anywhere. And I'm not dating anyone. You'll have your space, and I'll have mine. When it's right, we'll be together. We'll know when it's time."

She wanted to ask so many more questions, but they needed to get to Portia's office. They would have to finish the conversation after they got Jeremy's confession. "We have to meet them soon. I'm going. Please don't talk me out of it."

Jonathan nodded. "Okay. But don't do anything rash. I'm counting on you being my future."

Those words etched in her mind. He wanted her to be his future. Did it get more romantic than that? She decided he was right, and she would do this his way. Now she had to make sure the plan worked, so they had a future to work toward.

CHAPTER 32

They arrived at the office around noon. Michael brought two guns—one for him and one for Jonathan. They gathered around Jonathan's car to plan the last detail: how to get Jeremy to come to work on a Saturday.

Samantha stood next to the car, hands on her hips. "Amber and I should have a gun. We're the ones in danger."

"Absolutely not. You want to be the bait, fine. But you're not facing him with a gun. It's too easy for him to overpower you," Michael said.

Samantha sighed and shook her head. "You better have a good plan, then. He's mad we escaped. There's no telling what he might do."

Jonathan put his hand on her shoulder. "Remember what I said about doing something rash? Let's plan our every move. I need you to come out of this alive."

Samantha looked at him and smiled. She needed him to come out alive too. "Okay. But what's our plan? How do we coax him in the first place?"

"Portia's here. She can get him to come," Amber said.

"How can we convince her to do that?" Samantha asked.

"Tell her the truth about Jeremy. She'll help us when she knows he killed Elizabeth," Amber said.

Samantha bit her lip. "Cassie can talk to her."

"No. It needs to be from you. It will have greater impact if you tell her," Amber said.

Samantha closed her eyes, her legs shaking. "I can't do it. If I tell her about Lizzie, I'll explode. She has a part in this. She's the one who pushed Jeremy in the first place. I'm afraid of what else might come out."

Jonathan turned her toward him and met her gaze. "Maybe you need to let it all out. It's time you told her how you feel. Make her face what she did to you and Lizzie."

Samantha looked toward the ground. "I told you I was strong enough to face Jeremy, but I don't know if I'm strong enough to face Portia."

"You are stronger than you realize. Escaping Jeremy takes strength. Overcoming drug abuse takes strength. And being here with me, after all I put you through, takes strength. You can do this." Jonathan grabbed her hands. "And we'll stand behind you through it all. Remember what I said before—you don't have to carry this alone anymore."

She squeezed his hands and smiled. Being with him did take strength. Since she saw him at the diner, she resisted jumping into his arms.

"When he comes, where will he go? Does he have an office?" Cassie asked.

"Yes. His office is next to Portia's," Amber said.

"So, we corner him in his office," Michael said.

"Wait. What if Portia tips him off?" Samantha dropped Jonathan's hands and looked at Michael. "I don't trust her."

Michael crinkled his nose. "You think she would tip him off after learning what he did to you and your sister?"

Samantha closed her eyes and tilted her head skyward. "You don't know. I never told you." A tear started down her face.

"It's okay." Cassie put her arm around her and patted her back. "Portia neglected and abused Samantha since childhood. Mostly verbal abuse but she got physical as well."

Michael's face fell. "Why didn't you tell me? I knew you had a falling out, but I didn't know it was abuse."

"I didn't think it was abuse until one of Jonathan's sessions. And I didn't want to bother you with it. Honestly, I hoped it would go away."

Michael shook his head. "Did I make you think your problems were a bother? If I did, I'm sorry."

"It wasn't you. I didn't tell anyone, not even Lizzie. It took a group session to unveil the truth."

Michael put his arms around her. "If Samantha has to talk to Portia, we're all going with her. We'll make sure she doesn't tip off Jeremy," Michael said.

"What if she tries to help him?" Cassie asked.

"Simple. Lock her in her office." Michael grabbed the guns and handed one to Jonathan. "Have you ever shot before?"

"I'm no stranger to a shooting range, if that's what you're asking." Jonathan took the gun and secured it in the small of his back.

Samantha stared. She still didn't know so many things about him. She hoped they would have many years to learn about each other after today, but their relationship wasn't back on track yet.

"We need a better plan than cornering him in his office. He'll be armed, and he's not stable. We can't go in there, guns blazing. It's not wise," Amber said.

Samantha tapped her foot. "Amber and I will go in his office and talk to him. We'll get the confession. Cassie can watch Portia." She glanced at Michael and Jonathan. "You can hide outside his office and wait. If something looks wrong, then come in. Otherwise, we can handle this."

"I don't want you to be alone with him, but I think your plan makes sense." Jonathan glanced at Michael. "We do this together. If you move, I move. No vigilante garbage."

Michael nodded. "We're a team. Now let's get this party started."

Cassie, Amber, and Michael headed toward the office.

Jonathan tugged on Samantha's shoulder, turning her to face him. "I know we're still working out things, but I can't let you go in there without something."

Samantha stared, wondering what he meant. Her legs shook as she watched him take a small box from his car.

"This is a reminder. No matter what happens, no matter where life takes us, I want you to remember I love you, and I will always love you. Whenever you touch this, think of me waiting for you to return to me." He opened the box to reveal a heart-shaped silver locket with embroidered flowers.

Samantha sniffed back a tear. He gave her proof of his love. Whenever she doubted him, she could rub this through her fingers and remember. Why did he make her cry before she confronted her mother?

"Jonathan, I don't know what to say." Samantha shook as he placed the locket around her neck.

"Just promise me you'll be safe today. No rash decisions and no hero moves."

Samantha smiled. "Promise." She rubbed the locket between her thumb and forefinger, thankful for another chance with the man she loved. He was right; they were still working out things, but things looked better.

Hand in hand, they followed the others into the office, hoping they were prepared enough for whatever happened.

***

The group rode the elevator in silence to the top floor, exchanging uneasy glances. Samantha's stomach twisted, partly from Jonathan's unexpected gift and words and partly from her anticipated confrontation with Portia.

When they reached Portia's floor, Samantha closed her eyes and inhaled deeply. Cassie took Samantha's hand and squeezed. The two donned fake smiles and entered the reception area. Nora sat at the reception desk, unusual for a Saturday. Didn't Portia believe in time off?

Samantha stared, mustering her courage. Her hand went to Jonathan's locket. He believed she had the strength to confront Portia, even if she didn't believe it herself. She turned around and looked at her group of friends. They had supported her through everything, and they never left her. Even when she thought Jonathan had abandoned her, he returned when she needed him. With friends like that in her corner, she could face anything.

Jonathan came behind her and pulled her close. He encircled her waist and kissed her head. "You have tremendous strength in you. Believe in yourself, and confront your demons. You can do it."

Samantha put her hands on his and squeezed. She could do this. She turned around and hugged him. She swallowed and walked past the reception desk.

"Ms. Barrett. You don't have an appointment. Your mother's in a meeting."

Samantha brushed past Nora, ignoring her protestations. She focused on her end goal, her mother's office, not stopping until she stood in front of her door. She looked behind her and saw the others standing a few feet away. Cassie and Amber left the group and joined her, each clasping a hand. They stared into the office, gathering their courage to tell the story.

"Nora said she's in a meeting. Who would she have a meeting with on a Saturday?" Samantha asked.

"I don't know."

They peered through the floor-to-ceiling windows bookending the office door.

"Can you make out the person?" Amber asked.

"No. But we can't let this stop us. Stick to the plan."

They nodded at each other and opened the office door.

"Mother. You will sit and hear what we have to say." Samantha turned to the person sitting in front of Portia's desk. "I'm sorry, but this meeting is over."

"Isn't this a coincidence? I was telling your mother how worried I was about you. This saves us having to track you down."

Samantha froze. *Jeremy*. He had outwitted her again. Why was he here, and what nonsense did he tell Portia?

"Jeremy has shared some disturbing news, daughter. He says you're back on drugs. He saw you at a bar with some lowlife. Something about a bar fight? What's gotten into you?"

How did he know about the incident at Willy's? Had he been stalking her? Samantha glanced from Portia to Jeremy. He stood donning a wide grin, as if celebrating his victory.

"And I hear you've corrupted poor Amber as well." She grabbed Amber's hand. "It's okay, darling. You're safe from my daughter's machinations now." She turned toward Samantha. "You're a worthless piece of trash, and you'll always be a worthless piece of trash. I disown you."

Samantha pursed her lips. "So, you believe whatever Jeremy says without asking me about anything? You don't know him as well as you think."

Jeremy sat in the chair and folded his arms. "Is it story time? Do tell us what you think you know, Samantha." His gaze met Portia's. "Drug addicts are known for hallucinations. This should be interesting."

"It's not a hallucination. Amber can vouch for me." Samantha shot Amber an encouraging look, but she bit her lip and looked away. Great, she picked the worst time to give into her fears. Seeing Jeremy was a shock for both of them, but Samantha hoped Amber was strong enough to back her up.

"Jeremy killed Lizzie. Did you hear me, Mother? He killed her, not Cole. Amber was there, she knows. And he kidnapped me and attempted to rape me. Amber can vouch for that too. He's insane, Mother. There's no telling what he might do next."

Jeremy cackled. "A murderer, a kidnapper, *and* a rapist? That's quite a story. And where's your proof? You say Amber can back you up. What say you, sister? Is she telling the truth?"

Amber's face turned white. She wasn't ready to tell the truth in front of her brother. If only the others were here to talk sense to Portia. If she didn't believe her, Portia might listen to Jonathan.

As if on cue, the door opened, and Michael and Jonathan entered. Samantha breathed a sigh of relief, hoping they would bring sense to this interaction. At least Jonathan could remain calm enough to make Portia listen.

"Samantha, is everything okay?" Michael rushed to her side then looked toward Portia's desk. His eyes widened as he recognized Jeremy. He ran over and grabbed him by the collar, pulling him from the seat. "You pathetic little weasel. After what you did to Elizabeth and Samantha, you dare show your face here?"

Jonathan put his hand on Michael's shoulder. "Calm down. It's okay." He released Michael's grasp and patted Jeremy's shoulders. "Let me apologize for my friend. He reacts without knowing the whole story. I'm sure this is a misunderstanding. No one is low enough to murder their own fiancé, are they? Especially a fine, upstanding businessman like you."

Jeremy smiled. "I always thought highly of you, Doctor. I knew it wouldn't take long for you to see Samantha as the conniving bitch that she is. She'd say anything to frame me."

Jonathan pursed his lips and shook his head. "You had to say that, didn't you?" He grabbed him by the collar. "I've met plenty of scumbags in my work as a therapist, but you top them all. Hell's got a special place for what you did to your sister. And if I find out you placed a finger on my girlfriend when you held her captive, you'll wish you were dead."

"You believe everything that drug-addict bitch tells you, don't you? I thought you were smarter than that, Doctor."

Jonathan took a deep breath and looked toward the floor. Then he smashed his fist into Jeremy's nose, knocking him back on the chair. "Don't you ever talk like that about Samantha again."

He called her his girlfriend. And he punched out another guy for her. He had layers she hadn't uncovered yet, but she couldn't wait to explore every inch.

"Why do you always get to pummel the guys? She was my girlfriend first. I get to knock out the next one," Michael said.

Jonathan shot him a warning glance. "I'm hoping there won't be a next one."

Portia narrowed her eyes at Michael and Jonathan. "I expected this behavior from this degenerate but not from you, Doctor. You're obviously in an unethical relationship with my daughter, leaving you susceptible to her lies and manipulation. I'm sorry, but I have no choice but to report you to the psychiatry board."

She wouldn't. Yet she would if it'd hurt Samantha. She should be used to this behavior.

"Mother, you're the unethical one. You won't believe me about Jeremy. You're letting your daughter's killer get away, because you have something against me. You're believing a madman over your daughter, and you're willing to destroy Jonathan's reputation and career. For what? Because I failed you? I never understood your hatred for me. But now, I'm done. You want to disown me, fine. We're through."

Jonathan was right. Portia would never change. She didn't believe her about Lizzie's murder; she didn't believe Jeremy kidnapped and attempted to rape her. She thought she was a druggie bitch, just like Jeremy did. She couldn't recover from that.

Jonathan and Michael chimed in, arguing with Portia about her comment. With their attention elsewhere, Samantha left the room. She needed solitude to decide her next steps. Cassie and Amber would have to get the confession from Jeremy. She was too emotionally spent to deal with it.

She wandered into the hallway, tears streaking her face, when a hand covered her mouth and something cold pressed against her temple. Her body went rigid. It wasn't over.

CHAPTER 33

You pathetic whore. Thought you could escape and turn my sister against me? Nice try, but Portia will never take your word for it. As for your friends, well, it doesn't matter what they say. Logan won't turn against me, because that will implicate his involvement. So, I'm in the clear."

Samantha struggled against him, trying to dislodge his hand from her mouth. She scanned the hallway, hoping someone noticed Jeremy had left the office, but no one was around. As she struggled, her hand rubbed against the locket, reminding her of Jonathan. He told her that she had tremendous strength. She just had to harness it. She had escaped from Jeremy once; she could do it again.

"Don't think about biting my hand. Less harm will come to you if you cooperate." He pushed her into the elevator and hit the basement button. "No one will find us where we're going."

As the elevator door closed, she saw a figure standing by the reception desk. *Amber*. She saw Jeremy take her. Hopefully she knew where they were going and would tell the others.

"I see both of your boyfriends follow you around like puppy dogs. Did you think they could devise a plan to trap me? What were you trying to do, get a confession? As if I'm stupid enough to fall for that. No matter, your little plan won't work now."

He was trying to distract her, but he had a point. They thought their plan would work, but he had outwitted them. He used her mother against her, something she should have expected. She thought Jonathan's love was enough to protect her from her mother, but it wasn't. She needed something stronger. Something within herself, like Michael said, would help her deal. If she got out of this alive, she needed to talk to Michael and Cassie.

When they reached the basement, Jeremy pushed her to the warehouse floor. The cold concrete reminded her of younger days, when she spent time working in the warehouse. She used to know this place by heart. Escape should be easy.

"How did you get out of the office with four people guarding you?"

"Easy. Your doctor was so busy defending his reputation he didn't notice when I slipped out. Don't expect them anytime soon. Portia was a great help, threatening his career. It was genius."

Mother strikes again. Jonathan fell for her manipulation. Samantha doubted that Portia would report him, but it had created the perfect distraction for Jeremy's escape. Did Portia know the extent of Jeremy's madness?

He paced the aisles, looking for something. Samantha rubbed her hip and made note of the exits. She spent time during high school stocking shelves with new product for her mother. If she remembered correctly, there were two exits, one on either side. Jeremy was armed, so she had to carefully plan her escape, especially if Amber and the others figured out where Jeremy had taken her. She pulled herself to her feet and peered down the aisle. Jeremy focused his attention on a pile of twine and rope. He wanted to tie her up again. Was it a fetish or domination? Whatever it was, she wasn't returning to that situation.

As she tiptoed toward the opposite side of the warehouse, she heard a ruffling sound. Someone was here. She froze, trying to place the location. Did Jeremy hear it too? She glanced in his direction, but he was still focused on gathering supplies. A crash sounded from the aisle behind her. She scrunched her eyes, hoping to make out the culprit, but it was too dark to see anything. Before she could investigate, Jeremy returned with a nylon rope.

"Tying me up again? Not creative, are you?"

Jeremy's eyes narrowed. "Shut up. Do I have to gag you as well? I don't know how your boy-toys put up with your sass." He grabbed her hands and wrapped the rope around but stopped when a box crashed to the ground. "What was that? Did your harem follow you?" He dropped the rope and looked down the aisle.

Samantha picked it up and crept behind him. She threw it around his waist and pulled.

Jeremy stumbled but regained his footing. He reached for his gun and turned toward her. "Drop the rope, darling."

She stared as he cocked the gun. Without ammunition, she was in a precarious situation. She would have to tread lightly, if she wanted to escape unharmed.

Jeremy pulled her close and held the gun to her temple. "Don't be a hero. I'd hate to have blood stains on the concrete. They are so difficult to clean."

Samantha concentrated on the aisle in front of her. Someone was there. Could they help her escape, or did Jeremy have backup? She would have to stay sharp. When the person revealed themselves, she would have to make a quick decision.

Jeremy kept the gun at her head as he tried to tie the rope around her hands. She lifted her foot, poised to kick him when the elevator binged. Michael and Jonathan crept toward them, guns drawn.

"Samantha, no! Stay still. We got this." Michael's eyes locked onto Jeremy.

"What are you going to do, party boy? I can blow out her brains before a bullet will even hit me." Jeremy inched the gun closer. "Try it."

Jonathan looked from Michael to Jeremy and lowered his gun. "Stand down." He put his gun on the ground and raised his hands, palms front faced. "Let's talk. No guns, just a simple conversation."

"Are you crazy? He has her at gun point, and you want to talk?" Michael aimed his gun at Jeremy's chest. "I can take him out. One shot."

"Put down the gun. No vigilante moves, remember?" Jonathan met Michael's gaze. "Put down the gun."

Michael sighed. "If this doesn't work—"

Jonathan nodded. "What hurts? Something is bothering you. Lack of love from your parents? Bullied in school? Tell me about it."

He was trying to play the therapist. Samantha didn't think it would work, but she wasn't surprised he wanted to try,

Jeremy laughed. "Psychoanalyzing me, Doctor? Trying to figure out why I would do this? I hate to disappoint, but I don't have stories of abuse and neglect. Nice try, but I'm not interested in talking."

"Then what do you want? To go free? We can arrange that. Let Samantha go." Jonathan's gaze met hers. The usual look of calm was replaced with a look of fear.

"Not happening. She's mine, and I'm leaving with her. Thank you for making our escape easy." Jeremy yanked Samantha by the arm and backpedaled toward the exit.

The elevator binged again as Amber, Cassie, and Portia joined them. The three women raced toward the action, out of breath.

"Go back upstairs. It isn't safe," Michael said.

"We're not going anywhere," Cassie said.

Samantha's gaze caught Portia's. She stood to the side, eyes wide. For once, she was silent. Samantha wondered what she thought. Did she believe Jeremy was a threat now, or did she still think this was Samantha's fault?

Jeremy's grip tightened, shaking her from her thoughts. "It's nice to have an audience, but we're making our exit."

As Jeremy pulled Samantha toward the back of the warehouse, Amber surveyed the room. "Why are your guns on the floor? Giving up?"

"We're trying to have a conversation. Calm him down so he'll let her go," Michael said.

Amber shook her head. "We told you that he's insane. He won't listen to a conversation." She picked up a gun and approached her brother.

Michael and Jonathan moved to stop her, but Cassie held them back. "She knows him better than anyone. Trust her."

Samantha's mind raced. Jeremy had a gun pointed at her head. Jonathan and Michael had surrendered their guns, and Portia had come to the basement with Cassie. Now Amber wanted to confront Jeremy. Plus, with the strange sounds coming from the middle aisle, she didn't know what way to turn. She focused her attention in case she had a chance to escape his grasp.

Amber approached Jeremy, her hands shaking. "Let her go. She's not Elizabeth. She did nothing wrong."

"You turned against me, sister, after everything I did for you. Drop the gun before you get hurt."

"I'm not dropping it. And I'm not afraid of you. Let her go." Amber walked closer, the gun trained at his abdomen.

"If you're trying to kill me, you need to aim higher."

"Like this, brother?" She cocked the gun, raising it to his chest. "This has to end."

"Not wise, sister. You shoot me, she dies. Do you want another death on your hands?"

"Don't blame me for Elizabeth. That was all you."

"I know you're trying to get me to confess. But I can't when I'm innocent."

"I know the truth, and I'm not afraid to tell the police. You won't get away with it."

Jeremy raised the gun and pointed it at Amber. "Threaten me again, and you can meet your love, in Hell."

With the gun aimed in Amber's direction, Samantha turned and kicked him, laying him on the ground. Amber ran over and stepped on his stomach, pinning him. In the confusion, Michael grabbed the other gun and kneeled in the aisle, acting as backup.

She promised Jonathan no hero moves, yet here was a younger girl, still reeling from abuse and grief, stepping up and saving her. She stumbled toward Jonathan, not wanting to take her focus off the confrontation. He wrapped his arms around her and kissed her head. Neither spoke but focused their attention on Amber and Jeremy.

"I could be upset about what you did to me the past ten years. How you molested me and brainwashed me into thinking it was love. How you turned Mom and Dad against me, convincing them I was mentally challenged and needed your guardianship to survive. How you refused to let me have my own thoughts and desires. I could be mad at that." She inched her foot to his chest. "But that's nothing compared to what you did to Elizabeth. Are you too much of a coward to admit what you did?"

"Trying to get a confession out of me, sister? Won't work."

Amber moved her foot, so it rested on his throat. "You do what you want and call it love. It's not love. You destroyed me. My entire life, I did everything to please you so you wouldn't leave me. I was afraid to be alone, because I didn't know how to survive without you. But no longer. Elizabeth taught me love, and Samantha taught me strength. I'm not afraid anymore. If I must, I will shoot.

It will be a relief, giving you the same ending you gave Elizabeth."

Jeremy pushed her foot and toppled her to the ground. "Strength? You're weak. It was easy to manipulate you. Tell you that you're pretty a few times and you fell right into my hands. You would do anything to believe someone loved you." He leapt to the floor and pointed his gun at Amber. "As for Elizabeth, she was a conniving bitch too. She made you think she loved you, but she didn't. I did you a favor, taking her out. It saved you from the disappointment when you discovered the truth."

"Liar. I know the truth, and your manipulation won't work again. In fact, you gave me what I wanted. Was that a confession, dear brother?"

Jeremy's face reddened. He lunged for Amber; a loud bang resounded and a force pushed him backward onto the concrete. Blood filled the floor around him as he lay motionless.

Jonathan grabbed his wrist, checking his pulse. "He's dead." He looked at Michael, still aiming his gun. "I told you to stand down."

"It wasn't me. The shot came from the opposite direction." Michael lowered his gun and joined Jonathan.

Samantha watched as they exchanged words. It wasn't in the plan for Jeremy to die, but nothing went the way she hoped.

If Michael hadn't shot him, who had? She glanced down the middle aisle as a shadowy figure ran toward the side exit. As the door opened, the sunlight shone on an object sparkling in the dark. She glanced around. Amber stooped over Jeremy, eyes wide and body rigid. Cassie knelt beside her, placing her arm around Amber. Jonathan and Michael argued about who had fired the shot. In the back of the warehouse, Portia stood motionless. Samantha wanted to talk and see if Portia believed her about Jeremy now. But curiosity won out.

Samantha tiptoed toward the shining object—the only clue they had to identify the mystery shooter. Her eyes grew round when she picked up a detective badge—not any detective badge but Detective Logan's badge. What was he doing here? Was he afraid Jeremy would talk, so he killed him to protect himself? Samantha looked around then pocketed it. Logan wanted to frame Cole for murder. Why, she wasn't sure. But this badge and her knowledge of today could come in handy if he tried again.

"You okay?" Cassie stood in front of her, arms crossed.

"Yeah, I think so." Samantha glanced at Jonathan and Michael still arguing over the gunshot. "What should we do now?"

"Call the police. We'll have to give statements. We can't brush this over."

Samantha nodded and bit her lip. "Is Amber okay?"

"She will be. We're not abandoning her."

"Good. Lizzie would want us to take care of her."

Cassie nodded. "Portia's still here. Want to talk to her? She might be willing to listen now."

Samantha lowered her head. "I don't think so." She walked toward the elevator and curled up against the wall. She wasn't sure she could take anymore drama, especially from Portia. All she wanted was to curl up with Jonathan, safe in his arms. Without him, she felt exposed. How could she deal with it when he left again? A tear fell down her cheek.

As she shook, a hand touched her shoulder. "Mind if I sit, or am I not welcome?" Portia stooped next to her.

Samantha shook her head. "I'd rather you didn't, but I can't stop you."

Portia sighed and sat next to her. "Do you expect me to apologize? It looks like you were right about Jeremy."

"Of course, I was right, Mother. And can you apologize? I'm not sure you're capable."

"I don't know why you're so difficult. Ever since your dad died, I couldn't control you. You're a lot like him, you know."

Samantha chortled. "I wouldn't be so difficult, if you listened to me. You never cared what I thought or what I felt. Lizzie got all the attention. But now I realize she was playing a game. She did what you wanted, but she had secrets. Things I didn't know until recently."

"Elizabeth never kept secrets from me." Portia crossed her arms and looked away.

"Yes, she did, Mother. She wasn't in love with Jeremy. There was someone else. That's why Jeremy killed her."

"Nonsense. This is why we never got along. Such a vivid imagination."

"It's not nonsense. Ask Amber. They were in love, Mother. That's why she wanted to marry Jeremy. She was in love with Amber, but she was too scared to tell us."

Portia stared. "What are you trying to tell me? Are you trying to lay the blame at my doorstep?"

Samantha stood and faced her. "You have a part in it. If you had listened to me, if you had listened to

Lizzie, none of this would have happened. You only saw what you wanted. Jeremy was unhinged, yet you pushed marriage, because you thought you knew better. You didn't. That's on you. I hope you can live with yourself." Samantha turned to walk away.

Portia stood and placed her hands on her hips. "We're not done talking, daughter."

Samantha spun around. "We are done. Permanently. I thought I needed your approval, but I don't. The only person I need to rely on is myself. And it's about time I figure out how to do that. Goodbye, Mother. I hope you rot in your loneliness."

***

Samantha was exhausted after a long afternoon of questioning. Thankfully, Logan wasn't among the detectives sent to cover the case. She kept his badge a secret. The last time she shared evidence with the police, they indicted an innocent man. She wasn't ready to make the same mistake just in case she was wrong. And just in case she was right. If Logan decided to strike again, she wanted something to hold over his head.

After everyone had a chance to tell their stories, the detectives left with no word on Cole's release. She hoped it would be automatic, but it would take some time for the prosecution to drop the charges. In the meantime, Amber faced possible charges of her own. Jonathan promised to counsel her and testify on her behalf, if it came to it, and Cassie offered a free place to stay, for Lizzie's sake and for Amber's.

When they arrived at Cassie's, the five friends collapsed in the living room, worn out from the day's activities. Amber plopped in the armchair; Michael and Cassie laid on the couch, while Jonathan sat on the chair by the front door.

"Come sit with me." Jonathan tapped his lap.

Samantha gulped. She wanted to be with him, wrap her arms around him and never let go. But she knew better. They weren't together and wouldn't be anytime soon. Not until she learned to stand on her own.

"I can't. If I do, I won't be able to let you go."

Jonathan walked over and grabbed her hand. "Let's go out back and get some fresh air."

Samantha glanced at Cassie. She nodded in approval and shooed her away. "Okay. I guess we can do that."

They walked out the back door and sat on the porch swing. "How are you feeling? Any thoughts of Jeremy or your mother plaguing you?"

"Can you for once be my boyfriend and not my therapist? I don't want to talk about my feelings, and I don't want to relive the past forty-eight hours."

Jonathan took a breath. "I'll work on that while we're apart. Think Michael can give me lessons?"

Samantha laughed. "You don't want that. He's a great friend, but he wasn't the best boyfriend."

Jonathan turned and brushed back her hair. "So, rehab? Is that what you've decided?"

Samantha smiled. "Yes. Cassie is registering me at the same clinic Michael is attending. Six months feels like a lifetime."

"It's for the best. They can help you in ways I can't. I'll be here waiting when you get home."

Samantha approached the center of the yard. "I want you to wait, but I won't be ready when I get home. I thought about everything you said. I need to stand by myself. Once I have a direction and a future of my own, then, if you'll still have me, we can try again."

Jonathan joined her in the yard and raised her face to his. "Whatever it takes to get you back. I'm not in a rush. There will never be anyone but you, even if it takes years. I love you, Samantha Jane Barrett, forever."

He leaned down and raised her lips to his. The kiss was slow and tender, as if it was their last. She wound her arms around his back and held him tight. This embrace would have to last. It could be more than a year until she experienced his touch again.

She needed the memory of this kiss to get her through the hard months of rehab. Facing her demons and recounting her memories of Portia and Lizzie would be difficult, but, if it meant she could come back to him, fully healed, she would endure anything rehab threw at her.

Jonathan ended the kiss and pulled her close. She rested her head on his chest, beholding his smell. Lizzie would be proud. She was ready to find peace, for herself and Jonathan.

Chapter 34

Samantha adjusted the canvas painting, making it uniform with the others on the gallery wall. "This is your best work yet. How did you capture the faraway look on her face? It's a masterpiece. Amber will love it."

Gus smiled. "I hope so. She's a special person. I'm glad I had the chance to know her. Is she coming tonight?"

"Cassie and Michael are bringing her. She's come so far this past year. And we have you to thank. She came out of her shell during your painting sessions."

"Dr. Green deserves thanks too."

Samantha closed her eyes and nodded. Amber saw Jonathan twice a week for individual counseling sessions, and it was helping. Her confidence was growing, and she was learning to stand up for herself. Samantha wished she could tag along to get a glimpse of Jonathan, but they promised to stay away until they were both ready.

"Do you talk to Dr. Green? I mean, since Dr. Boyd has taken over our group, do you ever meet up with him? Talk about old times?" Samantha asked.

"You want to know if he asks about you."

She blushed. "Does he? I haven't seen or spoken to him in a year, right before I went to rehab. You don't have to tell me." Samantha walked to the opposite side of the gallery, perusing her contribution to the night's event. She'd grown over the past year. Her issues with Portia were managed. They weren't on speaking terms, but it was for the best. She had opened her photography studio, and business was booming. It gave her a chance to explore her dream taking candid pictures of Bracken Points residents. And it allowed her to pay back Cassie everything she had stolen and more. Life had a calm normalcy now, but one thing was missing.

Gus put his hand on her shoulder. "When I found out about you and Dr. Green, I was convinced it was a mistake. It wasn't real. But I've learned something this past year."

Samantha turned and bit her lip. "You were right about a lot of things. Our relationship wasn't healthy."

"Yes, but that doesn't mean you weren't in love. That you aren't still in love. I see it on your face whenever you battle the desire to ask about him. And I see it on his too. He does ask about you. In fact, that's the first thing he does whenever I see him. You love each other, and I think it's time you did something about it."

"When we're ready. That was the stipulation."

Gus motioned around the room. "I think you're ready. You've been clean for a year. Your photography business is growing, and we have a gallery show together. What else are you waiting for?"

Samantha fumbled with her bracelet. What else *was* she waiting for? A sign from Jonathan? They never discussed how they would decide to try again. "I'll think about it. Right now, we need to concentrate on tonight."

Cassie burst in the room, a package in hand. Amber and two other girls followed, eyes bright as they beheld the room.

"Sorry it took so long. Bex and Madeline couldn't agree on their outfits. Were we like this at twenty?"

Samantha laughed. Cassie's sister Bex and Michael's sister Madeline became fast friends the past few months. Amber tagged along, but she was much wiser and less impulsive. They made an entertaining threesome.

"Are these your photographs, Sam?" Madeline asked.

"Look at this one. Amber, isn't this your therapist? I wouldn't expect him to end up in a gallery show."

"Bex!" Cassie narrowed her eyes. "Be nice."

"What? I'm sure he's a nice guy, but he's not Michael."

Cassie shook her head. "I'm sorry. She has a crush on Michael."

Samantha giggled. "It's cute. And I don't blame her. I had a crush on Michael before."

"Yes, but that doesn't excuse what she said. Why did you include that picture anyway?"

Samantha sighed. "I don't know. When I looked through my photographs, I couldn't leave it out. If he can't be with me tonight, at least I can look at his picture and imagine him here."

"I don't know why you're still apart. Call him."

"I want to, but I don't know if he's ready. I guess I'm scared too much time passed and he isn't interested anymore."

"Stop talking crazy. Oh, that reminds me. This package came for you." Cassie set the box on a table in the middle of the room. "Bex! Don't touch the paintings." Cassie turned toward Samantha. "That sister of mine. Excuse me."

Samantha ran her fingers over the box. She wasn't expecting a package. Was it a congratulatory gift from one of her clients? She removed the tape and opened the lid. Her eyes widened as she lifted the contents from the box—the Nikon Jonathan had given her last year. She choked back a tear as she twirled it in her hands.

Returning this to Jonathan tortured her. And now she had it again. Was this his way of saying he was proud?

"There's more."

Samantha looked up and froze. *Jonathan.* He was here. Her eyes welled as she beheld him. He was dressed for the occasion and looked dapper in a black and white tux. A wisp of hair fell in front of his eye, adding to his charm. Despite being apart for a year, he stood stoic, controlling any passion he might feel. He hadn't changed. He was still Jonathan with the dancing brown eyes, and he still held her heart.

"Look in the bottom. I think you'll like it."

She put the camera on the table and reached into the box, her hands shaking. "*Emma?* You remembered."

"It's a first edition. It took me a while to find one I liked."

She opened it and read the note.

> *Samantha,*
> > *If I loved you less, I would talk more.*
> > *Mr. Knightley, Emma*
> > *I would love to be your plus one if you*
> *would have me.*
> *Jonathan*

She sniffed back a tear and nodded. Everything she experienced the past year led to this moment. The months in rehab, counseling sessions, confronting her ghosts, and defeating her demons—they all led back to Jonathan. He still loved her. "I wouldn't want anyone else."

He crossed the room and took her in his arms. She nestled her head in his chest and wrapped her arms around his waist. This is what she had longed for during the past twelve months.

"You're here. It's not a dream. You're really here."

Jonathan stroked her hair. "Tonight is important, and I didn't want to miss it. Besides, I couldn't stay away any longer."

Samantha met his gaze. "You won't disappear again, will you?"

Jonathan smiled. "No. Never again." He leaned down and took her mouth in his.

"Amber, is that your therapist with Samantha?" Bex stared at the couple, wide-eyed.

Cassie elbowed her in the ribs. "Shut up."

"What? Are you sure Samantha dumped Michael for him? Sorry, but I don't see it."

Cassie grabbed her sister's elbow and drug her toward the entrance.

"It seems we have an audience." Jonathan drew her close and smiled.

"Can we skip tonight and go back to your place?"

"And miss your gallery debut? We're staying, but I have something special planned for later."

She couldn't wrap her head around her new reality. He returned when she had least expected it. While she wanted to be alone with him, she feared disappointing him. She wasn't the same person. Rehab and her counseling with Dr. Boyd had changed her, made her stronger. What if she had changed too much?

The evening passed in a blur. Jonathan stayed by her side through the press interviews, the line of well-wishers, and interested buyers. The crowd grew larger than expected, and she ended the night with more clients than she had time. Gus had similar results and stood beaming at the picture of Amber. Although he had multiple offers, he gave it to Amber instead.

When the last guest left, Jonathan gathered her things. "Ready?"

She regarded the gallery and shuffled her feet. "I should stay and help Gus."

"He has plenty of help."

Amber, Bex, and Madeline surrounded Gus. The three girls proved a handful for most, but Gus handled them well. They busied themselves, taking down the photographs and paintings and wrapping them for storage.

"Back to your place?"

Jonathan nodded. "If that's okay. I hoped we could make up for lost time."

She'd imagined this moment the past year. Being alone with him, rediscovering their passion, ignited a fire within. But something deterred her. He'd showed up with no warning, no time to prepare herself or process her emotions. She wanted to connect, to feel his warmth against her, but she couldn't let herself relax. Too much was at stake.

Her brow beaded with sweat, and her knees shook. She steeled herself and took his hand. Nervous or not, she had to find out where this would lead.

They rode in silence, exchanging glances but afraid to speak. Jonathan grabbed her hand. She closed her eyes and smiled. His warmth poured through her, filling every heartbreak, every missing piece. She had to get this right. Losing him again was not an option.

When they arrived at his apartment, he rushed to open her door. "Let me be chivalrous for one night." He offered his hand and helped her from the car.

She allowed him to lead her up the stairs to his apartment. Memories of their magical night filled her head. Could they rekindle that passion or was a year too long?

He opened the door and stood back, letting her enter first. The living room glowed with candlelight. Red rose petals covered the floor, leading from the living room to the bedroom. Champagne glasses sat on the coffee table, chilled and waiting.

"You planned this. Cassie, Gus, Michael—they were in on it, weren't they?"

Jonathan smiled sheepishly. "Guilty. They helped me set this up. Well, Cassie did. She snuck out of the gallery before we left. Pretty good, isn't she?"

"It's gorgeous. Everything is perfect." She sat on the couch, bouncing her knee.

"It might sound creepy, but I've kept tabs on you. Even though we were apart, I knew everything. Cassie, Michael, and Gus were informative."

"Amber too? I wanted to tag along to her counseling sessions. It was so hard. Everyone else in my life could see you but me."

"Staying away was hard for me too. But knowing you were clean, dealing with your demons in a positive way and making a career of photography was enough to let you be. Tonight was your dream, and you shined. I wanted to be a part of that. I'm glad you let me."

Samantha bit her lip and looked away. Two dreams came true tonight, but she was still unsure about this one.

"I'm glad too. Although it was a shock."

"A good shock, I hope." He moved closer, their heads almost touching.

She took a deep breath as his hand caressed her cheek. He took her chin and raised her lips to his. The kiss was soft at first but grew demanding, his stored-up passion releasing. As he pushed her onto the couch, she froze then nudged him away.

"I'm sorry." She looked at the ceiling, trying to decipher her emotions.

"It's okay. We can take it slow, if you want. I've waited for this night. I want everything to go smoothly. Tell me what you need."

"I don't know what I need. So much time has passed. People change. Circumstances change. I'm not the person you fell in love with."

"I disagree. I fell in love with your passion, your care for others, and your amazing spirit. That hasn't changed. If you think you're a different person, I will get to know the new you, but the woman I fell in love with is still there."

"You say that, but how can I believe?" She shook her head. "I don't know what's wrong with me. I've dreamed of this. But I'm scared. What if we're fooling ourselves? Can we pick up from where we were a year ago? I can't lose you again."

"Is that all it is? I was afraid you didn't want me."

"Not want *you*? Jonathan, if you don't take me in your arms right now, I'm going to lose it. I want you more than anything."

He slid next to her and took her mouth in his. As they kissed, tears of joy dotted her cheeks. Jonathan with the dancing brown eyes was hers, and nothing would break them apart again.

EPILOGUE

Samantha slid into the passenger seat beside Jonathan. "Where are we going?"

"It's a surprise for the birthday girl."

"Is it Yancy's? Steak and mushrooms would be amazing right now."

"It's not food." Jonathan shook his head. "Is that all you think about anymore?"

Samantha patted her stomach. "Well, I believe you contributed to that problem, Doctor."

Jonathan laughed. "I hope you enjoy this as much as food. I promise we'll go out to eat later."

They pulled into the cemetery and parked. Samantha's eyes teared. "We're going to see Lizzie?"

"I thought you should spend part of your birthday together."

Samantha closed the car door and pulled her jacket around her growing belly. The autumn air swirled around her as leaves blew off the trees. The last birthday she had spent with Lizzie was four years ago, six months before she was murdered.

"We should have brought flowers. She loved yellow roses."

They neared her gravesite, hand in hand. "Already done. I have another surprise for you too."

Yellow roses covered Lizzie's grave. Jonathan spared no expense. But something looked different.

"Did you get a new headstone?"

Jonathan grinned. "Read it."

Elizabeth Barrett
Beloved sister of Samantha Barrett-Green

Samantha tried to restrain the tears but failed. "Thank you." She wrapped her arms around him and squeezed.

"Talk to her. I'll wait by the tree."

Samantha sniffed back a tear. She closed her eyes and looked toward the sky. *Lizzie. I did it. I found peace. And I'm not letting go.*

She stood for a moment, honoring her sister's memory. Her hand rested on her stomach as she thought of the children she was bringing into the world. She hoped they would be closer than sisters, like she used to be with Lizzie. And she would make sure they never lost their connection.

Jonathan put his arms around her shoulders. "Ready for food? You're eating for three, so I know you're hungry."

Samantha nodded. She had chased peace and found it within herself and again with Jonathan. Life couldn't get any better.

WANTING PEACE
COMING FEBRUARY 2020

CHAPTER 1

The world needed a fixer and Cassie Roberts was up to the job. There wasn't an addiction she couldn't cure, a mental health problem she couldn't counsel or a disease she couldn't beat. Until her mom got sick. That brought her to her knees, not that she wanted to admit it. She was used to talking her way out of situations or talking people into getting help. But no amount of help could cure stage four lung cancer.

She steeled herself as she pulled into the hospice in downtown Kingston. Since Gina Roberts was admitted a week ago, she spent a portion of every day at her bedside. Her diagnosis was sudden, and her health deteriorated faster than she hoped. Gina's time was limited, but Cassie hadn't come to terms with the reality.

The building sat back from the road, the small parking lot full of visitors and employees' vehicles. In her short time visiting, the staff knew her well and allowed her entrance without checking in at the desk. They knew Gina's prognosis and Cassie's reluctance to accept fact. Stopping her at the desk was an extra step they were willing to forgo.

Cassie breezed into her mother's solo room and stopped in the doorway. Two chairs stood by the bed; a small couch sat against the far wall. The room filled with natural light from the corner windows. Cassie fought back tears and composed herself. Gina's frail form took little space in the bed. Her once flowing red hair was replaced with a black and white headwrap. The cancer ate away at her, leaving sunken cheeks and an emaciated body. It was hard not to admit reality, but Cassie refused to let the cancer win.

"Where is Bex? She was supposed to meet me here." Cassie glanced at her watch. Her sister, Bex, was twenty years old and unreliable. While she wasn't surprised by her absence, she hoped their mother's poor health would prompt her to change. "I don't like the idea of her living in your house by herself. Until you come home, I think she should move in with me."

Gina attempted to sit, but her coughing set her back on the bed. "She's an adult. I can't make her do anything. Besides, what makes you think I'm going home? This is hospice, in case you haven't noticed. Most people don't have a long trajectory when they end up here."

Cassie grabbed her hand and smiled. "Don't say that mom. Positive thinking, remember?" Cassie wasn't used to this side of life. She was used to fixing problems, but she didn't know how to fix her mother. Instead, she stood by watching her deteriorate into a lesser version of herself. And she did it alone since her sister rarely appeared.

Gina patted Cassie's hand and smiled. "You were always a good daughter. The responsible one, but not so compassionate. In your line of work, I would expect more understanding."

"I understand where it is necessary, but nothing explains her actions." Cassie squeezed her mother's hand. "She needs to be here. You need her to be here."

Gina coughed and tried to catch her breath. Her words were slow and labored. "I'm fine. Bex will come when she's ready. She reminds me of your father. Impulsive and headstrong, but underneath she's nursing a wounded heart. You should know the signs."

Cassie shook her head. Her father was an unwelcome topic of conversation. He left them when she was ten and Bex was four. "Do we have to bring up father? I haven't seen him in sixteen years, and I'd like to keep it that way."

"Someday you will have to forgive. I have. He let his weakness take over, but he still loves you. And he's still your father." Gina closed her eyes and rested her head on the pillow.

Cassie spent sixteen years without a father, she didn't see the need for one now. Peter Roberts didn't see a need for a family, so she figured the feeling was mutual. He chose gambling over his wife and daughters. Cassie wasn't even sure he was alive.

"How do you know he loves me? He hasn't called or written in sixteen years. That's abandonment, not love."

Gina covered her mouth and coughed. Her body shook as she tried to speak. "He's afraid to talk to you. The big deal therapist scares him."

She scared her father. That didn't seem right. If he wanted to see her, why did he wait until she was an adult to try? He missed everything. Her first date, her first car, high school and college graduation, why was he interested now?

Cassie put her hands on her mother's shoulders and looked in her eyes. "I hear you and I'll think about it. Right now, you need rest. I'll visit you soon." She kissed the top of her head and walked toward the door. "If Bex comes by, tell her I'm looking for her."

Gina closed her eyes and clasped her hands on her stomach. She reminded Cassie of an angel. No matter what happened, her mother was her hero and the reason she was building a successful career. She stepped up when her father left and fought for her daughters education and wellbeing. Her greatest fear was letting her mother down. Cassie swallowed hard and walked out the door. She had a busy day ahead, and she would need the distraction.

Kingston was an hour from Bracken Point, the small town she called home. The drive gave her time to contemplate her mother's claims. Her father loved her but was too scared to connect. How did she know? Did she keep in touch with him? If she did, why wasn't she aware? She didn't like secrets. As she drove, she mentally compiled a list of questions for tomorrow.

An hour later, she pulled up to the small house she shared with Amber Martin and Samantha. Amber moved in when Samantha went to rehab six months ago. Soon, all three would share the house. Cassie beamed imagining the reunion. It was too long since she had a night of girl talk. In the meantime, she had an office to set up and a patient load to schedule.

She opened the front door and walked straight to her office. As she sat at her desk, her eyes fell on her psychiatry certificate. After years of study and multiple internships, she passed her boards and received her psychiatry license. The extra months learning from Dr. Boyd were useful, but she was anxious to work with Jonathan again. His style suited her own, optimistic, caring but realistic. But he wasn't expected back at the Bracken Point Clinic anytime soon.

As she put the framed certificate in her bag, a squeal came from the living room. It had to be Amber. What was she so excited about? Cassie rushed in curious about the commotion.

"Amber, is everything okay?" She entered the room and froze. Her smile grew wide as she took in the sight. "Samantha! I didn't know you were coming home today. Weren't we supposed to pick you up on Friday?" Cassie ran to embrace her friend. It was a long six months with only letters between them. There was so much to talk about, and she couldn't wait to share the latest news.

"Gus brought us home. He said you were busy getting your patient load set up. We didn't want to disturb you." Samantha squeezed her, then stepped aside.

"We?" Cassie looked behind Samantha and caught her breath. Michael. Six months were good on him. His white T-shirt clung to him, showing off his abs and biceps. She had to admit he was nice to look at, if only the rest of him matched. Michael was a party boy before he went to rehab. Cassie tolerated him, even started to care for him like a brother, but it ended there. He wasn't the settling down type, and six months of rehab wasn't enough to change him.

"Hi, Cassie. Hope you don't mind if I hang out for a while." Michael gave her a sheepish grin, accentuating his dimples.

"Of course. Make yourself at home." She looked toward the ground, trying to regain her senses. His dimples did something to her. That and his boyish charm cut to her core.

Amber grabbed Samantha's hand and led her to the living room. "Tell me everything. Did you have a nice doctor? Were the other residents nice? How was the food? I hear it's disgusting. There's so much to talk about."

Amber droned on, pulling Samantha onto the couch. Cassie and Michael stood in the entryway, neither making eye contact. Michael put his backpack down and stepped toward her. She gulped as he leaned close and wrapped his arms around her.

"I missed you. That sounds crazy, but it's true. There's only so much to do at rehab, and I spent a lot of time thinking of you."

He thought of her. The revelation made her stomach twist and heart sing. If only it meant something beyond friendship. "I thought of you too. I'm glad you're home."

He grabbed her hand and led her to the living room. "Still yellow? I was sure you'd paint it while we were away."

"That's my first task. I hate to get rid of Lizzie's design, but this room is disastrous," Samantha said.

"That can wait. We need to catch up. Tell us about rehab. How are you doing?" Cassie said.

Samantha rolled her eyes. "Rehab wasn't that interesting. It helped, don't get me wrong, but I need to catch up on real life." She took Amber's hand. "How are you? Cassie treating you well?"

Amber glanced at Cassie and laughed. "Yes. She's amazing. I'm in counseling twice a week and it's helping. Dr. Green is wonderful, so caring and patient. He says I'm making great progress."

Samantha's face fell. "I'm glad."

"Oh no. I shouldn't have mentioned him. Please forgive me?" Amber's eyes pleaded.

Cassie put her arms around Samantha and squeezed. "Do you want me to tell him you're home? I'm sure he wants to see you."

"No. We promised to stay apart until we're both ready. It's too soon." Samantha grabbed Amber's hands and gazed into her eyes. "And you're okay. Don't tiptoe around your life because of me. I can handle it. Jonathan is a part of your life, of everyone's life. It's a fact I will learn to deal with."

Amber wrapped her arms around her. "I'm so glad you're home."

"Me too." Samantha gazed at Cassie and Michael. They stood awkwardly in the middle of the living room, exchanging furtive glances.

"Amber, let's go paint shopping, I could use the distraction," Samantha said.

Amber's face brightened. "Can we? And get new furniture? A whole new look, so exciting."

Cassie shook her head. "You just got home. If you must go, don't stay out late."

Samantha and Amber locked arms and headed out the door, leaving Cassie alone with Michael. She tapped her fingers on her thigh, wondering how to fill the time. Before rehab, their relationship was easy. They built it around a love for movies and Samantha. Everything was different now. Samantha was sober and seemed content. And Michael. Had he changed?

"Rehab was the best decision I made, and I have you to thank. You're an excellent therapist. I wouldn't have made it through the first weeks without cocaine if you weren't beside me." Michael moved to the couch.

"Circumstances brought us together, nothing more. I'm glad you're sober. What are your plans now?"

"Haven't gotten that far. I need to see what shape my house is in, visit Cole, then make some decisions."

"Visit Cole? That's stupid. Aren't you worried about a relapse?"

Michael clasped his hands. "Cole is still my friend. I need to make sure he's okay. Logan is still out there, trying to pin any charge he can. If I can help him, I will."

Logan was a dirty cop. Last April he covered up Jeremy's role in Elizabeth's death, framing Cole. Beyond Amber's testimony, there was no evidence to convict him, so Michael and Cole had to tread lightly. Cassie didn't know why he was fixated on them, but she understood Michael's caution.

"You cut off your family because they were toxic. Shouldn't you do the same to Cole? He's not going to change."

Michael averted his eyes and crossed his arms. "My family is different. There are reasons we don't talk. Cole has his issues, but he's never let me down. He was there when I had no place to go. I owe him."

"You owe yourself the chance to stay clean. Going to his place is asking for trouble. Some people deserve to be cut out of our lives." Cassie sat down next to him on the couch. "Put your sobriety first."

"I'd expect a therapist to encourage mending relationships, not severing them. Is Cole any different than Samantha, or me? You didn't give up on us, why should I give up on him?"

Because she loved them. The realization threw her, but it was true. She loved Samantha like a sister. And Michael, that was a different story. Whenever he smiled, she melted. Cassie didn't intend for this to happen. In fact, she fought her attraction from the moment they met. Getting involved with an addict wasn't wise, but the more they hung out, the greater her feelings. She shook her head. He didn't need to know. She was a mousy psychiatrist, no match for his model good looks.

"If you want to be an idiot, go ahead. As your therapist, and friend, I advise against it." She stood up and walked toward the kitchen. Why was he insisting on ruining everything? If he went to Cole's, his old life would swallow him. Where would that leave her? And why was she concerned anyway? They had no ties to each other, except counseling. The more she thought about it, the counseling shouldn't continue. He needed to find someone objective.

Michael stood and followed her to the kitchen and sat down at the island. "I wanted to talk to you about the counseling thing." He grabbed a cookie and plopped it in his mouth. "I'm going with Samantha to Dr. Boyd's groups sessions. It's for the best, you know, avoid one of those conflict of interest things."

Cassie scrunched her nose. What was he talking about? "How do you figure it's a conflict of interest?"

Michael blushed. "Well, before rehab I thought we were, you know."

She didn't know. They were becoming friends, but nothing else happened. Did he want something else? Between her mother, Bex and the conversation about her father, she couldn't deal with this now.

"It's fine. Dr. Boyd is a great doctor." She grabbed a thermos of coffee and walked toward her office. Whatever Michael thought they had would have to wait. She grabbed her bag and headed toward the front door.

"I'm sorry, but I have to get to the clinic. Samantha should be home soon." She turned toward the door but stopped. "Michael, I'm glad you're home."

She shut the door, then closed her eyes and leaned against it. She wanted Michael, but she didn't have the energy to try. Why couldn't things go her way for once?

CHAPTER 2

assie drove to the clinic. Today was important. She had her own office and a new patient case load to schedule. No more relying on mentors—she could forge her own path. She pushed thoughts of her mother and Michael aside and concentrated on the task ahead. They would have to wait until she was settled in her new position.

The clinic parking lot was empty for a Wednesday afternoon. Cassie paused as she parked next to a green Nissan Sentra. What was Jonathan doing here? After his relationship with Samantha was discovered six months ago, he was reassigned to a clinic in Kingston. She didn't expect him at the Bracken Point clinic until Dr. Boyd cleared his return. And with Samantha back from rehab, it was wise to leave that separation in place.

She grabbed her bag and went into the building. Her new office was next door to the one she once shared with Jonathan, and recently shared with Dr. Boyd. She peeked inside her old office before she continued to her new space.

"Jonathan? I thought that was your car in the parking lot. What are you doing here? Transferring back?"

Jonathan looked up and flashed her a wide smile. "Not yet. I'm here to see you. Lee told me you passed your boards. I wanted to congratulate you in person."

Cassie smiled. Jonathan was always kind and polite. Two reasons why Samantha fell in love with him. "Thank you. I'm setting up my office and getting my schedule in order. Care to help? I could use your tips."

"Gladly." He grabbed his coffee cup and followed her next door.

"It's strange having a space to myself. I'm used to cleaning up your messes or tripping over Dr. Boyd's piles of books." She unpacked her bag, carefully removing her framed certificate.

Jonathan reached and grabbed it. "Let me hang this. Sit. Tell me the latest news."

Cassie smirked. "News about what? Samantha?"

"Is there news about Samantha?" He turned toward Cassie; his eyes round.

"Well, she came home today. Gus dropped them off before I left."

"Them? Michael is with her?" Jonathan put the frame on her desk and sat.

"Yes. Does that bother you? They're just friends." Cassie situated herself on the couch and stared at Jonathan. "Do you think rehab changed something between them?"

He shook his head. "No. I just know their history. Sometimes people lean on the closest person when they're down. I'm sure it's nothing."

It was nothing. Michael wasn't interested in Samantha. She closed her eyes and thought about his words earlier. He thought about her in rehab. Not only that, he thought something was going on between them before he left. She didn't give him a chance to explain himself and she wasn't sure she was ready to listen. Whatever Michael thought, he didn't believe in love, marriage and kids like she did. What was the point? Even if she gave into her feelings, he wasn't prepared to give her what she wanted, what she needed. So why give it headspace?

"Samantha still loves you. That's all I can say for now. You have to trust that she will find her way back to you."

Jonathan grabbed the frame and turned to hang it on the wall. "You're right. Knowing she's back hit me. I want to rush over to your place and see her, but I know it's not right." He stood back and straightened the frame.

"You will know. True love always finds a way, except in my case."

Jonathan sat next to her on the couch. "It will come when you least expect it. Make sure you leave yourself open to the opportunity. Don't scare him away."

"Am I scary? My mom said that I scared my father. I thought I was the warm, cuddly type."

Jonathan laughed. "Scary isn't the right word. Intense? Judgmental?"

Cassie's eyes bulged. "To hear you talk, I shouldn't be a psychiatrist. My mom says I lack compassion, Michael says I'm not understanding, you think I'm judgmental." She walked toward the wall and ran her fingers over her certificate. "Should I trade this in?"

Jonathan sighed. "No. That's not what I'm saying. You're good at counseling others. But when it comes to those you love, you tend to hold them to a high standard, one that they can't attain."

Cassie shook her head. "Is it wrong to want the people I love to act like civilized human beings? They keep making foolish mistakes."

"Yes, but you still love them. They need to know that. Don't shut them out because they don't live up to your ideal. And stop trying to fix them. Concentrate on your patients."

She hung her head and closed her eyes. Jonathan was the only one who could talk to her like that. His words made sense, but he didn't understand the extent of her issues. Bex and her father let her down. And Michael. He would let her down if she gave him a chance. It was better to walk away, save herself the pain. If she couldn't fix them, she didn't need them in her life.

She emptied her bag on her desk and busied herself arranging her office. Jonathan said to concentrate on her patients. That's what she intended to do. Until everyone else got on her game plan, her attention was better served here.

"I didn't come only to congratulate you. Lee told me your mother went to hospice last week. I thought you could use an ear."

"I'm fine. She's fine. Everything will work itself out."

Jonathan grabbed her arm. "Cassie. This can wait. Sit with me. You can't counsel others if you're not emotionally okay."

Cassie snorted. "I told you I'm fine. Can we please change the subject?"

"If you want to be an effective psychiatrist you have to take care of yourself. That's why it's suggested psychiatrists talk to each other, counsel each other. It's essential for mental health and you owe it to your patients."

"I know you're trying to help, but it isn't the time. My head can't handle anymore today."

Jonathan squeezed her hand. "I'm not finished with this conversation. We'll talk tomorrow. My office, nine o'clock in the morning."

Cassie nodded. He enveloped her in a hug then left the room. Jonathan's office was the last place she wanted to be in the morning, but he wouldn't relent until she talked about it. She would do the same for one of her patients, so she understood the need and the tactic. But she could handle this on her own. She sunk into her chair and hoped no one else would surprise her today.

***

Michael sat on the front porch, drumming his fingers on his thigh. This wasn't the reunion he hoped. He wasn't sure what he expected. But when she brushed him off it cut deep. She ruled his thoughts and he hoped they could explore their attraction. She couldn't deny it. They spent most of their time together before he went to rehab. Some of it was her practicing her counseling techniques. He was aware of his guinea pig status. But something else was up and he didn't understand why she ran from it.

Her letters told a different story. She wrote him every week he was at rehab. The letters and thoughts of her kept him going. He had a future to strive for, but now he questioned it. He reached into his back pocket and pulled out the last one.

Michael smiled as he read it for the hundredth time. It was well worn with creases in every direction. For a letter two weeks old, it showed its use. Cassie didn't write much about herself. She wrote about the latest movies and passing her boards. He smiled as she recounted the movies they watched together and how superheroes were growing on her. At the end, she told him how much she missed him and that she couldn't wait until he got home. They would plan a date. A superhero marathon of his choosing. Then she signed it: *All my love, Cassie.* All her love. Yet he could swear she was avoiding him.

He leaned back on the porch swing and gazed into the yard. Cole would be here soon. Samantha and Amber could spend the entire day shopping and he didn't want to wait for Cassie. He needed to sort his life out first before he figured out their relationship. Whether Cassie wanted to admit it or not, something was between them. He saw it in her eyes and felt it when they embraced. He wasn't giving up easily. He folded the letter and put it back in his pocket. This would have to wait until later.

A gray mustang spun into the driveway and honked its horn. Michael gathered his belongings and threw them into the backseat. "Thanks for coming. If I spent any more time here, I'd go crazy."

Cole laughed. "Didn't get the homecoming you wished for? After six months I thought she'd throw herself at you."

Michael shook his head. "She's not the type. Take me to my place. I need to see the damage."

"I checked on it as often as I could. Had to run out a few squatters every now and then, but it's in good shape."

"Thanks for looking out." Michael stared out the window. He had a lot of work ahead of him and it made sense to start sorting it out now.

"You okay? Is it that Cassie chick? Brush it off, man. There are more fish in the sea." Cole elbowed him in the side and smiled. "I'm throwing a party this weekend, in your honor. I'm sure you'll find someone to console you. If she's not into you, it's her loss."

Michael shook his head. "A party, huh? Don't think that's a good idea. You remember I went to rehab to stay away from drugs, not party."

"It's all good. Drugs, no drugs, I'm glad you're home and I want to celebrate."

"You should be lying low right now. Have you had any more trouble from Logan?"

"That low-life? He's been hanging around. We've caught him outside the house a few times, but we manage to run him off. He doesn't have a warrant, so he has to be careful. My lawyer is ready to pounce the first time he tries anything."

Detective Logan was a dirty cop. He tried to pin a murder on Cole earlier this year. Michael wasn't sure why he had it out for them, but he knew Logan would stop at nothing until Michael and Cole were locked away for good.

"Ever think about giving up the drug scene? Liam would fill the void. He'd throw a party if you retired."

"He'd love that. Can't let him win, you know? Everyone knows what they're getting with me. Liam's a wildcard. He's not safe. If I let him take over, I'm letting a bunch of people down that rely on me for safety. I'm in too deep."

He had a point. Liam was dangerous. After manipulating Samantha into taking speedballs multiple times the past spring, Michael didn't trust him. Despite Liam, Cole wasn't going to change. He would have to find a way to maintain his friendship with Cole while still recovering from his addiction. It didn't seem easy, but he didn't have another choice.

✳✳✳

Amber's car was in the driveway when Cassie returned home. She didn't get much done today, but she hoped tomorrow would be more productive. Samantha deserved her attention tonight. She grabbed her bag and opened the door, taken aback by the scene.

Samantha and Amber stood in the living room dressed in jeans and old t-shirts. The furniture was covered in drop cloths and painting supplies littered the room. Cassie shook her head. It didn't take them long to decide on renovations.

"Cassie! What do you think? Samantha thought lilac would be a welcome change. Oh, and don't worry about the furniture not matching. We ordered a new living room set. White leather and oak tables. It will be gorgeous!"

"I wish you talked to me before you started. Painting is a massive undertaking. How long will it be like this?" Cassie wrinkled her brow.

Samantha put her paintbrush down and glanced at Amber. "There's something you're not telling me. What's going on? You wanted this room painted as much as I did."

Cassie let out a breath and walked into the kitchen. She put her bag on the island and sat, nibbling on a cookie. Why did everyone want to know her inner thoughts?

Couldn't she deal with it on her own? She was trained to handle these issues. She didn't need anyone else.

Samantha plopped into a seat next to her. "You're not upset about the painting. Something else is going on. Spill."

"There's nothing to spill. I'm trying to get my office set up and my schedule straight. I'll be fine."

Samantha spun Cassie's chair around, so they faced each other. "I don't believe you. You're hiding something. If you think I'm too fragile to deal you're wrong. Whatever is going on, I can help. You were there for me, now it's my turn."

Cassie sighed. "You're not relenting, are you?"

"No. Get a shower and I'll meet you in your bedroom. It's time for some girl talk, just the two of us. I'll bring the cookies and the wine."

Cassie shook her head. She wanted to spend time with Samantha, but she didn't want to spill her baggage. She trekked to the bathroom, thinking of how she could avoid telling Samantha the truth.

She let the hot water fall over her as it washed away the stress of the week. Only Lee Boyd and Jonathan knew about her mother. No one else needed the burden. Samantha needed to focus on her recovery, not on Cassie's dilemma.

She dried herself and slipped into her plush gray and pink pajamas and settled on her bed. Girl talk could be light if she kept it focused on Samantha.

Cassie grabbed her journal and leaned against the pillows. Her entry could be lengthy tonight, if she wanted to remember everything. Instead of opening it, she closed her eyes and thought of Michael standing in the living room when she left. He had a forlorn look about him, like he was a lost puppy. He deserved a hearing, but she couldn't bring herself to talk to him. He set her off-balance and she couldn't deal with the emotions he stirred right now. She put the journal on her headboard and sighed.

"Going to sleep? I thought we were pulling an all-nighter."

Cassie grinned. "An all-nighter? Some of us have to work tomorrow. Can you settle for a few hours?"

Samantha put the plate of cookies and the wine on the nightstand. "I'll take anything I can get. You're a big improvement from my roommate at rehab."

Cassie wrinkled her nose. "That bad? I'm glad you're here and you don't have to worry about that anymore."

Samantha plopped on the bed. "Me too." She grabbed Cassie's hands. "Remember when you told me I didn't have to carry my abuse from Portia alone? Same goes for you. Whatever you're carrying, you have to share. Don't keep it inside."

"Everything is fine. Let's talk about you. I'm boring."

Samantha laid back on the bed and groaned. "Okay. Let's do this the hard way, then. We're playing Truth or Dare."

Cassie snorted. "I'm not in High School anymore. Don't you think that's juvenile?"

"No. It's perfect. If you don't want to tell me anything, just say dare. You know I'll think of some embarrassing things you can do, Dr. Roberts. I'll get my camera and document everything."

"That's blackmail!"

"Is it? Come on. It will be fun."

Cassie groaned. If I must. But I'm not happy about this."

Samantha squealed with delight. "You go first. Ask me."

"Truth or Dare."

"Truth."

"Was rehab helpful?"

"That's not a juicy question, Cass." Samantha rolled her eyes. "But yes, it was helpful. I have a direction now. Okay. My turn. Truth or Dare."

"Truth."

"Really? I have to make this count. Are you in love with Michael?"

Cassie's face turned red. "That's not a fair question."

"Of course, it is. Are you in love with him? I saw the way you looked at him when we came home today. And I know how you were before we left. Answer it."

"I can't. Michael and I are complicated. I don't have an answer."

Samantha shook her head. "Is that what's bothering you? Because you seem off, like something is eating your soul."

"I answered your question. Now it's my turn. Truth or Dare."

"Truth."

"Are you going to open your own photography studio?"

"That's an easy question. Yes, eventually. Now it's my turn. Truth or Dare?"

Cassie bit her lip. She couldn't handle another truth. If Samantha was going to push Michael, she needed to chance the dare. She didn't have answers about how she felt or what they were. And she didn't plan on having answers anytime soon.

"Dare."

Samantha's face lit up. "Feeling brave?"

"Oh no. What's going on in that mind of yours?"

"Just giving you a little push, like you gave me."

Cassie put up her hands and shook her head. "Oh, no. I don't need a push."

Samantha grabbed Cassie's phone and thrust it in her face. "Call him. You say it's complicated and you don't know what's going on between you. So, call him. Figure it out."

Cassie grabbed the phone and put it back on the headboard. "No. It's not as easy as you think. He's not Jonathan."

Samantha's face fell. "I know."

"I'm sorry, that was stupid of me. I didn't want to bring him up, but you kept pushing."

"It's okay, Cass. Michael isn't Jonathan. But he deserves a hearing. Just call him. Invite him over. Figure it out. You'll be happier if you do."

Cassie grabbed the phone. "You're not relenting, are you?"

Samantha shook her head.

"Okay, but if he comes over, no pushing. Promise?"

Samantha smiled. "Promise."

Cassie picked up the phone and dialed. As it rang, her bedroom door swung open. A young woman stood in the doorway. Her eyes were puffy, and her chestnut hair was plastered to her face.

"Cassie, it's time." She sniffed back a tear as she spoke. "Mom asked for you. They say she won't last the night."

Acknowledgment

This book is a culmination of a lifelong dream. I would not be here without the help and support of the following people. Rachel Burchett, Susan Harless and Megan Pelizzoni supported me from inception to final edit. Their critiques and encouragement helped make this book what it is. My Beta Readers, Kimberly Hunt, Rashmi Menon, Johanna Randle and Robyn Tillery were instrumental in improving this book. I would also like to recognize author JT Tenera for suggesting grass collecting as a stupid hobby. I appreciate your input and sense of humor.

Please leave a review after reading.
Goodreads Review
Amazon Review

For the latest news about upcoming releases,please visit my website and sign up for my newsletter for exclusive content including free novellas and short stories.
www.alainegreysonauthor.com

If you or a loved one is struggling with addiction, please visit—www.samhsa.gov/find-help/national-helpline for treatment options and support.

ABOUT THE AUTHOR

Alaine Greyson lives outside of Baltimore, Maryland with her husband, son and cocker spaniel puppy. She loves to push the envelope with her stories and strives to make her readers sympathize with characters from all backgrounds. Alaine is an avid reader and considers Jane Austen and Diana Gabaldon to be her literary heroes. She loves Mexican food, 80s music and is a Robert Downey Jr. super-fan. You will find mentions of things she loves throughout her books.

www.ingramcontent.com/pod-product-compliance
Lightning Source LLC
Chambersburg PA
CBHW051557100726
47898CB00001B/126